THE

I0553954

A MARVELLOUS SCHOOL STORY.

"Best for Boys" Publishing Co., 17, Gough Square, London, E.C.

REPLETE WITH STIRRING ADVENTURE.

GIANT JACK.

"Murdered!" Giant Jack cried. "Oh, you pack of wolves, did it take all of you to kill him?

LONDON: CHARLES FOX, 4, SHOE LANE, FLEET STREET, E.C.

GIANT JACK:

A Story of the Red Mountains.

"MURDERED!" GIANT JACK CRIED. "OH, YOU PACK OF WOLVES, DID IT
TAKE ALL OF YOU TO KILL HIM?"

No. 1.

◁ GIANT JACK: ▷

A Story of the Red Mountains.

-------◆◆◆◆◆◆-------

CHAPTER I.

NOTICE TO QUIT.

SOME years ago, when America, a young nation now, was younger still, and when some of the outlying states were barely rescued from their primitive condition, there lived at Broadpoint, a small settlement in Texas, a settler named Savage.

Where he came from no one knew. Round about the spot he had chosen for his home many other settlers gathered, but he held aloof from them all, and lived in a small shanty at the foot of the Red Mountains with no other companion than an only son—a boy about twelve years of age.

The mother of this boy had never been seen. The father brought the boy with him—a babe in arms—when he came to settle, and this child he for many years kept entirely apart from all those with whom he occasionally came in contact.

Two or three men had caught glimpses of the child, but no more.

If anyone approached the hut, from curiosity or any other motive, Savage sternly warned them away, and, being a tall, muscular man, with an unwavering resolution, none cared to disobey him.

The man was feared—he was the sort of man to cause fear—and few could look upon his giant form without feeling that it would be dangerous to thwart him.

The muscle and sinew apparent through the thin clothing he wore left no doubt as to his vast strength.

Once they had proof of this.

Some settlers were clearing a piece of ground, and a tree, in falling, knocked one of the men down and fell upon him.

He lay like one dead, but the motion of his lips showed that he still lived. The others, alarmed, were about to rush off for assistance to raise the tree when Savage came strolling by.

"Help—help, here!" cried one.

"What's the matter?" he growled, as he rushed up.

"Give us a hand here," replied the other.

Savage looked down and laughed.

"Help," he said, "who wants help? My boy could raise that."

Then, without further delay, he stooped down, seized the trunk by the roots, and tossed it aside.

The settler who had fallen had, fortunately, found a resting-place in very soft soil. He was much shaken and bruised, but not seriously hurt in any way.

Taking him up in his arms, like a child, Savage strutted away with him and placed him under the shelter of a hut. The other men followed.

"I guess," said one, "that you are pretty strong."

"It runs in the family," replied Savage, curtly; "my boy, I say, could have done all this."

"How old is your boy?"

"Twelve."

"Riddles and bib-tuckers!" said the settler. "I reckon he'll make a man if he lives long enough."

"He'll make a man for you to shake at," said Savage, turning away, "so don't you rile him, or it will go wrong with you."

From this time Savage became a noted man, but he was not popular. These settlers in a rough country, where might too often means right, had a doubt if it would be good for them to have much of the Savage blood about, especially as the Savage ideas seemed to be of the ruling sort.

Many tried to get a glimpse of young Savage, and a few, as we have said, had succeeded. Their report was to the effect that the boy was a wonder—as big as a man already; that he was a mass of muscle and sinew, like his father, and that his father called him Jack.

In a short time the fear of this father and son grew into dislike, and men said that "it was not good to have big, burly bullies about, who kept away from decent people," and that if "Savage and his boy Jack did not mix with the settlers round about there might be mischief."

Many of the settlers had by this time built tolerably decent homes, taken unto themselves wives, and raised families like decent men. These were particularly hard against the Savages, especially as the father was a great poacher, and shot over all and everybody's land.

Once a few of them, with Bob Griffin and Sam Turner—afterwards Mr. Samuel Turner, judge of the county—at their head, undertook to remonstrate with Savage on the subject, and to suggest to him the propriety of moving a little further off.

They came upon him coolly shooting within a hundred yards of Mr. Griffin's private residence, and, after a little hesitating preamble, put the case before him as clearly as they could.

"You see," said Sam Turner, "when the state was in the rough a man might shoot anywhere, but now the land's parcelled out, and a bit belongs to me, and a bit to another, the rights o' property must be respected."

"Look'ee here," replied Savage, coolly, "I

shot here years ago, when nobody growled, and I am going on with my shooting until I choose to leave it. What's more, my boy's now big enough to shoot, so he'll have his little run about, and if you think that any or all of you are men enough to stop us you had better try it."

As thus announced, Jack Savage came out shooting a few days afterwards, and not only trod most faithfully in his father's footsteps, but extended the field of his operations almost to the very doors of the settlers' houses.

This to men of newly-acquired property was unbearable, so time after time they remonstrated with the father, who only laughed, and when Sam Turner presumed to fall foul of young Jack the boy coolly knocked him down and went on with his shooting.

Smarting with rage, and with two black eyes, Sam Turner went running to the settlers and told the story, with this difference—he declared that the father and not the son had struck the blow.

"We can't expect to pick and choose our company much," he said. "In a new country most men are rough and ready, but I'm darned if we can put up with cusses of this sort."

This opinion soon became general. The Savages, father and son, were looked upon as dangerous, and it was decided that they must be got rid of.

But how?

Aye! there was the rub.

It was no use giving them a hint in the usual way, that had been tried and failed. It was no use saying to Savage that he had no right upon the settlers' land, as he only laughed and came again and again, just as he chose, and now here was the son, only a boy, acting in the same style.

It was unbearable.

The settlers round about the Savages numbered about two hundred, and it was a monstrous thing for them to be laughed at by one man and a boy.

But such a boy!

"I give you my word," said Sam Turner to his friends, "that the boy is bigger than most men, and he's got the limbs of an ox. There's a wild look about the beggar, too—something like his name in his eyes. They seem to punch a hole in a man, and you don't care to meet them. Then he doesn't wear a hat like a civilised being, but he's got a head of hair like a lion's mane, yet he's handsome—as handsome as paint—and I could not help liking him although he did put a smart tap between my eyes."

"I thought you said the father did it?" put in Bob Griffin.

"Did I say the father did it?" replied Sam, positively blushing.

"Of course you did."

"Well, it was the son, although I didn't like to say so at first; but, son or whatever he is, he's more than a match for me or any of you."

Bob laughed this idea to scorn, and very unwisely undertook to "tackle" the son, an opportunity being afforded him on the following morning to show his prowess.

He was going over his estate with a friend or two who had dropped in, as settlers did at that time upon each other, and was dilating upon the excellent prospects of coming crops, when young Jack Savage came sauntering out of a wood.

A noble figure the boy presented. Tall—far beyond his years—and broadly built, with a well-formed head set firmly on a fine pair of shoulders, and limbs that seemed to tread with an airy grace, but yet made the earth tremble as he walked. The figure of the boy was indeed remarkable, but the head was the most striking.

The features of his face were good—handsomely moulded, and full of expression; but the most remarkable thing about him was his hair, which was long, and thick, and tawny, giving Sam Turner ample reason for comparing it to a lion's mane.

His attire was simple—a rough shirt open at the neck, trousers and leather leggings, with a belt round the waist which held a knife, shotbelt, and pouch. In his hand he carried a gun.

He came on, neither looking to the right nor left, as if he would have passed Bob Griffin and his friends, but Bob, who would rather have let him go, felt his reputation at stake, and so hailed him.

"Hi! hallo! young Jack. Here."

The young giant swung grandly on his heel and looked at the speaker with lofty disdain.

"Don't you know," continued Bob Griffin, feeling rather uncomfortable, "that you are on my property?"

"Well, what of that?" demanded Jack.

"What of that!" remonstrated Bob, looking remarkably small. "You know it aint right."

"What ought I to do?" asked Jack.

"Well, being on another man's property," replied Bob, "you ought—you ought—to get off."

"Oh! is that all?"

"Aint it enough?" urged Bob.

"But why did you stop me to tell me this?" asked Jack, coming a step nearer. "Have you not said the same thing before, and have you not received an answer?"

"I believe that somebody—somehow—sort o' kind of mentioned it," said Bob, tamely; "but I—I repeated it in case you forgot it."

"We have not forgotten it," replied Jack, calmly; "we are not likely to forget it. But you waste your breath, as we shall continue to shoot as long as we please."

"Oh! will you?"

"Certainly. Have I not told you so?"

"Now, look'ee here," cried Bob, exasperated by the smiles of his friends, who had been looking on, much amused, "I'll bet you don't shoot here."

"You may bet if you like," said Jack, quietly, "but you will lose."

"You don't shoot here!"

"We shall."

"Then if you do," cried Bob, driven out of all prudence by a hearty laugh from his friends, "I'll shoot too, and I'll make a mark of you and your father too!"

"You had better not try it," said Jack, calmly; "neither my father nor I want to shed blood—we want to live, and we shoot the game to live on—but we shall not tamely submit to any attempt to murder us."

"If you come on my land," roared Bob Griffin, "I'll bring you down!"

"We will run the risk," said Jack, and walked quietly away.

When he was gone the settlers, although much amused, were compelled to admit that Jack was a very dangerous fellow, and not at all a desirable neighbour.

"But don't cross him," they said, as a parting warning ; "it'll be rather dangerous, Bob."

Mr. Bob Griffin was in a furious state of mind, so he went home to invent a plan for the extirpation of the Savages—father and son.

CHAPTER II.

JUDGE READY.

MR. BOB GRIFFIN, being in the main a prudent man, resolved not to attack the intruders upon his land without due notice. He therefore prepared a board, on which he painted the following warning :—

" NOTIS
IS HAREBY GIVEN,
THAT IF BULLY SAVAGE
AND HIS SON JACK
Come potterin' about the land of Bob Griffin
Bob Griffin will make cold meat of 'em."

This being worked out in large letters, had, in Bob's eyes, the appearance of a work of art, and with much pride he fixed it on a small tree which he planted upon a hill in the most conspicuous part of his estate.

Several friends were present at the ceremony of planting this tree, which was to bring forth such good fruit as the departure of Savage and his son.

"No man likes to be made cold meat of," Bob said, "and when they read this they'll go."

But the Savages did not go. When Bob went down next day he found the board gone, and on the spot the embers of a fire were still smouldering.

There were other signs about, which showed that not only had the board been burnt but that it had been used as a means for the cooking of a fowl—one of Bob's own fowls, which had doubtless served as a breakfast for the audacious poachers.

When he had arrived at the full extent of this outrage Bob swore a great oath and went home to fetch his gun.

His wife—Bob had a wife and three little ones—with a woman's instinctive tact, urged him not to interfere with the poachers, but Bob was blind with rage, and he was not to be defied with impunity.

"I'll have a shot at 'em," he said, "and I'll not come home until I've brought one or both of 'em down. A man may shoot any warmint as spiles his land."

He then bade his wife to be of good cheer, and, loading both barrels of his gun with a double charge of shot, went in search of the offenders.

The day passed and he did not return.

The night came on, and his wife sat through the dark hours waiting for his familiar voice, but she heard naught but the mournful soughing of the wind as it crept through the trees.

When the morning's light came she went to her nearest neighbour and spoke of the absence of her husband. Then a party turned out in search of him.

For a long time Bob could not be found, but late in the afternoon they came across him in the woods lying on his face—shot through the heart !

* * * * * *

Broadpoint was up and stirring—a murder had been done and the blood of the settlement was aroused.

All things pointed to the murderer. It could be no other than the man they now looked upon as an outlaw—Savage, the giant settler, had done the deed.

The settlement was small, and the framework of Texan life in general was in a very loose condition, but this sort of thing could not be passed by—murder must be met by justice, however rude in form.

At present the Broadpoint law was under the rule of Judge Ready.

Now we daresay most of our readers know what Ready Law is, but we must venture upon a brief explanation of it for the benefit of those who may never have heard of this rough mode of meeting and punishing crime.

When a crime was committed and the culprit arrested—any man could arrest him if he possessed the necessary courage and strength—twelve men were mustered to form a court. There was very little choice made. The first twelve who came together sufficed, and these generally tried, committed, sentenced, and punished the prisoner.

Now, when Bob Griffin was found dead, Broadpoint at once formed a court to carry out Ready Law, and to bring the supposed culprit, Savage, under its jurisdiction. Twenty volunteers, outside of the number selected to try him, were despatched to arrest him.

The number was very great, but they knew what a man they had to deal with, and so Sam Turner, who headed the party, declared there would not be many hands to spare.

The hut where Savage lived was well known. It was at the foot of the Red Mountain—a rough, wooden shanty, such as men in more civilised places reserve for cattle, but it looked pretty in the light of the evening sun as the party approached, and it was sufficient for those whose wants were few, such as Savage and his son.

The party proceeded without much noise, but all were on the alert, in case they should be fired upon. To their surprise nobody barred the way, nobody challenged them, and the door of the hut stood open, as if inviting them to enter.

"This may be some trick," said Sam Turner, pulling up.

"But they can't hurt us much," urged one. "At the most they can only fire two shots."

"Oh ! let us get on," said another. "Twenty afraid of two—absurd !"

It certainly seemed to be the case. Shame urged the party forward, and Sam Turner, having headed it hitherto, naturally felt compelled to keep in the van.

As soon as he entered the hut he recoiled a step and shouted—

"He's here—ready, lads !"

"Ready, lads !" repeated a deep, sonorous voice, in scornful tones. "Aye, I'm ready, but I would have been readier if I could."

Sam Turner looked down, and saw that Savage lay like a helpless log on the floor, breathing hard.

"You're wounded !" he said.

"Yes." replied Savage, "but, wounded or

not, I'm ready for you. I've looked for you all day. Come, be quick, and finish your work."

"You must be tried first."

"Take and try me, then."

"Where is your son?"

"Away," replied Savage; "he had nothing to do with it—knows nothing of it. I shot Griffin with my own hand. Here, take me, and get it over."

He seemed anxious, for some reason, to get them away from the hut, and they were nothing loth to go, so they tore the door from its hinges, and, placing him on it, bore him down the hill.

That he was sorely wounded they could tell by his deep breathing, but where they could not see, as his whole attire was a mass of gore —he was spotted and stained from head to foot with his own life's stream.

He remained perfectly calm, and when the men stumbled, as they did at times, with their burden, not a groan or complaint escaped him; but he remained with his eyes fixed upon the now darkening sky above, as if wrapped in thought.

The burden was heavy, for Savage was a huge man, and many times the bearers were changed. It was nightfall when they reached the place where he was to be tried, their rough-and-ready sense of justice having selected the place where the body of Griffin had been found.

The court was soon prepared, and darkness having set in a number of torches were lighted, those who formed the spectators holding them aloft.

The twelve men upon whose words the fate of Savage hung sat in a half-circle, the spectators forming the other half, and in front of the court, just within the circle, sat the widow and three children as accusers. The body of the dead man was near, upon a rough trestle, covered with a cloak.

Savage was brought into the midst of the circle and laid down. The widow rose with a wild look of denunciation and glared at him, but when she saw he was wounded and helpless she knelt down, and, covering her face, said not a word during the trial.

The prisoner, with a calm, unmoved look in his eyes, glanced leisurely round the circle, then composed himself, with his arms above his head, as one would settle himself down for sleep.

There was one of the settlers appointed to call over the names of the jury, and, having first demanded silence, he called out their names.

"Henry Snowden?"

"Here."

"James Barclay?"

"Here."

And so on, each answering to his name. The other ten were as follows—

"Tom Traver?

"Zepheniah Bisset?

"Charles Dean?

"Robert Packer?

"John Stepneroff?

"Theophilus Norman?

"Robert Norman?

"Reuben Brake?

"Arthur Scaler?

"William Newton?"

As the names were answered to Savage looked at the speakers one by one, without any appearance of emotion or curiosity. Of all the spectators of that scene he was the most unmoved.

And it was a solemn one.

Few could have witnessed it unmoved. The dark pines towering aloft, with the trunks and branches of the trees lit up by the torches, and the circle of solemn faces around, each and all conscious that a fellow-creature's life hung upon the verdict of the court.

Judge Ready lost no time. The witnesses were there, and they at once proceeded to business.

CHAPTER III.
THE SENTENCE.

THE first witnesses were those who were with the murdered man in the morning, when he threatened Jack Savage with death if he ventured upon his estate.

When the prisoner was asked if he wished to question them he simply said—

"It is true—Jack told me of it when he came home. Get on and finish your work."

Then proof was put in of Griffin having painted and fixed the notice-board, and of its untimely fate. At this part of the story Savage smiled.

"It was handy," he said, "and Jack burned it—used it to cook a fowl, but get on and have done with it. I shot him."

"We will be as fair as we can with you," said Henry Snowden, who had been appointed the head of the court. "We don't want you to confess."

"It will come to the same in the end," replied Savage. "I shot him, I tell you."

"How was it done?"

"In fair fight," replied Savage, raising himself upon his elbow—"in fair fight as far as I was concerned; but he was a coward."

"It is safe to slander a dead man."

"I don't slander him—he came behind me and put a charge in my back, and when I turned he put another charge in my breast, but then he was at my mercy—I shot him like a dog."

"Had you no words?"

"None!"

"Not one?"

"No. He came behind me, I tell you. I shot him fair, but it's murder in your eyes. I know your law, and I'm prepared for it."

"You were trespassing."

"Who made him master here?" cried Savage, fiercely. "The land was as much mine as his, though I did not draw a line as all of you have, and say that this was mine or that was mine. I only took the little I needed from it. It was not much."

"You broke the settlers' law, and we cannot live without it."

"I lived without it," replied the prisoner; "but there! have done with me. Say the word and get it over."

This was his continued cry.

He knew his fate and was prepared for it; but they had not done with him yet. The parent snake was in their power, but they wanted the brood.

The men whispered together for a minute or so, and then Henry Snowden addressed the prisoner again.

"You have a son?" he said.

"You know I have," replied Savage, smiling.

"Where is he?"

"Far away, I trust, out of your clutches."

"The better for him. We do not wish to

harm him, but he must not settle here."

"If he obeys me," replied Savage, "he will not come."

"It is well; and now have you anything to say why the sentence of the court should not be passed upon you?"

"Nothing," he replied; "and if I had it would not help me. Do your work and get it over."

Then the sentence was passed—a few short words, but pregnant with death.

To be hanged immediately upon the nearest tree.

It was cruel, wounded as he was; but they were rough men, living in a rough age, and they felt this to be a stern necessity.

It was their justice.

They carried it out. With much labour the big man they feared was hoisted in the air. Involuntarily he made a few frantic struggles for his life as he hung.

Then the men covered their faces and the women shrieked; but it was shortly over, and he hung still and lifeless, with the torch-lights giving a strange hue of health to his distorted face.

Now we do not suppose that these settlers were all naturally cruel, but out of those who had witnessed this scene only one had made a feeble protest against the execution.

This was a man known as Long Tom, his name being a playful sarcasm upon his exceedingly low stature—he being barely five feet high, and broad out of all proportion. He had said—

"I don't think we ought to hang him. Bob went out to get a pop at him and got the first shot, so it was all fair enough."

But Long Tom was barely a settler—he only squatted on a little bit of land—so they put him out of the question and hung poor Savage.

When all was over, and they were about to depart homewards, there came bounding through the wood, like a wild beast full of fury, the form of Jack Savage.

The noble boy, with his long hair flying behind him, came rushing through the underwood, and sprang into the midst of the startled men, crying—

"Father, where are you! I am here—Jack is here!"

"Poor boy!" muttered Long Tom, "he'll go mad when he sees his father hanging."

Then he signed to the torch-bearers to put out their lights; but they were too much occupied with observing the boy to heed him.

Jack was glaring from one to the other with the fire of fury blazing in his eyes. Fortunately for them he was unarmed.

Suddenly he espied the hanging form—then with a terrible scream he sprang towards it.

The men drew back, and the silence which followed was the silence of the grave.

"Oh! father, father!" cried Jack, "speak to me."

He held the body in his arms, and looked up at the ghastly face. Death was there, and Jack saw it.

"Murdered!" he cried. "Oh! you pack of wolves, did it take all of you to kill him?"

No answer. The majesty and beauty of the boy fascinated them all—they were like birds under the glare of the serpent.

"You shot him first," continued Jack, placing his hand upon the still bleeding breast, "and

then hung him—you dogs! you wolves! who trembled at the lion. Look to it, the cub lives."

With a quick, passionate movement he felt in his belt for a weapon—there was nothing there. Those who saw the action instinctively drew back, not entirely from fear—for some of the men were brave enough—but none cared to enter into a struggle just then.

CHAPTER III.
CONTINUED.

"GIVE me some weapon," Jack Savage said, "then stand before me, man to man. Here, you with the rifle there, stand forward."

It was Sam Turner whom he addressed, and Sam replied—

"I don't want to fight with you, poor boy. I'm sorry your father's dead; but he committed murder, and we are obliged to have laws, you know."

"Murder! Whom did he kill!"

"My husband!" cried the widow, suddenly standing forward, with the look of a tigress in her face. "He came behind him and killed him."

"You are a woman," replied Jack, softly; "let any man stand forward and say the same thing and I will give him the lie."

"He murdered my poor husband."

"He killed him in fair fight, if he killed him at all," said Jack, "and he did it alone. But it took all of you to kill him. Will none of you fight?"

"Not with boys," replied Sam Turner. "And now, neighbours, I think it's time we turned back. The night's half gone."

Gladly accepting this hint, the settlers shuffled off, a few throwing their torches away, the rest retaining theirs to light themselves and neighbours from the wood.

Taking up one of the cast-away torches, Jack waited until the sound of footsteps died away, then he burnt the rope through, and the body fell heavily to the ground.

Jack passed his hand over his father's heart—all was still there.

It was an action without hope, for he had seen death written in his face from the first.

"So they killed you because you were victorious in fight," he murmured; "killed you because you were the better man, and I was sent away to the west, and you were to meet me there. But I felt all was not well, and I have come back to find you dead.

"Dead!" he shrieked, and his voice echoed far away in the wood. "Dead! And I—I am alone. Oh! Great Father above—why was he taken from me? He loved me, and we were happy together. Why were these wolves allowed to hunt him to death? But I will hunt, too. Life for life. Let them sleep in quiet if they can, and walk abroad if they dare.

"The lion is slain, but the cub is alive, and the cub can fight as well as the lion. Look to it, Broadpoint. Woe to all who live there! I'll leave naught but widows and orphans to curse the hour they hung my father! The houses shall stand empty and the land shall want a master. Those who dare not stand shall flee away, and those who dare stand shall die."

The passion of the boy seemed to rend his

body, and with violent, choking sobs, he threw himself upon the corpse of his father.

The paroxysm was brief. When it was over he arose and dashed the tears from his eyes.

"My father," he cried, "I must bear you away and bury you—bury you in some place where they cannot find you—for wolves like these would wreak further vengeance on the dead."

He tried to raise the body, but the dead weight was almost too much for him. He dragged it a short way, then dropped it with a despairing groan.

"Don't give way, youngster," said a voice close to his ear, "let me help you."

CHAPTER IV.

NUMBER ONE.

IT was Long Tom who spoke. He stood close to Jack, looking up into his face. The boy looked down upon a squat little man as one looks for the first time at some great natural curiosity.

"Who are you?" he asked.

"Long Tom, at your service."

"A settler here?"

"Yes."

"Then you are one of my father's murderers!" cried Jack, with anger leaping into his face. "I have no rifle, but my arms are strong, and I'll have the life of you!"

"Hold hard, young 'un," cried Long Tom, dodging out of Jack's way; "don't be in a hurry. I'm a friend."

"It is a lie!"

"It is true, young 'un. I stood out against hanging your father; but one don't go far against so many, and I did no good."

"Are you speaking the truth?"

"Look into my face, young 'un," said Long Tom, "and if I lie blind me with the torch."

Jack held the torch aloft and looked long and earnestly at the face of Long Tom. At last he was satisfied.

"You do not deceive me," he said; "and you may help me to carry my father to his grave."

In sad and solemn silence the pair thus strangely brought together bore the body through the wood and up the hill to the hut which Savage, when in life, had made his home.

They laid him on the turf outside, and Jack, having fetched a pick and spade, they dug the grave and lowered the body, all dressed as it was, to its last home.

Jack filled in the grave, and knelt beside it for a few minutes, while Long Tom, with his eyes full of tears, looked another way.

The brief but solemn scene was soon ended, Jack rising and leading the way into the hut. Having the materials ready, he lighted a fire and ignited a lamp, which he placed upon the table—a very rough piece of workmanship indeed.

"There was not much in our house to make us enemies," said Jack. "I think they might have let us live in peace here."

"You see," hinted Long Tom, "you might have lived in peace if you had kept here."

"What do you mean?"

"I must put the truth to you, young 'un. If you hadn't gone on settlers' land against their will——"

"Who made it their land?" demanded Jack.

"The natural laws o' man," replied Long Tom. "I don't hold with hanging a man up sudden in the middle of the night, but I've lived long enough to know all about laws and so on. There must be masters of the land, or it won't be cultivated. No one won't cultivate land for other people to dance all over. And them as cultivates the land must have laws to protect em."

"I know nothing of men or of their laws," returned Jack, who sat with his head between his hands, looking thoughtfully into the fire. "I only know that they hung my father, and I know he would not have wilfully harmed any man. Tell me all about him—how he died."

"Perhaps it's better not to talk of these things," said Long Tom.

"I want to hear," said Jack, impatiently— "tell me."

Then Long Tom slowly related the events of the night. He was one of the party despatched to arrest Jack's father, and he could tell him all.

"It's a matter of law," he said, in conclusion. "All places, big and little, have laws, and them as breaks them suffers.'

"They suffer here," said Jack, calmly. "Now tell me the names of those who sentenced him."

"The court?"

"You know what I mean," returned Jack. "Give me their names."

"There was Henry Snowden."

"Henry Snowden," repeated Jack. "A tall man, with long black hair, who lives over by the Gully?"

"That's the man," said Long Tom. "What are you doing?"

"Notching a stick," replied Jack, suiting the action to the word.

"Tom Traver."

"Stout, with fair hair and blue eyes?"

"Yes. Zepheniah Bisset."

"Broad and tall, with one finger off his left hand?"

"Just so—you know 'em. Robert Norman."

"The man with the club-foot?"

"Aye. Theophilus, his brother."

"Very much like him, but two years younger."

"True as sunshine," said Long Tom; and in this way they went through the names of the whole court.

When they had finished there were twelve notches on the stick.

Without saying a word in reference to it Jack drilled a hole in the piece of wood and hung it on his belt. This done, he sat for a long time with his face again resting on his hands, looking into the fire.

Long Tom, with a vague presentiment of having done something wrong upon him, watched the boy, whose face, lit up by the wood fire, had a strange, weird appearance. He was, withal, very handsome.

Jack at length looked up and said—

"I have them all."

"All what?" asked Long Tom.

"Every man," muttered Jack. "All—all graven here."

"I don't understand you," said Long Tom.

"I was not speaking to you," replied Jack, quickly, but kindly. "I was thinking. Your name is Tom?"

"Yes."

"I shall call you by it. Tom, this is no home

for me."

"No, Jack, I'm afeared it aint."

"So I must move house. But I shall not go far away. Somewhere about the mountains.

"I think I'd make clean tracks out of the country."

"When my work is done, and not before," said Jack.

"Wheresomever you go, Jack, I'll go to."

"On one condition," said Jack, after a pause.

"What is it, my lad?"

"It's strange to hear you calling me a lad," said Jack, looking down upon him with a smile. "My condition is this—that if you live with me you neither question my coming or my going, or ask me what I have done. If it is good for you to know I will tell you."

"My lad," said Long Tom, "I'm not at all skewrious about other people's affairs, so I don't mind the condition, but let me give you a little piece of advice—may I?"

"If you will," said Jack, "but I don't promise you to follow it."

"Let bygones be bygones," rejoined Long Tom. "It's nateral for you to feel riled a bit to-night. Most chaps would feel riled under the circumstance, but they're too strong for you, there's too many of 'em at Broadpoint, and if you go agin em and put their backs up, they'll come on you in a body, and then you must get the worst of it. You're a fine lad—a wonderful lad, Jack—and you'll make a splendid man. Turn your back upon Broadpoint with me to-nigh , and never come nigh it no more."

"I shall leave it one day," said Jack, "but not now."

"The world's very wide," urged Tom. "There's a pile of land about. I know a place further south where a man may hunt and shoot all day, straight away cross country, and never come nigh a man as could say, 'You're on my land; git off, will yer.' There you can do as you like, Jack, if you will come with me."

"By and by, Tom, but not now. If you wish to stay with me you can, if not—leave me."

"I'll stay with you, Jack, for I've no tie at Broadpoint, and I likes you. But oh! do get further away."

"The time will come when we will go; for the present I have chosen my home. Help me to carry the few things I have."

"A table, two cheers, a pile o' skins, and a few airthenware pots," said Long Tom, making a verbal inventory of the household goods. "'Taint much, but it's enough to carry about—what's them in the corner, there?"

"My father called them books," replied Jack; but I know nothing about them. He said that learning had been a curse to him, and I should know nothing about them. What is learning, Tom?"

"Larning?" replied Long Tom, after a pause of doubt and meditation—"larning is a kind of skewrious thing which one chap gets inside of him and another doesn't. I aint larned myself, but I know it is so."

"I've often seen my father open those books," said Jack, "and look into them; then I have seen him frown, and sometimes he would laugh —I suppose they made him do it—then, when he went out, I have opened them and looked in too, but I never felt anything. How was that, Tom?"

"Because you could not read, I s'pose. I don't know. I can't read myself."

"But what is reading—my father would never tell me," persisted Jack; "he always refused to talk about his books."

"I've heerd say," said Long Tom, dropping his voice, as if about to make an awful communication—"I've heerd say that when a chap have been taught to read that the books know it, and they speak to him."

"Oh! nonsense."

"It's a fact, Jack; you'll hear chaps as can read say that 'the book says so and so.' I've heard it a hundred times."

"I should like to learn to read, Tom; will the books teach me?"

"I'm afeared not," replied Long Tom. "Why, I don't know, unless it's too much trouble for 'em; but there's heaps of men as could teach you."

"At Broadpoint?"

"Aye, and all over the world. Most men can read a little."

"We will take the books with us," said Jack. "Perhaps I shall one day find a man to teach me, and then those books, perhaps, will tell me about my father. But I don't want to be taught at Broadpoint. You take the skins. I will carry the table, the chairs, and the books."

"You've the most of the burden, lad."

"And am best able to bear it."

When they got the things outside Jack set down his burden, and bade Long Tom wait a bit.

"This house was my father's, and no other man shall live in it," he said, as he went back.

When he came forth again he shouldered his load, and bade Long Tom follow him. Without questioning the boy Long Tom obeyed, and the pair went on their way up the mountain. Half way up, Jack called a halt, and bade him look round. Tom did so, and beheld a fierce, red light at the base of the huge hill.

"It will be level with the ground directly," said Jack, "and the wind will scatter the ashes, therefore our home will not be desecrated by strangers."

"You've no larning, but you speak well," said Tom.

"My father taught me," replied Jack, "and as he spoke I speak. Let us go on, Tom."

* * * * *

With the morning came reflection to the people of Broadpoint, and most of them were sorry for the man who had died in the forest. They remembered his defence, and the fact that Griffin had gone out to bring Savage down—to shoot him, in fact—and in the course of events had met with the fate he designed for another.

There was another thing which the men remembered, and this was that the son was alive. An uneasy feeling arose in the breast of those who had played a principal part in the tragedy, and they wished that the boy had been killed with the father.

"Broadpoint is unsafe with him alive," was the general opinion. But most of the settlers had had enough of life-taking, and would have nothing to do with it.

But it was not so with those who had formed the court.

They felt the injustice dealt out to Savage most of all, for they had been the dealers of it, and the very terror of their conscience—terrors terribly awakened—spurred them on to attempt a still greater wrong.

They resolved to put an end to Jack.

This resolution was arrived at after a secret meeting called by Henry Snowden, who seemed to be under the influence of some mental fear.

For days after the trial he scarcely slept, and to those who were his nearest friends he solemnly declared that the figure of Savage swinging in the midnight breeze never left him.

"I'm haunted," he said, one day; "turn where I will, go where I may, I see his face lit up by the torches, and the staring eyes glaring down on me as if they cursed me, and then, somehow, the figure of the boy comes up before me. Last night I dreamt that he met me in the wood and took me by the throat, shrieking out, 'Number one!' It's awful! I cannot bear it, and I can't rest if the boy's left alive."

Quietly, one afternoon, the twelve men met, and went up to the spot where Jack's house had been; they found the ashes, nothing more, and the vague terror which had come upon all became confirmed.

These men, as before said, were not cowards, but they had the general common love of life, and they wished to live.

Were their lives safe with the big bold, brave lad at liberty?

It was doubtful.

"There was black blood in the father's looks," said Snowden, "and we shall find black blood in the son."

Seven days afterwards Snowden was missing.

The settlers of Broadpoint went out in search of him, and found him, shot back and front, swinging from a tree.

Hanging from his waist belt was a small stick with a single notch cut in the back.

"He's begun his work," cried Traver, "and that bit of wood signifies number one!"

CHAPTER V.

JACK'S MOUNTAIN HOME.

FAR up the mountain, near the summit, Jack Savage made his new home. This time he did not build a hut, but chose a huge cleft in the rock, shielded and almost hidden by the mass of underwood growing around.

The cleft ran quite through the rock, necessitating a roof, which Long Tom and Jack made of small branches and twigs. It was a rude kind of thatch, but it was all the two required, and they were satisfied.

Here, for about three weeks, they lived in a quiet way—Jack hunted and Tom stayed at home and cooked. But whenever Jack returned from a day's outing Tom always cast an anxious look upon the stick at his side, and invariably breathed more freely when he saw all the notches there.

One afternoon Jack was later than usual, and night had set in when he returned. Tom had prepared the supper, and was standing at the door when the young giant came, with a swinging step, leisurely up the hill.

A glance at the belt—twelve notches still.

"I thought he had begun," muttered Tom. "There's a look in his eye I don't like—he's unsettled a bit."

Jack put his rifle in the corner, and sat down by the fire. He had brought no game.

"No luck to-day?" said Long Tom, taking a pot from the fire and pouring its contents into a dish.

"None," said Jack. "At least, not what you would call game."

"It's bad luck coming home without anything," said Tom, making an attempt to laugh. "A weasel is better than nothing."

"I have shot something," said Jack.

"What is it, Jack?" said the other, bending down to get a look at his face.

"This," replied Jack, taking the stick from his side, and with his clasp-knife cutting off the first notch.

"Don't tell me you've done that!" cried Tom, starting back.

"Why not?" demanded Jack.

"It's no better than murder, lad—it aint right."

"It was not murder," rejoined the young giant, with a fierce gesture of his hand. "I met him and gave him a chance for his life. I offered to fight him. I am only a boy and he's a man. He would not fight, and I shot him like a dog—as my father was shot—and then I hung him on a tree to frighten the other rooks away."

Long Tom had been very hungry an hour before, but his appetite was gone now.

Forgetting all about his fast-cooking meat he sat down by the boy's side and put a hand upon his arm.

"Jack," he said, "you can't make it right; and, putting all right aside, it aint the safe thing to do."

Jack made no answer, but sat motionless, sternly looking into the fire.

"All Broadpoint will be up," continued Tom, "and although you're no chicken, and I'm pretty good at a pinch, I think they will be too many for us. We may pot a few as they come up, but we shall be potted at last."

"There's something in what you say," said Jack; "they may prove too many for us. You need not stay."

"I'm not thinking of myself," returned Tom, calmly. "It aint much consekens when I go off. I aint one of the world's wallyable pieces of furniture. It's no matter what becomes of me. You is a fine lad, and will make sich a man! Lor! I see you in a crowd, towering above everybody, and all of 'em turning to look at you, and everybody saying, 'There's a man!'"

"I don't want to be stared at, Tom."

"But think of life," urged Tom. "Think of what a lot there is to see and do in the world—fields, woods, perraries, with no end of buffaloes to hunt, and small game to pot, and big rivers to cross, and cliffs to climb, and redskins to fight."

"Where are all these?" asked Jack, whose eyes were gleaming with interest. "Are they near here?"

"A few days' footing will take us there," replied Long Tom, "and we shall be happy, and you'll forget this place."

"I cannot forget my father or his wrongs!" cried Jack, with sudden passion. "What business have I to think of fields, and woods, and hunting, while those who murdered him are above the ground? No, Tom, here I stay to do my work; then I go with you if you will."

"You will never go," said Tom; "they won't let us get clear away. But the supper's getting cold, Jack."

"I have no appetite," he said.

"Nor I," said Tom, pushing the table aside. "There's something curious in the air—it tastes of blood."

The last four words he muttered to himself, but Jack caught the expression of his face, and guessed their import.

"You think I am wrong," he said.

"My lad," said Long Tom, "I know you are. I don't want to say anything agin your father—he's dead and gone, but I think he was wrong from the first. He were too bumptious. A man likes to keep his own bit of land to himself, but he wouldn't let Bob Griffin do so, so they got potting away at each other, and both are dead, and now you are potting away at other chaps, and they'll come potting away at you, and so you'll go on until Broadpoint's extarminated."

"I long to see the day it is so," said Jack, gloomily. "Oh! my poor father."

"He didn't train you right," said Long Tom, sorrowfully. "I like a brave man, and I like brave deeds, but revenge aint brave. Ignorant as I am, I know that. You've got a sure hand and a steady eye, and you could put it to a better use than knocking over what I call your own flesh and blood—white men are that, you know. Now, if you must shoot men, try Injuns."

"Why Indians?" asked Jack.

"Because they're the nateral enemy of the whites," replied Long Tom, "and it aint no crime to shoot 'em."

"So you say," returned Jack; "but I see more harm in shooting the dirtiest wretch who never harmed me than in killing fifty who have wronged me as I have been wronged. Think of my father's death, Tom."

"I do think of it, Jack—it was a sad one."

"And l think of it, too."

"Come, Jack, let us leave this place, and go further away. If you keep in the same mind come back in a year or two and fall foul of 'em as much as you like. It's reasonable that if you keep your mind two years you'll keep it ever."

"Two years—it's not long," mused Jack. "I'll think it over, Tom."

"Don't think, Jack, but come away at once," urged Tom, who felt that it would soon be too late.

"I will think it over to-night," said Jack, decidedly, "and to-morrow you shall know what I have resolved."

He would do no more, and laid down as if to sleep.

Long Tom laid down too, but his senses remained stretched through the night to catch the slightest sound. Nothing out of the usual way occurred, and on the morrow he was up and stirring with the sun.

He pushed aside the brushwood and looked out. At that moment Jack raised himself upon his elbow and called out—

"Tom!"

"What is it, Jack?"

"I've been thinking over what you said, and I'll give the men of Broadpoint two years' rest."

"You've thought over it too long," replied Long Tom, coolly. "Broadpoint is up and stirring, and the men are swarming up the mountain's side."

———

CHAPTER VI.

CAPTIVE.

JACK stepped quickly to Tom's side, and saw that he had not deceived him.

The men of Broadpoint were advancing in a body, beating every bush as they came, and vowing and threatening vengeance upon the young giant.

"There's fifty or more," said Long Tom, gloomily, "and we're booked. Better have gone last night, Jack."

"Aye, aye, Tom!" returned Jack; "but you make a run for it now. I can stand alone."

"Will you give in?"

"When my arms drop by my side," replied Jack, contemptuously. "It would suit these fellows to have me lie down like a cur and lick their hands. No, Tom—I will fight."

"It's certain death," muttered Long Tom, as he took his rifle in his hand, "but it aint much odds what comes of me."

"I shall give them both barrels," said Jack, as he rammed the charge home, "then rush in with my rifle clubbed, and fight my way through."

"Aye! it's as good a way as any other," said Tom, savagely; "but why couldn't you go last night? Here they come, hollering like a lot of savages. I'm ready."

"You are not to fire," said Jack.

"Why not?"

"This is not your cause—it is mine."

"But I stand by you."

"Put down that rifle there, and get into the corner. Now promise me one thing, Tom.

"Aye, lad; out with it."

"None of these men know that you are here; when I fire and rush out you keep quiet."

"If I do I'm——"

"You will keep quiet," persisted Jack. "If I get clear away they will follow me. If I fall they will rest content, and your being here will not be suspected. If they take me prisoner you can help me better outside than in."

"There's good sense in what you say, Jack," said Tom; "but it seems cowardly-like not to keep to my word and stand by you."

"You cannot help me," said Jack, "unless you remain quiet. Lie there—flat and close—as there may be firing. I am going out."

Outside the cliff the settlers were coming up, for the most part in a cluster, but a few of the boldest were scattered here and there, examining brushwood, peering behind the rocks, and shouting to urge the others forward.

Foremost of all came the two brothers, Theophilus and Robert Norman, whom our readers will probably call to mind as a portion of the Court Ready which tried Jack's father.

These two men were brothers, not only in birth, but in appearance and disposition. Both were well known at Broadpoint as men fond of cock-fighting, bull-baiting, and all cruel sports.

They had been among the most eager for the death of Jack's father, and they were now proportionally anxious to capture Jack. Both were naturally bloodthirsty, and as they came upwards they reminded one of a pair of bloodhounds following a keen scent.

"He is not far from here," said Robert, the elder. "See these broken twigs, this crushed creeper; the young giant has been putting down his foot, curse him!"

"There he is !" cried the other, as Jack showed himself on the summit of a rock.

"Halt !" cried Jack, and they both halted— the rest were yet far down below, and out of rifle reach.

"Go back if you value your lives—I know you both."

The two brothers raised their rifles quickly and fired, but both bullets flattened against the rock and fell harmless.

Their weapons were single barrels, and now, of course, were useless. As Jack raised his rifle to his shoulder their full danger burst upon them, and they fled.

But it was too late.

Loud and clear his rifle rang out, and the two brothers rolled together over the mountain's side into the midst of their friends, who were hastily advancing.

"Three !" shrieked out Jack, then, with his rifle clubbed, he dashed down the mountain-path.

The tragic death of the two brothers startled the Broadpoint men, but they were prepared.

Jack sprang into their midst, dealing out blows perfectly marvellous for one so young.

Mr. Sam Turner was among the earliest recipients of Jack's favours, and, being knocked down, he prudently laid there, leaving the others to do the rest of the fighting.

"I should prefer the kick of a horse to another such a blow," he afterwards declaied. "I thought every bone in my body was smashed."

But to return to Jack.

He fought like a lion, but numbers prevailed. He made a dozen kiss mother earth, but the rest leapt upon him and bore him down.

Even then his struggles were terrific, and the men clinging to his powerful limbs were tossed about like so many monkeys, but he was at last exhausted by their persistent attacks, and then lay still.

Like a modern Samson, they bound his limbs with strong cords, and carried him back in triumph.

But their victory was saddened by the death of the two men, whom they brought down the mountain slowly.

The women and children came out to see Jack, and some, forgetting their sex, cursed him when they heard that he had killed two more men.

"Let him follow the old wolf !" they cried. "Hang up the cub !"

"Aye ! hang me up," cried Jack, smiling, "and then tremble, even as ye think of me quiet in my grave."

"The young braggart !" said Zepheniah Bisset.

"Braggart !" cried Jack, "loose these limbs of mine and see if I boast. But you will not."

Then, like his father, too proud to bear even the captivity of an hour, he bade them do the work they had to do.

But Broadpoint had its laws, and Jack must have his trial.

The boy was much bruised and beaten during the struggle, and the bonds around his limbs cut him in many places painfully, but he made no complaint and uttered no groan, even when, for greater security, they bound him with cruel tightness to a large tree. The men and women looked upon him with curiosity, and the children hung back and clung to their mothers' garments.

Jack bore his infliction very bravely, and gave back their bold looks with looks equally bold.

There was no lack of men ready to form a court. Jack had no relations likely to avenge him, and there was little danger in condemning a boy to death. So a dozen men volunteered, and the trial began.

The evidence was quickly given. They had found Snowden dead, and Jack must have killed him. This was the surmise, and the true one, as we know.

Jack did not deny it—he scorned to tell a lie —and he was prepared to give his life, but not without one last struggle.

The time spent in trying him had given him a rest. He had recovered his strength, and just as the head of the court, Zepheniah Bisset, was about to pass sentence, he suddenly burst his bonds, fairly electrifying his captors.

CHAPTER VII.
SEVEN YEARS AFTER.

A BLOW here and a blow there was given by Jack, then, seizing a rifle from the hand of Tom Traver, he dashed through the midst of the startled people and ran, with the fleetness of a deer, to a mound hard by.

"Men of Broadpoint," he cried, "I leave you now for awhile, but watch by your homes, and look to your lives as you walk abroad, for I shall return."

Then, waving in triumph the weapon he had seized, he ran towards the woods and disappeared.

*   *   *   *   *   *

Time has ticked off seven years from its endless roll, and we must now carry our readers on to a time when great changes had occurred in Broadpoint.

It was a hot morning in the middle of a Texan summer, when there came marching over the summit of the Red Mountains a body of men.

A strange, motley band.

Men of all nations, apparently none of the best, but a wild, reckless mass of humanity : those who will not submit to the laws of civilised life, but seek the liberty of untrodden lands, thus unconsciously becoming the pioneers of nations.

There was the Spaniard, the Frenchman, the Maltese, the Englishman ; Irish and Scotch were not wanting, although the latter were in the minority ; and of Russians there was but one, Russians not being a wandering race.

The various types of America were well represented—Yankees, Mexicans, Indians, and so on, to the number of about forty, and the band in a'l was at least two hundred strong.

They marched with apparently little order, each man walking as he liked, but a keen observer would have noticed that every eye was on the watch, that these men were accustomed to danger, and prepared to meet it at a moment's notice.

Of the men we will not speak particularly now, their individual peculiarities will crop up in the course of our story ; but we must devote a few words to those who appeared to be, and were, the leaders of the band.

First and foremost let us speak of the chief of all—the captain.

He was a giant—a broad-shouldered young man, fully seven feet in height, but so exquisitely proportioned, so handsome and noble-looking, that none particularly noticed his

◁ GIANT JACK: ▷

A Story of the Red Mountains.

GIANT JACK FAIRLY ELECTRIFIES HIS CAPTORS BY SUDDENLY BURSTING HIS BONDS.

extraordinary stature.

With the elastic step of youth he walked a few paces in front of all, like a lion and its jackals, for none of those who followed could compare with him.

He seemed in command. One who walked nearest to him was a complete contrast in every respect, being far under the average height of man, but very thick-set, and with great evidence of muscular power about him.

We need not describe them further—the pair are well known to our readers, being Jack Savage and his friend, Long Tom. Seven years had made very little difference to the latter, but Jack had developed from a boy into a man— a young man still, but with every attribute to make him worthy of manhood's name.

The next person who calls upon our pen for a little description was the third and last in command, one Will Larkin.

Will was an excellent specimen of that class of Englishman to be found in every quarter of the globe—he was handsome, young, genial, bold as a man need be, and invariably in excellent spirits.

He feared nothing, laughed at the idea of danger, and risked his life, when called upon to do so, at least a dozen times a day. As for his nationality, he generally, when asked a question on the point, answered in this style—

"I am a true Britisher," he would say; "my mother was Scotch, my father was Irish, while I was born in England, and if you can get a better born and bred Britisher than that you keep him close, for such articles are scarce."

The men were very fond of him and called him the "Cricket"—not at all a bad name, for Will had a pleasant chirping way about him, which was good for all he came in contact with —no matter how dull the company, how moody the men he fell in with, Will Larkin always acted like a sunbeam, and shed light and gladness upon all.

He was not walking with Jack and Long Tom, but with a few of the men, who were listening to his conversation with keen interest.

It may be here remarked that Will was still very young—not more than nineteen or twenty —but he had the air and confidence of a man of forty at least.

"Of course, it's odd how I came into this style of life," he said, pursuing a conversation. "Fellows like myself find the tight little mother isle too confined for us. We can't launch out —kick, you know—or if we do we are sure to hurt somebody, and then there's a row about it."

A great familiarity seemed to exist among the men and their officers—a familiarity engendered by their living in a country where the forms and ceremonies of society had not yet taken root.

One of the men replied—

"Ah! I tried to kick in the old country, but it ended in my having to run for it."

"Did you commit a robbery?" asked Will.

"No," was the rejoinder. "But a fellow insulted my sister, and I thrashed him within an inch of his life. The law called it an attempted murder, so I made a bolt for it, having a strong objection to stone walls."

"You did quite right," said Will Larkin, "and I commend you for it. But, you know, we don't care much for fellows who would steal here. A thief is generally a coward. We will not steal."

"Except the captain commands us."

"In that case," returned Will, "we must obey him, for one and all have sworn to do it. Obedience to him is our first law."

"Aye, aye, master! and it's a pleasure to obey such a captain."

At this moment Long Tom, after a brief conference with Jack, turned back and joined Will Larkin and those with him.

"As we have had a long march," he said, "the captain proposes to halt and rest, out of sight of Broadpoint. He doesn't want to be seen until the last moment."

"But we have most of the day before us," returned Will Larkin.

"And we have stiff work before us also, perhaps," said Long Tom. "We know what Broadpoint was seven years ago, but we don't know what it is now."

"True. But shall we not be seen?"

"A thousand to one against it. This is not a public road, I should say, for there's no signs of traffic hereabouts. The men of Broadpoint aint much reason for coming up here. They never had, and we can lie close. No fires to-night."

"Aye, aye!"

Long Tom went back to Jack Savage, and shortly after a halt was called.

The place chosen to rest in was well adapted for the purpose. It was near the summit of the mountain, behind a huge piece of rock, covered with lichens and creeping plants. The men were well concealed from the observation of any who might be below, but, by advancing a few paces, they could mark everything which passed on the lower part of the mountain and in the valley.

The main body of the men threw themselves down with careless ease, and Jack Savage, having first posted sentinels among the bushes, withdrew a few paces with Long Tom and Will Larkin.

There was a gloom upon the face of the young giant as he leaned upon his rifle and looked far away into the valley below. From the position he was in he could not see Broadpoint, but there were many spots near which were familiar to him.

Long Tom lounged carelessly against a rock, whittling a stick with his knife, while Will Larkin, first making a cigarette, stood at his ease, waiting until it should please his captain to speak.

"Seven years ago," said Jack, to the pair who stood by him, "I was a happy boy here. I had no thought but for the day—everything was gladness to me. In wood or field, on the prairie or mountain, I breathed the pure air of Heaven without a thought of ill. But now—ah! now!"

He paused, and a deep sigh swelled his heart. Long Tom, still whittling, cast a curious glance at Will Larkin, who appeared to be a little astonished at the demeanour of his chief.

"I swore an oath," continued Jack Savage, holding up his right hand, "an oath I'll keep. You," he added, turning suddenly upon Will Larkin, "you know nothing of this, but it's due to you that I should explain, as you must play your part in to-morrow's work."

"I am bound to you," replied Will Larkin, firmly. "You have but to command and I to obey."

"The story is simple," said Jack, sitting down upon the ground, and, with his eyes shaded by his hands, speaking as if he was in communion with himself. "I had a father. A settler sought his life, and fell in the attempt. They tried my father as if he had been a murderer, and hung him like a felon to a tree. Oh! my father."

It seemed as if the grief of his boyhood had returned as he uttered these words, his giant frame rocked with emotion, and the hot tears rolled between his fingers, but it quickly passed.

"And what comes out of this, Will?" he continued. "Can you not guess?"

Will could guess, but he was silent, and Jack Savage went on—

"Revenge! bitter revenge for the wrong done to me. I vowed it on all who had a hand in it when the crime was done, but I vowed more when they laid their hands on me."

Will Larkin looked at Long Tom, but that worthy continued his whittling as if the story were an old one to him, and he was not an interested party.

"I had slain one of their number," continued Jack, "when they came upon me. I fought my best."

"You fought like fifty," put in Long Tom.

"I made some of their pates ring," Jack Savage went on. "Boy as I was, I made them dance; but numbers were against me, and they got me down. Strong cords held me then, for I was weak; but when I gathered fresh strength I rent them asunder like flax and escaped, just as they had settled on my receiving the same treatment as my father. 'The lion is dead,' they said, 'but the cub lives, and he must die.' The cub is not dead, but is living, and he comes for revenge."

"On whom?" asked Will Larkin.

"On all Broadpoint," replied Jack Savage. "I will not leave a settler's home standing. I will lay waste the fields. I come in the harvest time, and if aught is saved from the ruin there shall be none but widows and orphans to gather it into the barns."

Jack Savage uttered this threat in a deep, sonorous tone, his knitted brows and compressed lips attesting how earnest and sincere he was.

Long Tom was not apparently disturbed—he had heard the same thing before—but Will Larkin was undoubtedly surprised, and a troubled look came into his face.

"Look you here, captain," he said, "when I joined you I didn't reckon upon this sort of thing. I don't hold with revenge. If a man hits me I hit him again—straight and fair, between the eyes. If he tries to pepper me with his rifle, ten to one I try to pepper him. Beyond that I don't go. I can't keep a wrong in my mind for years and then act as if it happened yesterday."

"Just my sentiments," said Long Tom, nodding his approval of Will's remarks.

"But such a wrong as mine," cried Jack Savage; "father murdered in cold blood!"

"It was Broadpoint law," said Long Tom; "but I don't arger."

"I have to obey," responded Will Larkin; "I have my oath to keep."

"And I mine," said Jack; "you are faithful to yours—let me be faithful to mine. To-morrow I will lay Broadpoint in ashes, and leave naught but widows and orphans to curse the hour they slaughtered my dear father."

"And then?" asked Will.

"Ask me not that," returned the young giant. "I have no thought—no wish beyond the hour of revenge. The oath sworn seven years ago shall be kept to-morrow."

So saying, he turned and walked a little way down the mountain's side, where he could commune with himself.

"It's bad," sighed Long Tom, "but he'll not go from his word. Broadpoint is as good as done for."

CHAPTER VIII.

A CHECK.

"It seems odd to me, Tom," said Will Larkin, "that one so generous as our captain should be so revengeful."

"It's the warp in the woof," replied Long Tom; "but I think it's more obstinacy than nateral badness. You see he said he would do it, and that's enough for him. He'd keep his word if he knew it was wrong."

"But on the score of mercy?"

"Ah! Will, that's a score as doesn't belong to many here. Mercy! Look at 'em, and say what mercy you could hope for from half on 'em."

"A rough lot."

"And chosen for the work, Will."

"And when the work is done will he leave them?"

"No—he's promised to lead 'em where they like for ten years, the place to be chosen by lot."

"I know that, and mind you, Tom, if some of them get the upper hand in voting, we shall have some queer work—sacking settlements, if nothing worse."

"Aye, lad!"

"Will you stay with them?"

"I will never leave young Jack while he or I have life."

"I am not so bound," said Will Larkin, "but I must say there is something in him which attracts me to him against my will. There's a power in him I don't understand."

"So there is," responded Long Tom. "Once he gets hold of a man he can't leave him. One look's enough. His eyes are rum 'uns."

"There is a supernatural power in them, Tom. He might have been one of the Chaldeans of old."

"Chaldayens?" repeated Long Tom. "Who were they? I never heard of 'em. Any tribe in these parts?"

"They lived long before your time," replied Will, with a smile. "But to return to the captain. When I joined you the band was already a hundred and fifty strong. How were these men brought together?"

"Some one way, some another," rejoined Long Tom. "Some j'ined because they were sort o' fascinated by him. He's so big, and so strong, and so handsome, you see, that men can't help coming over to him. Others he whopped into j'ining."

"Whopped?"

"Yes—beat 'em into it. You see Caderouse the Frenchman—and the biggest Frenchman I ever saw, six feet if he's an inch, and strong as an ox—he was the bully of Short's Run, down east, and no man dare hold up a finger to him.

He was cock of the walk, I can tell you."

"A determined-looking fellow."

"He's like a bull-dog. Well, when young Jack and I dropped down on Short's Run this Caderouse drops down on us. He didn't seem to make no count of Jack's size, but he comes at us slap straight away. Looks us up in our tent —we had a tent then—as free as possible.

"'Ah ! Mossoo,' he ses, sittin' down on Jack's skin bed, as if he'd shot the buffler himself; 'ah ! Mossoo, you come to de Run—yah !'

"Young Jack looks at him.

"'Get off my skin,' he ses.

"Caderouse laughed and tossed his nose scornful.

"Wal," continued Long Tom, "if you had seen what followed it would have done your heart good. Caderouse wasn't led out, and he wasn't kicked out, but he was shot out—ah ! a good dozen feet, and came on his back sich a buster that I'll bet he saw stars, and a good many of 'em. Then young Jack went and stood over him."

"Did he try to get up ?" asked Will.

"Get up," replied Tom, with profound contempt, "not he, but he kep' on his back, parleyvooing in sich a way that I knowed he was swearin' frightful. Jack didn't do no more to him when he found he didn't get up, but he leaves him there, and the next day Caderouse came on his own account to ax pardon. Then the captain tells him of a band he's forming, and Caderouse j'ines, and he's been civil to everything over five feet ever since. No man could be more perliter."

"It did him good."

"Ah ! it did, and Short's Run wanted to give young Jack a testimonial, I think they called it, but they couldn't agree as to what it was to be. One man wanted to send to Europe and get him a set of chainey, another said a folding-bedstead would soot, but we came away afore it was settled, so the captain didn't get nothing, and didn't want it."

"I joined because I couldn't help myself," said Will. "We met one night at a canteen, and he asked me to make one, and I made one as a matter of course—had no idea of saying no."

"That's his way," rejoined Long Tom ; "and once he's got the power over you there's no getting away from it. It's magic like."

"Do you know anything about electro-biology ?" said Will.

"Never heered on him," replied Tom, after a little reflection.

"It's not a man," returned Will, laughing, "but a strange, mysterious power which some men hold over others. I've seen a man stand up before another and ask that other to strike him in the face, and the man couldn't do it. I've known money to be offered, but the effect was the same."

"I wish some man—a rich 'un—would offer me five pound a blow," said Long Tom, grimly. "I'd precious soon make a fortune."

"You think so ?"

"I know it."

"It all depends upon the man," said Will. "Now, I'm sure that if the captain chose to exert his will that neither you nor any other man could strike him. He may not know of the power within him, but I have watched him for some time, and I am sure he has it."

"Could he stop a bullet ?" demanded Tom, feeling very sceptical.

"The bullet being inanimate," replied Will, "he could have no power over it, but I am sure he could control the majority of living men."

"He's a tough subject," said Tom, "and that's the least we can say. But no more now—he's coming this way."

Jack Savage sauntered up with a thoughtful air, and his officers knew by his look that his mind was troubled.

"I have been looking over Broadpoint way," he said, "and it looks but little like the old place, and yet I cannot tell where the change is. The houses stand the same, the woods the same, and the fields much as of old, but there is something wrong."

"Perhaps if I looked I could tell," said Tom. "Broadpoint was well known to me from this spot. Shall I take a peep ?"

"Do so."

Long Tom clambered to the summit of the rock, then, stretching himself at full length, he took a long and earnest look below. Presently he slid down, and presented himself before Jack Savage and Will.

"The place itself is just the same," he said ; "but I know what made it seem different to you —there aint a creetur moving !"

"That's it !" cried Jack.

"No cattle—not even a dog," said Tom ; "and sure the place do look strange."

"I cannot account for it," said Jack, "unless they have seen us."

"No," said Tom, "that's not it. Had they only seen the corners of our hats they would naturally have been runnin' about like an ant's nest when a stick's poked into it. Maybe there's a great bee on."

"What's a 'bee' ?" asked Will.

"Not know what a bee is !" returned Long Tom, with ill-concealed contempt. "Where was you raised ? A bee's a general presarving day, when the fruit's put by, and all the neighbours come to help."

"It is too early for that," said Jack ; "the fruit is not yet ripe."

"Look'ee here," said Long Tom, "the Broadpoint people have nothing ag'in me—they don't even know for certain that you and I went away together. Suppose I go down and see what's the matter ?"

Jack thought a little while, and then agreed to the proposition.

"It can do no harm," he said, "but be back before sunset."

Putting aside all arms and making a few alterations in his attire, so as to give himself the appearance of a peaceable settler, whose mind was entirely bent upon agricultural pursuits, Long Tom sauntered down the mountain side and was speedily lost in the intricacies of the winding-path.

While he was gone the captain and Will Larkin conversed on general topics, and during the conversation an event occurred which showed the great power the young giant held over his men.

Some half-dozen of them were playing cards, and as the fifty-two pieces of pasteboard are about the best invention for getting up a quarrel, in this case they were faithful to their mission, and hot blood sprang up between the players.

In an instant knives were drawn, and they began slashing right and left. The lookers-on endeavoured to interfere, but the enraged men were blind and deaf to all their efforts until the captain stepped into their midst.

In a moment they were still, and drew back panting, casting furtive looks of apprehension at their leader's face.

"Put up your knives," he said in a low, clear tone, "and the next man who draws one shall feel the pressure of my finger and thumb. I'll wring his neck."

He held up his huge but well-shaped hand as he spoke, then dropped it, and returned to Will Larkin's side.

The men who had been quarrelling sat down upon the ground and renewed their game, talking to each other in the mildest tone of voice.

Jack invariably remonstrated once, threatened once, and then kept his word.

The day previous there had been a quarrel over the cards, when he remonstrated, and the men knew that the next quarrel his promise would be kept.

The afternoon passed in tolerable quiet, and the evening came on, but Long Tom did not return.

Just before sunset Jack Savage went to the rock and took a survey of the mountain. His faithful servitor was not in sight.

"I cannot think what has detained Tom," he said, addressing Will. "Unless they suspect my coming they have no cause to arrest him."

"It's a stiff journey," replied Will, "and perhaps he will return at nightfall."

Jack was obliged to rest content with this hope, and darkness slowly afterwards set in. The men rolled themselves in their warm coats and wraps and lay down to sleep. Jack Savage and his second officer, Will Larkin, sat silently waiting Tom's return.

About two hours after dark the cry of a whip-poor-will was heard, and Jack, springing up, answered with the hooting of an owl. Then Long Tom's voice was heard.

"Show a light here, will you? All's clear straight away."

Jack struck a light and fired a few sticks, which had previously been gathered together in case of such a need, and Long Tom came panting up, dragging after him what at first appeared to be a bundle of old clothes, but which afterwards proved to be something in the semblance of a man.

"Lie there until you are wanted," he said, "and move if you dare."

"I don't want to move, good sir," piped a weak, thin voice. "I wouldn't run away for worlds."

"You dare not," said Tom, coolly; "don't wriggle in that way."

"I am sure, sir, that I don't want to wriggle," replied the same voice. "If you don't wish it, sir, I wouldn't wriggle for——".

"Worlds—I know," said Long Tom. "I say, Captain Jack, you see that small critter there?"

"Yes, I see him."

"Well, captain," said Long Tom, speaking very slowly and very distinctly, "that's all that is left of the people of Broadpoint!"

CHAPTER IX.

WHAT BECAME OF THE SETTLERS.

"PERHAPS, captain," continued Long Tom, "you don't know this party, but I remember him. His name's Snip; he settled down here some nine years ago, and got a living by mending and making toggery—didn't you, Snip?"

"I'm sure, sir," whined Snip, "that I always did my best, and charged fair. It's very hard work, and I wouldn't wrong anybody for——"

"I went down," interrupted Tom, addressing his leader, "and the first house, you know, is Barclay's. I found that empty—not a soul, or a bit of furniture, or live-stock, or anything —all clean gone. Then I went on to Stepneroff's, and there it was the same; and so on, from one to the other, all empty alike, until I came to Arthur Scaler's barn, where I found this critter cowering like a rat, and has him out."

"And what story did he tell?"

"One that will astonish you a bit," replied Long Tom, "and as I thought you would like to have it at first-hand I brought him here to tell it."

"Make up the fire," said the young giant, "and bring him before me."

Long Tom made up a good fire with brushwood and sticks, then he brought the quaking Snip near to his chief, and bade him begin.

"And don't you put in no lies," he added, "or it will be the worse for you."

"I am sure, sir——" Snip began.

"Attend to me," interposed Jack; "tell your story without any superfluous assertions— you remember me?"

Snip shifted his eyes uneasily, and coughed gently twice or thrice ere he replied.

"I think I do, sir."

"You know you do," said Jack, sternly.

"I—I was present when—when your late lamented father—did as—as I might say—die," stammered Snip, "and I saw you then."

"And you remember my oath?"

"I wouldn't accuse you, sir—of the habit— of swearing, for——"

"Bah!" exclaimed Jack, impatiently; "get on with your story. Tell me of Broadpoint. I hear it is deserted."

"I am the only man left, sir."

"The only man!" repeated Jack. "Well, go on."

"I remember the time, sir," Snip began, getting more at his ease as he proceeded, "the time when you—you objected to being bound, and broke away like—like a raging tiger, as I might say, although I wouldn't compare you to such a ferocious beast for—for any amount of worlds.

"Well, sir, shortly after you got away— which it was a clever get away, and completely knocked them, as I may say, off the board— shortly after that people began to get uneasy at Broadpoint. I don't know exactly how it arose first, but I think it began with the cattle dying. Bob Scraggs's cow was found dead, and after that the cattle went off like sheep with the rot.

"'They're p'isoned,' everybody said, 'and it's young Jack Savage as is doing it.'

"I ax your pardon," said Snip, humbly, "for even repeating such an accusation against you, respected sir, but they said it, and I am obliged to repeat it to make my story good."

"Go on," said Jack.

And Snip proceeded—

"This feeling growed so strong that the Broadpoint men sat up in batches to watch, and all carried arms. They meant to put a bit of lead into you, respected sir, and I being timid-like and not used to weppings, being cockney-born and led away to emigrate, I do assure you, sir, that I could not sleep at night for thinking of you."

"Thank you," said Jack, drily.

"It's above nateral kindness," put in Long Tom.

"But the cattle dying did not stop here," Snip went on. "The horses in the stables went next—first they was taken a little poorly, then they hung their heads and looked stupid, then they lay down, and then they finished off the job and died.

"After this sort of thing had gone on for some time it stopped, and as you had not appeared they made up their minds it wasn't you, but something else, although what it was not a man-Jack of them could tell.

"Still, they were uncertain about you.

"Many of 'em expected you back, and kept a good watch for you; but you did not come, so they soon settled down into their old ways, and a year passed on. Then another misfortune came upon them.

"The crops failed.

"It wasn't exactly a blight which came, but something that just nipped everything in the bud, so as it didn't dewelop. Corn and green crops was just the same, all went bad, and there was precious little for man or beast to feed on.

"They couldn't lay this to you, so they put it down to the weather, and, making the best of a bad job, managed to keep going until the next season.

"Then the crops showed well.

"Everything was as good as man could wish for.

"But one night a terrific storm came on, and the rain came down in cataracts—everything was swept away, the fields were like mud pools, and there was nothing gathered in, not enough to feed a sparrow for a week.

"It was total ruin for that year, but they bore up.

"The fields were sowed again, with seed fetched from the settlement at Stony Gap—fourteen miles away—and from this seed they got a fairish crop; but next year things were bad again—the fields were black with blight, so then a meeting was called, and they tried to make out the cause of it.

"Tom Traver was the first to speak; he had called the meeting, and he had a right to be first. He starts—

"'I'll tell you what it is, neighbours, this blight aint no common blight, it aint in the country, but it's in us, and I'll tell you what brought it.'

"They were all eager to learn, and you might have heard a pin drop as Tom looked slowly round, then said, solemnly—

"'It's the ghost of old Savage as is haunting us.'

"A few looked solemn at this, but the most of 'em laughed, and Dean said he wasn't afeared of any ghosts. Then Tom Traver went on—

"'You may believe it or not, as you like. I do, and I'm off in the morning. Broadpoint is going to the dogs.'

"According to promise Traver went away the next day, and hasn't been heard of since. The rest kept on, and next year the crops were good, but other things went wrong—cattle died, houses caught fire, children got drowned. One man was thrown by his horse and dragged in the stirrup until he was dead. Nothing but accidents and horrors everywhere, until people began to think and talk of what Tom Traver had said, and thought it might be true.

"Another meeting was called, when it was decided to leave Broadpoint and form another settlement a little further south, and Sam Turner and Dean went out to pick the land.

"They found the place, and everything was settled upon. All that could be taken was packed up, and they started one morning and have not been back since."

"Why did you not leave with them?" asked Jack Savage.

"The fact is," replied Snip, "that they told me of the hour for moving, but I overslept myself."

"And why did you not follow?"

"I have been making up my mind ever since," returned Snip. "Day after day I have said I would go, but it's a lone country—there's savages, both man and beast, and I might lose my way—so altogether I thought it best to stay, especially as they had left no end of corn, and so on, behind them."

"And where is this settlement?"

"Away south, somewhere. That's all I know of it, except its name."

"And what is that?"

"They intended to call it Mount Restore—at least, so I heard them say."

"I must find it at once. South, you say?"

"Yes, respected sir."

"Don't fawn upon and crouch before me," said Jack, sternly, "but stand up like a man, Tom, this ninth part of a human being will go with us. I leave him in your charge."

"I'll take care of him," replied Long Tom, "and I'll make him useful, for some of us are in want of needle and thread."

CHAPTER X.

THE MARCH TO MOUNT RESTORE.

JACK felt sadly disappointed at the evacuation of Broadpoint, but this feeling was not shared by his officers or his men; the former were averse to the whole affair, as we know, and the latter, being of a class of men but little likely to sympathise with aught which did not concern themselves, were profoundly indifferent. It mattered little to them whether the Broadpointers were there or not.

Having ascertained through Snip that the houses were deserted, some of the men expressed a wish to go down and see if anything in the shape of plunder could be obtained. They solicited leave of absence from their chief, and Jack, although impatient to be off, knew how to do a thing graciously at the proper time, so he gave them permission.

About a score went down the next day, and roved from house to house, fishing up all that was left, which was not much, and firing each habitation as they left it.

The smoke and flames were easily seen from the camp on the mountain, and Long Tom, calling the attention of Jack to them, said—

"I think, captain, that you might consider your word kept. There will be precious little of Broadpoint left after our men have done with it."

"My oath is yet unfulfilled," replied Jack, gloomily. "I swore to it by my father's grave. It must be kept. Pray trouble me no more on the subject, Tom. To-morrow we march for this Mount Restore. Those who wish to go must fall in at sunrise; if any want to hang back let them leave to-night. My oath must be kept."

"He's determined on it," said Tom, to Will Larkin. "If he's left single-handed he'll go on with it."

"We are bound to follow," rejoined Will, a little sadly. "But who comes here?"

"The foraging party, with Caderouse at their head."

Caderouse came marching up the hill, laden with window-curtains and wraps of various materials. The others followed, each with something from the deserted homes.

The Frenchman was very proud of his English, and generally spoke it. It was, like all Frenchmen's English, of rather a complex nature, and exceedingly confounding to his listeners.

"I shall come to Broadpoint," he said, throwing down his load, "vith tings of de window, and of bed de curtain. Yah! it is good."

"Some of the things will come in," said Long Tom, turning them over with his foot. "We will make tents of the curtains, and Snip shall stitch them together."

"I go for the house of Snip," said Caderouse. "I look de door in, and I say 'Snip vith us.' Ve catch ze goose for Snip; in my pocket I shall have him—he is the bird of iron."

So saying Caderouse drew from his pocket that peculiar instrument of the tailor craft, and tossed it to Snip, who was sitting on the ground. He eyed his property with thoughtful melancholy, but made no response to the Frenchman.

"Monsieur Snip shall goose my clothes," continued Caderouse. "If de sun shines Caderouse shall have of clothes de finest. I shall vith de peacock vat you call compare."

"You won't have anything done by me," said Snip, surlily.

"Mend dis jacket mine," said Caderouse, loftily, tossing it towards him. "De vind and vater make too free—dey come in so. De door is open, dey not knock, but come in straight to de skin of Caderouse—tickle."

"I'll not mend a Frenchman's togs," said Snip, throwing back the jacket.

"Vat you say?"

"I won't mend a Frenchman's togs," repeated Snip, very pale.

"Vy not? Sacre, you dog!"

"We licked you at Waterloo," replied Snip, expanding his breast. "My great-uncle was there—he shot a man or two, and I've seen the gun he did it with."

"Sacre? you Vaterloo of me speak?" cried Caderouse. "Yah! dere was no Vaterloo, no battle—all lies of de English. Bah! mend my coat."

Snip's answer was of a most startling nature, for he deliberately spat upon the Frenchman's garment and kicked it near its owner with his foot.

"I'm a son of bold Britannia," he cried; "I'm a ruler of the sea, and I answer you—never! I'll die on my beam-ends first."

In all probability he would have died on his beam-ends, or some other part of his anatomy, but for Long Tom. The Frenchman, enraged at the insult, drew his knife and sprang towards Snip, but Long Tom stepped between.

"No, Caderouse—no, friend," he said; "you're too big a man to pitch into one of his size."

"He speaks of Vaterloo," hissed the Frenchman; "he my clothes spit."

"You should keep your clothes on your back," said Tom; "put up your knife, or I shall call the captain."

Caderouse muttered something of a very personal nature with regard to Snip, then he sheathed his knife and sat sullenly down.

"As for you," continued Tom, addressing Snip, "don't you get up quarrels here, or they will make a cullender of you. A tailor's only the ninth part of a man, and he shouldn't run his head against a whole one."

"I come of a brave family," replied Snip, who, now that the excitement was over, was as pale as a ghost. "My uncle was very brave—he fought at Waterloo; my father was also brave—he was always fighting. Black eyes was chronic with him. If his friends met him without a black eye they didn't know him."

"Well, you bottle your bravery," said Long Tom, drily, "and keep it until it's wanted. I daresay we shall find it useful."

"In the hour of peril," said Snip, striking an attitude, "you will find me there. Ha, ha! Lead me on to the battle! to the battle! Ha, ha!"

Tom was at first disposed to think that Snip had gone mad, but, calling to mind some of the peculiarities he had exhibited when he knew him at Broadpoint, he at length concluded that he was only a little dramatic.

This was, indeed, Snip's great forte—he was dramatic at all times when not overcome by a little natural nervousness, which some people might call cowardice, such as he had exhibited when first captured and brought to the camp in the Red Mountains.

"He's an amoosing creetur," said Long Tom, after he had told the story to his captain; "'specially if you lets him have his way a bit. They was always having fun with him in the settlement. I wonder they left him behind."

"He may say or do what he pleases," said Jack, "so long as he doesn't exercise his folly upon me."

Will Larkin rather took to Snip. He knew that he was an arrant coward, and only brave when certain of victory, which he really felt sure of when he quarrelled with Caderouse. Big as the Frenchman was, he was only a Frenchman in the eyes of Snip.

"Frenchmen are but rats," he said, addressing an amused audience, consisting of four or five of his countrymen. "They only fight when you get them in a corner."

"But Caderouse is a giant in strength," said one.

"Gird on my sword and buckler," returned Snip, "and I will to the field with him. What shall I, Sir Pandarus of Troy, hold back, and by my side wear steel? Nay, then, Lucifer ake all ?"

CHAPTER XI.

RUBY PLAIN—A TEST FOR SNIP.

VITHOUT exactly seeing what reference the uotation made by Snip had to the Frenchman, is listeners told the vain-glorious tailor that e was undoubtedly very brave and bold, and hat he would be of immense service to the ompany.

"I only want a chance," said Snip, "then ee what I will do. I was a little bit out of orts last night. You saw me before the aptain ?"

"Rather ! you shook like a leaf !"

"All my fun," said Snip, lowering his voice o a whisper. "Of course I am not a match or the captain, but I am not afraid of him. So ong as he did not lay a hand on me I pretended o be afraid, but if he had touched me—if he 1ad only ruffled a hair of my head—then, hunder and blue bricks ! you would have seen 1 fight."

Those who were listening scarcely knew what o make of Snip. He was so small, and with as ittle of the fighting man about him as one of the Peace Society would wish to see, but he had certainly shown a bold front to the Frenchmen, and now, as he spoke of the happily-avoided encounter between him and the captain, he looked so fierce, and every hair of his head bristled with so much fury, that an impression came upon them that the little tailor must be brave.

Snip was clever enough to see that he had made a favourable hit, and was keen enough to follow it up.

"There's not much of me," he said ; "but I'm plucky, true to the core, bold as a lion—a tigress robbed of her young is not more terrible when my dander's up. Ah ! you should have seen me fight Ben Caunt."

"Champion of England ?" asked one of his astonished listeners.

"Yes—that's the man," said Snip, nodding his head. "He's retired from the ring now ; but we fought, about a week before I sailed from England, for a hundred pounds a-side—catch weight, of course, on account of the difference in our size."

"I should like to hear about that fight," put in Will Larkin, who had silently joined the group.

"You shall, respected sir," replied Snip, with a slight return of his old humbleness. "I challenged Caunt in a moment of liquor, for when a man puts rum on the top of four half-an'-half there's no knowing what he may do ; but when I got sober I stood to my word. 'I can't only get beat,' I said, 'and if Caunt's ready for me I'm ready for him.'

"Caunt *was* ready for me," Snip continued, "and the next day we met. Caunt thought he had only to look at me to lick me, but there he was a little out. I got first knock-down blow and drew first blood, but Ben was the heavier man, and he beat me, but not afore he'd knocked me down thirty-six times, and I had pounded his face to a jelly."

"A remarkable fight," said Will.

"It was, respect—ahem !—sir, it was," returned Snip, "and the papers was full of it. They wanted to show me about, but I aint fond

of that sort of thing, so I came out here."

"Very modest indeed," said Will, as he walked away.

"Your friend Snip," he said to Long Tom, "if he is nothing else, is a remarkable liar."

"I think he has that weakness," returned Tom ; "but lor, most people do fib now and then."

"But lying is worse than stealing. Still, if the fellow confines his lying to simply folly he won't do much harm."

"If he lies any other way," said Tom, "I'll skin him."

Jack interrupted the conversation. He came to give orders about the morrow.

"We will start with the first gleam of light," he said, "and rest in the heat of the day. I think I have an idea where this settlement of Mount Restore can be found. You will be ready ?"

His officers said they would be, and shortly. afterwards, the sun setting, the camp settled into repose.

With the first faint streak of light in the eastern sky the avengers were up and on their way to the settlement of Mount Restore.

*　　*　　*　　*　　*

Ruby Plain is one of those vast wastes so familiar to those who have travelled in America —commonly known as prairies. It lay about twenty miles to the north of the Red Mountains, and at the time of our story was seldom trodden by the foot of civilised man.

It was the favourite haunt of the buffalo, and thither the Red Indian resorted to indulge in his favourite pastime—hunting. White trappers never attempted to cross it alone.

But there was little danger for Jack Savage and his band.

The Indians were but little likely, however great their numbers, to make an attack upon him, so the first night they halted the camp fires were boldly lighted, and the men sat around them laughing and chatting, as much at their ease as if they had settled down in a Parisian restaurant.

The common talk among the men was the feats of their chief.

He was their idol and their hero, and when they looked at his towering form a feeling akin to that which pervades a heathen's breast when he looks up to the huge image which represents his god took possession of them.

Snip was seated with a party who were speaking in the highest terms of their leader, and one of them, a broad-built, thick-set German, opened the conversation with a story.

"He is dat strong," he said, "dat he take up men and throw them about like cannon balls. I vas strange to him ven he come to de hotel, vot you call de Tiger, down at Thunder Flat. Dere vas a row in de place—two men quarrel about cards, and de captain say—

"'You fellows, dere, stop dat row."

"They not stop, so he take dem—one—two—and knock dere heads together until dey ring like crack basins. Yah ! it vas goot."

"Especially as one of the heads happened to be your own, Carl," put in a listener.

"So," replied Carl, "it vas true—de strongest head vas mine, and t'other man got his broke. He lay very quiet when the captain done with him."

"Was he killed ?"

"No, though he vas stupid for a veek. Yah !

he never forget mine head," said Carl, laughing ; "but here comes Mister Tom and Mister Larkin."

The pair indicated joined the group, and Long Tom, running his eye over them as if in search of some particular individual, singled out Snip.

"Hi !" he cried. "Snip, the brave—you're wanted."

"I'm your man, and am ready," replied Snip.

"In fact you wouldn't fail to be ready for worlds," said Will Larkin, with a sly look ; "it's well, as you are wanted for a service of great danger."

"Danger !" repeated Snip, turning ghastly pale.

"The fact is," said Will, calmly, "we are not alone on the prairie. There's human creatures of some sort near us—Indians, or something of the kind. We are not afraid of them, but we don't want to be caught napping, so we intend to post sentinels."

"And for such sarvice," added Tom, with a malicious grin, "we must have our best and bravest men, and Snip's one of them. You don't mind, do you, Snip?"

"I—I—oh ! dear no. Why should I ?" said Snip.

"You rather like it, I should think ?"

"Oh, oh !—of course."

"You comes of a family as glories in danger,' pursued Long Tom, with another grin.

"Just—just so," said Snip ; "but don't you think—think that it's rather—rather lonely, and in case of surprise wouldn't it—it be better to have another man to run back with the news?"

"One truly brave man is worth a dozen of the common ruck," said Will Larkin. "Shoulder your rifle, man, and follow your nose about five hundred yards, then stand at attention, and keep a good watch."

"Oh, oh !—yes, certainly," stammered the wretched Snip, "but have you such a thing as a drop of rum about you ?"

"That would supplement your bravery with Dutch courage," said Will. "No—go out as you are. Shoulder arms !—march !"

Snip had no recourse but to obey, so, shouldering his rifle, he tottered away into the darkness.

"Is there any real danger?" asked Carl, looking up at Will.

"There's somebody on the plain," returned Will, "but who and what they are we don't know."

"What's your idea for sending him ?" asked Carl.

"Just to try him," replied Will. "The fellow brags so that it is a pity he should not have an opportunity to prove himself a liar."

"But he will be a bad sentinel."

"The best of sentinels, Carl, my boy—the fall of a leaf will be sufficient for him to give the alarm."

The two officers then returned to Jack Savage, who was sitting before a fire, his tall form looking the mightier for being wrapped in the skin of a bear.

It was not the night for such a precaution, but he had complained of cold, and Will had thrown his rug over him.

Jack Savage scarcely noticed the act, but sat with his eyes fixed upon the hot embers, his face resting in his hands, much as he had sat

in the hut that night when he and Long Tom returned from the execution of his father. Tom, looking at him as he came up, was reminded of it, and whispered as much to his companion.

The pair sat down beside him, and neither moved nor spoke until Jack raised his eyes.

"I have been," he said, "with my father."

"With whom ?" asked Will, startled.

"With my father," repeated Jack. "There are times and places when I can call him before me and commune with him."

"Impossible !"

"Not only possible but true," returned Jack ; "only a minute ago he was with me and spoke to me."

"This must be a trick of the imagination," said Will.

"Oh, no !" replied Jack, smiling with intense meaning ; "my imagination is never tricked. This is not the first time he has been with me. I saw him the night I sat in the hut with you, Tom, and I have seen him a hundred times since."

He paused for a moment, and looked fixedly at the fire. Then he went on—

"Sometimes he is away for months, sometimes he comes twice in a day, but he never appears except when I flag in my purpose, and then he brings me a message."

"And what does he say ?" asked Will.

"He bids me go on !" cried Jack, rising suddenly. "He demands the punishment of those who slew him."

"You must imagine all this."

"Do you doubt the possibility of seeing spirits ?" demanded Jack.

"I have never seen any," said Will.

"And will you believe only what you see ?" rejoined Jack. "Can you see that which we call life ? Can you see the great spiritual lever which moves all creation ? Yet you do not doubt its existence ?"

"You mean a Creator ?"

"Aye, I do."

"The man who doubts the existence of a Creator," said Will, "is a poor, silly, purblind fool —one whose head is like an addled egg. Instinct, reason, and everything else teaches us differently."

"Or, to come lower," pursued Jack, "will you doubt a power I have within me, and yet which you cannot see ? Look at me."

Will looked straight at Jack, who made a rapid pass with his hands.

"Raise your arms," he said.

Will tried to do so, but they hung like lead at his side.

"It was my will," said Jack, "that you should not raise them. Now I will it otherwise. Up with your hands."

Almost without thinking, Will raised his hands above his head. Jack looked at him steadily.

"Now drop them," he said.

Will tried to do so, but his hands remained in the air.

"Strike me," said Jack.

Will shook his head—he felt powerless to do anything except stare at Jack Savage in dismay.

"Now to break the spell," said Jack. "Will Larkin, you are free."

In an instant Will was himself again, as far as muscular action was concerned, but he was mentally much perturbed. "Doubled up inside and out," as he expressed it.

"Do you doubt that power?" asked Jack.

"No. I should be an ass if I did," said Will.

"Can you see it?"

"No."

"Can you tell me where it comes from."

"No."

"Neither can I," said Jack, "but I have it, and can use it upon some men when I will—with others I am powerless. Now, I know not the reason, neither can I tell why, my earthly eyes see the form of my dear father, but he comes to me, standing as plainly before me as you do, and his message is, 'Go on, leave none alive,' and I will travel on to the end."

"I cannot make you out," said Will, shuddering. "I am afraid of you."

"Would you leave me?"

"I would I had never joined you," said Will, frankly. "But I have sworn an oath, which I will keep, let what may come of it."

"Let me tell you one thing," said Jack, as he coiled himself up in the skin and lay down to rest, "there are very few of you who could leave me, except I so willed it. If you think I lie try it, and if you succeed you are free from your oath."

"I don't know what they call the power he's got," said Will Larkin to Long Tom, as they stood side by side watching their sleeping chief, "but he has it, and I cannot leave him. I have heard of this sort of thing before, but never believed in it."

"What can it be?" mused Tom.

"It's impossible to say," replied Will, "but it has existed in all ages and in various forms. The Chaldeans of old practised it, the learned men of the middle ages possessed it, but no man yet could say from whence it came or whither it goes. It is a strange, mysterious, terrible power for a man to hold, but Jack Savage has it and I must obey him even to the end."

*   *   *   *   *   *

If any of our readers ever walked over a lonely heath alone at midnight, with naught around them but the heather below and the starlit sky above, the place having the reputation of being the favourite haunt of footpads and murderers, they have some faint idea of the feelings of Snip as he stood out upon the prairie to keep watch and ward over his friends and fellow-adventurers.

Snip declared that he came of a brave family. Perhaps he did, but bravery is not at all times hereditary—talents possessed by the father do not always descend to the son, and certainly Snip, of brave descent, was as arrant a coward as need be.

His situation would not have been pleasant to a brave man.

A lonely prairie is dismal at the best of times—at midnight it is decidedly depressing—and Snip, full of vague terror, sat upon his haunches, looking about him like a startled hare, ready to bolt on the first appearance of even the shadow of an enemy.

During his life at Broadpoint he had heard many stories of the cruelties of savage tribes—of men flayed, boiled, and roasted alive!

"IF I was only back in old England," Snip muttered, "you wouldn't catch me emigrating. Don't I wish I had hold of that fellow who wrote in the papers and said that this was a land of gold, where it could be picked up if one only stooped for it, with everything growing spontaneous and without any trouble, from a cabbage to a bottle of port wine. Oh! don't I wish I had him here. What's that? Oh! lor', I'm a dead man."

It was only the rustling of the grass near him, and in a minute it was still.

But, slight as it was, it had a thousand terrors for Ship. The little bravery he might have possessed—it was not much—oozed out of his finger's ends, and he sat down upon the ground in an agony of terror.

"I hope it's nothing savage," he murmured; "I never saw an Indian, except at a distance, and he didn't look nice even then. Scissors! what's that?"

A slight crashing sound, like the breaking of a twig, fell upon his ears.

Snip now felt as if his last moment had come, and cowered closer to the ground.

"The wind don't break sticks," he thought, "at least, not such a wind as this. It must be a footstep. There's another and another. I'm a dead man!"

He had barely uttered these words when he felt something hover over him like the wings of a huge bird, and then he was enveloped in a soft substance, while an iron band seemed suddenly to close round his waist.

His first thought was to cry out, but prudence came to the rescue, and he was silent.

Then he had some notion of firing his gun, but thought was again his friend—he dropped it instead of firing, and the next moment he was raised in the air.

The position he was in—one trying even to a man of strong nerve—confounded him, but he had enough mind left to realise the fact that a cloak or sack had been thrown over him, and a man, with his arms tight around him, was carrying him.

Carrying him!—ah! but where to?

That was the question.

And a serious question to Snip, one fraught with matter of considerable moment, and the speculations he ran over were none of the most agreeable.

But speculation neither makes nor mars events, and Snip was compelled to do what others in the same position must have done—he waited the issue of events.

The man carrying him made light of his burden, and strode on with the ease of one carrying a child.

Suddenly the man halted, then he placed Snip upon the ground and removed the covering.

"Now you open your mouth without being spoken to," said a voice, "and I'll blow your head off."

"Don't be violent, sir," pleaded Snip, in tremulous tones. "I wouldn't speak against your will, sir, for worlds."

"Silence!"

Snip inwardly resolved that no earthly power should make him speak until he had permission to do so.

"I am going to leave you here a minute or two, but bear in mind that there are those watching you who will put a dozen bullets into your insignificant carcase if you only dare stir."

So saying the speaker moved away.

Poor Snip remained on his knees, perfectly

immovable and silent for a few seconds, which seemed hours to him, when he heard a rustling in the shrubbery round him, and a voice said—

"Hist! don't speak, I am a friend. I dare not release you, but I can leave you a gun, so that you can protect yourself."

Poor Snip groaned, inwardly thinking how little use the gun would be to him.

Ere he had time to answer the sound of footsteps fell on his ears, and almost before his unknown friend had time to hide himself in the undergrowth, the bandage was torn from his eyes, and he found himself confronted by two determined-looking settlers, armed with guns and pistols.

"Now, no noise—follow us quietly, and all may yet go well with you."

With this they raised him to his feet and led him from the bush, where they had left him on the prairie.

He ventured to look round—the scene was not very cheering.

The only light visible, save that of the stars, arose from the camp-fires of his friends in the far distance.

Nearer he could see about a dozen shadowy figures—the forms of men—and these, to his joy, he could perceive were clad in civilised costume.

These figures gathered close around him, and one proceeded to examine him in a very positive manner, taking him in hand as a judge might take a prisoner who was expected to prove refractory.

"First, your name?" he said.

"Oh! if you please, it's Snip."

"Give your answer without any superfluities—short and to the point."

"I will, respected sir," said Snip.

"Who are those men by the camp fires?"

"My friends, sir."

"Their names?"

"Well, sir," replied Snip, "there's such a pile of 'em that I must have a little time to think."

"Time to hatch a lie or two. Speak at once. Name your leaders—I don't care for the tag-rag and bob-tail, so you can give me them in round numbers."

"Well, sir—respected sir—there's Mr. Larkin, Mr. Long Tom, and Mr. Jack Savage."

"Good Heaven!"

The tone of the speaker was altered now, and the other figures moved uneasily, as if they had suddenly received intelligence of danger.

"What is he doing here?" the speaker asked, after a pause.

Snip hesitated a moment, and a lie rose upon his lips, but he burst out with the truth—

"He's been to Broadpoint, and, finding it deserted, he is going on to Mount Restore. He's after the man who hung his father."

"Now, Snip," said the speaker, "I know you, but you don't know me."

"Indeed, respected sir," said Snip, "your voice seems familiar like. I have heard it before."

"Can you not guess when?"

"No, respected sir."

"You are more polite than when I saw you ast. Let me give you a help—how about Zepheniah——"

"Not Zepheniah Bisset?"

"The same," replied the other, "and here's

Tom Traver, and Jack Stepneroff, and a few others who settled old Savage. I wonder what young Jack would do if he knew we were so close?"

"He'd come down upon you like thunder," replied Snip, dropping his superabundant respect; "he'd bile or roast half of you, and bury alive the rest."

"Would he?"

"Yes, he would," said Snip, growing bolder, "and I can tell you that I'm a bit of a favourite of his, and it will go very hard with you if you damage a hair of my head."

"Now you begin to bully," said Bisset, "but it won't do, Snip. You draw it mild, or we will bile or roast you—at least, we will make an end of you."

"I am sure you couldn't think of serving an old friend so," returned Snip, timidly; "it would go against your nature, Zeph. I am sure it would."

"You are more sartain of it than I am," said Bisset; "but we are not going to harm you at present, Snip, as we want you. First, tell us how many men this Savage has?"

"About two hundred."

"Humph! that's a pile. And well armed?"

"Covered all over with daggers, knives, and pistols, and all of 'em as bloodthirsty as wolfhounds."

"Now you're at your old game again, but it won't do. So they are going to Mount Restore?"

"Sich is their intention."

"Well, they can come," said Bisset, "and we will be ready for them, but they must not come yet. You must keep him away for a week."

"I?"

"Yes, you."

"But how, Zeph? Don't you think you put too much upon me?"

"I don't think so, Snip, whatever you may say. You must do it. Tell any lie—you can lie as well as any man, I know—and you can work it how you like, when you like, and where you like—it don't matter to me, but you must do it."

"I'll try," said Snip.

"You had better," returned the other, in a meaning tone. "If you fail you will suffer. You will find it difficult to keep clear of us. Now go—here's the gun you dropped. The camp fires are straight before you, and you cannot miss your way."

Snip took the rifle, which one of the men held towards him, and, with a dolorous sniff, he turned towards Jack Savage and his men.

"I'm in for a fine sort of thing," he muttered, as he footed his way across the prairie. If Savage finds me out he'll do—what won't he do, and if I fail to keep my word with Zeph then I'm as good as a dead man! Bother all of them! Confound Jack Savage, and blow the whole of the Broadpoint people! That's my sentiments."

Muttering in this fashion, he made what speed he could to the camp, where he found Long Tom impatiently awaiting him.

CHAPTER XII.

SNIP AS AMBASSADOR.

"WHERE have you been?" demanded Long Tom.

"I—I," returned Snip. "Oh! I've been over

◁ GIANT JACK: ▷

A Story of the Red Mountains.

SNIP FOUND HIMSELF CONFRONTED BY TWO DETERMINED-LOOKING MEN, ARMED WITH GUNS AND PISTOLS.

there—sentinel—you know."

"But you left your post !" said Tom. "I've been up there and could not find you. A man shouldn't leave his post."

"Except when he thinks it's his duty," said Snip.

"But was it your duty ?"

"When a man hears what he thinks is savages," replied Snip, " it's his duty—even at the risk of his life—to go and see what the row is."

"Humph !" exclaimed Long Tom.

"I'm not the man to funk my duty," said Snip, growing bold. " I heard what I thought was savages on the trail, and I went after them to make sure before I fired my rifle and roused the camp."

"Did you find any ?"

"No."

"In course not," said Long Tom; "none but a jackass or a tailor would have gone humbugging about the prairie in search of what can't be found. But go to the captain—he wants you."

This intimation was received by Snip with a great amount of self-complacency. He could not dream otherwise than that the captain required him for some important office, and with the strut of a turkey-cock he marched towards Jack Savage.

The young giant was seated by a fire in his favourite attitude, with. his face resting on his hands. As Snip approached he rose up, and stood in such a position that while his face was in the shade, he could see and read Snip's with perfect ease.

"Stand still, there !" he said.

"Yes, respected captain," replied Snip.

"Spare yourself the breath and me the needless hearing of complimentary terms," said Jack. " Now, Snip, what are you ?"

Snip paused a moment, as if to collect his thoughts—the question certainly surprised him —and then he replied—

" I was a tailor, respect—ahem !—sir."

" I do not care for your trade," returned Jack Savage, impatiently; " what are you, an honest man or not ?"

Snip could say nothing to this—the question was so different from what he expected that he was dumbfounded ; but he thought of Zepheniah Bisset and his friends, and trembled.

"Are you not a liar ?" demanded Jack, with an imperious frown.

"I—me—a liar !" exclaimed Snip, as if he had been the most virtuous person in the world, and accused of picking a pocket.

"Yes, you—are you not a liar ?" said Jack. " But there, why do I trouble you with the question—when I know you are ? Have I not the gift of reading men as other men read what they call books ? You cannot keep your inmost thoughts from me. You are a liar !"

The power which Jack boasted of troubled Snip very much, and he wondered if the young giant, his captain, had any inkling of his meeting with the men of Mount Restore. On this head Jack speedily relieved him.

"The gift I possess," he said, "tells me that you have met men on the prairie this night. I saw you and them in the fire, but I know not what you said. Tell me, and tell me the truth, if you wish to live another hour."

"The other was a pretty go, but this is a prettier," thought Snip, the very hair of his head standing erect. Then he said, aloud—

"The men I met, I met against my wish. They were Zepheniah Bisset and a few of the old Broadpoint men. They said—ahem !—they said——"

"Give me the truth," rejoined Jack, firmly, " and nothing but the truth."

"They asked me all about you," said Snip, fairly driven into a corner, " and—and——"

"You told them !"

"I was obliged to, respected captain—that is, I meant to say, sir."

"Did you tell them the truth ?"

"As much as I was obliged to, sir; but I did my best to serve you," returned Snip.

"Thank you," said Jack, sarcastically. Then he stood in silence for awhile, consulting the fire, as was his wont.

"As you seem to know both sides well," said Jack, " you will be the best agent I can employ. I intend sending you to them with a message."

"And once away I don't come back again," thought Snip.

"I read your thoughts," continued Jack, instantly. " You think that once away from me you will be free. Poor fool ! Try it, and you will find that you must come back again, even against your will. Move now !"

He made a few rapid passes before Snip, who in vain endeavoured to stir a step. He was as secure as one bound in bands of iron.

"Why don't you move ?" asked Jack.

" I can't," returned Snip, trembling, but otherwise still as a statue.

"No," said Jack. "And why ? Because it is my will. Would that I could exercise it upon all men—but stand free !"

Snip experienced a sensation as if being delivered from a spell, and the young giant went on—

"Go now, at once, to the people of Mount Restore, and give them this, my message. Say that if they will give over the men who tried my father, to be tried by me—the rest shall be spared ; but, if they refuse, tell them this, my second message—I will not leave a man amongst them alive. I will even destroy the male children, and uproot the names of all from the earth. You understand ?"

" I do, sir," replied Snip, thinking to himself, " and a very pleasant message it is for a chap to deliver."

"I give you two hours for rest," continued Jack. " By that time the sun will be above the horizon, and will afford you the little help you need to guide you on your way."

His manner intimated to Snip that this was his last injuction, that the interview was ended, and the brave tailor of Broadpoint retired to get what rest he could in the two hours allotted to him.

As for Jack, when alone he paced to and fro like a restless spirit.

There were thoughts within his brain which troubled him—promptings of conscience he would not listen to. He was bent upon an errand of vengeance, and his strong will urged him to fulfil it.

By-and-bye a step aroused him.

He turned and beheld Will Larkin.

"Come here and walk with me, Will," he said, with a sad smile on his noble face.

Will came, and the two paced for awhile in silence. It was broken by the chief.

"Will, you know I love you as a friend."

Larkin looked up quickly, surprised at this style of address, for Jack was not given to utterances sentimental.

"I believe you have a sincere regard for me," Will said.

"But more than that, Will. I was drawn to you the first time we met."

"Gad !—so was I drawn to you," returned Will, with a laugh, "and now you hold me pretty tight."

"You are free to leave me, if you will."

"Never !" returned Will, warmly. "I am bound to you in a hundred ways, without naming the strange power you hold over me."

"Ah ! that power," said Jack, in a musing tone. "My father used to say that our ancestors learned it from books, and he was always reading to find it. One day the books told him the secret, and he tried his power over me."

"Did he succeed ?"

"Yes. He bound me as if by a magic spell. He bade me go, and I went—he asked me to return, and I came—his will, and not my own, moved me. I obeyed that at all times, whether I would or no."

"But how came you with the power ?"

"I suppose it came from him. I know that it grew within me as I grew—that as my early boyhood left me it came. I was first made aware of it by Long Tom. He was my first victim."

"I should like to hear the story," said Will, whose curiosity was strongly excited.

"It can be told in a few words," returned Jack. "One night we were out upon the prairie, sitting by the fire, and I had been, as usual, looking into the ashes, where I saw, as I had seen a hundred times before and since, the spirit of my father. What he said to me that night was what he always said, 'Go on, go on' —but let that pass.

"I sat there some time, until I heard the hooting of an owl. Suspecting the presence of Indians, or strangers at least, I rose up, and walked a little way into the darkness.

"Tom followed me. ' You need not come,' I said, ' there is no danger. I can go alone.'

"' And you might have gone alone,' replied Tom. ' I did not want to come. I came because I could not help it.'

"' Not help it !' I exclaimed.

"' No,' said Tom, ' I could not help it. You seemed to draw me like a magnet, and I can't go back without you.'

"' Go back !' I said, but Tom stood still.

"I was rather inclined to be angry with him, thinking that Tom was joking, when suddenly there burst upon me the memory of my father's power—a thing I had almost forgotten. Wondering if this had descended to me, I made what he used to call the passes of relief, and Tom turned back instantly, when I knew the power was mine."

"And you have exercised it since ?"

"Now and then, Will," replied Jack ; "but I must be frank with you. It is very hard work. When I use it all my strength seems to leave me for a moment, but it quickly returns. But were I sick I should be powerless— wounded the same. If my father had not first been shot, I doubt if all Broadpoint could have taken him. But they took him," added Jack,

"and his murdered spirit calls for vengeance."

"I wish you could abandon that idea," said Will.

"I cannot."

"There is a glorious life before you," said Will Larkin, growing warm on the subject. "A field for mighty adventure, whither every man here assembled would follow. You would be victorious wherever you went, but the greatest victory would be the forgiving of these Broadpoint people."

"Ah ! Will—but how forgive ?" replied Jack, doubtingly.

"Will murdered husbands, weeping widows, burning homes, and orphaned children bring back your father to life ?" pursued Will Larkin. "Can bloody deeds turn right into wrong ? Your father certainly defied these people and broke their laws. They tried him by their laws, and he paid the penalty. They were wrong, I know, but he was wrong also, and will that which you are bent upon put either right ?"

"But his spirit urges me on."

"Not his spirit, Jack, but the spirit of some devil who would ruin you," returned Will. "Such work as vengeance on these people is not worthy of you. Your deeds should be nobler, for you are noble. Down farther south, in the most lovely part of this beautiful land, ruffianism of every degree is rampant—rogues from every clime are mustered there, and deeds are done daily which should shake the earth."

"I know, Will—I have seen it."

"There lies your field," cried Will. "In days gone by, when old England was befouled by crime, good King Arthur and his knights purged the land. Be you the King Arthur of this land and we your knights. Bid us work and fight against savage hordes and bloody ruffians, and we will fight, and fighting die, if need be."

"Ah ! Will, you are brave and true."

"Be you brave and true, Jack, to the better and nobler part of your nature. Rise up against the demon who urges you to do a wrong to others and yourself."

"Leave me, Will, for awhile," said Jack ; "I must sit by the fire and think. Your words touch me to the heart, but my answer must come from the fire."

Will left him, and Jack sat by the fire until the sun peeped above an eastern line of cloud, then Will came back and stood before his chief.

"What says the fire ?" he asked.

"On to Mount Restore," replied Jack.

"On to Mount Restore !" mused Will, as he mustered the men, "and then—ah ! then—on to where ? This deed will never be sanctioned by the Heaven above."

CHAPTER XIII.

THE AMBASSADOR AT MOUNT RESTORE.

"So you are going as ambassador to Mount Restore, are you ?" said Long Tom, addressing Snip, who was getting ready for his departure.

"I go by the commands of my noble captain," returned Snip, with a proud air. "He can't trust nobody else."

"Can't he ?"

"So he told me," replied Snip. "He said that out of the two hundred men around him he could trust none of 'em but me."

"That's the way he soft-soaped you over,"

said Tom. "Such chaps as you can't get on without soft soap. But look'ee here, my ambassador, you mind this—it aint no rosy office, for when a ambassador goes on his errand it's allus ten to one against his returning alive."

"Lor!" ejaculated Snip, turning ghastly pale.

"That's a fact," said Tom, shouldering his rifle; "but you are the sort of chap as comes of a brave family, and fighting's your forty, as the French say, so you'll rather enjoy this little trip; but keep clear of Injuns, for they are the cusses as toast a man afore they kill him—adoo!"

With this parting salute Tom turned on his heel and walked away.

The thoughts of Snip were none of the pleasantest, but the camp was now alive, and if he had no other reasons for obeying the injunctions of his captain, the fact of the men being around him would have checked any display of actual cowardice.

He, therefore, took a gun under his arm and assumed a valiant air.

The news of his mission had gone forth, and the men crowded around him to wish him good speed. Even Caderouse was there, and Snip, on the impulse of the moment, held out his hand to him.

"When a man is on the brink of a fearful grave," he said, a little mournfully, "he ought to part friends, even with his enemies."

"It shall be the best of frens ve must part," replied Caderouse, and Snip walked out of the camp with the swinging step of one conscious of his important mission.

The way to Mount Restore lay across the prairie, but the exact distance neither Jack Savage nor his ambassador knew.

Jack had an idea that it might be about twenty miles, and put it down as a day's journey for Snip.

Twenty miles in a civilised country is not much to trouble about, but twenty miles in a land where savages were still plentiful as blackberries, and where the scattered civilised communities were of the roughest sort, was a very different thing, and Snip felt it was so.

"Once back again in old England," he thought, at least a hundred times during the first mile, "and I'll do any amount of jobs at any price. Bread and cheese and an onion there would be better than roast beef and plum pudding here. I'll bet a hundredweight of the finest diamond-eyed needles to the skin of a gooseberry that I'm toasted and eaten before the day is out. Now, if I had only defied this brute, Savage—if I had only stood my ground and refused to go, what would he have done? Just taken my neck between his finger and thumb, and I—I, Snip, the tailor—would have dropped on my back as dead as mutton."

In this way Snip mused during the entire journey.

Fortune favoured him, for no savages crossed his path—the Indians do not care for daylight or open spaces—and he was spared to reach Mount Restore, and deliver the message with which he had been entrusted.

A word about Mount Restore.

It was a large hillock, in the very heart of the prairie, rising to a considerable elevation.

In extent it was about six miles from side to side one way, and four the other.

The land was exceedingly rich, and easily cultivated; there was a fair amount of wood and water, and all things necessary for a small community to begin with.

The spot had been chosen partly for its richness—it was, indeed, an oasis in the desert-like prairie—and partly from its elevated position, many parts giving a very extended view of the vast plain around.

With very little watching the people were secure from the secret approach of an enemy, and on three of the highest points stockades had been erected where the settlers could flee for safety in case of attack.

The houses, built entirely of wood, were dotted about on the various pieces of land which had been parcelled out to the men when they came from Broadpoint, and the rough but comfortable structures looked very picturesque even in the eyes of Snip as he left the prairie and marched up the rising land.

He saw no living creature, save a few cattle grazing, who turned their heads and stared at him as he went by.

But one vicious old buffalo bull made for Snip, and it would have gone hard with this ninth part of a man had he not summoned up sufficient resolution to attack the bull.

Poor Snip had been so inured to danger from human enemies latterly that he was quite brave in comparison when it was only an animal he had to deal with, so, throwing down his rifle, he literally caught the bull by the horns, and had it out with him.

The bull, not being used to this style of combat, was soon glad to give up the struggle, and Snip was highly elated with his unexpected victory as he trudged on his way.

Climbing over a rude fence he entered the yard of the nearest house, and advanced to the door and knocked.

No answer.

"They can't be gone to bed," thought Snip; "it isn't above four o'clock!" and then he knocked again.

No answer, as before.

"It's skewrious," muttered Snip, stooping down, and screwing up his eye to get a peep through the latch-hole. "I don't see anybody about. Hallo! house, there!"

While his voice was yet echoing, a heavy hand descended upon Snip and smote him.

As might have been expected of such a brave man, he fell in a huddled heap upon the ground, and gave a dismal yell.

"Silence!" cried the voice of Zepheniah Bisset; "don't you know me, man?"

"What do you mean by coming upon a man behind?" demanded Snip. "Can't a man look into a house without being knocked down like a bullock?"

"I GAVE you greeting, that is all," said Bisset, in reply to Snip's query; "but enough of this. What brings you here?"

"I bring a message from the great and mighty captain, Jack Savage," replied Snip.

"Do you remember the orders I gave you?"

"It was no use," said Snip. "I tried to carry them out, but the captain was too much for me, and he will be too much for you. I bring a message from him."

"To whom?"

"To the people of Mount Restore."

"Humph!"

"Where are they?"

"In the northern stockade," replied Bisset; "we saw you crossing the prairie this afternoon, but knew you not."

"And I frightened the lot," grinned Snip.

"One vulture is but a pilot for a hundred," said Bisset, sternly. "How could we tell who was on your ugly track? Danger is near us, that we know, and our wives and children are dear to us. Where is your captain?"

"He is following me."

"Father of mercies!" ejaculated Zepheniah Bisset, passing his strong hand across his brow. "Is he so near. How shall we escape?"

"You can't escape," said Snip, solemnly.

"What is your message?"

"Shall I give it to you alone?"

"Yes—but stay, better all should hear it. Follow me."

He passed round to the back of the house, where the ground rose abruptly.

Some rude steps had been cut—a narrow pathway for one—and up these he led the way.

On the summit of the cliff was a deep fringe of bushes.

Through these they went to another rugged rising of the ground, similar to the first. On the highest point of this was the stockade.

As Bisset advanced he called out "Broadpoint!" And immediately a rough wooden fence was crowned with a line of heads, most of them familiar to Snip—being, in fact, the property of the people of Broadpoint.

The stockade was very strong, and fairly constructed; but Snip saw at a glance that it could not hold out long against Jack Savage and his men.

Then, again, there was the important question of provision.

The stockade contained more than a hundred and twenty souls—men, women, and children—who crowded round Bisset and Snip as they came in.

The men were moody and frowning, the women pale and frightened, the children wondering—some of the youngest were amused with the novelty of being altogether in the pretty stockade.

"It's only Snip," said one of the women, "come back at last."

"He comes as a messenger from the Wolf," said Bisset. "Stand around, comrades and friends. This man will tell you what Jack Savage has to say!"

Snip took advantage of an empty barrel and mounted thereon. He felt that he had now an opportunity of distinguishing himself which, if neglected, might be lost for ever.

"Ladies and gentlemen——" he began.

"No foolery, man!" interrupted Bisset, sternly. "Remember, this is a matter of life and death."

"Jack Savage's message," said Snip, sobering a little under the rebuke, "is in two parts, and the first part refers to me."

"Go on, man."

"He wishes it to be known that I brought this message against my will, and that he hopes that you won't harm me."

"You are perfectly safe," said Bisset, with profound contempt. "Go on, man."

"His next message was to this effect—that is to say——"

Snip could not help making the most of the situation. He saw the anxiety on the faces of his listeners, and he paused a moment before continuing his communication. Then he went on.

"He, Jack Savage, says that if the people, late of Broadpoint, now of Mount Restore, will give up the men who tried his father, the rest shall go scot-free."

There was a silence for some minutes after this intimation. Then Zepheniah spoke.

"And what will he do to the men when they are in his power?"

"Try them as they tried his father," replied Snip.

"Aye, he would be judge, jury, and executioner, no doubt," returned Bisset, bitterly; "and what if we refuse?"

"In that case," said Snip, getting down from his tub, "he has made up his mind to slaughter the lot."

"Men, women, and children?"

"Men, women, and children," repeated Snip; "he won't leave one—or, in his own words, he means to exterminate the breed."

"A goodly threat, and one which requires a little discussion. In private, too. Will you have the goodness to retire to that knoll while we consult a bit?"

Snip went to the spot indicated and sat down. Then the settlers consulted together in an undertone. The talk was brief, and Snip was summoned back.

He came with his hands upon his hips, swaggering like a rover of the seas.

Bisset, as spokesman of the party, took him again in hand.

"You are certain," he said, "that your captain sent that message?"

"I gave it word for word."

"And he wants an answer?"

"Yes."

"Then he must come here for it."

"And I?" said Snip.

"Will be kept here," replied Bisset.

Snip began to look very uneasy.

"What for?" he asked.

"That you will know in good time," replied Bisset, as he turned away.

"I don't think I can get into a deeper hole than this," muttered Snip, the cold dew of concentrated cowardice standing on his brow. "I thought the lonely life at Broadpoint bad enough, but this—well, it's the prettiest go I was ever mixed up in."

CHAPTER XIV.

JACK SAVAGE'S REVENGE.

THERE was a solemn sadness among the people of the stockade. The women kept close to the men, and the children clung to their mothers with a vague sense of coming danger which was truly touching.

The men were all armed, but the weapons they bore were bad, even for that time, and so far inferior to the weapons of the present day that they would be useless now.

Old Brown Bess rifles, heavy in the stock and not very certain in the barrel, were all they possessed, and these they loaded with a dogged air.

"We can but die," muttered one, "so we may as well die fighting."

Among them all not one could be found
desirous of giving up Zepheniah Bisset and the
rest of the court which had condemned Jack's
father, but there were many who looked upon
the advance of our hero with a secret trembling,
in which self had no part.

They were husbands and fathers, and their
thoughts were for their wives and children.

Some sat apart from those they loved, others
kept them near, and gave what comfort they
could to their dear ones in smiles and hopeful
words.

Above all, upon the summit of a mound in the
centre of the stockade, a sentinel sat.

It was Tom Traver.

He sat with his chin upon his hands, his eyes
fixed on the fair horizon, while most of the
settlers kept their eyes on him.

And thus the night came on.

The sun goes down quickly in the west, and
the short twilight died out as rapidly as hope
died away from the settlers' hearts, leaving
them in utter misery.

Once there had been a suggestion from a
settler to flee across the prairie. This was met
with an objection from Bisset.

"Well enough," he said, "if we had had a
few days clear ; but now the wolf would be upon
us ere we were half across the plain. No—we
must stay here and fight—if need be, die—
leaving ourselves in the hands of a just and all-
wise Providence."

The moon arose slowly before midnight, and
its light fell upon the sleepless people awaiting
the coming of the avenger.

It also fell upon Snip, under the guard of Sam
Turner and Charles Dean, both resolute men.
Snip had received a slight warning from Sam.

"If you so much as wink," he said, "I am to
put a bullet through you, so sit quiet, and
don't make noise enough to disturb a mouse.
You hear ?"

"I'm not deaf," returned Snip, surlily ; "but
I warn you that the captain will make some of
you smart for this. I am a tremendous favourite
of his."

"All right," returned Sam, carelessly ; "you
sit quiet, and we will take what follows."

The light of the moon was so brilliant that
objects could be seen far away on the prairie—
far enough for the unhappy watchers to receive
intimation of the avenger's coming.

But the night passed, the white prairie lying
like a sheet before them, and the sun uprose as
the moon went down.

As its golden rays glanced over the country
around the watchers on the mound uttered a
startled cry. In an instant all was commotion.

"What is it ?" shouted Bisset.

"A band of men coming across the prairie."

Some of the men, actuated by an irresistible
impulse, knelt down, and the women fell a-weep-
ing. There was a sound, too, of ramrods—a
ringing sound, being used, as the men loaded
their guns and sent the charges home.

Snip scarcely knew whether to feel elated or
depressed. Under ordinary circumstances he
might have considered that Jack's coming
would save him, but, as matters were, he was
doubtful if it would not be a signal for his
death.

The men under Jack advanced across the
plain until they arrived within a quarter of a
mile of the stockade, when they halted.

Then one came from their midst bearing a
white flag—a flag of truce.

Snip, jerked forward by Sam Turner, came
and stood before the leader of the settlers. The
brave man had never been so cowed before.

"You know many of these villains," said
Bisset. "Tell me who comes here ?"

"Wait—let me see, sir," returned Snip. "I
think you asked me who was coming."

"I did."

"I am too far away, sir," replied Snip. "If
I could be allowed to go nearer—down the hill a
little way——"

"You will be allowed nothing of the sort.
Who is it ?"

"Now I look again," said Snip, amazed by
the peremptory tone of Bisset, "I think it is
Mr. William Larkin."

"You know it is ?"

"Yes, sir, I know it."

"And who is Larkin ?"

"A sort of lieutenant, sir."

"Friends and neighbours," said Bisset, turning round, "I am going to meet this new-comer
man to man—no great harm can come of it."

There was no objection raised to this, and
Zepheniah Bisset descended from the stockade.
Those above saw him cross the intervening space
and meet Will Larkin.

The two men halted without any greeting,
and a few words passed between them.

Then Zepheniah Bisset waved his hand to his
friends, and he and Will Larkin went on to
where Jack Savage and his men were waiting.

"He's gone to his death," cried Sam Turner.
"The Wolf has him in his power."

With sadder faces than before, the settlers
remained watching, until they saw Bisset
returning.

This time he had a companion, but not Will
Larkin.

By his side walked one above the common
height of men—a tall, majestic figure—Jack
Savage himself.

He and Bisset came on alone.

The two hundred men composing our hero's
band lay quietly upon the ground, their gun-
barrels gleaming in the sunshine.

"He's mad to come here," muttered Dean, a
tall, powerful man. "I'll have a shot at him if
no other man will."

"You couldn't harm him," said Snip. "No
man could fire at him unless he chose to let
him."

At this some of the listeners laughed, for they
could not help it—Snip's reverence and belief in
Jack seemed so ridiculous.

"Aye, you may laugh," continued Snip,
"but I tell you that he can do as he likes with
any man in his camp, and no one can raise an
arm if Jack Savage chooses to keep it down."

"I guess I'll try his power," muttered Sam
Turner—and the time was near for doing so, for
Bisset and Jack were coming up the side of
the mound, and soon they were in the midst of
the settlers.

As the men looked at the young giant they
ceased to wonder at the power he held. He was
certainly of noble presence, with a mien they
had never dreamt of before.

He stood for at least a minute gazing calmly
at them, Zepheniah Bisset standing by his side
with an unmoved face.

"Well, men of Broadpoint," said Jack, "I

,am here at last."

There was a little uneasy shifting as he spoke, but none ventured upon a reply.

"My father died by your hands," pursued Jack; "he is at peace, I hope, but should be living now. You were his accuser, judge, and executioner all in one, and I am here with the power to be your accuser, judge, and executioner. The time may come when I may think fit to carry out my vengeance—but not now. I will give you the chance of redeeming yourselves, meanwhile I command you one and all to follow me wherever I lead."

They were awed by him. The magical power of his presence and his voice subdued them, so that they became as children.

A respite! Well, it was something, and all hoped they would be spared, but they had not prophetic eyes, and could not dive into the future, where so much that is dark and terrible ay hidden.

"It's the act of a man," cried Sam Turner, "and he's every inch a man. Three cheers for Jack Savage. Hip, hip, hurrah, boys!"

Up went their hats, and the air was rent with their shouts of joy.

The noise was heard in the camp below, and the followers of Jack responded with a lengthened cheer.

Then Jack held up his hand for silence, and every voice was hushed.

Even the children ceased their prattle, and stood gazing quietly at the big, handsome man, who made a splendid picture as he removed his sombrero, and, with his hand resting negligently upon his hip, prepared to address them.

"Men of Mount Restore," he said, "your thanks are not due to me, but to a friend of mine—Will Larkin. I will call him."

He gave a great shout from his powerful lungs, and not only Will, but all the followers of Jack, came running towards Mount Restore.

For an instant a thought of treachery flashed across Bisset's mind, but one glance at Jack's open face dispelled the doubt, and he allowed the men of Jack's camp to swarm up the side of the mount and into the stockade without a murmur.

Cordial greetings were exchanged, and Will was quite mobbed by the women, half of whom fell in love with the good-looking fellow.

A little later Jack announced his schemes for the future.

"I am not fit for a quiet life," he said. "My career must be one of adventure, or I should die. Now, further south, there are knaves and rogues who have grown fat and rich in sin—plunderers of the settler and the traveller. It is my intention to rid the land of these leeches; but there will be times when I shall want to rest from my labours—to remain in some spot which I may consider home. Men of Mount Restore, shall I rest here?"

CHAPTER XV.

THE PIRATE'S HAUNT.

AN affirmative shout responded to the query, and Jack went on—"If I make wealth you and your children shall share it; if I fail, you will give me and mine a crust of bread and a cup of water—will you not?"

Again they shouted the reply he needed, and Jack continued—

"My first journey will be to the haunt of the tiger who calls himself Don Ricardo. You have all heard of him—a pirate on the sea and a highwayman on land. Hitherto he has kept his hiding-place a secret—has defied all search—but I know it, and to-morrow I start to unearth him."

"And I tell you what I'll do," said Zepheniah Bisset, "I'll go too. We owe you something, and I don't think that it will hurt me to serve you for a year or so. My dame can farm while I am away."

"But what says your dame?" asked Jack.

"She bids him go," returned Bisset's wife. "He is a man, and can fight like one."

Then other volunteers stood forth, and from them Jack selected those who had formed the court when his father was condemned to death, but there was no demur. The men were willing, and the women bade them go.

Leaving their land to be tilled by their wives and neighbours, they joined Jack Savage, and on the morrow the parting came.

Much good-will was expressed on both sides, and Jack went forward with ten additional men added to his strength—as good men as ever handled a gun, and volunteers to boot.

That night, as Jack sat by the camp-fire, Will Larkin came to him.

"Is it good or ill?" Will asked.

"Good," returned Jack. "Good in every way. Ah! Will, after that last exhortation of yours I saw my father in the camp-fire, as I see him now."

"Is he changed?"

"Much."

"And what says he?"

"That I have done well," replied Jack, "and he bids me go on with the work I have in hand."

"And you will?"

"To the end. Let the knaves and pirates tremble. I will wipe them out, as the rising waters wipe out footprints from the sand—they shall melt before me as snow melts before the sun."

"But they may prove very tough, Jack."

"I know my power," returned Jack, calmly, "and I neither brag nor boast. I have a work to accomplish, and I shall not die until it is done. There lives not the man who can take my life, or even turn me for a moment from the path I have chosen, and which you and I will tread together."

*   *   *   *   *   *

A brisk wind blowing from the sea sent the blue waves dashing against a mighty rock and turned them to snowy foam.

This huge rock, standing like a pinnacle near the shore, its crown tinged with the light of the setting sun, seemed to smile upon the efforts of the waves and calmly defy them, as it had long and successfully defied the hand of Time.

The entire coast appeared rugged, barren, and forbidding; but there was one spot, in the very heart of a group of rocks, which afforded a snug retreat.

The place was naturally protected. On the seaside the giant rock sheltered it, the lesser rocks keeping it from harm on the land side, and here a band of men had chosen to make their home.

We have called them men—we should have said demons, monsters, anything but men—for they were pirates of the deep, with Don Ricardo, a recreant Spaniard, at their head.

.The deeds he did have died away—wiped out by the sponge of Time—but at the time our story treats of his doings were known east, west, north, and south, and men cursed while women shuddered at his name.

It was the habit of this villain, when successful in plunder, to retire to the haunt we have described, and there carouse a month or so away. With curtains hung about the entrance of the caves and alcoves, and with a rude kind of luxury within, he and his followers managed to make themselves tolerably comfortable.

Of their lawless doings we will not speak—all that could be imagined they were guilty of, and they lived on in their sin, sweltering in vice as a toad swelters in the dim corners of some reed-tangled marsh.

Don Ricardo, their leader, was at home, lying upon his back in the shade of a rock, which, if it could have moved of its own will, would have fallen upon and crushed the wretch who lay beneath, calmly smoking his cigarette and drinking coffee.

A number of men lay around, many of them sleeping off the effects of the previous evening's debauch.

One and all were well dressed, and several were gaudily attired, but no dress could hide the stamp set upon their faces by the seal of Nature, which declared them to be rogues and ruffians everyone.

Presently Don Ricardo turned lazily upon his side and called out—

"Pedro!"

A lithe, swarthy man responded to the call, and stood respectfully before his chief.

"What is the hour, Pedro?" he asked.

"In an hour the sun will sink and night will be here," replied Pedro.

"Santa Maria! so late?"

"So late, your excellency."

"And Tesana not in?"

"He said he would be here before sunset, and the sun has yet an hour to the good, your excellency."

"True," muttered Don Ricardo, resuming his cigarette; "leave me, Pedro."

The man bowed and left him, then clambered up one of the rocks with the help of a rope dangling from the summit.

He stood there for awhile gazing inland, then he came down again and returned to his chief.

"Your excellency?"

"What is it, Pedro?"

"Tesana is coming."

"Indeed!" cried Don Ricardo, becoming suddenly interested; "and is he in good company?"

"He comes alone, your excellency."

A frown crossed the swarthy face of the Spaniard as Pedro spoke, but he merely lighted another cigarette and said—

"When Tesana arrives bid him come to me."

Pedro bowed, and five minutes later hailed Tesana from the summit of the rock. Tesana, a nimble half-caste, scarcely in his teens, came sliding down the rope, which appeared to be the only means of exit and entrance to the haunt, and dropped upon the sand as lightly as a cat.

"His excellency wishes to see you."

"I have no wish to see his excellency," muttered Tesana; but, nevertheless, he went to the pirate and announced himself.

"So you have returned?"

"Yes, your excellency."

"And alone?"

"I am not to blame," returned the boy, hanging his head, "I was robbed of the lady on my way."

CHAPTER XVI.

SNIP PROVES HIMSELF A HERO.

"ROBBED!" cried Don Ricardo.

"Aye, your excellency—robbed," replied Tesana, his boyish face full of fear and woe. "I gave her your message, and the Lady Ximena, saying that she was your slave, came along with me. We travelled half the day, and towards noon halted upon the plain which lies beyond the sands. While there a band of men came suddenly upon us, and took from me the Lady Ximena, but I escaped."

"You fled and left her," said the Don, fiercely.

"What could I do?" returned the boy, earnestly. "My feeble arm against two hundred men."

"Two hundred men?"

"Aye, your excellency. At first I thought it was some of those who serve you, otherwise they had not come upon us so readily; but I was speedily undeceived, and then it was too late."

"What were they like?"

"All well armed, and English for the most part; but there was one who rose like a mountain above the rest. He appeared to be their leader, and when some of the men levelled their guns at me I heard him cry 'Harm not the boy!' and so I escaped to tell the tale."

Don Ricardo was sorely troubled, it was plain, but he strove to hide his perturbation from the boy.

"The news you bring is strange," he said. "But why should I trouble? I will scatter this band of fools like chaff before the wind! Send hither Cassaban."

Tesana bowed and hastened away. In a few minutes Cassaban, one of the officers of the pirate, appeared before him.

"Your pleasure, excellency?"

"Good Cassaban," replied Don Ricardo, "there are strangers in our land—intruders on our ground."

"So I have heard," returned Cassaban, quietly stroking his moustache.

"They number two hundred at the least, so Tesana tells me," continued the chief; "too large a band for us to despise."

"Much too large, your excellency."

"How many do we muster?"

"Three hundred here, and the crew of the Fire and Flame, two hundred strong, expected to-morrow."

"Five hundred in all. Humph! a goodly number. We should be more than a match for the new comers."

"We should be," returned Cassaban; "but whether we shall be is another thing. I do not like these wandering bands of English."

"Not all English."

"But British led, your Excellency, which is about the same thing. They always give us no end of trouble."

"A plague upon them!" muttered Don Ricardo. "Am I never to be at peace?"

Strange that a man who lived by fire and rapine should talk of living in peace; but such are the inconsistencies of some natures. Cassaban marked the petulance of his chief and inwardly smiled.

"We must meet this foe," continued Don Ricardo, after a pause, "by stratagem first of all. We will resort afterwards to arms if need be, although I would rather avoid it—not that I fear anyone living."

"Fear is unknown to your excellency," replied Cassaban.

"It is, good Cassaban. We will begin with stratagem. Send out some spies to mark their movements."

"I will take half-a-dozen men with me and go in person," replied Cassaban.

"Well said," returned Don Ricardo. "I shall expect you on the morrow."

The greater and lesser villain then separated—Cassaban to choose half-a-dozen men he could best trust for courage and cunning, and Don Ricardo to smoke and drink while he thought over this unexpected blow to his quietude.

Early the following morning Cassaban returned with his men, bringing with them, in great triumph, a prisoner.

They dragged him, bound and gagged, into the presence of their chief, who, with his inevitable cigarette, awaited their coming.

The prisoner had been terribly mauled, and every hair of his head seemed to bristle with fear and rage as the pirate chief looked him up and down.

It was our old friend Snip.

"And pray who is this?" demanded the pirate chief.

"We found this man on duty outside the camp of the strangers," replied Cassaban.

"As sentinel?"

"Yes. I struck him down, and bound him hand and foot."

"And you hit me on the ground," cried Snip. "Yah! coward."

"Silence!" said Don Ricardo, sternly.

"Silence yourself," returned Snip; "you will get into trouble over this. Blow winds and crack your cheeks. Flow cataracts and hurricanes spout. Kicked was I by a foreigner, and he half a nigger."

"If you are not quiet," said Don Ricardo, "I will have you toasted alive."

"If you do you will be cut up piecemeal by our bold and noble captain, with whom I am an immense favourite. I am the very apple of his eye."

"Who is your captain?"

Snip was at first inclined to tell the simple truth, but his love of bombast overcame all other feelings as he replied—

"Lord John Plantagenet Savage, Admiral of the Port of London, and Chief Commander of the Royal Cavalry of Great Britain and Ireland—that's what he is, and you mind how you treat me."

Absurd as these titles were, they appalled Don Ricardo.

He, like most men of his class, saw much in a big name, and there was a thousand terrors in this string of titles bestowed upon our friend Jack Savage by Snip.

"The British Government has sent out its full power against me," the pirate thought. "Ah! they know and fear me."

He could not, even in his terror, help smiling complacently at his importance. Beckoning to Snip, he bade him come nearer.

"How can I come?" demanded Snip, "bound up as I am like a bag of wool?"

"Remove his bonds," said the pirate.

Snip's bonds were removed, and he stamped about for a minute in a frenzy of pain, the result of returning circulation.

The pirates roared with laughter at his antics.

"You may laugh," said Snip, "but if any one of you will stand up before me for five minutes I will make you laugh the other way."

Snip then and there perpetrated a few insane movements, which he supposed were connected with the science of boxing.

This time the pirates did not laugh, and the chief called Snip to order.

"If he doesn't stand still, Cassaban," he said, "put your sword through him."

Cassaban drew his sword, and Snip prudently retired, with commendable promptitude, into his shell, becoming meek and patient in a moment.

"Now," said the pirate, "describe your chief."

"He is as big as two people and as strong as ten," returned Snip, instantly. "He can take trees up by the roots, draw them like teeth, and sling them about like cricket balls."

"He must be a strong man."

"He is," said Snip. "I'll tell you what he did, and it's a fact, as true as that I came from Wapping. Yesterday morning he was out on the plain with the female Spanish party—who fell in with us sudden—when they came upon half-a-dozen buffaloes lying in the grass. Up jumps a bull and rushes at the Spanish party, when Lord John Savage takes him by the horns and turns him on his back in a twinkling. The bull was so knocked over by this that he got up and went away as quiet as buttermilk."

Snip was not given much to truth-telling, but this was, indeed, a fact—Jack Savage had acted as narrated above.

"You speak of a Spanish party," said Don Ricardo. "Whom do you mean?"

"A gal—a lady," replied Snip.

The pirate chief leaped up as if he had been stung, and his face flamed up like a blacksmith's fire aroused by the bellows.

"Were they friendly? In close communion?" he asked.

"Uncommonly close," replied Snip, "close as wax—sweet as honey—regular nuts. I haven't seen such a case since I saw Brown Betsy and Bill Swash, who lived in Toddle's-court, Wapping, and they never left each other a minute, except on Monday morning, when Bill went up to the westry to get the weekly relief."

Snip had time to volunteer this statement, for Don Ricardo was indulging in a fit of furious meditation.

He came out of it as Snip concluded, and bade Cassaban come closer to him.

"I am mad, Cassaban," he said, "mad with fury, to find the Lady Ximena forgetting herself with this stranger. Send out and watch their movements, and let me have news of both."

"It shall be done," replied Cassaban. "And

what shall we do with this fellow ?"

" Kill him and cast him to the carrion crows," replied the other. " Stay ! we will have some sport with him. He shall fight for his life. Let him choose his man. If he conquers he shall go free—if he fails, he dies."

Cassaban imparted this piece of intelligence to Snip, who received it with better grace than might have been expected. He was one of those who believed that being an Englishman by birth was sufficient to make him more than a match for any man born of any other tribe or nation.

" I'll have a go in," he said. " Right is might, and while Britannia rules the waves no Britons shall be slaves. So I am to have my choice of a man, am I ?"

" You can select whom you please."

" Then," said Snip, " as I always had the courage of ten people, I'll have a go in at the big pot."

" Who ?"

" The big pot—your chief. He don't seem to do much except lie on his back and smoke, so I'll have a fire at him."

" Impossible," said Cassaban.

" Then why do you tell me I can choose which man I like," said Snip, " when you say ' impossible' to the very first I select ? Perhaps your chief is funky."

Don Ricardo overheard these last words, and asked what they meant. Cassaban, with much hesitation, and no little fear, told him.

" So he would fight with me ?" he said, with a smile ; " well, be it so. I like excitement—it is my food. I will give him his choice of weapons. Bid my men assemble, and they shall see me kill a cur."

Cassaban then led Snip to an adjoining alcove, where a vast number of arms of various descriptions were piled up.

These were part of spoils of many a plundered ship, and had evidently been cast carelessly aside, as of little worth.

" There," said Cassaban, " you can have your choice."

Snip ran his eyes over them, but saw very little to please him. He knew very little concerning weapons and it really did not much matter what he chose, but he wished to appear critical.

Turning them over with the air of a judge, he came upon an old-fashioned English mace, with a handle about four feet long. The top was an iron ball, about five inches in diameter, with a liberal allowance of spikes sticking out in various directions. This took Snip's fancy, and it pleased him mightily.

" Here's the very thing for me," he said, " and if I land one on the nob of your big gun I think he will know it."

" But it is a weapon of a bygone age," said Cassaban.

" That's no business of yours," returned Snip, obstinately ; " it's a favourite in my family. My grandfather fought with it in the wars of the Red and White Roses, and no man could stand against him. He left the weapon he used to the king, and it is kept under a glass case in the private parlour of St. James's Palace."

" His excellency has given you your choice," said Cassaban, " therefore I suppose you must have the weapon. You had better rest a little while, for in half an hour the arena will be cleared for the fight."

CHAPTER XVII.

RIGHT AND MIGHT.

THE pirates gathered in a circle around the open space, their swarthy faces full of evil glee as they anticipated the pleasure of seeing Snip slain by their redoubtable chief.

They had seen Snip, and knew instinctively that he was not familiar with the use of weapons, so any chance of their chief failing to make short work of him did not enter the mind of any man assembled there.

It must be confessed that Snip had a strong suspicion that he would cut a poor figure, for the mace, although very promising to the eye, was a cumbersome weapon and exceedingly unwieldy, insomuch that he had much ado to handle it at all, to say nothing of doing so with perfect ease.

" It's frightfully heavy," murmured Snip, " and when once I get it up I must hit him with it, or it's all over with me. He could poke that thin sword of his into me a dozen times before I could get the mace up again, and then it would be farewell to all. I should never see Wapping again."

We are not sure that Snip cared very much about seeing Wapping again, but he was rather sentimental, and thought it was the right thing to think mournfully of it during what might possibly prove to be his last moments.

With a tolerable assumption of boldness he entered the arena, and was the first there.

The pirates received him with a mocking cheer, and Snip bowed graciously.

" They know and respect me," he thought. "Oh ! blow this thing, what a weight it is. I shall never get it up in the air before he comes down upon me."

Don Ricardo stepped lightly into the arena, toying with his sword—a fine Toledo blade, supple and gleaming.

He surveyed Snip and his weapon with a calm smile, and bowed with much grace.

Snip also bowed, until his nose nearly touched the earth, then he took up a defiant attitude, which would have done credit to any super at the old Vic.

" That is your weapon," said Don Ricardo.

" It is the weapon of my family," answered Snip. " We have been accustomed to it for hages."

" Ready !" said Don Ricardo.

" Ready !" cried Snip, and with a violent effort he hoisted the mace in the air.

" If I can only hit him," he thought, " how he will holler."

But the Don had no intention of permitting himself to be hit. He was quite as much aware as Snip was that a blow from the iron spikes would be very unpleasant, and instead of advancing he awaited the attack.

" Advance, senor !" he cried.

" You come on," urged Snip. " You have got nothing to carry, and it isn't fair to make me run about with this thing."

But the Don declined to advance, and Snip, feeling that he must drop the mace sooner or later, staggered forward with the sweat of his labour on his brow.

The Don quietly awaited his coming.

Down came the mace, and Snip went with it.

upon his nose. He expected to be instantly impaled, but nothing of the sort occurred ; the Don, instead of stabbing him, began to curse roundly.

Snip looked up quickly, and saw what did his heart good and gladdened his eyes. The mace had fallen upon the fine Toledo blade and shivered it to pieces.

"Wictory !" Snip cried, leaping to his feet. "Onward ! Forward ! Down with the tyrant ! Oh ! come, it aint fair to run away. Stand and take your gruel like a man."

The Don, however, steadily retreated before him, keeping an eye upon the mace, which Snip had succeeded in elevating once more. The pirates involuntarily roared with laughter, and Don Ricardo, with a savage gleam in his eyes, drew a dagger from his belt.

Staggering and fuming, Snip followed him up, loth to drop his mace again without a tolerable chance of success.

The glitter of the dagger held by the Don was very unpleasant, and the point, also, had anything but an amusing appearance. Snip shuddered as he looked upon it.

"It aint fair," he gasped, "to have two weapons. One ought to be enough for any man. It's all I've got. You drop it."

The Don smiled, and simply said, "Come on, you English dog !"

Snip felt he must go on or fall, and at that moment a slight quarrel between two of the men diverted the attention of the Don. He only looked away for a moment, but Snip took advantage of it.

Rushing forward, he aimed a blow at the pirate's head. It fell rather short, but the mace alighted on Don Ricardo's breast and sent him to the ground with a crash, where he lay still and motionless as if dead.

"Let me have another cut at him !" gasped Snip, making an effort to raise his mace again ; "only one more."

But Pedro and Cassaban held him back, and several of the pirates raised up their chief and bore him to the alcove, where they laid him on his couch.

"I claim my liberty !" cried Snip. "It was promised to me if I was victor."

"Liberty !" sneered Cassaban. "You are more likely to be roasted alive."

"He promised me my liberty," urged Snip.

"I have nothing to do with that," said Cassaban. "If he wishes you to be released he will say as much when he recovers, if he ever does."

"And if he don't ?"

"The men will cut you up piecemeal."

"This is pleasant," thought Snip. "I fight for my life, and if I've killed the fellow they intend to cut me into bits. Where's the justice in this country, I wonder ? I wish that I had never left Wapping. What now ?"

"The chief is recovering," said Pedro, "and he desires to see the English dog."

"Now for the boiling and roasting," muttered Snip. "I wish it were over. All this comes of being sprung from a brave family."

Don Ricardo lay propped up with cushions, and when Snip appeared before him he gazed at him long and earnestly.

"Your nation is very brave," he said at last. "The men are mostly stalwart and tall—you are small and weak—but you are brave."

"I'm braver than most men," returned Snip, modestly. "You do not find many men of my pattern."

"I believe it," said the Don ; "your race overrun the earth—you are everywhere—you rule everything. A curse upon your people !"

"Now he's getting vicious," thought Snip, his knees feeling very much inclined to knock together.

"If I had the power to exterminate you all," the Don, "I would do it."

"No doubt," thought Snip.

"But, as I have not, I tremble at your name," continued the Don. "You fought with me, and I promised if you were victorious to give you your life.'

"Ah ! that you did," said Snip, eagerly.

"Take it and begone !" cried the pirate.

"Eh ?" said Snip.

"I give you two minutes to clear out," the pirate continued. "After that I loose my men upon you. Begone !"

Snip was overwhelmed with amazement, but he had sufficient sense left to realise the shortness of the time given.

He was unaccustomed to rope-climbing, but he went up by that means of egress from the pirates' haunt like an old professional acrobat, and leaped from rock to rock with the agility of a goat, until he reached the sands.

"I never hoped for this," he thought. "But only two minutes—it isn't much—and if they can run I'm a dead man."

There was a wood not more than a quarter of a mile from the shore, and towards this Snip went at a marvellous pace.

When half the ground had been covered he heard a shout from behind, and, looking back, he beheld the pirates, like a pack of wolves, in full pursuit.

Terror gave wings to the legs of the brave man, and he skimmed over the ground like a swallow, with his eyes fixed upon the wood and an earnest hope in his heart that he might reach its shelter before they overtook him.

"Once there," he muttered, "I'll get up a tree, and if they bowl me out I'll throw myself off and break my neck. It will be much better than being either toasted alive or cut up into pieces."

CHAPTER XVIII.

JACK SAVAGE'S ADVANCE.

"A SENTINEL missing, sir."

It was Long Tom who spoke, and he addressed Jack Savage, who lay before an expiring fire in the light of early morning.

"Who is it, Tom ?"

"Snip."

"Where did you put him ?"

"By yon group of trees," said Tom ; "there's a sign of feet, but not much appearance of a struggle."

"I suppose some of Don Ricardo's scouts have fallen foul of him," said Jack.

"If so he's a dead man," replied Long Tom.

"I'm sorry for him," said Jack ; "he was rather amusing. Is the trail pretty clear ?"

"A child could follow it with his eyes shut."

"Then if there is any hope for him we will go forward at once. You will guard the Spanish lady in the rear, Tom. Will and I will lead the van."

◁ GIANT JACK: ▷

A Story of the Red Mountains.

SNIP LITERALLY CAUGHT THE BULL BY THE HORNS, AND HAD IT OUT WITH HIM.

"I'll take care of the purty dear," said Tom. Then he muttered to himself, "but I do wish we could lose her quietly, without hurting her. Women aint no good in a camp. They never do anything but mischief in it, 'specially when they are like this one, with eyes that make you quiver all over as if you had received a prod with a bayonet."

In five minutes the band was moving, with Jack and Will Larkin leading the way.

They soon came upon the trail, which was broad and clear, showing the footmarks of at least a dozen men. It led towards the sea.

"They have got him," said Jack, "and, as there are no signs of blood, let us hope he is alive."

"Perhaps they have taken him to their haunt?"

"Snip will then, unconsciously, become our guide," said Jack. "Are all ready behind there? We may have rough work presently."

"Aye, aye, sir !"

"Every firearm loaded ?"

"Aye, sir !"

They were not more than three miles from the sea, and presently its dark blue water came into view.

There, too, was the giant rock, rising high above every object around, and apparently frowning upon these intruders into the haunts of vice.

"That's the place," said Jack, pointing to the rock. "It answers the description I received. So we have lighted upon our bird at last. Close there !"

"Aye, aye, sir !"

"Tom !"

Tom came forward for orders, and Jack drew him aside.

"Is the lady safe ?"

"As eggs," replied Tom ; "we've got her in the moving shanty there."

Tom pointed to a rough sort of palanquin, made of branches and boughs, borne upon the shoulders of half-a-dozen men.

"It was a good idea of yours, Tom, and I thank you for it in the lady's name," said Jack. "You will remain behind here and guard her. Choose half-a-dozen men."

"And you ?"

"We go on to fight the pirate Ricardo. Yonder is his haunt."

"It would be better work for me to go forward fighting with you," muttered Tom, "than to stop here to look after a woman."

"I leave her to you, Tom," returned Jack, "because I can trust you. I know that if danger threatens her you will shield and guard her with your life. It is a sacred charge, Tom, and one I would leave to few men."

"If that's the case, replied Tom, cheerily, "I'll stop and do my duty like a man ; but it's the first time I've left your side in the time of danger—that is, since we have been really together—and I feel it, Jack."

"All right, Tom. I fully appreciate your good feeling."

The giant and the dwarf shook hands, and Jack went back to Will.

Long Tom chose several of the men whom he thought most trustworthy—all of them volunteers from Mount Restore—and these gathered round the leafy palanquin, wherein the Lady Ximena remained hidden from view.

Before going forwards Jack came up and stood by the palanquin, but made no attempt to part the screen.

"You know my mission ?" he said, in a soft whisper.

"I do," came the answer, as musical as a bell.

"I am near him now," said Jack. "Do you approve ? Shall I go on ?"

A small, white hand came from between the leaves. This was the reply. Jack kissed the little hand and went back to Will Larkin.

"Let us go on," he said, and the men followed their chief to the cluster of rocks where the pirate lay.

Their coming had not been unheeded.

Don Ricardo's sentinels had espied our hero and his men, but his coming was badly timed for the pirate.

More than half his men were away in pursuit of Snip, and had not yet returned.

How the pirate cursed his folly in allowing the men to leave.

Don Ricardo thought they would run him down in a few minutes, but an hour elapsed and still the men were away, little suspecting the arrival of Jack Savage and his followers.

The pirate still had more than two hundred men by him, enough to hold the stronghold for awhile, if fight he must ; but, resolving to evade this if possible, he bade his men lie close and wait the course of events.

He had not long to wait. Jack was full of action, and, having scented his prey, he rushed at once on the tiger's lair.

Like a torrent he and his men came pouring over the sides of the rock, dropping into the arena like cats, and ere the pirates had recovered from the surprise caused by this sudden attack a third of them were slain.

All was confusion—the air was filled with pistol reports and the clash of arms, mingled with the shrieks of the wounded and the dying. Where the slaughter was thickest there was the giant form of Jack, with Will Larkin by his side, both fighting like young lions.

The pirates knew that victory or defeat was a matter of life and death to them, and fought well, but they did not fight with the courage which the consciousness of a good cause always gives, and soon they were driven into a corner of their haunt, where some sixty or seventy of them clustered together in affright, like rats in a pit.

"Throw down your arms !" shouted Jack, and his voice sounded like thunder in their ears.

"Quarter ! quarter !" they cried.

"Throw down your arms !" repeated Jack, and the beaten knaves cast them down, crouching upon the ground like whipped dogs.

"Collect the arms, bury the dead, and look to the wounded," was the next command, and a portion of his well-organised force hastened to obey.

Jack had lost five men, and about a score more were wounded.

Our hero's next care was to look for the pirate chief.

He had a tolerable description to go by, but he could not find him among the dead or wounded, nor was he among the prisoners, and the fear that the greatest villain of all had escaped dawned upon him.

Singling out one of the men, he bade him

come forward. It was Cassaban, and he came forward with an abject air.

"Your chief," said Jack—"where is he?"

"He is not here," replied Cassaban; "he has fled."

"When did the coward turn tail?"

"I do not know," said Cassaban; "he was not in the fight, so I suppose he went away at the beginning."

"Have you another haunt near?"

Cassaban hesitated. Jack repeated his question sternly.

"Ten miles from here," Cassaban said, "there is the Pearl Grotto, where sometimes our chief goes. He has had time to get clear away. The fight has lasted an hour."

"Scarcely that," said Jack, looking at a watch he wore. "But he has had, as you say, time to get clear away. Coward feet fly fast, especially when they carry knaves. In what direction lies the grotto from here?"

"By the alcove—west."

"Good! we will get on," said Jack, "and you shall go with us. If we fail to find the grotto, or your chief, you shall answer for it."

Cassaban turned pale, and his lips quivered as he stammered out—

"I fear I have made a mistake. The grotto lies to the east."

"A timely correction," returned Jack. "What now, Will?"

Will came rushing up to his chief with a face full of excitement and alarm.

"The Lady Ximena!" he cried.

"What of her?" returned Jack.

"There is firing from where we left her."

"I cannot hear it."

"Come outside and gain the surface of the rocks, then you will hear it plainly."

"Guard well that man," cried Jack, pointing to Cassaban, as he followed Will.

As soon as he reached the open ground Jack heard the firing plainly, but he could see nothing, as the spot where he had left Ximena was hidden by a clump of trees.

Suddenly the firing ceased.

"Let fifty men follow me!" Jack cried.

The young giant was fleet of foot, and those who went with him had hard work to keep up with their leader.

The clump of trees was soon reached, and then Jack and his men gained the spot where the Lady Ximena had been left.

The rough grass was trampled down, and there were bullet marks upon the trees, but that was all they could see, except one man, who alone remained of the party left to guard the lady.

And he lay upon his face, with a bullet through his heart, as inanimate as the stones around him.

* * * * * *

With fast faltering steps and a heart that beat about one hundred and fifty to the minute, the valiant little tailor, born in Wapping, gained the woods.

His pursuers, about three hundred yards in the rear, came howling after him, and they set up a yell of rage and disappointment when he gained the trees, which afforded the little man temporary safety.

But the pursuit was not over.

Snip knew that, and, although the wood was

comparatively a haven of rest and safety, yet he did not trifle away a minute's time, but sped on, looking for some place which would afford him additional security.

CHAPTER XIX.

SNIP IS UP A TREE.

PRESENTLY Snip came to a tree which afforded him some chance of hiding—a big tree, whose branches grew low, and whose trunk was short.

Moved by the desperate nature of his position, Snip made a run at it, and, grasping the lower boughs, scrambled up the trunk. Just then he heard a shout behind him, when, being half-blinded by fear, he made a second plunge, and in an instant was in total darkness.

This sudden change was very startling in itself, but there was a yet more startling phenomenon—the world appeared to be turned upside down, for Snip was standing on his head.

"I can't be dreaming," he gasped. "I am in a wood up a tree, and yet how is this—I am on my head?"

Then the truth burst upon him, and he realised the fact. The trunk of the tree was hollow, and he had plunged head-first into it.

Fortunately the dimensions of the hollow were sufficient to allow him to recover his normal position, but it was not done without a struggle, and when he had succeeded Snip stood still and listened.

He heard voices outside, certainly, and they were the voices of the pirates.

"I am sure I saw him about here," said one. "He disappeared very suddenly."

"Gone away," said another.

"Or got up a tree," suggested the first.

"I wish I could get a look at them," muttered Snip, "but I can't reach the top of this hollow, and if I could I dare not peep out."

Turning slowly round, he discovered a small hole—the work of some insect—in the trunk. Through this he could get an occasional glimpse of what was going on outside.

The pirates were moving stealthily up and down, gazing furtively into the trees, as if they expected to see the legs of their victim dangling in the air. All had their swords drawn, and several carried cocked pistols in their hands.

"I never saw such venomous wretches," muttered Snip. "They run a man to earth, and then want to kick him when he's down. They know I'm not far away. Ah! I thought so."

"He's close at hand," said one of the pirates, coming forward. "There's not a mark in the brushwood around."

"He'd better show," cried another, speaking louder than usual, for the especial benefit of the concealed Snip. "It will go worse with him if he doesn't!"

"Who wants to harm him?" said a third. "Not I, I'm sure."

"Or I," said the others, in chorus.

All of which failed to bring Snip forth. The hidden little man was not to be caught with chaff, so he simply laid a finger upon his nose and murmured—

"Walker!"

Finding their blandishments of no avail, the

pirates tried the other move, and threatened him with all the pains and penalties ever inflicted by man upon man if he did not come forth, but Snip turned a deaf ear alike to both and refused to show.

Then the pirates sat down upon the ground doggedly, and loudly declared their intention to wait for him, if they stayed there until the next year.

"We can see you!" bawled one, "up among the top branches there, and here we will stay until you rot and drop off. Come down, will you?"

"Ha, ha!" muttered Snip; "but I am not in the top branches, my friends, and you will wait some time before I drop down upon you—and yet don't I wish I could! I would not mind a bruise or two if I could break one of your precious necks. Murder! what's that?"

Something was crawling over Snip's neck, and presently an earwig about an inch long was wriggling in his clutch.

"Of all things," he muttered, with a shudder, "I have a supreme horror of earwiggles, and—oh! murder! get out!—there's another, and another! The place is full of 'em. I can't stand this."

Overcome with horror and affright, he sunk to the bottom of the tree, and the insidious little insects, feeling something warm in their vicinity, came rushing upon him by hundreds—his face, arms, and neck being literally covered with them.

"Anything is better than this," he cried. "Here, make short work of me. I'm coming out!"

No answer.

"Can't you hear?" roared Snip, as he scrambled up. "I'm coming out. If you mean killing me aim at the wital place, and don't hack a man."

He reached the summit of his hiding-place, recklessly threw his legs over, and then looked down.

Not a pirate was to be seen.

Astonishment drove all thoughts of his insect foe out of his head, and he sat staring, with a stupid look upon his face, at the empty space below.

The earwigs, being introduced to daylight, tumbled off him as quickly as they came, and crawled away to their dark hiding-place, so in a few seconds Snip had been relieved of both his foes.

"I'm either a lunatic or a wisionary," muttered Snip. "Was them pirates or not, and was I smothered in carwiggles? Is this Wapping or Hepping Forest? Have I had a Saint Monday, and been out in a wan? Have I made too free with my drink, and mixed my liquors? Can anybody tell me? Perhaps I'm in a coffee-shop. I don't know."

Bang! went a gun close at hand—apparently just behind—and its effect upon Snip was very unpleasant.

Relaxing his hold, he fell backwards into his hiding-place, carrying with him hundreds of earwigs equally alarmed.

"Bang! bang! bang!" sounded several more guns, and this was followed by the clash of swords.

"Hooray!" cried Snip; "it's Jack Savage and his men. Hooray! Up with the banner of old England, and raise the brave standard of Wapping! Give 'em pepper, my boys! No quarter to the pirate dogs! And remember your brave Snip's coming to help you!"

Despite the verbal encouragement Snip gave, he made no very great effort to go to the assistance of his friends, but, climbing once more outside, he sat upon a branch and listened to the sounds of warfare.

"Perhaps it may go the wrong way," he thought, "and, if so, then the trunk of a tree is better than nothing, and earwiggles may be got used to."

The fighting seemed very desperate. He could hear the men shouting, and knew some of the voices—one in particular was very familiar to him.

"That's Long Tom," he said, "and he's a tough 'un if he is a little 'un."

The scrimmage was not of long duration, and soon a lull ensued. Then he heard voices and the sound of footsteps.

"Somebody's coming," he said; "but is it friends or foes?" He caught a glimpse of the foremost, and saw it was a foe—one of the pirates, bearing in his arms what seemed to be a woman.

Snip dropped inside the tree again with the alacrity of a cat, and, ignoring the earwigs and all other insect foes, he fixed his eye to the little hole.

"Yes," he muttered, "it is a woman, and—no—yes—it's the Lady Hardname, Jack Savage's delight, and a pretty one she is, bless her! And who's this? Long Tom and some of the Mount Restore men, bound like bundles of faggots. But where's Jack—the bold, big Jack? Killed I suppose. Well, I didn't think there was a man in the world who could settle him; but you can never tell. Only think, the whole band is licked by these pirates. Who'd have thought it? It must be a dream—my old head is muddled—it can't be real, and I shall wake up in a minute in Wapping, with my master hollering out for me to get up and take down the shutters. They may do what they like with me now—they can't harm me. They may toast me alive. I've dreamt before of sitting on the hot goose, and it didn't hurt, so get your fire ready, my boys, and I'll come out and ask you to toast me. What's the odds? Rule Britannia!"

CHAPTER XX.

TO THE RESCUE.

LET us leave Snip to battle with his fate for awhile and return again to Jack Savage and his men.

"Where is Caderouse?" cried Jack.

The giant Frenchman came forward and bowed with the politeness of his nation.

"You are good on the trail?"

"Even so, Sar Jack."

"Take up the trail, then, and lead the way."

Caderouse bowed again. He never did anything without bowing in the politest manner. If he killed a man in fight he invariably bowed before leaving him.

The trail was strong and led into the wood. Caderouse went on at a swift pace, and the others, like avenging shadows, followed him.

A hundred yards in the wood one of the guns carried by the men exploded. Jack turned upon him angrily.

"I forgot it was on cock," said the man, apologetically.

"You have startled the wolf, perchance," said Jack, "so silence is useless now. Forward!"

Then they rushed on, giving mouth like hounds in pursuit, and the crash of the brushwood as they trampled it down with their feet resounded through the wood.

"Here they have rested for a minute," said Caderouse, pulling up close to the hiding-place of Snip.

"But they are not here now!" cried Jack. "Forward!"

"I hear a voice, sar."

"Forward!"

Caderouse could not disobey this peremptory command, and he recommenced the pursuit.

"They have left but a little while, I hope?" said Jack, running close by his side.

"The nest is warm yet," replied Caderouse.

"Then our coming alarmed them," muttered Jack, "and they cannot be far in front."

Loosening his sword, to have it ready at a moment's notice, he kept his eyes fixed ahead, hoping each step to catch sight of those who had carried away the Lady Ximena. But the time for her rescue had not yet come.

A little later the track of the pirates led them to a small open space, and then all signs of them disappeared. They searched the wood and ground in every direction, but not a broken twig or bent blade of grass gave out any signs to guide them further.

There was a problem to solve, and Jack and his men were puzzled. Caderouse tilted his cap on one side and scratched his bullet head. Will Larkin, who stood near, asked him where he thought they were gone to. The Frenchman looked up at the clouds.

"They are not gone that way," said Will. "Gently of their stamp go the other way."

"Den I not know to where they go," said Caderouse, in despair. "Dere no hole in de earth, and no wings dey have."

Jack stood moodily by, with his right hand in his bosom. He was the sorest tried of all, and he could not fathom the mystery of the disappearance.

"They must have some hiding-place near," he said. "Some cavern, with the entrance covered with earth, perhaps. Stamp around, my men."

Jack's followers began rushing about, stamping like niggers among the sugar canes, until Caderouse cried out that he had found something.

"It hollow here," he cried. "Listen! It sounds like him drum."

"Up with it!" cried Jack, slashing the grass away like a madman. "Here is the wolf's lair!"

The men had nothing but their swords and daggers, but strong arms and willing hearts do much, and the metal of their weapons was soon ringing against stone—the bed of a trap-door bound in iron.

When the turf was scraped away Jack knelt down and tried to force it open with his sword, but the weapon would have snapped had he not given up the attempt. The door was secured within, and he chafed and foamed like a tigress robbed of her young.

Then he attempted to cut through the wooden door, but iron bands traversed it in all directions, foiling him in every way. The men gave what help they could, but the lair of the pirates was famously guarded by its door, and it kept them out.

"I'd give ten years of my life," cried Jack, "to be the other side of this sheet of wood and iron. Dig further round, my men. Let us get at the foundation of the masonry."

A deal of the ground was cut away, but the mass of masonry proved to be so large that Jack presently cried out to them to desist, and then he sat down upon the ground in utter despair, with his face in his hands, looking at the masonry as he ofttimes looked into the fire.

Jack was strong, and he possessed a strange hold over most men, but he had no power to move the barrier between him and the charming Ximena.

The thought of her being a prisoner almost drove him mad. What was her fate?

In the hands of lawless pirates bent upon her estruction, perhaps. But for the presence of his men he could have thrown himself upon the ground and wept.

But Jack was a man of action, so he cast aside his own grief for the moment, and called out for Caderouse.

"You said something about a voice as we came through the wood," he said; "what was it?"

"I hear him voice," returned Caderouse, "like smother."

"As if it were smothered?" returned Jack. "Did you know the voice?"

"I know him."

"Whose was it?"

"The voice of Snip."

"His voice!" cried Jack, in surprise; "and what did he say?"

Caderouse paused a moment, to give effect to his answer, and then replied—

"Him say—'Hallo! I say! Stop a minute!'"

Jack could not help smiling, for the communication was not of very serious import. Caderouse thought it right to smile too. He also bowed.

"Go back," said Jack, "and see if you can find him."

Caderouse did not care much about the office, but he said nothing, merely bowing and making a grimace—then he went his way.

The road back was clear to him, and he walked straight to the tree now so familiar to Snip. There he halted, put a hand on each side of his mouth, and bawled—

"Mistare Snip!"

"Here," said a feeble voice.

"Vere?" asked Caderouse.

"Here," replied the voice, again; but Caderouse looked up, and down, and around him, and was no wiser.

"If you shall say vere you can be, Mistare Snip," he said, "I shall tank you."

"I am inside this tree," replied Snip. "Stop a moment—I am coming up."

Then, to the astonishment of Caderouse, our friend Snip appeared, apparently coming out of the very heart of the tree. The face of the little man was a study.

"Is it a dream, or isn't it?" he asked. "Am I here, or in Wapping? Is my name Snip, or is it Brown, Jones, or Robinson? Will anybody prick me with a pin?"

"Your name is Snip," replied Caderouse,

" and you are avake vide."

Snip, still doubting, alighted on the earth.

" Pinch me," he said ; and Caderouse pinched him heartily.

" Oh ! that'll do," cried Snip. " I am awake —thank you ; no more at present. You are very kind, but I would rather not."

" Sure ?" said Caderouse, anxious to have another grab at him.

" Quite right," said Snip. " Are you alone ?"

" Mistare Jack shall be close by," replied Caderouse.

" Lead me to him," said Snip, with an impressive air. " I have news to communicate —important news."

The pair trotted to the spot where Jack was moodily waiting, and the young giant greeted Snip with a smile, nodding good-humouredly.

" Glad to see you amongst us again," he said.

" It's something to be thankful for," returned Snip, " but I have news for you—rare news— wonderful news !"

" Indeed !" said Jack, indifferently.

" Of the Lady Ximena," continued Snip, and in an instant Jack was all eager attention.

" What of her ?" he cried.

" While I was hid in the tree," said Snip— " that is, concealing myself so as to get news for you—the pirates brought her, and Long Tom, and some more prisoners near me. They rested a moment, when they heard a gun go off, then up they all leaped, and I heard them cry, ' To the Pearl Grotto !' "

" The Pearl Grotto ?" said Jack.

" Yes. Then one said they would never reach it, another said he knew of an entrance to it close at hand—in the wood—and away they all ran like rabbits, before I had time to get out of the tree and stop 'em, which I should have done, and kept them there until you came up."

" No doubt," said Jack ; " but your news is valuable about the Pearl Grotto. Then the other entrance to it is by the sea. I'll haste to my pirate prisoners, and force one to be my guide. But I must leave a guard here—two or three will be sufficient. Caderouse—Snip !"

The two in question stood before their chief ready for orders.

" I am going back to the pirates' haunt," said Jack, " and my intention is to obtain a guide to the other entrance of this grotto. I leave you two to guard this trap-door."

" To guard this door ?" gasped Snip.

" Aye—who dare venture forth with an enemy here ? Only one man can come up at a time, and his life is in your hands. Besides, you can pile more earth upon it in a quarter of an hour than any man can raise. I leave that work to you. You are both brave, strong men, and will no doubt do it well."

Jack smiled a little sarcastically as he spoke, but as his orders never admitted of any dispute, Caderouse and Snip submitted to his will, and in another minute the two watchers were left alone.

" I can't be awake," murmured Snip. " I'm no sooner out of one mess than I am into another. It's just like a dream after a pork-chop for supper. Nothing would surprise me—a few dragons from the clouds, or a shower of pickled whelks instead of rain. I would ask Caderouse to kick me, only he is precious strong, and his boots are so thick ; but it's a dream, an 'orrible dream, and I must soon wake up in Wapping."

CHAPTER XXI.

SNIP DISTINGUISHES HIMSELF.

IT shall be very unpleasant to be alone here," said Caderouse.

" It don't matter—it aint real," said Snip, despairingly.

" Yah !" muttered Caderouse, " it real enough if some pirates should come."

" It's no use thinking about it," said Snip ; " what I have gone through in the last twenty-four hours is more than man can bear. I'm tired out."

" Sleep, den," said Caderouse, sententiously.

" Will you watch ?"

" Yes, Mistare Snip."

" Then here goes for forty winks," said Snip. And the little man, who was indeed utterly worn out, stretched himself upon the grass and sank into a deep sleep.

Then Caderouse, to make sure against surprise, took his seat upon the trap-door, and began to ruminate over the memory of the vineyards of France, where he had spent the days of his youth.

Snip was too tired to dream, and it was a complete blank with him from the time he stretched himself upon the grass to the moment when Caderouse shook him by the shoulder and aroused him from his sleep.

" What's o'clock ?" growled Snip, yawning.

" Hush ! there shall be fighting," muttered Caderouse. " Listen !"

" Still in this 'orrible dream !" growled Snip. " Where's the fighting ?"

" In the ground. Put your ear down and him shall hear !"

Snip laid his head flat on the ground and listened. Fighting was going on, and he could faintly hear the clash of swords.

" Yes," he said ; " they've come together. Did you wake me for that ?"

" They shall come through the door-trap soon," said Caderouse. " Den we chop him head off !"

" How long have I been asleep ?"

" Two hours."

" Two minutes you mean."

" Two hours," repeated Caderouse, emphatically, " and your nose snore like one grampus.'

" I come of a snoring family," said Snip. " But we shall have those fellows here presently."

" They shall come soon."

" Pile up the earth."

" No, Mistare Snip," said Caderouse ; " we shall wait, and I, Caderouse, shall have pleasure much in chopping him head off."

Saying this the Frenchman drew his sword and tightened his belt.

Snip, coming of a brave family, could do no less, and the pair stood by the trap-door like terriers at a rat-hole.

The sounds of fighting grew louder, and soon they could hear mingled oaths and cries ; then there came a thump at the trap-door.

Snip's heart leapt within him, and he began to feel as if the scene were very real indeed, but he was in the presence of a Frenchman, so he stood firm. ●

" Coming !" said Caderouse.

" Coming !" repeated Snip. Then there was the noise of shooting bolts and the falling of chains, and the trap-door flew up.

Out popped a dark, swarthy face, and Snip made a slash at it. His aim was rather defective, but it sent the pirate back howling.

"Here's sport!" cried Snip, dancing round about the opening like a madman. "Why don't they come up half-a-dozen at a time—I'm ready for 'em!"

"So!" cried Caderouse, as another appeared, then his sword flashed through the air, and a head rolled upon the grass.

"Good!" he said, as he wiped his blade.

"Neat as wax," added Snip; "but don't be covetous—let me have the next cut."

An arm and hand appeared, and Snip sprang forward. A stunning report followed, then Snip fell upon his back.

"Shot through the heart!" he moaned. "Oh, Mr. Caderouse, if my aged father in the union could but see me now!"

"Bah!" exclaimed Caderouse, "if him shoot you, how you holler out—eh?"

"I'm hit somewhere," said Snip, feeling about his waistcoat. "I heard something break and thought it was my bones. I was right—see! the bullet struck one of my buttons."

"THE hand which fired him bullet lies dere," said Caderouse, pointing to a hand severed from the wrist, which lay upon the grass, with a pistol close by still smoking.

"Oh, Mr. Caderouse!" said Snip, shuddering; "how very unpleasant!"

"Them or us," replied the Frenchman.

"Just so," assented Snip. "Look out!"

Quick as a flash of thought a man leaped through the opening, brandishing a glittering weapon. Snip, heated by excitement, sprang upon him and passed his sword through his body. The pirate made one effort to return the blow, and then fell, with a malignant scowl upon his face.

"Good!" said Caderouse.

"I hope it is, I'm sure, but I feel frightfully bad," said Snip, wiping the dew of perspiration from his face.

During all this time the fighting was still going on below, and the shrieks and cries drew nearer and nearer. They could distinguish the shouts of their friends, which gave both Snip and the Frenchman additional courage.

The entrance to the trap was so small that they could see nothing without peering over, and this was too risky for either of them to attempt, so they stood watching for another foe, listening to the uproar of the contest below.

"I hope this is real," thought Snip. "I've killed a man. Now, if one of the pirates would kill Caderouse, I would swear that I had killed the three."

"Look about!" roared Caderouse, as another man leaped forth—a gigantic built fellow, who attacked the Frenchman furiously.

Snip had no time to help him, for another sprang forth, and another, and another, but the two latter were wounded, and Snip had only one to fight with.

The little man would have fled, but he forgot even the use of his limbs, so, like a stag at bay, he fought for his life.

He knew as much of swordsmanship as he did of astronomy, which was nothing, but the very want of knowledge on this occasion saved him.

He danced about and flourished his sword in such a manner that the pirate, a practised hand

in the art, was utterly confounded.

He made several thrusts at Snip, but he might as well have tried to stab a will-o'-the-wisp, and while he was yet looking for an opening, Caderouse, who had killed his man, came and cut him down behind.

"This is noble work," said Snip. "In my native land I should be made commander-in-chief for it."

Caderouse pointed to the open trap-door, as a hint that all danger was not yet over, and while he was yet pointing another head appeared.

"Death to all murderers and villains!" roared Snip, as he flourished his sword.

"Hold hard! What are you up to?" roared the voice of Long Tom. "Don't you know a friend when you see him?"

"Is it possible?" cried Snip. "You free?"

"Can't you see!" growled Tom. "Get out of the way."

"Where are the rest?"

"Below, with the chief."

"And the pirates?"

"Dead to a man! All except that scoundrel, Don Ricardo, and he didn't show himself."

"Are our friends coming?"

"Directly—the chief's attending to the Lady Ximena. She has been stabbed by one of the scoundrels."

"Sacre!" muttered Caderouse. "So young, so beautiful, so charming, so exquisite!"

And then he bowed, as if the lady was present listening to the compliment.

"She's all that," said Tom, "and more. But I'm afraid its all over with the poor thing. Here comes the chief."

Jack came forth, bearing Ximena in his arms—a lovely Spanish girl, about twenty years of age. Jack held a handkerchief to her bosom, and it was dark with the life-stream flowing from a ghastly wound.

"Mourn not for me," she said, in a musical tone, gazing tenderly into Jack's face.

"You must live, or I shall die too," he murmured; "without you what have I to live for? The last few days have told me what it is to love."

"My big, brave boy!" she whispered.

"Oh! my darling!"

And the young giant, so strong in all things else, broke down under the power of love, and wept.

The men made a couch of leaves, and Jack laid her thereon. Then they retired, and left Jack with the girl he had learned to love.

"Let me look to your wound," Jack said. "I may yet save you."

"No," she said; "my fate is sealed. Sit by my side and look into my eyes. To die thus is all I wish."

"What a miserable fate is mine!" groaned Jack. "I have but to love a thing to lose it. Oh, Ximena, with you the world would be bright indeed."

"This world has naught to do with me now," she said. "Our parting is near, darling. I feel my life is going—but you love me, Jack?"

"Better than my life."

"Then we shall meet again," she murmured, "in a better and purer world than this. "Oh, my brave hero! forget not my love—come nearer."

"Yes—darling!"

"I cannot see you, Jack—you have never kissed me."

"No, darling; I was not sure you loved me."

"Kiss me now, Jack."

He put his lips gently to hers, and held them there. The kiss he gave received a feeble, fluttering response, and the spirit of the Spanish girl, the lovely Ximena, left its tenement of clay.

"My darling! my darling!" cried Jack. "Come back to me, my love! Oh! Ximena, leave me not thus!"

But the fast-glazing eye looked not into his, and the fixed lips gave him no response. All was over, and Jack covered the fair face with his cloak.

Then he called aloud for Will, and Will came. Jack, with his back to him, said—"Leave me here for an hour, then come back and help me to lay her in her grave."

When Will came back at the appointed time he found Jack quite calm, waiting to help him make the grave.

The two dug it easily in the soft, peaty earth, and then buried her as she was, with Jack's cloak upon her face.

"Let it remain there," Jack said. "It is all the covering I can give her. Can you pray, Will?"

"Aye, I have not forgotten it yet," said Will.

"Say what is right, then;" and in a voice broken by emotion Will said a few simple appropriate words, and then they covered her in.

"Whither go we next?" asked Will.

"I must rest by the fire first," replied Jack; "then you shall know more."

"Still haunted, Jack?"

"Still haunted, Will. This night there will be two spirits in the fire. Ximena lies not there, she will be with me, wherever I go, unto the end."

"Forget her, Jack."

"I will—when the stars fall from the heavens, Will. I loved her with a love that was new to me—with a love as fresh, and holy, and beautiful as anything in this world. It lay upon me as the dew lies upon the flowers, it lent a radiance to my life, and it made me feel a better man."

"The night is coming on," said Will, after a pause. "Shall we rest in the wood?"

"No—go out upon the plain. Are the prisoners safe?"

"Chained together with their own chains, and guarded by men who will shoot the first who rattles his chains too musically."

"Good! Let us encamp—the men will be glad to rest and eat. They stand in need of their supper."

"Supper!" thought Snip, who happened to overhear the last words, "if they don't want it I do. I don't think I have had anything to eat for a week—but people are never hungry in dreams. *Is* this a dream! No, it isn't, for the internal rumblings say I am awake, and have this day done my duty for the honour and glory of Old England. Shoulder arms! Forward! Quick march!"

CHAPTER XXII.

NEW WORK FOR JACK SAVAGE.

AFTER the capture and dispersion of the pirate gang Jack resolved to give his men a rest.

Don Ricardo had escaped, but that could not be helped. As he was almost powerless without his men, our hero resolved to leave him for the present and trust to time to bring about a meeting.

They went back in a body to Mount Restore, having first collected and divided all the pirates' wealth, and their return was hailed with joy. The men who had hitherto accompanied Jack—that is, the settlers of Mount Restore—now resolved to remain at home and till their land, a resolution in which Jack cordially concurred.

Our hero was somewhat puzzled as to what was the best course to be pursued with regard to his pirate prisoners, and being averse to cold-blooded murder he offered them their liberty if they would promise not to return to their vicious course of life.

But the men refused this.

"We do not want our liberty," they said, "unless it is to serve you. Take us with you—prisoners if you will not trust us, brothers in arms if you believe our word. We will fight with you, and die for you, if need be."

What could Jack say to this? How could he decline such hearty volunteers?

"It is not for me to judge of your past lives," he replied; "your sins must rest upon your own heads. I will be your ruler and chief, but my government is stern. The man who disobeys me dies. I must be absolute. Will it suit you to serve me?"

They declared that it would, and shouted with joy when Jack declared the compact to be complete.

These men were then formed into an extra corps, and Caderouse was appointed as their deputy commander.

Snip desired to be placed at their head, but when Will Larkin maliciously called his attention to their murderous looks, and to the probability of their cooking and eating him one night for supper, Snip prudently retired from the candidature, and lapsed into his old position of full private in the general body.

Our tailor friend had some idea of settling down at Mount Restore, and, with a view of having a home of his own, made certain matrimonial proposals to the only single lady in the settlement, one Priscilla Norton, but the reception he met with was not flattering, and Snip precipitately retired from this venture also.

"I'm not to settle, I suppose," he soliloquised. "I'm cut out for glory, so I may as well go in for it. I wonder where we shall next tramp to?"

That question was shortly settled by Jack and Will Larkin.

The two young fellows sat by the camp-fire one evening, as Jack loved the open air, and never went within a house, discussing the best field for adventure, when Will mentioned a piece of news he had heard in the settlement that day."

"You have heard of Short's Gully?" he said. Jack nodded.

"It is a settlement of about a hundred people," continued Will, "or rather it was so, but about a fortnight ago a cloud of redskins came down upon it and murdered all the men, then they retired up country with the women and children."

"The brutes!"

"They belong to the Pawnee tribe, and the

fellows fight well. I think they will give us good work if you are disposed to go in for them."

"Their hunting grounds are west from here?"

"Yes."

"Then we will start to-morrow and hunt the monsters," said Jack.

When the men heard that a new field of adventure was open to them they were delighted, and half through the night they were polishing their arms and making other necessary preparations for the journey.

Their property they left in the hands of their friends at Mount Restore, and Zepheniah Bisset was made treasurer, a post he promised to fulfil faithfully.

We cannot say whether Snip was really pleased or not at the prospect before him, but he appeared to be so in the eyes of his friends.

Putting on a joyous swagger, he went about among the men, talking to and encouraging them in the following style—

"Nothing like fighting, my boys," he said; "what's life without fighting and glory? I haven't had a cut at anybody lately, and I feel like a man who has been a week without his dinner. Fighting is wittles and drink to me. Cheer up, lads! there's great work before us, and if the Injuns only knew we were coming wouldn't they tremble in their boots?"

"Injuns don't wear boots," said one of his listeners.

"I used boots as a flower of speech," returned Snip. "Boots is the poetical way of putting it. Ordinarily I should say mocashings, but mocashings is wulgar, and I therefore says boots. I don't come of a wulgar family—ahem!"

"He is all 'family,'" said Caderouse, turning up the white of his eyes. "I shall nevar see a man vith so much family."

"I shouldn't think you are very proud of your'n," said Snip, as he walked away.

CHAPTER XXIII.

THE EVE OF THE MARCH.

JACK, who since the death of the Lady Ximena had been very sad, was pleased to find an opportunity for action. He wanted something to turn his thoughts from the hopes which had now faded away, at any rate in this world, with regard to the Lady Ximena.

He did not sorrow, as most people do, nor idly think her lost for ever.

"She comes to me at night with the spirit of my father," he said to Will, "and when all Nature is at rest I see them both."

"Are you still sure these visions are not fancy?" returned Will.

"Fancy!" cried Jack. "What fancy can there be in a thing which is more real than the things of this world? Fancy! Ah! Will, you have yet to learn the joy I feel when the spirit of those I love is near me."

"But the spirit is unreal," urged Will.

"No," returned Jack. "The body is the house the soul of man inhabits. Pleasure and pain affect the body, but they are not the body."

"What is pleasure and pain?"

"Neither I nor any man can tell you," replied Jack. "Who shall say whence they come or whither they go? The same with the spirits of my father and Ximena. I cannot see them with the eye, yet I do see them. I cannot touch them with my hand, yet I feel their presence. I know they are with me, and their presence is more real to me than anything in this world."

"You talk strangely, Jack."

"I talk truly, Will. I know such things are not common to men. Some are artists, others musicians, but the great multitude are only recipients of the pictures and music painted and composed by talented men. So is this spirit-seeing of mine. It is a gift, and as such I value it. So, also, is the strange power I hold over many men. That is a gift likewise—a dangerous one I know—and one which may be used for good or evil."

"You make me afraid of you, Jack," said Will Larkin, looking at him in wonderment.

"You need not fear me," returned Jack Savage. "I would not use my power for evil purposes to save my life. I have work before me, I feel—rough, but good work. When I met her who lies beneath the ground I hoped to have laid aside my rifle and sword for ever. But it was not to be, and as the gallant old king went forth to smite the wrongdoer and the oppressor so go I until my life is done."

"Noble Jack."

"Ah! Will, it falls to the lot of few to be noble. The chances are few, and men too often throw them away. Is all ready in the camp?"

"All ready, and the men are eager to start."

"How far is Short's Gully from here?"

"One hundred and fifty miles."

"We can march there in seven days, then, and allow ample time for rest."

"We cannot be there too soon, Jack."

"No—dreadful work has been done, without a doubt. We are too late to help that, but some of the children, at least, may be rescued. I think we had better start an hour before dawn."

CHAPTER XXIV.

SHORT'S GULLY—THE TRAIL.

SEVEN days later Giant Jack's band arrived at Short's Gully. Very little of the country traversed was blessed with a decent road, and the men were tired and worn out. As for Snip, he limped like a lame dog, and the boots he wore had lost nearly every vestige of sole or heel.

Jack allowed one day's rest, and then resumed his march, Caderouse leading as before.

Prior to leaving Short's Gully, Jack went round the settlement to view the mischief wrought by the Pawnees, and found the ruin of the place complete.

Every house had been burnt or razed to the ground. The goods and chattels were broken and destroyed, and everything which could not be carried or driven away had been slaughtered.

The murdered settlers had been left upon the ground, with their heads showing the mark of the villainous scalping-knife. These Jack caused to be buried, and Will Larkin said what was necessary over the graves.

Our hero wondered what kind of men they could be who had committed these atrocities, and well might he wonder to find such devils existed in the bright, beautiful world.

A great deal has been said and sung about the kind instincts and good humour of the noble savage. Romance has done much for him, but the truth is that the general run of savages were, and are, nothing better than dirty, howling, thieving, murderous beasts—creatures of the lowest instincts and most grovelling tastes.

That is the reason why your savage retires before the advance of civilisation—the reason why he is ousted by the better race, who come to his shores and make the land habitable for man.

These remarks apply to savages of every degree, be they Sandwich Islanders, Pawnees, Hottentots, or Mohicans.

The trail led them across a great plain, then through a forest, and afterwards out upon another plain, where they could see the hazy outline of some hills or mountains in the distance.

The Pawnees had been careless of their trail—wonderfully so for Indians; but their numbers were great—five hundred at least—and Long Tom accounted for their carelessness by saying that it was a sort of defiance or challenge for those who might choose to follow them.

"They may live to regret their challenge," replied Jack, with a grim smile.

"They will regret it if I come across them," said Snip. "Lor! if I could only kill a red Injun, and take his scalp back to Wapping, what a reception I should get!"

"You would probably be pelted with brickbats," said Will Larkin, "and serve you right. The idea of an Englishman soiling his hands with their dirty scalps!"

"I thought it was the correct thing to do," said Snip, humbly; "and I was not aware that their scalps were dirty."

"Do you know what a scalp is?"

"Well, a scalp—a scalp," said Snip, "is—ahem!—a scalp is—is—a scalp."

A roar of laughter greeted Snip's ignorance, and the little man looked very indignant, especially at Caderouse, who enjoyed the joke most of all, wriggling and skipping about as only Frenchmen can.

"Laugh on," muttered Snip, "but I mean to have a scalp, and to take it back to Wapping."

A little further out upon the plain they came upon a spot where the ground was hard. The trail would have been difficult here but for a cleft stick thrust into the ground, with a feather in its top, pointing the way the Pawnees had gone.

This piece of impertinence brought a smile into Jack's face, the first which had appeared there since the death of Ximena.

"The fools," he said; "they court their own death. They call me to my duty, and the task shall be performed."

Just before sunset that eve they came to a place where the traces of men on foot disappeared, and the ground was literally trodden into a mire with the hoofs of horses.

"Here," said Long Tom, "they left their horses, and here they came and mounted again. They will give us a smart run now."

"Horses or no horses," said Jack, "I will track them down. Let them flee as they may, their time is approaching, and their doom is sealed."

All that day and the next they kept on, with the marks of the hoofs guiding them unerringly, the distant mountains still laying like a cloud on the horizon.

The next day a dark belt arose before their view. This, Long Tom said, was a forest, which the Pawnees doubtless made their home, using the plain as a hunting ground.

"If we wish to circumvent 'em," said Long Tom, "I guess that we had better go on in the night and get into the forest before sunrise."

Jack, who had a very great opinion of the sagacity of his officer, adopted Long Tom's plan.

So they lay quiet throughout the day, and at night crept forward to the forest.

As they passed beneath the trees the hooting of an owl was heard.

Every man, according to instructions, was walking very lightly, and the cry was heard by all. To the ears of most it had no significance, but Long Tom was of a very different opinion.

He was walking between our hero and Will Larkin, and, turning to the former, he said—

"We might as well have come in by daylight —the skunks have diskivered us."

"That was their cry," said Jack.

"It were," replied Tom. "Not a bad imitation of the real thing, but I know the difference."

"This place is hardly safe for us, then?"

"Depends on circumstances, Jack. They may attack us, or they may not; but I guess there's a body of them about. A single Injun would have stole away and not opened his mouth. They've too much respect for their hides to risk that."

"I don't care to turn tail from them," said Will Larkin.

"Nor I," said Jack.

"Let us light up fires and defy them!" interposed Snip.

"And wouldn't they just pot a few of us off!" said Tom. "If you are tired of your life I am not. What's the good of coming all this way to be shot like a dog in the dark?"

"Tom's right," rejoined Jack. "No work ought to be done unless it is well done; but I do not care to retreat. We can rest until dawn without fires. The night is not cold, and every man has his blanket. Set the usual number of men to watch, and the rest may sleep."

Nothing was heard throughout the night, not even a repetition of the hooting of the owl, and Jack was inclined to think that Tom must have been mistaken in the significance of that cry, while even Tom himself was wavering on the point, when a roar of laughter rang through the morning air.

"Silence, there!" cried Jack, leaping to his feet. "Are you mad? What is the cause of all this?"

"Your pardon, sare," said Caderouse, "but Snip made de laugh."

Snip himself came forward at this moment, with an arrow in his hand.

"Shot through the tails of my coat as I lay sound asleep," he said. "Here's a narrow escape of my life—another foot or so and I should have been a dead man."

"The feathers are dipped in blood," said Jack, taking the arrow from his hand. "The Pawnee defies and threatens us. A bold dog brought it here."

"It may have been discharged from a bow," suggested Will.

"No—your Indian never trusts his messages of defiance to chance," returned Jack. "Snip!"

"Yes, respected sir."

"How found you this arrow?"

"By the first rays of morning light," Snip began, preparing himself for a very dramatic version of the story. "When I awoke, thinking I was in Wapping, I tried to turn over for another gentle snooze ere I was called for the duties of the day, but I found myself a fixture."

"Be as brief as you can, for we have little time to lose," said Jack.

"Finding myself a fixture, I knew I wasn't in Wapping," continued Snip, "so I lay back to think it over, when my eye fell upon the arrow, sticking upright like a—like a young geranium growing out of the tails of my coat."

"Was it thrust far through it?"

"Half a foot of the arrow, at least, was in the ground, and I was a fixture. I never felt so queer before. I thought of Shakespeare——"

"Never mind Shakespeare," said Jack. "You have told your story, now go back to your post. We shall have work for you to do presently—some hard fighting, perhaps."

"My soul's in arms!" cried Snip, shouldering his rifle. "Only bring me an Injun before me, and see what I will make of him."

Jack smiled. He had his own opinion of what the Indian would make of Snip, but he said nothing.

Jack held a council of war that morning with Will, Tom, and a few of the best men. All were of opinion that the arrow had been planted in Snip's garment by the hand of some bold Indian, and that they were surrounded by a murderous and dangerous enemy.

"It's a scout who did the trick," said Tom. "If he could have brought the main body up they would have fallen foul of us in the night, but he gave us this bit of cheek to let us know he was not afraid."

"I'll make a few of them tremble," rejoined Jack. "We will get on at once, and Caderouse shall beat them. He is as good as any wolfhound."

"Better," said Tom, "because he will keep on the scent, and never bark to give warning."

"Let every man fill his can with water," said Jack, "and use it sparingly, for, judging by the soil, springs are scanty hereabouts."

There was a spring near, and the men went down in batches to fetch the water, among the last batch being Snip.

He had mislaid his can, in the hurry which followed the discovery of the arrow, and while he was searching for it his party started.

In a minute or so he discovered the can, and started on what he believed to be their track. As the plain was not far away he could not think it possible he had made a mistake, so he kept on for some time, but came not in sight of his people.

"It's very odd," he thought. "I am certain that we were not five minutes' walk from the plain. Hallo! there. Hallo!"

His shout echoed through the forest, but echo alone gave him a reply.

"I've got on the wrong road," he groaned. "Just my luck—everything goes amiss with me. I shall have nothing to drink, and the others will have none to spare. I must go back."

He paused a moment and reflected, then a feeling of despair came over him.

"I've been turning and turning about," he thought, "until I've lost my way. This is worse than anything yet. Pirates are angels compared to Injuns. I'm as good as boiled and flayed alive. I've as good as lost my scalp. I'm a dead man!"

Utterly overwhelmed with horror, Snip sat upon the ground and tried to think out his position. It was terrible, and can best be given to our readers in his own words.

"If I go on, or try to go back," he thought, "I am nearly sure to go the wrong way, and shall walk straight into the arms of the Injuns, perhaps. If I shout for my friends I may bring enemies upon me. And if I sit here, and neither friend nor enemy comes to me, I must starve."

It was a pretty pickle to be in, and Snip was scarcely the man to meet such an emergency. He lacked true courage, and his tact and judgment were none of the best.

———

CHAPTER XXV.

MORNING DAWN.

VERY little difficulty bewildered Snip, and a moderate amount of danger overwhelmed him.

"If I could only see the sun," he groaned, looking up at the dense foliage above his head, "but there is not a patch of sky to be seen. The light comes through the trees as it would through a fine sieve."

Snip thought he would shout again, and opened his mouth to do so, but the fear of Indians was upon him, and he refrained.

Then he thought of firing his gun and getting up a tree to watch the effect, but the trunks of the trees near him were all tall and straight, with no substantial branches for many feet from the ground—all very nice for a practised climber, but quite beyond the powers of Snip.

"I had better wait," he thought; "perhaps they will come to look for me. They can't leave a valuable man like me behind. I'm the life and soul of the camp, and Jack Savage is very fond of me—at least, I hope so. What's that? Oh, murder! It's all over! Don't upset a man as never hurt a worm in his life. I'm only a poor tailor, sir, fresh from Wapping. Don't be too hard upon me."

The latter part of his speech was addressed to a tall young Indian, who came from between the trees with the silence of a shadow, and now stood before him.

There was a composure in the face of the young savage which was very striking. There was no paint upon it to mar its beauty, and the even outlines of the features looked beautiful as he stood with his eyes fixed calmly on the agonised Snip.

His dress was plain, being garnished here and there with only a few beads and feathers. In his belt was a tomahawk, at his back was a bow and arrows, and that was all. He wore no head-dress—nothing but the long, flowing black locks which fell upon his shoulders.

"The little paleface is in pain," he said, calmly.

Partially reassured by the tone of his voice, Snip looked up. The Indian shifted not his ground or removed his eyes.

"My pale-faced brother is in pain," he said.

"Yes," replied Snip, who thought that by some extraordinary power he held the Indian in subjection; "I'm subject to such things if I eat vegetables for breakfast, and this morning

⊲ GIANT JACK: ⊳

A Story of the Red Mountains.

SNIP WENT UP THE ROPE LIKE A PROFESSIONAL ACROBAT.

I've had nothing else. They are werry trying to some constitutions."

"My brother is better," said the Indian, calmly, as before.

"I am," replied Snip. "I soon get over these attacks—some men are laid up a week by them."

"My brother's name is Snip," said the Indian.

"How did you know that?" asked Snip.

"I heard his brothers call him so," replied the Indian.

"Perhaps you will oblige me with your name?" insinuated Snip.

"My people call me Morning Dawn," was the reply. "I am a chief of the Pawnee tribe."

"A chief?" said Snip to himself. "Well, if I can awe him, how about the common ruck?"

"I have seen my little white brother before," said the Indian. "I came to him in the night, when he was sleeping."

He took hold of Snip's coat and pointed to the hole made by the arrow.

"My brother sleeps well," said the Indian, "but he makes much noise in his sleep—with his nose."

"I come of a snoring family," replied Snip, "and I flatter myself that I keep up the credit of the breed. But you don't happen to know which way my friends have gone? It's getting late, and I must be off."

"My little pale-faced brother," said the Indian, "must come with me."

"Oh!" exclaimed Snip, in dismay, "I was not aware that you wanted me particularly."

"My little brother," said the Pawnee chief, "is wanted by my people. They have a sacrifice to make."

"Toasted alive!" groaned Snip. "Here's an end of a man like me!"

"My little brother must hasten," said the Indian; "he will find his lightning-tube heavy. The Morning Dawn will carry it."

With a quiet but quick and dextrous movement the chief of the Pawnees jerked the rifle out of Snip's hand and put it across his shoulder. Then he beckoned for our friend to follow him.

"I suppose I must go with you," said Snip; "not that I should be of any use. I'm——"

"If my brother will not come with me," said Morning Dawn, "I must leave him here."

"The very best thing you can do," returned Snip, hastily. "I should only be a burden to you. I am a horrible bad walker, although I come of a walking family."

"If I leave my brother here," said the Indian, calmly cocking the rifle, "I must leave him dead."

"Dead!" stammered Snip.

"Ah!" said the Indian, putting the weapon to his shoulder.

Snip reeled and fell, and shouted—

"Hold—hold hard! I'll go with you anywhere! Don't fire!"

Morning Dawn put the butt of the rifle upon the ground and beckoned again. Then Snip arose and followed the Indian into the depths of the forest.

CHAPTER XXVI.

THE FIRST SHOT.

"ALL ready, Will?" asked Jack. "Is everyone here?"

"One missing," said Will Larkin.

"Who is that?"

"Snip."

"The troublesome fellow," said Jack, impatiently, "where is he?"

"He missed the water party and has not been seen since."

"Perhaps he is at the spring."

"No—I have sent down, and he is not there."

"Where was he seen last?"

"By the tree, yonder."

"Has he left a trail?"

"Caderouse thinks he can find it."

"Put him on at once—we can follow. If he has been snared by the enemy he may lead us to their hiding-place."

Caderouse, the bloodhound of the band, was forthwith put to work, and he soon declared that he had found Snip's trail. Following it quickly, he easily led Jack and his men to the spot where Snip had sat down in despair.

"Rest here," said Caderouse. "Ah! vat dis—one—two foot—white foot—Indian foot!"

"It's the skunk who left the arrow with us, I'll bet," said Long Tom.

"I see no signs of a struggle," said Will Larkin.

"Mistare Snip go enough quiet," grinned Caderouse, "he no fight."

"He showed pretty good fight to you," said Long Tom; "don't run a man—and it may be a dead man, too—down behind his back."

"He not dead," said Caderouse, "here shall leave four feet."

"Four footsteps!" said Jack. "Lose no time—get on."

Caderouse bowed one of his most polite bows, and then ran forward upon an easy trail. The men followed as best they could.

The forest grew thicker, and, in addition to the increasing number of trunks of trees, they had now to encounter a troublesome undergrowth, which impeded their footsteps and caused many of the men to fall.

They were not hurt beyond a scratch or a bruise or two, but the impediment retarded their movements as a body, and Caderouse shot ahead, leaving the whole of his comrades about fifty yards in the rear.

Jack kept with his men, but lost not sight of Caderouse until they came to a denser part of the forest than they had hitherto met with, and then the Frenchman suddenly disappeared.

"Forward!" said Jack, in a low tone; "we are losing our hound."

"We have lost him," said Will Larkin. "Where did you see him last?"

"By the tree, yonder," replied Jack.

"He is not there now, and I see no signs of him."

"If we keep on," said Long Tom, stepping forward, "we shall be all right. We might miss him, but he won't miss us."

The next moment Tom stumbled and fell. Jack laughed, but changed his tone as Tom arose with a look of horror upon his face.

"What's the matter?"

"Caderouse!" gasped Tom.

"Where?"

"Here! I fell over him."

With an involuntary cry Jack, Will, and several of the men sprang forward. There, indeed, lay the Frenchman upon his face.

"Shot through the heart !" cried Jack, raising him up.

So saying, he pointed to an arrow sticking in the Frenchman's breast—an arrow with a bloody feather, the very counterpart of the one left in the camp.

"Clean work," said one of the men, with the air of a connoisseur ; "the fellow who shot this could split a hair."

"Poor Caderouse," cried Will. "We could very well have spared a better man."

Regrets were useless, so a hasty grave was dug and the dead man laid therein—a sudden and fearful end to a life which had been none of the best. Death comes to men at strange times and in strange places. Man is oft the agent of the Great Destroyer, but there are occasions when Death does the work with its own hand. The appointed time arrives, and the man falls.

The mourners, in their strange dress, looked more like a band of murderers than men burying a friend.

Deprived of their guide the band were rather at fault. The keen instinct possessed by Caderouse is not given to many men ; but Long Tom was of opinion that he could follow the trail with tolerable accuracy.

Tracking a person is an instinct—that is, unless the ground is soft and the marks tolerably clear. In the present instance there was nothing which the ordinary eye could see to guide them, and Tom had a stiff job before him.

Long years before, when a younger man, he had spent some time with the Indians, and knew a little about their arts, which now helped him, so he kept on with tolerable ease until they came to a small brook, which ran babbling through the forest.

Here all trace of the captor and captive was lost, and Long Tom called a halt.

Bidding all stand quiet, so as not to blot out any footmarks, he went carefully to and fro on one bank, then crossed over and examined the other, but found nothing.

He came back with a puzzled look upon his face—he was foiled.

"The Injun took to the water," he said to Jack, "and when a man does that neither dog nor man can follow his trail."

"We will rest on the bank of this stream,' said Jack, "then the Indians are sure to return and attack us. In appearance we will camp carelessly, but let every eye be open and every ear stretched for the slightest sight and sound."

"Aye, aye, sir !" said Tom.

So the pursuers pitched their camp, and remained there throughout the night.

Sentinels were posted, and every precaution quietly taken, but nothing was heard throughout the night. No arrow or further message from the enemy, and no signs of Snip.

Perhaps, as a fighting man, Snip was as useless as a man could be, but he was a prominent person, nevertheless, and he was missed very much.

He was amusing, and that was a great deal to men who were out in a wild, uncultivated land, going they scarcely knew whither—in fact, our little tailor friend was mourned for much more than their man-bloodhound, Caderouse.

Jack Savage and Will Larkin held counsel together, but they came to no satisfactory conclusion.

There were but two courses open to them—to stay there and await the enemy or to follow on.

The latter was impracticable, as they knew not whither they were going.

To remain was decidedly trying, both to leaders and men, but there was nothing else to be done, and they resolved to wait.

"The Indians won't rest with us on their ground," said Will. "If I know anything of them—and I know a little—they will come back again."

"As sure as the sun will rise to-morrow," returned Jack ; "but the waiting chafes and irritates me."

"You are impatient."

"Aye, Will, I am impatient. I am so full of life, so full of energy and activity, that I cannot rest. I feel as if it is to be my lot to wander about the earth until I die."

"You are hipped, and have been thinking of Ximena."

"Oh, wise Will !" said Jack ; "as if she were ever from my thoughts. She rests in my heart by day, and at night she always comes and sits with me by the fire."

"Strange dreams and fancies, Jack."

"No, Will ; neither dreams nor fancies. She is with me—so is my father. One on each side they sit, and we hold council together ; but there are—are—— What was it you were telling me the other day your great poet said ?"

"There are more things in heaven and on earth than are dreamt of in our philosophy."

"That's it," said Jack. "Man, in my opinion, even the wisest, knows very little. If the visions I see at night are not real, then there is very little that is real in this world."

"You are a strange fellow, Jack."

"You have said that before, Will. I am strange, and I know it. I am not like the general run of men. Look at my body—feel my hands. Was there ever bone and sinew like this ?"

"Rather a rare article, I must confess," said Will.

"And what is this strange power I hold ?" pursued Jack. "Whence does it come ? What is it ? Where is it ? Move, Will !"

He made a few rapid passes, and Will was fixed. He had lost all power to obey the command.

"Raise your arm, Will."

"You know I cannot," returned Will, half alarmed, but nevertheless amused. "Release me, for I do not care for this sort of confinement."

"You are at liberty," said Jack, and Will once more moved and breathed freely.

"If it is all the same to you, Jack," he said, "I would rather that you practised on one less susceptible. Tom is less so—try him."

Tom at this moment came up, and Jack made a few passes before his face.

Tom twisted and fidgeted about, but he could still move.

Jack made a few more passes, and Tom was still.

"You are always up to some game," said that worthy. "Come, Jack, don't be hard on an old man."

"All right, Tom," said our hero, "you are free."

"That's better," replied Tom. "Thank'ee— no more of that just yet, if you don't mind. I came to say I've heard the owl again."

"Ah ! they are coming."

"Some of 'em," said Tom, "and I've got a game for 'em. I am making up a sentinel."

"Making one up ?"

"Yes, a dummy—a figure of a man stuffed with moss. I am going to plant him outside our circle, and see what follows."

"No, Tom," said Jack, reflecting, "let that be my duty. I want something to excite and amuse me. I am dull, and my blood runs cold."

"You must not go," said Will. "Suppose you are killed ?"

"I shall not be killed," said Jack, quietly. "When my time is at hand I shall know of it."

"Another dream ?"

"If you like to think so, Will ; but it's all real to me. Make up the figure, Tom, as well as you can, and I will start with it soon after dark."

"I'll make it so like a man," replied Tom, "and so handsome, that a woman coming by would try to kiss him."

"Very good," said Jack, smiling ; "but you must be quick, for the sun will soon be down."

Tom nodded and went away, and in less than an hour he came back, bearing the figure in his arms.

It was not all he promised, but it was an excellent make-up, and pleased Jack exceedingly.

"You have done well," he said.

"You ought to have been a sculptor," added Will. "If you can do this much with a few old clothes and a barrow-load of moss, what would you have been able to do in modelling clay ?"

"I flatter myself," said Tom, with a complacent air, "that there's many a man living a deal uglier than that crittur."

Shortly after the sun went down, and Jack strode away with his burden, under the cover of darkness, into the depths of the forest.

Bearing his load as if it were a feather, Jack walked on until a good half-mile was placed between him and the camp, then he halted and placed the work of Long Tom upon the ground.

Darkness was now fully upon the earth, but it is seldom so dark that the practised eye cannot see something of the objects near him, and Jack was able to perceive that the trees were unusually large, with a tolerably wide space between.

"Here is the very spot," he thought, and, dragging the imitation man into the open, he fixed it upright with the help of several forked sticks, which he had brought for the purpose.

Knowing the Indians well, he had walked boldly to the spot where he now stood. This was done to give a watcher, if there was one, an inkling of his whereabouts—just the thing Jack wanted.

Fixing the sentinel was a matter of some difficulty, but with the help of an additional rifle he had brought it was done. Then he took shelter behind one of the large trees near him, and lay down upon the ground to watch.

He had barely stretched himself at full length when the hooting of an owl was heard.

"Ha, ha !" thought Jack. "I shall not have long to wait."

Again the sound was heard, probably a reply to the previous cry, and Jack smiled with hopeful anticipation.

He had no fear—such feelings was a stranger to him.

One Indian—a dozen—fifty—a hundred—it was all the same to Jack Savage. He was prepared for anything that might transpire.

As for death, he never thought of that. He had a conscience like other men, but what crimes he had committed appeared not as crimes to him, for he thought of right and wrong as most of us think—as he had been taught.

An hour passed and no change had occurred.

The forest was still—not a breath of wind ruffled the tree-tops, and no sound, save the creaking of twigs and branches—a sound which never ceases in large forests—disturbed the serenity of the midnight air.

Patient as a cat watching for a mouse Jack lay prone on the earth.

The ground was cold, and the dew was gathering on every object around, but he was inured to such things—his frame was strong and hardy, and they gave him no trouble or pain.

———

CHAPTER XXVII.

JACK TAKES A PRISONER.

ANOTHER hour passed, and Jack was still watching.

"They can be cunning," he thought, "and so can I. But why is the owl so quiet ?"

As the question evolved itself in his brain, he heard the hoot again, and his pulse beat a little faster, for the cry was nearer.

"What fools they are to think that they are deceiving me. Hark ! a footstep that," he muttered ; "there is a clumsy Indian abroad to-night."

His eyes were now used to the darkness, and he could see some yards away. Close at hand was the form of his dummy sentinel—a very tolerable imitation of a man. But he saw more than this. Behind the sentinel was another form—not erect, but lying on the ground.

Inch by inch he could see the dim outline moving along the earth—so slowly that it would have deceived almost any eye.

It was an Indian decidedly, but an Indian apparently unarmed.

Jack could see no signs of a weapon—the arms and legs were extended, and the back bore nothing. As for anything underneath, it seemed impossible to carry arms and crawl thus.

"He is unarmed," thought Jack ; "a mad eak for one of such a cunning race."

Then a sense of chivalry and fair play came over him, and he took his hand from the rifle which was lying by his side.

The Indian drew nearer to the sentinel.

Jack removed his knife from his belt and placed it beside his rifle.

Then the Indian sprang upon the figure with a guttural, hissing sound, and the next moment he was enfolded in Jack's arms, when our hero discovered that he was armed with a tomahawk.

"Ugh !" exclaimed the Indian.

"Fairly caught !" said Jack.

"My white brother is strong," said the Indian, quietly ; "he will crush my bones."

"I will be more gentle," said Jack, "but do not attempt any tricks or I will kill you."

"If my brother will take a Pawnee's word," said the Indian, "I will go with him. I am his captive, and he is my master."

"I will take your word," returned Jack, releasing him.

Then the pair stood still for a moment in the darkness, taking such stock of each other as they could.

"My white brother is tall," said the Indian; "will he give me his name?"

"I am known as Jack Savage among my men."

"My brother is the giant the little paleface spoke of?"

"You mean one of my men—Snip?" returned Jack.

"Aye," exclaimed the Indian.

"Is he alive?"

"The little paleface is with my people."

"Are you a chief?" asked Jack, with surprise.

"I am the chief of the Pawnee people, and my name is the Morning Dawn," was the proud reply given.

"And you are out alone on a midnight expedition?" exclaimed Jack.

"My brother, the white chief, is out alone," retorted the Indian, quietly.

"Right,' returned Jack, laughing. "What is good for one chief is good for another, I suppose. But your name is the Morning Dawn—rather a strange one for an Indian."

"My people gave it to me," replied the Pawnee, "because they say I am gentle, but yet have about me the fire of the day. I am calm when the sun rises, but there is lightning in my bosom, and the thundercloud comes sometimes o'er me, when my people tremble."

"You struggled well," said Jack, "and have much bone and sinew."

"But my brother has the bone and sinew of ten men."

"Yes—I have never met my match. But come, we must go back to the camp."

Jack picked up his rifle and replaced his knife, then he beckoned to the savage to follow him.

Morning Dawn pointed to the figure on the ground, and asked—

"Will he not come?"

"Not just yet," said Jack; "it is only a dummy."

Morning Dawn bent over the dummy and touched it with his finger, then he arose with a look of disgust upon his face.

"I am getting old and blind," he said. "I cannot see. My people want a better chief."

"It required a good eye," said Jack, "to detect the cheat on such a night as this."

"I am a fool—I cannot see."

Then with a stately step he followed the young giant through the wood. Captor of Snip, he had been made captive himself. The little tailor was a prisoner in the Pawnee camp, but he was a prisoner among the palefaces. An excellent hostage for our little friend—the bold Wapping man descended from so remarkable a family.

CHAPTER XXVIII.

AMONG THE PAWNEES.

SNIP, brave Snip, was a captive among the Pawnees. In a deep hollow in the middle of the wood the camp lay, the wigwams covered with branches, and every precaution taken to prevent anything giving a hint of their whereabouts.

The glade itself was surrounded by a very dense portion of the forest, impenetrable to man, except in one part, and even here branches and brambles were strewn about, so as to hide all signs of a pathway.

To ordinary eyes the place was unapproachable, and no mere passers-by would have dreamt that some five hundred men, with a number of captives, lay hidden there.

But so it was, packed like rabbits in a warren captors and captives lay, and among the captives none was more unhappy and apprehensive than Snip.

The Pawnee chief brought him in and left him among his people, while he went out again to watch, as was his wont, the advance of the foe he had but too much reason to dread.

He started at sunset, but the morning came and he did not return.

It was his custom to come back with the dawn, from which he partly gained his name, and the Pawnees were so used to this that they invariably arose before the first ray of light to give him welcome.

While it was yet dark the principal warriors gathered in the bottom and stood silently awaiting his coming.

Soon a ray of light came through the leafy arch above, and fell upon the wigwam of their chief, which had been so placed as to catch this earnest of the morning sun.

The dawn was there, but where was the chief?

Unaccustomed to betray any emotion, the warriors stood in silence, without even exchanging a glance to show the apprehension which was growing in their breasts.

The ray of light became diffused, and the air was full of broken beams of the morning sun—the day had arrived.

Then a warrior, older than the rest, stood forth and spoke. His voice was low and clear, but every word was heard by those present.

"The sun is high," he said, "but where is our chief, the Morning Dawn? He is not an idler—he sleeps not in the forest—and he loves his people. Why is he not here?"

"Last night he went forth with the Wolf," said another, "and neither the Morning Dawn nor the Wolf are here."

"Perhaps our chiefs have fallen among the palefaces," said the old warrior.

"The Red Tiger speaks badly, but he should know—he is old, and a warrior," said the previous speaker.

"If he has fallen," said the Red Tiger, "we must have another chief. Who is it to be?"

Pride and ambition were already springing up in the old man's breast, as it was springing up in the breasts of others, and firing their glittering eyes; but for a moment it was foiled, as there came gliding into their midst the Wolf—the midnight companion of the Morning Dawn.

"The chief—the chief!" said a dozen voices.

"Is he not here?" asked the Wolf, calmly.

"The Wolf knows he is not," said the Red Tiger, with scorn in his face.

"The Red Tiger lies!" replied the Wolf. "I know nothing of the Morning Dawn."

"Is he dead?"

"I know not."

"The Wolf must tell his story," said one of the Indians, and then all but the Wolf sank quietly to the ground.

He stood erect, one hand toying with his tomahawk, the other resting on his hip, and thus he told his story :—

"When night spread her dark mantle last the Morning Dawn and I went out to watch the palefaces. Silently we passed through the wood until we drew near to the enemy, and then the Morning Dawn bade me watch the camp while he followed a footstep we had heard in the wood—the footstep of a sentinel going to his post. I laid still until the cold chill of night had fallen long, and the Morning Dawn not coming back I sought him—sought him and found him not. Then went I through the wood with the owl's cry, but no answer came to me from our chief."

"The Wolf is deaf," sneered the Red Eagle.

"The Wolf has ears," was the quiet reply, "and eyes—but he saw and heard nothing."

"He could not hear the dead speak," said the Red Tiger, rising and pointing at him, "and he did not care to see the chief whom he had killed."

"The Morning Dawn is alive," said the Wolf.

"Where is he, then?" asked the Red Tiger.

The Wolf could not reply to this, and a murmur arose among the warriors, for the words of the Red Tiger had taken root.

"If the Morning Dawn is alive," pursued the Red Tiger, "why is he not here?"

"He may be a captive among the palefaces," replied the Wolf.

"A captive and alive!" sneered the Red Tiger. "The Wolf knows not the Morning Dawn."

"The Wolf knows this," he retorted, "that if the Red Tiger says he has slain his chief the Red Tiger lies, and a liar must fight or die."

"If the Morning Dawn returns by noon, or if he is found among the palefaces, the Red Tiger will give his blood to the Wolf," said the old Indian. "If he does not the Wolf must die."

"The Wolf is content," he replied, and the rest murmured their approval.

"We shall know more if our people make a sacrifice," said the Red Tiger, after a pause. He was an old man, but the thirst for blood which had gained him his name in his youth was still upon him.

"Who shall be the sacrifice?" asked one of the Indians.

"The paleface captive was brought home by the Morning Dawn," answered the Red Tiger.

"Good!" was the guttural rejoinder of most of the Indians present, and the word was passed to bring forth Snip.

From a wigwam where he had been kept, a prisoner bound hand and foot, they brought him out into the light of day.

Poor Snip! He was a little man, not of the most muscular kind, and he had been badly used. Being a captive of their chief, the Pawnees had bestowed extra care upon him, and he had been so bound and trussed that the circulation of his blood had suffered much.

Pale, rumpled, and dejected, he was dragged out and placed in the midst of the tawny ruffians, who veiled their ferocity and love of blood under a cool demeanour, and hid their love of vice beneath a cloak of haughtiness.

Snip was no sooner in the presence of his persecutors than his usual propensity to babble broke forth. Bound as he was, he could not improve his rhetoric by action, but his tongue could wag, and he set it going at a great rate.

"Look here, gentlemen," he said, "this is not quite according to Cocker. It's bad enough to truss anything after it is dead, but to truss a live man is against any Act of Parliament ever written. It aint justice, and you can't make it so. If you didn't want me to run away I would have given my word, and the word of my family is as good as a bond. None of us ever broke our word, except my Uncle Tim, who gave his landlord to understand that he would pay his rent the next morning, and then moved everything in the middle of the night. He went clean away, and was never heard of again until he turned up without a shoe to his foot, when he borrowed a shilling of my father, who was glad to get rid of him at any price. But to go and regular cut up a chap with these bits of leather is too bad, and if any of you had any feeling you wouldn't do it."

"My brother talks much," said the Red Tiger.

"It's enough to make any man talk," returned Snip. "The way I have been treated is infamous—a dog wouldn't stand it. Look at my arms—look at my legs. Confound you all for a—ah! would you?"

One of the savages clapped a hand over Snip's mouth, and the little tailor thought he was about to be strangled, but it was not so. The savage simply kept his hand there a moment, then he made a sign to the prisoner to be silent.

"Will my brothers have the sacrifice now or after noon?" asked the Red Tiger.

Some were for the immediate death of Snip, but others were for the postponement of the interesting event. The latter, after a brief debate, carried the day, and Snip was pushed down on the ground like a log of wood, to remain there until wanted.

"I will go to the camp of the palefaces," said the Red Tiger. "If our chief is there I will find him; if he is not, and he does not return in the meantime, the Wolf dies."

"The Wolf will die as a warrior should," said the Wolf; "but the Red Tiger must not speak lies when he returns."

"The Red Tiger never lies," was the reply, and the savage went as swiftly and as silently as a cloud upon his way.

Then the other warriors sank into sitting or reclining postures on the ground and spoke no more, waiting, with the phlegmatic indifference of their race—real or assumed—the issue of events.

Snip lay close to the Wolf, who had taken up his quarters close by, and our friend, albeit interested in his own affairs, could not help feeling a little sympathy for one who was, as the saying goes, in the same box.

The Wolf kept his eyes upon the ground, and toyed lightly with his tomahawk, as he revolved within his mind the perplexities of his position.

He was, as our reader knows, innocent of the death of the chief; but at the same time he was ignorant of his fate, and herein lay his danger.

What if the chief could not be found? He must die!

The sun once at the meridian, and the camp without a leader, his doom was sealed.

Flight was useless. His first attempt in that direction would lead to instant death—that he knew.

The eyes of the other warriors were upon him in spite of their assumed indifference, and were he to rise and attempt to move away a dozen tomahawks would cleave his skull into as many pieces. It was but hurrying his fate to attempt such a thing.

He was thinking this over when a voice fell upon his ear. It was Snip speaking in a low tone.

"I say, Mr. Wolf," whispered that gentleman.

The Indian stared at him haughtily, but made no reply.

"We are both of us in a precious mess," pursued Snip. "You cut my cords, and we will make a run for it together."

"The little paleface talks riddles," said the Indian.

"Riddles be bothered!" returned Snip. "I never liked them, and never could make 'em out. Where's the riddle in cutting these cords, which are sawing me in two, and then making a run for it?"

The Wolf resumed his meditations. Snip, perceiving that his proposal had failed, became meditative too, and the whole camp was soon buried in silence.

About twenty feet from where the warriors sat were two wigwams, larger than the rest, and in these were the captive women and children whom our hero came to save.

In number they were about forty—twenty-two women, and the rest children.

Standing over them were several Indians, who, with tomahawks in hand, threatened instant death to anyone who broke the silence by word or cry.

The poor captives were huddled together terrified. They had no desire to live, and all who were old enough to understand prayed to die.

Had they not seen all the men of their village slain they might have had some hope, but the cruel work had been too complete, and they had no hope.

Upon some the bloodstains of the fight still remained, and one poor woman in particular held sacred a few drops of blood bespattered on her arms, which she hid with her dress, lest savage tongues should bid her wipe them way.

It was the blood of her husband—all that was left to her of the man she loved.

The women had asked for death, but their captors had denied them. They would have destroyed their children, but a careful watch was kept, and the children still lived.

What would be their fate? Aye, what was in store for them? The mothers thought of this and shuddered.

After his vain attempt to induce the Wolf to become his companion in flight, Snip thought over the various unpleasant items of his position, and he felt a sensation like that of cold water trickling down his back as he thought them over.

But thinking would not help him. He was still speculating on his fate when the Red Tiger came back as swiftly and silently as he went.

The warriors arose to their feet and gathered in a circle, with the Wolf and the Red Tiger in their midst.

CHAPTER XXIX.

THE WOLF IS DOOMED.

LIKE statues the Indians waited to hear what the Red Tiger had to say, and he, with a calm and impressive air, began his story.

"I have seen the camp of the palefaces," he said. "It is full of men, with a giant paleface for chief, but there is no Indian warrior there. The Morning Dawn is dead!"

There was a murmur among the listeners, and a few bent their heads, but none spoke aloud, so the Red tiger went on.

"When the Wolf came back with a lie upon his lips the Morning Dawn, the greatest chief the Pawnees ever saw, was lying dead. He had been slain by the Wolf, who wished to be our chief. Will he not tell us where he made the grave of the Morning Dawn, that our people may weep over his ashes?"

"The Morning Dawn yet lives," returned the Wolf, "and the Red Tiger lies. He has not been to the paleface camp."

"My brothers have heard me and have heard the Wolf," replied the Red Tiger, sitting down; "let them judge between us."

"The Wolf has lied," said every warrior, in a monotonous chant, "and the Morning Dawn is dead."

"Will not my brothers hear reason?" urged the Wolf. "If I killed the Morning Dawn why did I come here to ask for him?"

"Because the Wolf is false and subtle," said the Red Tiger, "and he thought that we were blind, but he was a fool, for we can see."

"I do not think any Pawnee a fool," returned the Wolf, "and only an idiot who had slain the Morning Dawn would have come back to this camp to talk to his people."

"The Wolf is cunning," responded the Red Tiger; "we hear him but we are not deceived. He lies!"

"The Wolf never lies."

"The sun is past the moon," said the Red Tiger, "and the Morning Dawn has not returned."

"He will come ere the sun sets," urged the Wolf.

"He will not," said the Red Tiger. "The dead cannot rise from their graves—when the heart is still not even a Pawnee can walk. The sun will rise and set many times, and the Pawnees shall all die, still the Morning Dawn will not return."

"He will," said the Wolf. "Why are my brothers so hasty? I am not a coward and can die, but when the Morning Dawn returns they will weep over the grave of the Wolf, whom they have slain without a cause."

"Is the Wolf a woman?" asked one of the warriors, scornfully.

"No," replied the Wolf. "My heart is strong, but it loves the people of my tribe. Why should I leave them while my blood is warm and my eyes bright as the stars? See, my hand is steady—my aim as true as ever. So!"

As he spoke he suddenly drew forth his tomahawk and hurled it at the Red Tiger. Straight and true to his head it went, but the savage was on the alert, and caught it dexterously by the handle.

"The Wolf is more than a woman—he is a

child," said the Red Tiger, with a sarcastic laugh. "He cannot wield the tomahawk— his hand trembles as he thinks of his murdered chief, the Morning Dawn."

"The Wolf must die !" exclaimed a dozen voices, and his doom was sealed.

He gave one glance round the circle—not an appealing one, for that he knew was useless, but an interrogative look—to see if there was one friend amongst them all.

Not one. The Wolf had always been a favourite with the Morning Dawn. This had been sufficient to make him no favourite with his fellow-warriors, which, added to their instinctive love of bloodshed, made them eager to take his life

"The Wolf must die !" they said again, and the Wolf, like an Indian, made preparations for his fate.

His wife was summoned and she came. Young and beautiful. It would have touched any heart but that of a savage to see her cling lovingly to his neck and look into his eyes, which were brimful of the agony of his soul.

He kissed her once, whispered a blessing in her ear, and put her aside. Then he removed his beads from around his neck, his belt from his waist, and placed them at her feet. Afterwards he kissed her again, folded his arms, and stood still.

There was a strange hush upon the camp. Death is a solemn thing, even to the most brutal of mankind, and a man was about to die.

To the Wolf the great mystery would soon be unravelled—the veil of "the future" drawn aside.

Let men argue as they will, and deaden their hearts with scepticism and miserable philosophy, they cannot shake off the probings of their conscience, which is always saying, "Wish as you may, your soul is immortal, so look to its keeping."

This is alike the gift of the savage as well as the civilised being. All have hopes and fears of the life to come. All love to dream of the great Eternity. So sure as the light of the sun gilds the hill-tops at morn the endless life—the immortality of man—is true.

On the brink of this life stood the Wolf.

With head erect he waited the blow which was to lay him low, and he knew who would deal it—the Red Tiger.

He was at once accuser, judge, and executioner. This was Pawnee law—the unjust law of the savage, barbarous people.

Perhaps of all those who were watching the scene none were more interested than Snip—not only interested, but terrified.

He was about to witness the fate of a man— a fate which might prove to be but the forerunner of his own—and the natural interest excited by the event in all breasts was augmented in his own by the consciousness that he would, in all probability, travel the same road.

The Red Tiger, with the light of triumph gleaming in his eyes, which he could not conceal, drew his tomahawk from his belt, and slowly ran his thumb down the edge, to test its keenness.

So cold, and yet so bloodthirsty; it was strange to watch the savage whose hand was about to slay one of his own people.

But, as he felt the edge, he looked towards the squaw, who had taken her leave of the Wolf, and that look showed that he had another cause to hate the man he had doomed.

Then he poised the tomahawk aloft. The aim of the Red Tiger was known to be sure, and, with sinews nerved, he was about to hurl the weapon, when a hand grasped his wrist and wrenched the tomahawk away.

With a cry of rage he swung upon his heel, but the exclamation changed to one of terror when he saw the Morning Dawn !

CHAPTER XXX.

RETRIBUTION.

"WHY are my people at play ?" asked the Pawnee chief, sternly. "The palefaces are near—it is no time to idle."

The Red Tiger stood silently before his chief, but he had nothing to say. Then the Wolf came forward and addressed the Morning Dawn.

"The Pawnees are not at play," he said ; "they were in earnest. The Wolf was condemned to die."

"For what ?" demanded the chief.

"For having killed the Morning Dawn."

The chief laughed.

"This is childish," he said. "But who accused the Wolf ?"

"The Red Tiger," said several.

"What proof had he ?"

"The Morning Dawn was missing," said the Red Tiger, "the Wolf came back alone, and the Wolf desired to be chief of the Pawnees— it was said that he had killed the Morning Dawn !"

"Said by whom ?"

"By me," replied the Red Tiger, "for I loved my chief and my heart was sad."

"Why did you not seek me ?" asked the Pawnee chief.

"I sought my chief.'

"Where ?"

"In the wood and among the palefaces."

"If you had sought me there," said the Morning Dawn, "you must have found me. But you lie !—I see it in your face. You never liked the Wolf, and this was a means to take his life."

There was a murmur among the savages, and several of them cast looks of hate upon the Red Tiger. His turn had come, and his end was approaching.

"I sat in the midst of the palefaces," continued the Morning Dawn, "free and unbound. Their chief is great and noble, and I came hither by his command. But more of his will anon. Let us judge the Red Tiger—he has lied and must die. The sun is going down—let it be done."

Thus was his sentence passed, and, with a sullen look, the Red Tiger bent his head to the stroke. There was little or no ceremony. One of his brethren struck him down, and he lay like a log upon the earth, never to rise again.

Some of the Indians bore him away to bury him, and the chief resumed his address as if nothing of great interest had happened.

"The white chief says that if you give up the captives we may go free. Shall it be so? Will my brothers agree ?"

There was a murmur of dissent at this. It was not at all suited to the Pawnees' tastes or wishes.

"'Shall it be so?" asked the chief again.

"'No!" was the general reply. And the voice of the Wolf was loudest.

"Why should the Pawnee yield?" he said. "The land is wide. If we cannot fight we can flee, and the paleface, if he follows, will starve, for he cannot hunt—he knows not how to secure the hare and the fox, and roots are poison to him. Let the Pawnee take his captives and go away."

"Is that your answer?" asked the chief.

"It is!" was the general reply, and the Morning Dawn gathered his buffalo robe around him.

"I must take that answer back," he said; "the palefaces will expect me before sunset."

"Will the Morning Dawn return again?" asked the Wolf.

THE Pawnee chief smiled sadly as he replied to the Wolf's question.

"If the sun rises and sets three times, and he is not back, let the Pawnees choose another chief, for they will see him no more."

A wailing cry ran round the group, and the Wolf's squaw held out her arms beseechingly— she was a woman, and was allowed thus to express her emotion.

"I promised the big paleface that I would go back to him," continued the Morning Dawn. "Will my people have me break my word?"

There was no reply to this. The honour of their chief was dear to him they knew, and no man dared hint at anything which would destroy it.

At this juncture a happy thought dawned upon Snip, who had been listening to the conversation with the keenest interest. Raising his voice, he called out—"I say, look here one moment. You need not go back to Jack Savage."

The Morning Dawn turned an inquiring gaze upon him.

"Send me," continued Snip. "I can tell them to cry quits. They will lose you, but they will get me."

"Will that be keeping the Pawnee's word?" demanded Morning Dawn.

"Not to the strict letter, perhaps," returned Snip, "but they won't think bad of you when they see me. I am a very valuable man among them, I can tell you."

The Pawnee chief smiled. "I know," he said, "your value among the palefaces. You were my captive—I am theirs. I go back to my bondage, and I leave you to my people. Fare-well!"

"Oh! but do listen to reason," cried Snip, in an agony. "Suppose you don't turn up, what will be the end of me? These savage fellows are sure to take it out of me; be reasonable, and tell me what I ever did to you."

"The little paleface came upon the war trail," said the Morning Dawn; "if he was afraid to die he should have stayed at home."

"Don't I wish I had," groaned Snip; "but who is there living in Wapping that would suspect there were such a set of beasts as you Pawnee chaps? You are not men—you are monsters."

"My paleface brother," said the Morning Dawn, sternly, "will do well if he talks better. The Pawnee does not like hard words."

"Oh, go it!" groaned Snip; "but there. I might as well talk to stones."

Utterly cowed and beaten, the little man lay flat upon the earth and said no more.

Then the Pawnee chief took a dignified but simple leave of his people, and went back to his captivity. But before leaving he bade them quit their present hiding-place.

"The eyes of the palefaces are good," he said, "and if they find my people here many warriors will fall. Let them go from hence and keep with the sun for three days. If I am free I will come to them. If not I shall be no more."

Then he walked out from his people with a slow, measured step, and was lost to sight in the maze of the surrounding forest.

For a long time after he had disappeared the warriors stood still, with their eyes upon the ground. The Wolf was the first to break the silence.

"The light of day will soon be gone," he said. "Shall we move now or wait for another sun?"

A brief debate arose, and it was settled to remove at once.

But for their prisoners they would have left the ground in a few minutes, but a number of captives, however desirable, are necessarily a source of more or less embarrassment, and it was half an hour before all was ready.

Snip was the only one who was bound, and by urgent and earnest entreaty he succeeded in getting his hands loosed.

"My people took your chief's word," he said. "You take mine."

This the Pawnees flatly refused to do, but they loosed his cords, and quietly informed him that if he attempted flight a tomahawk would be immediately despatched after him.

Snip felt the edge of a tomahawk held towards him, and went so far as to say that he thought he should go quietly, and would give them as little trouble as possible.

"A man had better make up his mind for the worst," he said, "especially when there is no help for it."

Strict silence was then enjoined, and the Pawnee camp moved forward, with scouts before and behind and scouts on either side.

They did not think that Jack Savage or his men were near, but they were a people accustomed to war and bloodshed, and it was not their wont to neglect any needful precaution.

Snip was very angry at the refusal to take his word. The little man was a bit of a fool, but he had an inkling of what was due to the dignity of man, and he was disgusted with the Pawnee's want of faith.

If they had taken his word he would have kept it. As they had refused it he resolved to flee.

"Half a chance," he thought, "and I am off. A tomahawk may stop me, but anything is better than being toasted alive."

He tried to imitate the phlegmatic indifference of the Indians, succeeding tolerably well, and the amount of dignity he summoned up in his emergency was perfectly marvellous.

"I'll let 'em know how the palefaces can suffer," he muttered, more than once. "These Injuns don't think any small beer of themselves, and they shan't think any small beer of me. I'll do credit to 'Rule, Britannia.' Now, then, what do you think of that?"

The Pawnees, in reality, thought very little

about him; they saw the majestic strides he took, but their minds were busy with the foe behind, and they had little time to devote to Snip.

The afternoon was soon gone, and after a short twilight—so short that an Englishman would have thought there was none—the night came on.

As the darkness fell, swiftly and silently, the hooting of an owl was heard. This caused a momentary commotion among the Pawnees, but they rallied quickly, and closed in, waiting to learn the cause.

The scouts came speedily in, and the word was passed that the palefaces were approaching rapidly.

One of the rear scouts had seen them, and he told a very strange story.

"They are coming along," he said, "close on our trail, led by the Morning Dawn."

So startling a piece of news—proving their chief a traitor—roused even the Indians from their quiescent state, and a universal "Ugh!" was heard.

"Blackfoot must be mistaken," said the Wolf.

Blackfoot, the scout, repeated his story quietly, and declared that the palefaces were coming on apace, guided by the chief of the Pawnees.

"He walks beside the big paleface," said the scout. "They are coming on together."

Marvel upon marvels? What strange power had changed their chief? Had he sold the blood of his people? If so the tribe was doomed.

Amazement and despair took possession of all, and in the darkness they moved quickly to and fro muttering to each other their comments and proposing plans for their deliverance.

Snip saw his opportunity and seized it.

With an ease and alertness which would have done credit to an Indian, he slipped through his foes and made for the spot where he considered he should find his friends.

One alone saw him—the Wolf.

He hurled his tomahawk at Snip, but the darkness was profound, and his aim not sure.

The tomahawk whizzed by Snip's head, just grazing his ear, and buried itself in the bark of a tree.

"Whew!" gasped Snip, "that was close enough."

Then he gathered himself together and ran on, his eyes having grown sufficiently accustomed to the darkness to guide him on his way.

The Indians were too busy to follow him, but the air itself was full of pursuers to him, and he ran like a hunted hare.

It was a flight from death, and when men run from the Great Destroyer they generally run well.

Through the wood he went, past long lines of giant trees, through dense masses of brushwood, under vast overhanging boughs, until the sweat poured down his face like rain.

Sometimes he fell, but he was up again like a ball, and so he ran on until nature gave way and he fell exhausted.

"I'm done now," he groaned, but no hand was laid upon him.

He lay and listened. The night was still and the forest was impressive in its silence—a silence broken only by the buzzing of the insects and the creaking of the boughs—and the darkness was intense, but not for long.

Soon there came something like a star dancing towards him. It alighted on the trunk of a tree, which it illuminated for a yard or more around. Then came another and another—then a great number.

"I'm either dreaming or in fairyland!" thought Snip.

But he was neither dreaming nor in fairyland—he was only in a favourite haunt of the fire-fly.

CHAPTER XXXI.

SETTING AN INDIAN TO CATCH AN INDIAN.

WHEN the Morning Dawn left his people he went straight back to the camp of Jack Savage and his men. Two things compelled him to do this. First, his innate sense of honour—a feeling not entirely strange to men of savage life, and often very strong among the chiefs of wandering people—and, secondly, a marvellous power Jack had obtained over him.

We have seen the influence of our hero among his own men, but the amount of power he held over the savage leader has yet to be seen.

All men of mark have their influence, and he who meets with one more than his match invariably submits and ever afterwards looks up to his superior.

So it was with the Morning Dawn. He had encountered Jack and experienced defeat; he at once acknowledged Jack's superiority, but it did not end there.

Our hero soon perceived that the savage looked up to him with more than ordinary admiration, and remarked that he showed a docility totally foreign to the Indian nature. He was, in fact, more than a captive—he was a voluntary slave.

Nothing pleased him more than an opportunity to render Jack a service, no matter how trifling. He would fetch his gun, fasten his belt, and help him to adjust his dress with all the eagerness of an attached and faithful servant.

When he went away on the mission to his people he went sorrowfully and slowly, when he returned he came again to the camp with eagerness and joy.

Jack was, in fact, his hero and his idol.

Our hero had no thought of turning this idolatry to account—it simply amused him, but Will Larkin saw that it might be made of use if his leader would only consent.

"The Indian would do anything for you, Jack," he said; "why not make use of him?"

"How?" ask Jack.

"Put him on the trail of his people," replied Will. "Caderouse is dead, and although Tom does his best he is not keen enough for those mocassined imps."

Jack was struck with the idea, but he did not think it would work.

"There's a limit to all things," he said, "and I am afraid he would not do that."

"Try it," said Will.

The Indian was close handy, leaning against a tree, with his eyes fixed upon Jack, eager to obey his slightest sign.

Jack, with a good-humoured smile, went up to the Morning Dawn, and put the case without any beating about the bush.

"We are on the trail of your people," he said, "and it is difficult to follow. White eyes are not keen enough. Will you help us?"

The Indian bowed low, his face wore an inquiring look, and Jack went on—

"Will you lead us on their trail?"

"If my white brother wishes it I will do so," replied the Morning Dawn; "if he bids me climb the highest tree and throw myself down I will do it. I will obey my big white brother in all things."

"If your people give up their captives they may go," said Jack, "if not there will be blood-shed."

"If my people are wise they will bow to my white brother," said the Indian, and at once he made preparations for following the trail.

In a few minutes the whole camp was moving, with the Indian at their head, leading the pursuers to the hiding-place of his people.

A marvellous sight, and when the men saw it they vowed a yet stronger allegiance to their youthful giant leader, who held such a strange power over them all.

But the Pawnees were on the alert, as our readers are aware. They knew the whites were approaching, and when a savage flies he flies quickly.

Capture would have been out of the question but for the captives, who rather hampered their movements, but their flight was nevertheless swift, and when the night came on they still kept moving.

They originally intended to halt after dark, but the news brought by their scouts changed their tactics, and they resolved to keep on.

Before moving on they elected the Wolf for their chief—any community without a head is no community at all—and then, with hearts embittered against the Morning Dawn, they resumed their march.

No effort was made to conceal their trail—that they knew was useless—their numbers were too great, and the eyes of the Morning Dawn too keen, for them to escape without leaving information of their whereabouts.

So they kept on throughout the night, which was so much time gained by them, for it was impossible even for their recreant chief to follow a trail when darkness was upon the earth.

In the morning they halted, and a rude breakfast was partaken of.

The captive women and children were worn and weary, but the Indians, accustomed to rough life, thought little of the extra fatigue.

Some of the women begged that they and their children might be killed at once—their present and prospective fate overawed them, and they wished to die.

But the Pawnees turned a deaf ear to their appeals, and bade them be quiet and prepare to resume their march.

While they were doing this, with much pitiful wailing, an idea entered the head of the Wolf which promised to give them a respite.

Calling the chiefs of the Pawnees together, he held a short council with them—a council which gave most of them, apparently, much satisfaction.

When the council was over the Wolf and about a dozen others lagged behind, the rest moved forward slowly, which gave rest and ease to the captive women and children. At night they came to the margin of the forest, beyond which lay a small prairie, and then a range of hills.

Here they rested for an hour, and then started across the plain, indifferent to the light of a full moon, which cast its rays upon their path.

Before the dawn they reached the hills, and upon the summit of the nearest they halted. The spot was well chosen—three sides of the hill sloped precipitately down, affording no foot-hold to man, the fourth was rugged and uneven, and difficult to traverse, therefore, if defended with a spark of spirit, the position was simply impregnable.

Glad of a place of rest, the captives lay down to sleep, but the Indians kept an earnest watch throughout the darkness, until the first golden pencil of light swept athwart the sky.

Their eyes were fixed eagerly upon the plain, in the direction they had traversed during the night.

As the increasing light began to reveal the larger objects, their watch became keener, and soon an involuntary cry burst from the lips of the foremost brave.

He pointed to the plain, and his brethren gathered eagerly around him. A body of men were approaching.

At first it was difficult to tell what people they were, but soon the light revealed their nation and character. They were Indians—Pawnees.

They came on in a close, compact body, bearing a burden in their midst which looked like a log of wood in the distance, but as they came up the hill the watchers could see that it was a human being bound hand and foot.

Then another cry burst from the watchers, not a loud cry, but a pent-up moan from angry and agonised hearts, while some clasped their hands and others bowed their heads in anguish.

"The Wolf is a great chief," said one.

"He is worthy to be a Pawnee leader," said another.

"His hand is as swift and as sure as the lightning," added a third; "his feet move with the wind, and he walks as silently as the clouds cross the sky."

The march up hill with their burden was heavy, and the Pawnees came on but slowly.

At their head walked the Wolf, with the air of a victor, doing no part of the labour, as became a chief, but walking with the conscious look of one to whom they were indebted for success.

The Pawnees in the camp made great preparations to receive the Wolf and his assistants.

The captives were awakened and arranged in a half-circle, while the Pawnees themselves completed it, standing several deep, and leaving a small opening for the entrance of their companions with the captured man.

The Wolf came first, stalking into the midst of the circle with a step which would have done justice to a conqueror of the world.

"My brothers," he said, "it is good—our work is done."

"The Wolf is a great chief—the greatest of all the Pawnee chiefs!" cried several of the tribe, and the Wolf drew himself up another inch, looking like Cæsar and Pompey combined.

All this is natural to your true Indian—without braggadocio he is nothing, and unless he had the prospect before him of being allowed to sing

◁ GIANT JACK: ▷

A Story of the Red Mountains.

"HERE'S A NARROW ESCAPE!" EXCLAIMED SNIP. "ANOTHER FOOT AND I SHOULD HAVE BEEN A DEAD MAN!"

day and night about his victories he would not fight.

There is great satisfaction to an Indian in being allowed to howl about every petty triumph of his life—he enjoys it very much.

But this was no light triumph for the Wolf.

He had, in fact, performed a very daring deed, for in the night he had stolen into the midst of the white men's camp and brought away a captive, assisted by those who had gone with him.

This captive they had bound, gagged, and carried from the camp, without disturbing one of the sleepers or giving a hint to any of the sentinels that an intruder was near.

It was, indeed, a great feat, and the Wolf might very justly be proud of it, although, as we have hinted, he might have had a little less braggadocio in his walk and look.

"I came swiftly," he said, "for my feet are light when they bear good news. The feet of my brothers are light, too, but they carry a traitor."

The other Indians came toiling up the hill, bearing the captive man upon their shoulders, and the face of every one of them wore a proud look—the reflex of the countenance of the Wolf.

The form of the captive was quite still—not a muscle moved, and naught save the eyes gave any signs of life. These glanced restlessly to and fro, but there was no apprehension in their gleam.

Slowly the captive was lowered to the ground, and then the circle closed in, firm and compact, leaving no chance of escape.

Every head was bowed, and every eye was dim with sorrow, but the sorrow was mingled rage, and none wore a pitying look.

"When the god of day was at rest we walked into the paleface camp," said the Wolf. "The Indian foot is as the mists which rise in the valleys and go silently up and down the hills. He is as the shadow of a cloud upon the earth—he can come and go as he will, and the paleface sleeps on."

"The Wolf is a great chief," chorussed his hearers.

"The Wolf said he would do it," continued the Wolf, "and he has kept his word. Do I lie? See—here is the traitor. Unloose his bonds."

The thongs around the captive man were cut, and with an unrestrained air he arose and revealed to the Pawnees the form of their recreant chief—the Morning Dawn.

"Behold the traitor to the Pawnee people!" said the Wolf.

"Who calls me a traitor?" asked the Morning Dawn.

"Let Blackfoot speak," said the Wolf.

And Blackfoot—the scout who had brought the intelligence of his chief being on the trail—stood forward and repeated his story.

It was heard amidst the most intense silence, and when it was all over the Wolf spoke again.

"Does Blackfoot lie?" he asked. "If so let the Morning Dawn say so. And let him tell also why he slept in peace, unbound, in the midst of the paleface camp."

"Blackfoot does not lie," said the Morning Dawn, calmly. "And I am no traitor to my people."

"The Morning Dawn's words are like trees in a mist," said the Wolf. "We hear but we cannot understand."

"Here I am a leader of my own people and would fight and die for them," replied the Morning Dawn, "but in the paleface camp I am the slave of its big chief. I am not myself. I am in his power. He bids me do a thing and I do it. I cannot say nay or turn aside. But here I am free and can do as I will."

"Again the Morning Dawn speaks and we do not understand," said the Wolf.

"I do not understand either," returned the Morning Dawn. "I can only say that it is so. not why it is so. But it is true, and I do not lie. The paleface is a man of great power, and when he is near I am his slave."

"You led him on to the trail," said the Wolf.

"He bade me do so and I obeyed," returned the Morning Dawn.

"He left you free."

"He bade me keep within the camp, and I remained."

"His arms were near and you had no weapon."

"He bade me touch them not and my hands were still," replied the Morning Dawn.

"Is this our mighty chief?" said the Wolf, appealing to the Pawnee people; "is this the Morning Dawn, the great chief we have fought with and bled for? Is this the mighty hunter and the great scout, who could follow the trail of a cloud and track the breath of the morning? Would he have bowed down and bid the paleface put a foot upon his neck? Would he have slept in the hated enemy's camp while the vultures waited to feed upon his people? Answer me—my brave Pawnees. Is this the Morning Dawn?"

"The Morning Dawn is dead," they said.

"Aye, he is dead!" pursued the Wolf, "and the spirit of some traitor took possession of his body. The palefaces killed him, and filled his heart with wickedness towards the Pawnee people."

"But I love the Pawnee people," said the Morning Dawn. "Away from them my heart was bad, but now it is good again, and I love my people."

"The Morning Dawn sings two songs," sneered the Wolf; "one he sings in the paleface camp——"

"It is not so."

"It is—and the other he sings here. But I do not accuse him—he speaks for himself."

"He speaks the truth," said the Morning Dawn.

"He lies!"

"The Wolf lies!"

"The Wolf is your friend—he cannot lie."

"He was my friend, but he is now my enemy. If he doubts me let him go to the paleface camp and learn the power of its giant chief."

The Wolf laughed scornfully.

"I love not the paleface," he said, "and I am no traitor to the Pawnee people."

"The Wolf is traitor to his chief."

"Who is my chief?"

"I, the Morning Dawn."

"It is a lie! I am your chief, chosen by the Pawnee people to judge a traitor. The palefaces—bah! Are they not traitors? What is their faith? Have I not seen a number of them assail one of their own race? Have I not seen them even apply fire to a helpless prisoner? They are fiends in human shape. The Wolf is no paleface. He is a great warrior, and the head of the Pawnee tribe."

"Is that the voice of my people?" demanded the Morning Dawn.

"It is!" they said, and then there was a moment's silence, which was broken by the Morning Dawn, who, in a sorrowful tone, thus addressed them—

"Be it so, my people. Your hearts are turned from your chief, and he cannot do better than die. I go to the happy hunting-grounds of my fathers, where ye will come anon and learn the truth. If I have lied ye will not find me there, but if ye meet me ye will know that I was no traitor in my heart to those I loved. My blood be upon the head which strikes me down. I am ready."

There was a hush upon the camp—the dead silence which comes when doubt and pity touch the hearts of great multitudes. Not a hand stirred.

"If I speak the truth I am still your chief," said the Morning Dawn. "If I have lied I have earned my death. Who strikes the blow?"

Another silence, and no hand was raised to strike. There was a radiance upon his face, the radiance of truth, which none of them could face.

But the Wolf had tasted power.

For a few hours he had been chief of the tribe. He had performed a daring feat, and brought one whom he deemed a traitor out of the very midst of his enemies, to have him punished before his people, and now that very act was bidding fair to dethrone him.

"The Morning Dawn talks well," he said, "and touches the hearts of the Pawnee people. But what is talk? It is but as the idle wind, it is not proof. The Morning Dawn led the palefaces upon the trail of his people."

"Ugh!" ejaculated several of the Indians, and their faces darkened ominously.

"The greater the chief the greater the traitor. Do I speak well?" urged the Wolf; "or have the Pawnee people turned traitors to themselves? Have they adders' ears when the truth is spoken, and only listen to a lie!"

"The Wolf wishes to be chief of the Pawnees," said the Morning Dawn, quietly; "he forgets the friend he loved."

"Words are nothing," said the Wolf. "If I lie kill me—if the Morning Dawn has lied he must die!"

"He shall die!" said several, and there was a stir among the Indians.

"If there is one who loves the Pawnee tribe more than the rest let him kill the Morning Dawn!" cried the Wolf, and immediately a dozen arms were raised to slay the chief they had once so truly loved.

*   *   *   *   *

We left Snip among the fire-flies, and, as a matter of duty, we now return to him.

The strange nocturnal insects mustered in great numbers around our friend, illuminating the air in fairy fashion, and making the whole scene at once novel and astounding.

"I may be awake," thought Snip, returning to his favourite idea of his present life being a dream, "but I don't believe it. Flies don't go about in civilised places with little lanterns hanging to their tails. It's all bosh, for you see nothing of the sort outside a pantomime. No—I'm fast asleep and dreaming."

Resolved to insist upon this idea, Snip stretched himself at full length, and endeavoured to forget all around him. Fatigue helped the little man, and in a short time he was sound asleep.

He lay quiet until the day was far advanced, and when he awoke the rays of the sun, such as could penetrate the dense foliage, came down almost perpendicularly, thus showing that that luminary was high in the heavens.

CHAPTER XXXII.

SNIP FINDS THE CAMP OF HIS FRIENDS JUST IN TIME TO BE TOO LATE.

SNIP was bushman enough to see that the sun was at his meridian, and understanding it, with a cry of surprise he sprang to his feet.

"I've overslept myself," he said, "and Captain Jack and the others have gone on without me. No, that's not right—let me think. Haven't I been a prisoner among them greasy savages? Yes, I have. And didn't I bolt for it, and make clear away? To be sure I did. I see it all now. And the little flies with lanterns hanging to their tails—all true, too, I suppose, and if it isn't it's all the same. What's the use of bothering about the past? Let me think of the present. Where's Captain Jack? I must find him."

Easy to say, but very difficult to perform. Daytime gave Snip courage, and he walked boldly forward, looking for some signs of his comrades.

Fortune favoured him, and he walked straight to the spot where Jack Savage and his men had camped during the previous night.

But they were gone. Snip found plenty of indications of their presence, even to the extent of a fire which had been lighted at early dawn to cook some food, and their trail was clear—clear enough even for the little tailor, who was about as useful to track anyone as a giraffe would be under similar circumstances.

"If I keep on," he thought, "I must overtake them—that is, if nothing stops me by the way."

Unpleasant thought.

At such a time, and in such a place, impediments were apt to arise in the form of a few bloodthirsty Indians, or a bear, and as Snip followed in the footsteps of his friends he trembled.

"A man's life is not worth much in these parts," he thought. "They can kill you and stow you away, and if anybody does find you they don't care two buttons about you. I never heard of such an outlandish place. Hallo! murder! help! what's that?"

Only the falling of a rotten twig, although sufficient to alarm the lone man, and to bring him up sharp upon the road. But he was quickly reassured, and moved on again, with the swinging trot of a man who is upon a dangerous track.

His friends had several hours' start, and he was far behind, but lopped boughs and downtrodden bushes cheered him on, and by noon he reached the outskirts of the wood.

Beyond was a broad plain, fringed with a long line of hills. The plain was clear, and nothing, as far as he could see, was moving on the hills.

Suddenly a thought flashed upon him—a terrible, bewildering thought, and he sat down upon the ground and groaned aloud.

"I've made a mistake," he moaned. "This is the way we came, and I've doubled back upon the old trail!"

Utter prostration, engendered by fear and want of food, overcame him, and he lay upon the ground with his eyes fixed upon the hills.

Ah! what is this he sees? A small white puff of smoke. Then another—then a number of them.

What is this he hears? The report of rifles rolling over the prairie, followed by the shouts of men—outbursts of triumph and pain from the victorious and the dying.

"Hooray!" cried Snip. "I'm on the right road. Jack's among the redskins, and it's a precious pickle they're in, I'll bet. Keep the game alive—I'm coming. But stay, let me think."

Snip paused.

"Suppose," he soliloquised, "the redskins are too much for them, then I shall only be rushing into the jaws of death. But nonsense! who can beat glorious Jack? Who can beat the trapper-king? Nobody. He is a match for the lot, and I'll go and share his glory. 'Rule Britannia! Britannia rules the waves! Britons never—never—never shall be slaves!'"

Finishing the popular song with a flourish, Snip set out upon his march across the plain.

The fighting was still going on.

The little white puffs of smoke increased each moment in number, and the clear air bore towards him the reports of the rifles and the clash of arms.

But above all this he could hear the terrified shriek of the Indian as he fought for his life and liberty, and the loud shout of the paleface as he did great havoc among his foes.

"I'm sorry I'm not there," said Snip, aloud, "for I am wanted just now."

He walked on briskly, never moving his eyes from whence came the sounds of warfare, but beyond the smoke he could at present see nothing.

Soon the view became clearer, and he could mark that something was moving ahead.

As the objects became more distinct he saw the palefaces and the Indians struggling hand to hand, the tomahawks gleaming in the air, and the deadly knives flashing in the sunlight. He could see the women captives trembling on the edge of the fray, covering their eyes with their hands as the slaughtered victims fell to the earth, and the sight filled his heart with awe.

"The redskins fall fast," he muttered, "but what a lot there is of them."

Faster and more furious grew the fight. The redskins seemed to swarm, but the arms of their adversaries were powerful, and they fell like grass before the scythe of the mower.

Dreadful work.

Who so remorseless and cruel as man when he is pitted against man? Who thinks less than man in the midst of a bloody, angry fight?

Suddenly a change came o'er the scene, and the redskins, as if actuated by one impulse, turned and fled.

They came tearing down the hill straight towards the hapless Snip, who saw his danger, and pulled up sharp in the middle of the plain.

Where could he go? What could he do? Where hide his terrified head?

There was nothing bigger than a mole-hill upon the plain, and this offered very little shelter to a man, although he was but five feet high.

"If ever there was a man born to hard luck," gasped Snip, "I'm that creetur. Confound 'em! Why could they not run t'other way?"

They either could not or would not, and a body of howling, furious savages came straight down upon the little man.

Close behind them came the whites, rifle in hand, firing and loading as they came.

"I'm done for now," thought Snip; "I've nothing to defend myself with, so I had better lay down and take my death-blow quietly."

Snip, therefore, threw himself upon the ground, and, coiling up like a hedgehog, awaited his fate. But now comes a strange part of our narrative.

The Indians, usually so clear of vision, did not perceive the little man even when standing erect—their eyes were probably blinded with fear, and the first of the flying men fell over him.

The savage, in falling, tramped heavily upon Snip, and hurt him very much. Furious and terrified, Snip laid hold of his legs, and immediately a second savage fell over the first.

In ten seconds twenty men, without knowing the cause, were in a heap; in five seconds more their white pursuers were upon them.

Snip heard the shouts and knew the voices—foremost and loudest was that of our friend, Long Tom.

"Settle the lot!" he bawled; "don't leave one alive! No quarter! Fire in among them, lads, then finish the work. Death to the redskins!"

The shrieks and struggles of the savages were awful, and their kicks terrific. Snip tried to shout for help, and thus give his friends notice of his whereabouts, but every particle of breath was knocked out of his body, and he could only gasp and groan.

"Death to the redskins!" shouted the white men, and the savages were one by one drawn off the body of the little man and slaughtered.

At last they came to him.

Long Tom laid hold of his leg, crying out—"Hallo! here's a curisome critter. Stand by, lads, and let us see what it is."

Then he dragged Snip up and turned his face towards him.

"Snip!" he cried.

"Yes—it's me," gasped Snip, "and glad I am to be here."

"Why didn't you show afore?" asked Tom; "and why did you run away with them?"

"I didn't run away with them."

"Did they carry you?"

"No. I ran away from them last night, and a pretty time I have had of it, I can tell you. I've been in a place where—but there, it's no use talking, you won't believe me."

"Anyhow, I'm glad to see you," said Long Tom. "It's good to see any friend safe out of the clutches of them brutes. But we've made mincemeat of 'em."

"Killed the lot?" asked Snip.

"All except them cutting across the plain. A few are sure to get clear away, but not many, and up on the hill they lie like spring blossoms arter a heavy shower."

"You have had some stiff fighting I should think, Tom?"

"I guess we have," said Tom. "Lor! we

came upon 'em on the sly, and a score or two were dead afore they knowed we were there. You should have heard the women shriek with joy when they saw us, and you should have heard the savages yell as we cut 'em down."

"I heard something of it, Tom."

"But nothing to what happened up the hill. You should have seen our captain, like a giant as he is, taking them up in his hands and casting 'em down like rats. Ah! it was a sight, I can tell you."

"I wish I had been there, Tom."

"You lost something by not being there, for you see we meant and mean to extarminate the varmints. They've no feeling, and can't expect much from us. There's not a man left alive in Short's Gully, and we didn't mean to leave one of them as murdered 'em breathing on the earth."

"It was awful slaughter, Tom."

"Awful slaughter? Well, I suppose it was for them as isn't used to it. I don't know that it is right, and I don't know that it is wrong. I've been among fighting men all my life, and I'm not squeamish—but there is some as would say that it was wrong to kill them Injuns."

"It may be so, Tom."

"So it may, but I don't know nothing about it, Snip. I obeyed orders, and it were sharp work. Will Larkin came out strong for a young 'un, too. He aint so tall nor yet so strong as our captain, but he lost no time in setting about his work, and he made that cutlass of his fly about like a flash of lightning. Many a redskin's head felt it once, and then the redskin forgot everything in this world. He's a well-made and good-plucked youngster, and I like him more than a little."

"So you ought, Tom," said a voice behind him, "for I respect you, old man, and respect from the young secures love from the old."

It was Will Larkin, and as he finished he held out his hand, which Tom grasped heartily.

"If you'd fallen under a redskin, Will," he said, "I must ha' died too."

"But we must not, either of us, think of dying," said Will. "The fighting is all over and the redskin is settled. All those who have not fled have turned up their toes, and there are more toes turned up than are flying through yonder wood. Hallo, Snip! you back again? I never saw such a man for disappearing and turning up again."

"And I never read of such things as I have undergone," returned Snip; "what I've done since you saw me last would fill a book, and a big one. But I'm always here when wanted. When them savages came tearing down the hill I stopped at least a dozen of 'em, and handed the wretches over to the sword of justice."

"Indeed!" said Will, with a sceptical look.

"It's a fact," corroborated Tom; "he stopped more than a dozen, and there they lie. The bravest among us could not have done it better, and he did it unarmed, too."

"Upon my word," exclaimed Will, "I fear that I have hitherto done you a great injustice. An unarmed man stopping a dozen infuriated savages! It was a bold, brave deed, and one the captain shall hear of."

"I don't think you need tell him," said Snip, modestly; "it's hardly worth while. Lor', if you start talking of my brave deeds to him you might do nothing else. What I have gone through would fill a library. My family have always been a suffering family, but none were ever like me."

"But why should you be overlooked?" urged Will.

"Snip's not the man to talk of his doings," said Tom, his eyes twinkling with fun. "Suffice it to say that he stopped a dozen—or nearly a score—savages, and I saw him do it. If any man says I tell a lie I'll make him eat his words."

Will was puzzled. There was something in the story he did not understand, but as neither Snip nor Tom offered an explanation he sought none.

"Here comes our great captain," said Tom, and as he spoke Jack Savage advanced with an Indian by his side, and that Indian was the Morning Dawn.

The Indian walked calmly in the company of Jack, casting every now and then looks of admiration and wonder at our hero's face.

Jack came up and shook hands with Tom and Will, saying—

"We were only just in time it seems. The tomahawk was raised to cut down the Morning Dawn, but our sudden and unexpected arrival saved him. Who's this? Snip back again! We feared you were dead."

"I've had a narrow squeak for it," said Snip, with a modest look; "but perseverance and pluck will carry a man through anything."

"You have had some curious adventures, I suppose?"

"There was never anything like it before," said Snip, "and never can be again."

"Almost too painful to relate, I may venture to suppose?"

"Not a bit of it, respected captain," said Snip; "if you are ready to listen I am ready to tell."

"Not just now," observed Jack—"but when the men have had their breakfast they will be glad to hear you, without a doubt. Now leave me with the Pawnee for a moment. We have a few words to say to each other."

Will, Tom, and Snip moved away, and Jack and the Morning Dawn were left together.

"So you are resolved to leave me?" said the former.

"I love my big white brother," replied the Morning Dawn; "but I must, if he will allow, go away. My heart is dead—I must live henceforth alone."

"You think so now?"

"I am sure it will be so until I die," said the Indian, sadly. "My people are dead; they lie like the leaves of autumn on the plain, for my paleface brother and his men are strong. The Pawnee cannot look into their faces—they are so bright."

"If kindness could have saved my captive people," said Jack, "I would not have struck a blow."

"The Pawnee is used to the war-trail," rejoined the Morning Dawn. "Peace was strange to them, and they knew it not when it came. My big brother would have been merciful, but they would not hear him."

"They did cruel work, and their cruel work brought me here."

"It did not seem cruel to me then," said the Morning Dawn, sadly, "but I see it now. The Indian is born in blood, lives in blood, and loves it. Before the paleface came he fought with his brethren, and the prairie and the forest were dyed with blood. Where the Indian fell thickest there the poppy grew, with its blood-red leaves, warning them of the time to come; but they would not heed, and then the palefaces entered our land, and the lightning-tube smote them to the earth."

"There is no reason why it should be so," said Jack; "the land is wide enough for us all."

"Oil will not mix with water," said the Morning Dawn, "and the paleface and redskin will never live together. No—I love you, my big brother, well; but I cannot live with you, for your hands are red with the blood of my people. If you will not let me go, kill me now."

"Why should I kill you?" returned Jack. "My object is gained. I have saved the captive women and children. No, you are free. Go!—gather together the remnant of your people and live in peace."

"Should I be happy with my own people?" said the Morning Dawn; "would they love their chief? No—they would think of this morning, and they would curse their chief, who led the palefaces to their wigwams."

"I am sorry I influenced you to do it," said Jack.

"It is better so," returned the Morning Dawn; 'better that the Pawnee should die than that the white women and children should be wronged. We were cruel to them—I know it now—and our crime brought punishment upon us."

"If you must go," said Jack, after a short pause, "at least take a rifle with you."

"No," said the Morning Dawn; "my hand is cunning, and I can catch all I need to eat. What would a rifle avail me? I should soon use the fire-powder you give me, and to get more I must come back again among men—that I will never do. I go away to live and die alone."

"But men will cross your path."

"Away there," replied the Indian, pointing south, "many days' journey from here, is a hunting-ground where man never goes. There I can live, as I have said—there I will hunt the buffalo, make a wigwam of his skin, and trap the fox and wolf with his sinews."

"Take a day or two to think it over before you go."

"No—my big brother is kind, but I cannot remain here. The air is full of Pawnee blood; the sun is red, and the ground is wet with the life of my people. No—if my big brother says nothing I will go."

"I like you," said Jack, "but I cannot urge you to stay. You will have some food before you go?"

"When the heart is full," said the Morning Dawn, "we do not need food. I cannot eat. I only wish to go."

"Then farewell!" returned Jack, extending his hand, "and all good go with you."

The Indian took it between his two palms, which looked small and woman-like beside the big ones of Jack, and yet the Morning Dawn was a strong man.

"If my big brother could come with me alone I should be glad," said the Indian; "but it cannot be so. While the Morning Dawn can see the sun, or think of the past, he will remember his big palefaced brother; when he forgets him the Morning Dawn will die."

Then he pressed the big hand again, and, turning on his heel, left Jack behind him for ever.

He went straight away, and Jack stood watching him until his figure was a mere speck in the distance.

"A savage man," he said aloud, "and the offspring of a savage people, but with a deal of good in him, as there is in most people, I guess."

"You are not far wrong there," replied the voice of Will Larkin. "I have seen some preciously bad men in my time, but I never found a man without some good in him."

"Most men have some redeeming quality."

"Even Rough Sawny had. You remember Rough Sawny?"

"Not just now, Will."

"He murdered a settler and his family near Moreton—murdered them all in their beds!"

"I remember now—the scoundrel!—he was hung."

"Yes—but even he had a good point, Jack. I went to look at him in his cell. Curiosity took me there, as it did other people, for, if you remember, this wretch murdered a whole family for the sake of a copper kettle."

"I believe so."

"Well, I went to see him," continued Will, "and there he was in irons, looking as much like a devil as a man can look, I should think. He scowled at us, but he said nothing until I was going away, and then he shouted out—

"'I say, Mister.'

"Not knowing that he was addressing me, I kept moving until he shouted again.

"'I say, Mister—you with the brass buttons—come here.'

"I wore brass buttons on my coat then, and seeing that nobody else had them, I concluded that he must mean me, so I went up and spoke to him.

"'Do you want me?' I asked.

"'Yes, I do,' he said. 'You've got a kind-looking face of your own, and I think you will do a dying man a favour. I am more than dying—I'm as good as dead—so don't refuse.'

"'If I can do you any good I will,' I said.

"'But you can't do me any good,' he replied, 'no more could any man. It's not good to me that I want done—but you know my hut?'

"'I can't say I do,' I said.

"'It's two miles west from the settlement,' he said; 'anybody will tell you where—it's only a mud hut. Well, go there and loose a dog as you will find. Take care on him, mister, and give him a bit of grub now and then. He aint great shakes in the point of breed, but he's faithful, and he won't give you much trouble. Will you do that for a dying man?'

"I promised I would, and left him. The next morning he was hung, and his last words were a hope that the chap with the brass buttons would take care of his dog. There was his good point, bad as he was."

"True," said Jack. "Did you fetch the dog?"

"Yes, but the dog had his good point, too. He found out where his master was, and even found his grave. There he stretched himself out, and, refusing all food, starved himself to death."

"Faithful creature!"

"True as steel. But that's not the only instance of such a spirit; you will find it all over the world—in men, women, and even children—and the lesson we should learn from it is that, in spite of the evil and sin around us, the world is better than we are apt to think it."

"I think so, Will."

"Now we will leave our moralising, for breakfast appears to be ready. Won't you have some?"

"Not now, Will. You go on—I will come to you anon."

So Will went to his morning meal, and Jack, as he had often done of late, walked moodily to and fro—alone.

*   *   *   *   *   *

The breakfast party was a noisy one. Men who spend their lives in the open air are proverbially light-hearted; they are accustomed to live for the moment, and to take the sweets and bitters of life as they come and go.

The fight in the morning had not been without loss to the white men.

Seven had fallen to rise no more, and about a score were more or less wounded. But the dead were buried, the wounded were looked to with rough surgical skill, and there was an end to the matter.

Of course the acquisition of the women to the camp made a great difference. They were widows, and full of sorrow; but woman at the worst has generally a brightening influence, and the men were glad of their company.

They treated them well.

This was enforced by the commands of our hero, who threatened death to any man who dared insult one of the poor creatures under his charge, and they knew Captain Jack was a man to keep his word.

There were also the children—bright little things, for the most part too young to comprehend the loss they had undergone, and these ran about among the men, talking and laughing like little fairies—their bright, pretty faces quite in unison with the morning sun.

Jack stood watching the scene with a variety of emotions contending within him, until Will had completed his breakfast and rejoined him.

"You are sad?" said Will.

"Nothing unusual for me," replied Jack, "for I am troubled, Will."

"Troubled! What with?"

"Thoughts."

"Of what?"

"I am in doubt, Will. You know my father was a strange man—I have told you of my young life—and I sometimes think that he must have been more than a rough settler."

"I am sure he was."

"What makes you think so, Will?"

"He had some excellent books—I know they were by the description you gave of them. It is a pity they were destroyed, although you cannot read."

──❦──

CHAPTER XXXIII.

JACK'S DESIRE.

"I AM sorry I cannot read, Will, because I feel it is a great loss, and doubt arises."

"Doubt?"

"Yes, of my father. Why should he wish me not to read?"

"I cannot understand," replied Will; "because it is a credit to a man to have learning."

"That's the point with me, Will. I begin to think that my father was wrong to keep me in ignorance, and there is a thirst within me. He, perhaps, did what he thought was best; but he may be wrong, and I want to read."

"It is easily acquired."

"Will you teach me?"

"With all my heart."

"I was sure you would, Will, and then you must teach me to do what you call writing. You cannot think how strange it seems to me to see one man scrawl his thoughts upon a piece of paper and another man tell him what they are."

"It is easy enough when you understand it."

"No doubt. I have got a conviction upon me—where it comes from I don't know—that as soon as I learn to read and write my whole nature will be changed. I often feel now as if I were not exactly myself—as if I were under the influence of something."

"You certainly are a marvellous fellow, Jack; but what about your early life?"

"My boyhood?"

"No, go further back—to your infancy."

"All my early life," said Jack, "seems to me like a dream; but I remember pretty well that before we settled at Broadpoint we went from place to place, sometimes with a party, sometimes alone. Before that——"

"Aye, Jack, before that?"

"Before that time I have a very faint recollection of a place covered with houses, and bright lights, and a number of horses, with finely-painted carts and wonderfully-dressed people in them."

"Carriages, I suppose?"

"Perhaps so—I don't know, Will. And then I remember a number of people, hundreds and thousands of them, hooting and howling like wolves, and my father and I standing up somewhere on the top of a house, looking down upon them; but it is all so vague and faint, and only like a dream."

"Do you remember anything more?"

"Yes—there is a complete blank after this, but then I come to the time when my father and I were upon the water for days and weeks. I think we must have been upon the sea, for the water was very rough, and we had lightning more than once. I can also call to mind my father holding me up in his arms to see the big fish playing on the surface. I know the sun was very hot, and something white was put over my head to keep me cool."

"It is plain to me," said Will, "that you and your father belong to another land, and came across the sea, but where from is the question? Can you remember what the people were like?"

"I can only remember that their faces were white, and they were so numerous that the whole ground appeared to be covered with them, but nothing more."

"What were the houses like?"

"Tall, and with big windows. I can tell you nothing more."

"Not much of a clue," said Will, "but something may come of it. In the meantime we will devote ourselves to the art of reading and writing. Hallo! they are hoisting our friend Snip up—he is about to tell his story."

"Truth itself, no doubt."

"Certainly," returned Will, with a laugh; "but let us draw near and listen to it."

Snip was, indeed, about to relate his story,

and, for the purpose of telling it effectively, he had been placed upon a piece of rising ground, where, as Will and Jack came up, he struck an attitude, and announced himself as being ready to begin.

The men, women, and children gathered in a body around him, reclining upon the grass. Work was over for the present ; they were to have a little rest, and the amusement offered them by Snip came in most *apropos.*

"Friends, Britons, countrymen, and—widows and orphans," he said, "lend me your ears, and be silent that you may hear. But before I begin just tell that child to take his thumb out of his mouth. A child with a thumb in its mouth drives me mad, and takes all my horrytorrical powers out of me."

The obnoxious thumb was removed, and the child taken upon the lap of a woman near, then Snip proceeded—

"I daresay," he said, "that what I am about to relate will startle you, and it is possible that some may not feel inclined to believe it, but that will be their look-out, and neither the fault of myself nor my story.

"On the morning when I left the camp to get the water I wanted, I went, as one may say, up the wrong alley, and lost my way. Instead of going straight to Aldgate Pump—by which I mean the spring on the prairie—I got into Smithfield, among the butchers, by which, you must know, I mean the Injuns.

"I came bang across about forty of 'em, armed to the teeth and eyes, and they fell upon me, calling upon me to lay down my arms, which naturally I didn't, for that's not my way of doing business. I've too much respect for my family to cave-in, so, my rifle not being loaded, I ups with the butt-end of it and knocks the face of the first savage in as if it was a hat-box.

"Down he went, and I ups with the rifle again, catching another under the jaw, then I fetches one a stunner on the side of the head, then I bangs all the breath out of another's body, and then they gets me down."

Snip paused, while the interest appeared to be intense, although a few quiet winks were exchanged, and Long Tom seemed to be troubled with a cough.

"When down," pursued Snip, "most men give in, but not me. I fought and kicked until at least twenty of 'em were howling, and I saw nine of 'em at one time holding tight to their shins. If you laugh again, Long Tom, and look as if I was lying, I've done."

Long Tom promised to behave better, and Snip, after a few indignant glares around, resumed his story.

"Forty to one is too many," he said, "thirty too many, at least. I don't mind ten, but forty overcame me, and bound me just as them dirty Italian chaps bind their legs, only about four times as tight. Then they carries me away in triumph, saying, in a sort of song, that they had captured the White Man King, and were jolly glad they had him.

"Such a persition," pursued Snip, "is in some p'ints flattering, but when you come to think that they always give the great people a little extra toasting, it spiles the whole thing, and, although I didn't give way, I had a sort of feeling upon me that it would be much better to be out of that hole than in it.

"They took me to the camp, and then I was brought before the chief—as bloodthirsty a looking villain as ever you wish to see."

"The Morning Dawn," added Long Tom.

"The Morning Dawn," said Snip, a little confused for the moment, he having, in the excitement of his story, entirely overlooked that individual. "The Morning Dawn wasn't the real chief, he was only a sort of leaftenant—a kind of second fiddle—a good sort of Injun in his way, but nothing to the chap they brought me before. No—he wasn't a patch upon him, and that's as true as a pig wears bristles.

"'So you are the paleface warrior?' he says.

"'I am,' I says, as bold as brass.

"'You come here to make war upon my people?' he says.

"'I does,' I says.

"'And if I let you go free will you go back and leave us alone?' he axes.

"'No,' says I, 'for the first p'int with every Englishman is dooty—the dooty of the brave and the free.'

"'All this is cheek,' he says. 'Take away the paleface and toast him.'

"There was wenom in his eye, and I saw it ; but I despised that wenom, and told 'em I was ready.

"'Take me to the stake,' I says ; 'England have had its martins long ago, and I'll keep up the Magnum Charter. I'm ready—come on, and don't keep the company waiting !'

"'That's more cheek,' says the Indian chief ; 'give him a double dose—skin him.'

"Where's the man who could have heerd them words without trembling? And do you think I trembled? Not a bit ; but I stands up bold as a lion and says, quite offhand—

"'Lead me to the torture-chamber. I defy you.'

"This took 'em back a bit, and they put their heads together, when I hears one say to the real chief—not meaning the Morning Dawn—he says—

"'Aint it a pity to kill such a plucky chap as this?'

"'No, it aint,' replies the chief. 'If we don't kill him he will kill us. There's nothing else to be done with him.'

"Then they gets a lot of faggots and piles them up together, while all the savages goes to work sharpening their tomahawks, quite joyful like, and I hears them talking about the lark it was to have a white man to cut up.

"In half an hour all was ready, and then I makes up my mind.

"I knew they would cut some of the cords off me, so that I could walk up to the pile of faggots, which they did, and then I bursts the rest, gives the chief one between the eyes, which rolled him over and over, and ran for my life.

"I own it weren't plucky to run away," said Snip, modestly, "but a man can't be expected to fight a whole tribe, so I ran, and they ran after me. But I comes of a running family. My father's brother won the ten-mile champion cup several years running, and another brother ran away with all the cups and pawned them, so you may guess Injuns weren't much use to me, and I gets clear away.

"But getting clear away and finding you are two different sorts of coats, and I had to pass a night on my back among the bushes, where I saw no end of flies and beetles, carrying Roman candles, squibs, and crackers in their tails, which they let off, and then cheered like a lot of boys on a Guy Fawkes' night.

"They was certainly the strangest flies I ever saw, but I didn't mind 'em; nothing could ruffle my composure and I slept beautiful.

"In the morning I got upon your trail, and comes to the prairie, where I heard firing.

"'Ho, ho!' says I, 'here's a pity—they've got at the Injuns and I'm away. I hope they won't get licked.'

"Now, I knowed that you were all pretty good, but at such a time every man's a man—especially one like me—and I comes tearing across the prairie to help you, when I sees the Injuns running down the hills.

"Then a brilliant thought struck me.

"'If they see me,' I thinks, 'they will turn about and bolt another way, and so they will escape, but if I sits down on the grass I may ketch a few.'

"So I sits down, and as they comes up I ketches hold of their legs and holds them until Long Tom arrives, when he finishes them off, which is all I have to say. What do you think of my story?"

"It is all a darned lie," replied about a score of voices, without the slightest hesitation.

"A lie!" said Snip. "Come, now, you're joking."

"No, we aint," was the response, and a general murmur confirmed it.

"But I stopped the Injuns," persisted Snip; "didn't I, Tom?"

"I found a dozen or so on the top of you," replied Long Tom, gruffly, "and you was a-squealing like a pig at the butcher's."

"I'm ashamed of you, Tom, to turn against a friend that way."

"I don't turn agin yer," replied Tom. "I tells the truth—nothing more. You was a-squealing, and you was precious white when I lifted you up."

"It's unkind to take away my laurels of victory," said Snip."

"Laurels be blowed!" returned Long Tom; "you come and sew a button on here, that's about the best thing you can do."

"I have got above that sort of work," urged Snip.

"You do it sharp, or it will be the worse for you," said Long Tom.

Snip sighed and produced his needle and thread, and while he was fastening the button on Tom gave him a lecture.

"You've been lying," he said, "and lying is about as mean a thing as a man can do. Besides, all liars are fools, and everybody soon knows one. A liar is never open, and he's generally a coward. Any man could see when you was a-speaking that you was lying, and what's the consekens? There aint a man in the camp who doesn't turn up his nose at you in p'int of real pluck. If you want to be respected, drop lying, and talk like a man, then you'll get along better in the world. That button is werry nicely put on. Now you go to Banks; he's got a rent in his coat as will be all the better for a little needle and thread."

Long Tom was right.

Lying is a mean thing, and the braggart never deceives those around him. He only lowers himself in their estimation, and, in time, loses even his own self-esteem.

Never lie, my boys. It's about the worst trick you can be guilty of, and as an investment it never pays.

CHAPTER XXXIV.

THE SALOON—AN OLD FRIEND.

A CHANGE of scene now comes over our story, and we must bear our readers to the thriving town of Marena. It was a new place—everything was new in America just then—but it had rapidly risen into a town of some importance, being the depot of the buffalo hide trade. Thither, too, a large number of gold diggers resorted—men who made their wealth one week and spent it the next, on the principle of "lightly come, lightly go."

Being a new place, much frequented by a lawless set of men, it had its gambling saloons, and these haunts of the vicious brought upon it the inevitable curse.

Murder was common, and every night the sounds of contention were heard in the streets, invariably ending with the groans of one or more hapless wretches left to die.

In the morning the bodies were cleared away by a sort of special constable, elected every month, and the dead were buried just outside the town. Their property, if any was found upon them, which was not often the case, was put into the public funds, and there was an end of it.

Liberty is one thing, license another, and these lawless scoundrels, swaggering down the street armed to the teeth, thought they were the very emblems of liberty until it came to their turn to fall under the assassin's knife or pistol. Then their opinion of affairs undoubtedly changed.

The visitors who came for play alone were numberless, and some of them won extensively, while others lost every penny in a night. This was the secret of perpetual bloodshed.

The winner will boast, and the loser will give way to remorse and rage—the paltry gold is more precious to both than life, and murder is the issue.

These gambling saloons were of various sizes —some were small and others were large—but the finest of them all was known as Croupier's Saloon.

Here assembled all the *élite* of ruffianism, and men lost and won heavy sums, often going home rich or ruined.

Drink was provided, and stood ready for the players—nothing to pay. "Drink what you please and play when you wish," was the motto of the proprietor, and no doubt it was an excellent motto for his hellish purpose.

With this saloon we at present have to do.

It was a hot evening in autumn, and the place was full. The windows had been taken out to let in air, for the number of the players were so great that the atmosphere was oppressive. Not half assembled in the room could get near the table to play, and those who were thus deprived of their favourite excitement either lounged impatiently about or sat upon the balcony under the verandah, looking with lack-lustre eyes at the peaceful sky and glorious moon.

Among the latter were two Spaniards, who sat as far as they could from the rest, and talked in whispers, casting furtive glances around occasionally to see if they were overheard.

"It was bad luck," said one. "Who would have thought of your being bowled out? But these Englishmen have such long noses you cannot keep clear of them."

"This fellow," said the other, "is no common Englishman. He is the terror of the land, and it is said he keeps his attention fixed on such fish as ourselves."

"I should like to see him."

"Once is often enough," returned the other, grimly. "There is a look in his eyes alone which is enough for most men—they pierce you like a stiletto, curse him, although I got out of his clutches."

The speaker was none other than Don Ricardo. The pirate stroked his moustache and frowned upon the sky. His companion rested his chin upon his hands and grew thoughtful.

"I have heard of this fellow," he said, "and the stories told of him are wonderful. Have you heard of that affair at Short's Gully?"

"The murder of the settlers by the Pawnees?"

"Yes. Well, he has been in pursuit of the Indians, recaptured the women and children carried away, and brought them back. I hear that some of his men married the widows and repopulated the Gully."

"Indeed!"

"But he has no lack of men. If he wanted a thousand he could have them. They flock to him as the knights of old flocked to the banner of the Crusade."

"But what need has he of them?"

"Who can tell? I suspect he has some wild notion of purifying the land, by driving out all the evil and keeping the good—a very excellent idea if it will only work. They say he is as tender as a child. In a skirmish one of his men was seriously wounded, and the giant made for him a bed of rushes, then sent for the man's wife to administer to his wants, while he remained on sentry by his wounded follower all night. His men love him like a father, and their children cluster round him as he passes."

"Ha! I wish him well," said Don Ricardo, sneeringly.

"This morning," continued the other, "I received a letter directed to Don Jose Santioff, Marena. It was brought by a short, thick-set fellow, who tossed it impudently in at the window as I sat at breakfast, and then rode away. Shall I read it to you?"

"Can you make it out?"

"Certainly," replied Don Jose; "the moon is bright and the writing large. Listen!"

Then he drew a paper from his breast and read as follows—

"To DON JOSE SANTIOFF,—You are a man of influence, and a magistrate of Marena. Take heed. Marena must be made cleaner. If men will not govern themselves rightly they must be governed. If there isn't a change in Marena shortly a broom will come and sweep it clean. How can a place be pure if those in authority haunt the gambling saloons and set the fashion. Be warned in time. RIGHT AND MIGHT."

"Now what does that mean?" said Don Jose, as he refolded the paper. "Who is this 'Right and Might,' and what will he do?"

"It is our long friend, Jack Savage, I suspect," returned Don Ricardo; "and if you don't take steps to make this place a little better he will turn you inside out."

"What can I do?" asked Don Jose.

"Shut up half the gambling saloons, or a few to begin with."

"But I get a royalty from each, and if I shut up one I must shut up all."

"If you don't he will."

"A stiff job for him."

"There will be fighting without a doubt, but he is not the man to speak without his book. What he says he will do he means to do. I intend to give him a wide berth."

"But, confound the fellow!" said Don Jose, with a savage look, "what has he to do with us?"

"Everything in his own ideas. What have we to do with other people we often interfere with? What has any man to do with another? And yet here we are always putting our fingers into other people's pies."

"Just so."

"And this Jack Savage will put a finger in your pie, and such a large finger it is, my friend. Gad! it is larger than any man's thumb."

"But the men here won't stand it."

"Men? Call these curs men? How many will fight for a gambling-house, do you think?"

"I don't know."

"I do. Not any of them. It is not like a man fighting for his home, or his meat and bread. They can gamble anywhere—if not here on the prairie; if not on the prairie in the forest. No, Don Jose, if this fellow comes down upon Marena, Marena is as good as gone."

"The remembrance of your own defeat has made you nervous," replied Don Jose.

Don Ricardo winced under this stroke, and his brother Don laughed a little, for he considered that he had said a good thing.

There was a pause after this, and both sat looking at the moon and stroking their moustaches with a thoughtful air.

"There is only one way out of it," said Don Ricardo; "at least, only one as far as I can see."

"What is that?" asked the other.

"Kill the leader."

"Jack Savage?"

"Yes."

"Easier said than done."

"You may think so," said Don Ricardo; "but I am not so doubtful."

"Would you undertake it?"

"No—but there are scores who would do it at a price."

"He is such a mighty fellow—so strong—so brave."

"What of that? Given time and opportunity, the meanest assassin could lay him low."

"An assassin? Ah! I see your drift now."

"What did you think I meant?"

"I was thinking of fair fight."

"Bah! I'm not such a fool. No, an assassin must do the work. This Jack Savage will be here shortly. He is sure not to be long after his message."

"I fear not."

"When he comes hold parley with him. Promise a great deal. Put on a friendly face. Visit his cave. Watch the position of his sleeping-place. He is as fearless as a man can be, and will hide nothing. When you know all, hire your man and put him to work."

"I like the idea," said Don Jose Santioff, "and I hope we may be successful. Have you played to-night !"

"No."

"Shall we go in?"

"Yes. I hate such a night as this—so calm and peaceful. It clashes with my feelings."

"You are more fiery."

"What has yon sky to do with a life like mine?" asked Don Ricardo, bitterly. "Look at fair Luna—she is all purity and peace. Look at the sky—smooth, unruffled, and without a cloud. Then compare me with Luna, and my life with the sky around her."

"Not much alike."

"No, Santioff," said Don Ricardo, laying a hand upon the shoulder of his companion, "they are not much alike. Would to Heaven they were! Would that the sky above was an emblem of my life; but it is not so. I can look at that sky, but I dare not look at my life. Could the mother who bore me see me now she would weep her heart out."

"Some say the spirits of the dead look down upon us."

"I hope it is not so. I dare not think of the pure woman who brought me into the world looking on me now. The thought would kill me. I am not all iron."

"You are a bit mellow to-night, and grow sentimental."

"A man ceases to live when all sentiment dies within him. Ah! my friend, I sometimes think of the quiet vineyard of my father's, where I was born. I can see the slanting rays of the setting sun gilding the peasants as they wend their way homeward, singing such things as I dare not listen to now. The good is all dead in me, and the purity of others is poison to me."

"You are a man, Ricardo, and yet you talk like a girl."

"I talk as I feel, Santioff. You know I am not over tender in my nature, yet these thoughts will come. Life is but a brief span after all, and it ends too soon."

"But you may live a good score years yet?"

"What is a score years for repentance? Will it wipe out the sins of fifty—and such a fifty as I have passed? Man should be a helper to his race—what have I been?"

"That's best known to yourself," returned Don Jose, shrugging his shoulders.

"It is known," returned Don Ricardo, "and known but too well. Murder and rapine have been my pursuits. I have lived by doing wrong, and have been a blight and a curse upon my fellows—now I end by being a blight and curse upon myself."

"This comes of an idle life," said Don Jose, with a sneer; "men like you should always be actively employed. But there is good work for you getting ready, and a week in the field will set your blood in motion and drive this folly away. Come into the room."

"Stay! what is that?" asked Don Ricardo.

Both stood still and listened. The usual excited roar of the gambling-room had changed to a murmur of surprise, not so loud as the usual noise, but much more impressive.

Don Jose Santioff drew near to one of the windows and peeped in.

"What is it?" asked the other.

"Our friend is here."

"Who?"

"Jack Savage."

"Impossible!"

"Look for yourself."

Don Ricardo lost no time in obeying the injunction, and he then saw that what his companion had said was correct.

Walking calmly down the centre of the saloon, with every eye upon him, strode Jack Savage, and on either side of him were Long Tom and bold Will Larkin.

Apparently unheedful of the many startled and angry faces around him, Jack Savage compassed the entire length of the saloon, then he turned on his heel and surveyed it.

His entrance had wrought a strange change in the scene. All gambling had ceased.

The noisy gamesters cursed and swore no more, the croupiers toyed with their knives or stealthily slipped the loose money from the tables, and the attendants, who had been busy drawing corks and handing drin about, stopped suddenly in their vocation.

To most of the assembly Jack was an entire stranger; but some had heard of him, and to a few he was known personally, and these latter knew that his presence there boded them no good.

His appearance was certainly striking.

Dressed in a suit of deep rich maroon velvet, with a cashmere shawl around his waist, he looked like some hero fresh from a fable. The dress, close-fitting and superbly made, looked magnificent.

His face lit up with the bloom of youth, and his flashing grey eyes added to his imposing appearance, and those who looked at him could not help admiring nor avoid trembling with apprehension while they admired.

The coolness of his demeanour was well seconded by Long Tom and Will Larkin, both of whom seemed, like their leader, to look down with quiet contempt upon the scene.

After a few moments' survey Jack retraced his footsteps the whole length of the room again, until he had reached the door by which he had entered. Then he took out his knife and cut a notch upon the doorpost, and walked away as quietly as he had come.

His disappearance released the voices of the tongue-tied men, and immediately fifty questions were asked—

"Who is he?—what is he?"

"He is Jack Savage!" cried Don Jose, stepping into the room. "A man who takes upon himself to correct other men as if they were naughty boys."

"He's a precious big 'un," said a voice.

"He comes here," said Don Jose, "to put down the gambling of Marena. He objects to gambling."

⁂

CHAPTER XXXV.

A CRY FOR HELP.

"By Jupiter! I object to gambling," put in a tall, rakish-looking man, who was listening to Don Jose's remarks. "It never does anything but empty my purse."

"This Savage," continued Don Jose, "intends to shut up every gambling-house in Marena—that is, if he can. If we are not men, but old women, he will do it; but if we are men we shall fight him while there is a pinch of powder or a shot in our pouches."

"Let those who like fight for a gambling-hell," said a big, burly-looking fellow. "I don't. I've

◁ GIANT JACK: ▷

A Story of the Red Mountains.

"UGH!" EXCLAIMED THE MORNING DAWN.   "FAIRLY CAUGHT!" SAID JACK.

got a better use for my powder and shot."

"Hear, hear!" said a score of voices.

"If Jack Savage comes and makes firewood of this place," continued the burly man, "you must move the tables elsewhere. I guess there's a good many towns round about which can make room for 'em—but as for fighting, I reckon I don't do it, and if I know the men about there's not many will fire a shot to try and save what ruins them."

This opinion was endorsed with laughter, and then the play was resumed by the careless, thoughtless men.

"I see you were right?" said Don Jose to his friend, who came up to him with a smile upon his face.

"Aye, I was," replied the pirate.

"So we must go to work another way. Jack Savage has but just left. Let us after him."

"For what purpose?"

"To see where he goes to, and if a chance offers, do the necessary work myself."

"Be careful."

"Never fear. I love my skin too well to risk it idly."

The two hurried down into the street and looked about them.

Jack was not in sight, but a brief inquiry of a man who was lounging about near gave them the information required.

"Straight down the road opposite," he said, and they hastened on in the direction pointed out.

The bright light of the moon soon revealed the form of Jack and his attendants as they walked at an easy pace through the town of Marena, looking neither to the right nor to the left, and apparently as careless of everything as if they were in a peaceful, well-protected city, instead of being in a place where ruffianism held entire sway.

The two Spaniards kept in the shadow, with their eyes upon the trio, who walked in the moonlight, and they followed them the whole length of the street, when Jack and his lieutenants stopped and appeared as if they were about to part.

Jack held out his hand and Will grasped it, showing by his actions that he was endeavouring to induce his leader to go with them, but our hero resisted this as well as the kind solicitations of Long Tom.

Waving them away he stood firm, and when they turned back again and again to him, he still waved them away, until they disappeared in the shadows of the night.

"Favoured by the gods," said Don Jose—"the time and opportunity are here."

"Seize it, then," said Don Ricardo.

"Will you help me?"

Don Ricardo shrugged his shoulders and stroked his moustache. He was doubtful.

"Are you a coward?" demanded the other.

"Aye, a little, when I look upon our tall friend," said Don Ricardo.

"Stay here," was the angry reply. "I will do the work alone."

Then Don Jose Santioff, still keeping in the shadow, crept cautiously after Jack Savage, and Don Ricardo as cautiously followed him.

Jack, with the same ease and nonchalance hitherto displayed by him, walked down to the end of another street and turned the corner.

Don Jose by this time was close upon him,

stealing on like a thief in the night.

He, too, turned the corner, and just at that moment Don Ricardo beheld something glitter in the hand of his friend.

It was a stiletto!

"Santioff strikes swift and sure," he muttered; "if he does not fail now I am avenged."

The little good which had dawned in him a short time ago was gone, and evil was again paramount. He had no thought but of his defeat, and thirsted for revenge.

He came to the corner also, and looked down the street. The light of the moon fell on it straight and full, and every plank of the rough wooden houses and the ill-shaped windows were revealed.

Half-way down was a bridge, under which a swift river ran, and across that bridge sauntered Jack Savage, at the same easy pace.

But where was Don Jose?

Not in sight.

Save Don Ricardo, Jack Savage was the only living thing in view

"Santioff is skulking in some doorway," thought Ricardo; "the moon is too bright for him."

Involuntarily attracted by the water, he halted and looked at it, silvered all over as it was by the moonlight.

At that very moment the face of a man rose to the surface, and a fearful shriek rent the air.

It was Don Jose Santioff!

"Help!—help! Murder!" he cried.

What help could Don Ricardo give? And the cry brought no other to his rescue, so the swift waters bore him under again.

Don Ricardo, spell-bound, stood watching the turbid stream until he saw his friend rise once more to the surface, and again he heard his piteous shriek for help.

A fearful cry.

It has no parallel on earth, this shriek of a despairing man—it teems with horror, and once heard is never forgotten.

The peaceful air seemed to be rent by it, but shriek as he might no help came to save him, and the waters bore him away a corpse.

"The giant must have stunned him," thought Don Ricardo, "and then thrown him over. Well, he was my friend," he soliloquised, "and I suppose I ought to grieve for him. I would if I could, but grief for others and I have long been strangers. It was rash of Don Jose, as he should have made sure of his man before he struck a blow. My giant friend is unconquerable. I expect all men will have to bow before him. If others don't I will, so I shall go away to-night and leave this place to him."

Don Jose Santioff had reckoned without his host, and Don Ricardo was now doing the same.

He proposed to leave the country, and he felt inclined to halloo before he was out of the wood. Many do this sort of thing, and find out their folly when too late .

He was correct in one thing, however, and that was with regard to the encounter of Jack Savage and his would-be assassin. Our hero heard a footstep close behind him, and, turning, beheld a glittering dagger close to him.

It was no time to ask questions.

Swift as thought his strong arm lashed out, his huge fist struck the Don full in the throat, and the Spaniard reeled.

The rail of the bridge was low, and ere Jack

could put a hand out to save him he was over and under the swift, cold water.

The blow stunned the Spaniard, but the water revived him, and when he came to the surface he instinctively shrieked for help; but no help was near, and, as our readers have already learned, he died the death he so richly deserved.

CHAPTER XXXVI.
OUR HERO'S CAMP.

JUST outside Marena, under the shelter of a hill, was the camp of Jack Savage, and there at least thirty tents stood white and ghost-like in the moonlight.

These tents were large, sufficiently so to accommodate ten men in each. They were arranged in a circle, and within the circle were a number of mules and mustangs, the beasts of burden required to carry their baggage.

As for Jack and his men, they marched on foot. Jack had always been accustomed to use his limbs for walking purposes, and his example was followed by all, so they had no more beasts with them than were necessary for the purposes we have named.

The main object of the new expedition was to search for gold, several of the trappers who had joined the party having declared their conviction that it would be found further west. As seeking gold was in itself a harmless and perhaps profitable pursuit, Jack encouraged the idea, and agreed to carry it out on condition that his men obeyed him in other matters.

One object he had, we know, and that is what concerns the town of Marena. Jack had heard of the doings there, so he resolved to do something towards the establishment of order, and thus show himself to be a pioneer of better times than those the hapless town had hitherto known.

As for gold, our hero had little taste for it, but he knew that the necessaries for such a band as he commanded must, if honestly obtained, be paid for in gold or some equivalent, and therefore he willingly lent his aid to procure wealth as a necessary means of locomotion.

All the married men he had left behind, but he had enlisted many recruits—all good men for the work cut out for them, and all prepared to look up and to obey him.

Will Larkin and Long Tom were with him, as we have seen. Snip was with him too.

The little tailor had some notion of remaining at home, but the prospect of gold-finding was too much for him, so, having treated himself to a spade and pick-axe, he most valorously joined the party.

"It must be better than fighting," he thought; "besides, I'm rather fond of digging —I used to help the sexton at Wapping sometimes to shovel in. Lor! what a delicious sensation it must be when one hears the spade ringing against lumps of gold! It's enough to make a man's mouth water."

When he heard that his leader intended to stop at Marena, and that a bit of a fight might probably ensue, he became very dejected, and entered a mild but ineffectual protest against such a proceeding.

"If we are going for gold we ought to go," he said; "but as for fighting on the way, it's downright absurd—almost wicked. Suppose a man gets killed, then gold's no good to him; and if he's only wounded—loses a leg, perhaps —what is he to do then? A man with one leg is no use for digging."

This protest was made to Long Tom, who only grunted and growled a bit about a certain person known as General Funk, hinting that that was the sort of person Snip would serve best under.

"If you mean that I am caving in," said Snip, "you are mistaken; but fighting is one thing and gold-seeking another. If we come out to fight let us fight like one o'clock, but if we come out for gold let us dig for it like—like——"

"Two o'clock?" suggested Long Tom.

"Of course," said Snip, "that's what I meant. You put it to the captain."

"Put it yourself," said Long Tom.

"And if I do—what then?" asked Snip.

"He would most likely knock your head off," replied Long Tom, as he went away.

The result was that Jack never heard of the suggestion of his able assistant, Snip, and the next day Long Tom delivered his message to Don Jose Santioff.

Then Jack Savage and his two officers went boldly into the town, as we have seen, and, strolling back, our hero bade the others return to the camp.

"Go!" he said; "the men are alone, and, although I have no great apprehension of danger, yet it is as well that someone should be ready to command, in case of need."

"And you?" asked Will.

"I am going to the end of the town," he said.

"What for?" asked Will.

"Although I have never known this town by name, I have, I am convinced, been here before," replied Jack. "I have a remembrance of the place, and I am sure that my father lived with me for a time in a hut upon a hill yonder. If the hut is there I may find something of interest, for I remember that, before leaving, he took up a part of the flooring and buried some books and papers."

"This is good news," said Will; "but why go alone?"

"Why not?"

"The place swarms with murderers and villains."

"They prowl about alone, Will," said Jack, "why, then, should I fear?"

"I do not suppose you fear," said Will; "but useless risk is always foolish. Let us go with you."

"No, Will—you must get back to the camp. I shall be there by the morning."

Finding his leader could not be persuaded, Will and Tom returned to the camp.

Both were tired, but neither thought of sleep, and they sat waiting for the return of Jack, until the light of morning arrived.

The sun came back to them with its life and light, but the captain did not. Then they grew uneasy, and as the men came out of their tents and prepared for the early meal it was whispered about that the captain was missing.

"He's gone down to the town," said one; "he started last night, and they've fallen foul of him."

"If they have," returned Snip, "let 'em tremble in their boots."

"Don't you begin to bray again," was the response; "you are all very well at stopping a runaway Injun, but I'm darned if I think you can do much with white flesh and blood."

Snip muttered something about somebody being an ass, and somebody wanting their noses pulled, but as he did not specify the person or persons, either by word or deed, nothing more came of it.

As for Will, he was in a terrible way, and if he had followed his own inclination he would have mustered the men and gone up to the town in search of his leader; but he knew that if Jack was alive he would not approve of such a step, and if dead it could not help him.

So he stayed where he was, impatiently awaiting the issue of events.

Long Tom was uneasy, too.

But he was of a more phlegmatic nature, in addition to the wondrous faith he had in the powers of his leader, whom he almost worshipped.

Jack had promised to return, and return he would, Tom felt certain.

"You may make your mind easy," he said to Will, "and have a bit of breakfast."

"But he may have been murdered," urged Will.

"Murdered!" repeated Tom, with contempt. "Bosh! Where's the man as dare try that game on, or where's the man as could murder him? Jack's a match for any of 'em."

"He's not a match for a bullet or a knife behind him."

"No man could hit him, I feel sure."

"Nonsense, Tom—look at his size."

"What of that, Will? I say as no man *could* hit him. He's been in the thick of many a fight, and no man ever touched him yet. You know that much."

"But the best of men get in the way of a bullet sometimes."

"He's more than the best of men," said Tom, staunchly; "don't talk to me of Jack being shot. Here's the coffee, hot and sweet, and here's the bread. You take something, for I'm sure you must want it."

Will ate a little, but he had no stomach for food, and the bread passed to him by Tom was left lying almost untouched.

The others ate and drank with the relish of men who live in the open air, and then lay about chatting and cleaning the bright metal parts of their arms.

Will went to the outskirts of the camp, watching for his captain, but another hour passed, and still there were no signs of him. Then he went back to Tom.

"I'm afraid he's been murdered," he said. "It's no use looking sceptical."

"I don't know what you mean by 'spectacral,'" returned Tom, "but I don't think Jack's come to any harm."

"I do, Tom."

"You're wrong, I'll bet."

"I am right, and I can't rest any longer, so I shall go up to the town and search for him."

"Alone?"

"No—what could I do alone?"

"Just my notion. But we can't all go. Suppose the captain comes back and finds the camp empty?"

"You can remain here."

"Not I. If you go to Marena I must be of the party."

"One of us must remain," said Will, de-cidedly. "Look here, Tom, we will divide the men. Half shall go to the town, the other half remain here. You shall have one party and I the other. Now here, between my fingers, are two pieces of stick, one short and the other long. The long one goes to Marena and the short one remains here."

Tom nodded and drew a piece of stick.

It was the shortest, but the length of his face made ample amends for its sparsity.

"I guess it's my luck," he muttered; "but duty is duty. Pick your men, Will."

"Call them out and take them as they come," returned Will.

The men were then summoned, and the nature of the duty required explained to them.

More than the number required volunteered immediately, and about a hundred and fifty men were portioned out to Will, all eager for the expected brush with the inhabitants of Marena.

With one exception—our old friend Snip.

He had wished in his heart to be left at home in peace, but fate was against him, and it came about that he was selected as one of the attacking party. Will ranged his men in front of him and favoured them with a few words.

"I intend to search every nook of the town," he said. "If it can be done without fighting, well and good. If not, I intend to fight for it, and the man who does not wish to fight with me had better stand out now, as it may be too late by-and-bye."

Of course none stood out, although Snip longed in his heart to do so; but a feeling of shame kept him silent, so, putting his best face on the matter, he marched off with the rest.

As they drew near Marena they saw some men running towards the town, then others came out to look at them, and these ran away too, much to their amusement.

"No fight in that lot," said Will. "We shall have an easy scamper over the town."

Snip overheard the remark, and his heart was considerably lightened. It also gave an airiness to his footsteps, and he became, as one of the men expressed it, "quite cocky."

"They are a set of cowards," said Snip. "The very look of us frightens them."

"I don't think they are cowards," returned another. "They are not organised as we are. They have nothing to fight for as we have. It make all the difference. No man cares about blood-spilling unless there is something to be gained by it."

"But honour and glory, you know," suggested Snip.

"Not much honour and glory is gained by fighting against a gambling hell," was the quiet reply; "and the town itself aint worth much—a lot of wooden shanties and gimcrack saloons."

By this time they had reached the city and entered its streets, which were quite deserted.

There was no life to be seen in the houses either, and, in obedience to a command from Will, the men began to search them.

He himself walked forward to a rising piece of ground overlooking the town and beyond it. There he saw a strange sight.

Far beyond the houses was a moving body of men—a perfect exodus of knaves and gamesters, running away from they knew not what.

But "Conscience makes cowards of us all," says the great bard, and these men were flying from an unknown and therefore a dreaded foe.

"The town is deserted!" cried Will. "It is ours."

Snip hitherto had been cautiously helping his comrades; but when he heard this cry he became exceedingly energetic, and went to the fore.

"Come on!" he cried; "let us find our noble captain or perish in the attempt! This way, my men, this way!"

CHAPTER XXXVII.

A SLIGHT MISADVENTURE.

THERE is an old and trite saying which tells us that "Fools rush in where angels fear to tread," and this much of it is certainly true—that a fool will often go blundering about in places where wise men would prudently decline to go.

Snip was a fool. There is no doubt about that point. On this occasion he demonstrated it by rushing ahead of the general body and choosing one of the biggest houses to search upon his own account.

Snip tried the door, then he tried the windows.

The first was secured, but the second opened to his touch, so having looked in to see that nobody was there, and finding the place perfectly empty, he valorously entered.

Once inside he paused to breathe and think for a moment.

The place seemed to be entirely deserted, but it was possible that some ferocious ruffian might be concealed somewhere.

"Hullo! hullo!" he shouted; "anybody at home?"

His voice rang through the house, and echo alone brought a reply.

"If there is anybody," cried Snip, "he had better make haste and get out of the back-door or window. I give him a minute to do it in. I'm rather an awkward chap to deal with if it comes to fighting."

Again his voice rang through the house, and, as before, echo alone furnished him with a reply.

"Quite empty," muttered Snip. "Now to search the place."

He chose the top of the house first, and walking up to the landing he looked around him.

There were six doors, leading into six rooms, and the doors were all open.

After a preparatory cough, as a warning to any man who might have the audacity to linger, Snip entered one of the rooms, poking his rifle in before him as a sort of bogey.

The room had been used for sitting purposes and was well furnished.

In the centre was a polished walnut table, with books and music strewn about it, and on the ground, where it had fallen, lay a guitar.

"Whoever lived here," muttered Snip, "made themselves pretty comfortable, and there's a bottle under the couch there. I suppose they drank a bit, too."

Not finding more than we have described, Snip left the room and went into the next. This was a bedroom, with a most luxurious couch near the window. Snip felt it, and finding it was blessed with a feather bed, he could not refrain from having a roll upon it. Feather beds and he had not met for many a day.

Then he got off and looked under the bed.

Nothing there, so he went to the next room.

This was almost empty.

In one corner stood a long chest, about the size and shape of a corn-bin, and that was all.

"That looks like a plate chest," thought Snip. "Suppose the plate is there it is mine by our laws, and I'm a rich man. Here goes, and good luck help me."

First depositing his rifle in the corner, Snip went over and tried the lid.

Locked!

"The plate must be there," muttered Snip, elate with triumph; "but how am I to get it open?"

He tried to raise it again, but it resisted his efforts. He had a knife, but that would do little with so strong a lock, so he was compelled to give up the attempt.

"If I am not sharp," he thought, "the others will be here, then it's share and share alike, and a precious small share mine will be—not so much as the lid of a silver coffee-pot, I reckon."

He was in despair. Cupidity was strong upon him, and he was thirsting to know what the chest contained. Suddenly a brilliant idea came to him.

It was to blow off the lock.

"Hurrah!" cried Snip, capering. "I've got him. The row will bring the others up, but it will be too late to claim a share."

Taking up his rifle, he thrust the muzzle into the lock and pulled the trigger.

The report was loud and the recoil terrific. Snip was knocked over upon his back, and then in the midst of the smoke he saw the lid open and a man leap out.

A fierce, swarty, angry man, who threw himself upon Snip and seized him by the throat.

"You dog!" he said, "would you murder a sleeping man?"

"Come, draw it mild," cried Snip, wriggling. "I didn't go for to hit you."

The man swore, and held Snip fast. Snip wriggled and groaned. But even in the midst of his struggles our little friend marked the features of the man, and knew him.

It was the pirate—Don Ricardo.

Almost at the same moment the Spaniard recognised Snip, and with a cry of surprise he let go his hold.

"The little English beggar!" he cried.

"Not quite a beggar," returned Snip, "for I gave you a whopping."

"Enough," said the Spaniard, loftily. "What are you doing here?"

"Searching for the captain."

"Savage?"

"Yes."

"Is the dog lost?"

"He went away last night and hasn't come home," returned Snip, backing towards the door, and making preparations for a grand skedaddle.

"Stay where you are," said Don Ricardo, savagely, drawing a knife from his belt. "Now, tell me about your chief."

"I've told you all I know," returned Snip, doggedly.

"And told the truth?"

"Yes—every word of it."

"What fools and cowards we have all been,' muttered the Spaniard to himself; "without their giant leader the men are but ordinary people, and we outnumbered them ten to one. Here, you sir !"

"Snip is my name."

"Confound your name! Tell me—— Ah! what's that ?"

It was a shouting outside, and the noise of men hammering lustily at the door.

"They heard me fire," thought Snip. "I am saved."

"The report of your rifle has brought them here," said Don Ricardo. "Quick—into that box." •

"Get into that ?"

"At once—there's not a moment to be lost. It is my only chance. Do you hesitate ?"

He held up his glittering knife, and Snip obeyed. With a groan he put his leg over the side of the box, and laid himself down.

"You burst one of the springs," said the Spaniard, as he also got into the box, "but there are others to hold it. Lie quiet."

"We shall be smothered if you shut down the lid," groaned Snip.

"Both lid and sides are perforated," returned the Don, "and it is not the first time a man has been hidden there. Hush! I hear them coming."

Then he pulled down the lid and lay close to Snip. It was a tight fit, and the hot breath of the Spaniard fell upon the little tailor's face.

"Do you know the feel of this?" hissed the pirate, as he placed the blade of a knife upon Snip's neck.

"Oh !—don't I !" replied Snip, with a shudder.

———⚓———

CHAPTER XXXVIII.

MATTERS MEND VERY LITTLE.

"BEWARE !" rejoined Don Ricardo. "If you move a hair's-breadth, or if your friends attempt to raise this lid, I will cut your throat !"

"I'll lay quiet enough," groaned Snip; "but I can't help what my friends do."

"Silence and obey!" hissed the Spaniard, menacingly.

"There never could have been such luck as mine," groaned Snip in his heart. "Things were bad enough before, but they grow worse and worse every time. The hollow tree with the earwiggles was a place of luxury, and the night among the Injuns was joy in comparison. Why on earth I came here I don't know. Other men don't get into such awful scrapes. I dursn't move an inch, for these chaps are uncommon ready with their knives. But it can't be real! All the other may be right enough, but this must be a dream. No man in his waking senses ever was put in a box with a Spaniard who's got a precious long knife. No— it's a dream at last."

"Your friends are coming," hissed the Spaniard; "move, and you peril your life !"

"Dead as a doormat !" groaned Snip, and he lay perfectly still.

Just then the door was kicked open, and a number of men, Will Larkin at their head, entered the room.

"There is the smell of smoke," Snip heard him say, "but there is no one here."

"And nothing but this old chest," returned one of the men.

"Anything in it ?"

"Don't know, sir."

"See, then."

Don Ricardo laid a hand upon Snip's throat, and our friend felt that his last moment had come. He must have cried out but for the terror which tied his tongue.

The man tried to open the chest and announced it to be fastened.

"It is only an old clothes chest," said Will, indifferently. "If there is any gold or jewels in it—which I do not suppose there is—they will rattle. Tilt the box up and see."

Two men laid hold of the box, and, first standing it on end, tilted it over.

Down went the box with a crash, and Snip and the Spaniard knocked noses together.

Snip could not avoid a low groan of agony as Don Ricardo pricked him with the knife.

"Silence, on your life !" he whispered in Snip's ear.

"I haven't said a word," returned Snip. "I can't be no silenter."

The box was perforated with an infinite number of holes, but these gave very little air, and the prison-house of the two men was intensely hot.

The perspiration rolled down their faces, and Snip felt his clothes sticking to his back, but he dared make no complaint. Any life in the fix he was in was better than none.

The men heard the thud of the two bodies as they fell over with the box, and laughed aloud.

"A linen chest," said one.

"More likely dirty clothes," returned another.

"The gun was fired in this chamber," broke in the voice of Will, "but nobody is here. The question is—who fired it ?"

"None of the enemy," said one.

"I should say not," replied Will. "The rifle was not fired at any of us in the street, for the window is closed, and we saw nobody escape."

Will walked to the window and looked out, while the others stood still in the centre of the room.

"Oh! why don't they go?" thought the agonised Snip. "It's my only chance of life. If they try the box again this blessed Spaniard will settle me."

It really appeared so, for Don Ricardo held Snip lightly but securely by the throat, and every now and then the cold point of the stiletto touched the skin of his prisoner.

Snip was, indeed, in a very sore strait.

"I see nothing to explain the mystery," said Will, coming back; "but I cannot leave the house until I have ascertained the cause of the report. Our leader himself may be here."

"Or one of our men."

"Just so. Is there anybody missing ?"

"Yes. Snip has not been seen for some time."

"Where is he ?"

"Aye, that's the point," said Snip to himself; "where is Snip? If you only knew you would pity and respect me."

"He went ahead of us," said one of the men, "and disappeared. That is all we know of him."

"It is most mysterious that rifle being fired," said Will, musingly. "As for Snip, he is all right, and is sure to turn up again."

"I wish I was as cocksure about it myself," thought Snip; "but that is just the way with people who are out of the ditch. They see another man in it, and always feel perfectly easy about his getting out."

After a little more doubt and hesitation Will and his men left the room, and the two perspiring inhabitants of the box heard them running about and searching the house.

They could hear the slamming of doors and the overturning of furniture, and the Spaniard called down all sorts of evil upon them for making such havoc amongst his private property.

"It's the way with those beggarly English," he muttered ; "they destroy everything."

Snip thought that the Don must have done a little in the destructive line himself, but he said nothing, and they lay side by side listening.

For nearly an hour the men were moving about the house, but at last the footsteps ceased.

The Spaniard was cautious, for the silence might be a ruse, so he lay with his ear stretched to catch every sound.

Snip listened too, not with any hope of being saved by his friends, but with a longing to escape from his dreadful prison, the heat of which had now become insupportable.

At last Don Ricardo was convinced, and he uttered a little sigh of relief, while Snip sighed in concert.

Then the Don spoke.

"They are gone," he said, "and we are at liberty to leave this hole, my friend."

"I can't say I shall be sorry," replied Snip, "for I was never nearer being biled in my life."

The Don turned over and touched the spring, but the lid of the box remained still. Then, with an impatient movement, he placed his finger upon it again.

The same result.

"God of my fathers !" he cried, "we are lost ?"

"Lost !" cried Snip.

"Yes—lost !" shrieked the Spaniard. "We are fixed in here. The box has been turned over upon the lid, and the spring won't act. If no one comes to help us we must starve to death together."

"Shriek for help," yelled Snip.

"Too late," groaned the Spaniard ; "they are gone !"

CHAPTER XXXIX.

NEWS OF JACK.

LITTLE thinking whom he had left behind, Will Larkin went down into the town, and there stood meditating upon the next step to be taken. The street was alive with his men, who ran in and out the houses like bees in every respect but that of finding honey, for no signs of Jack were discovered.

Marena was not a large place, but the houses were sufficiently numerous to make the task Will had undertaken a very troublesome job. However, he belonged to the energetic order of men, and his hesitation arose from no sense of unwillingness to proceed, but from a conviction that Jack was not within the town.

"He may have got clear of it," he thought, "and is now in the hut—perhaps he was murdered there. I will go and see "

He never had seen this hut, but Jack's last words gave him sufficient clue, and he struck across the town, calling on the men to follow him.

But while he was yet calling another voice was heard, and Long Tom was seen coming up behind shouting like a madman.

"Hallo, there ! Stop the search," he said. "The captain's found !"

"Hurrah !" shouted Will. "That is good news if he is well."

"Sound as a bell," replied Tom. "He has just come into the camp."

"I hope he will not be angry with me," said Will.

"Not a bit," returned Tom. "He laughed when I told him you were gone, and said it was like you to be always thinking about him."

"He is a noble fellow."

"Right you are, Will. He sent me after you as he wants you particular. Go back at once, and I will stay and muster the men."

Will stayed to hear no more, but ran back at once to the camp, where Jack Savage was awaiting his coming.

Jack greeted him with a smile and an outstretched hand, and Will felt much relieved, for, despite Tom's assurance, he was not certain that his movements might meet with approval from his leader.

"Very good of you, Will," said Jack ; "but I told you there was no danger."

Indeed, there seemed none to Will now that his captain was back, and he could not help feeling that he had been somewhat premature in his search.

"You promised to be back at dawn," he said, "and as you did not come I became anxious."

"I was later than I intended to be," said Jack, "but the time slipped away without my heeding it."

"You found the hut ?"

"Yes—not quite as we left it years ago, but I found it. Just sit down and let me spin the yarn to you."

Will stretched himself upon a sloping piece of ground, and our hero placed his massive limbs beside him.

"The hut," Jack began, "lies there, over to the west. You see that clump of trees ?"

"Near the yellow sand-bank ?"

"That's the spot, and just in the very heart of those trees stands the hut I told you of. By the way, your fears were not entirely without foundation. Some Spanish fellow did make an attempt upon me, but he went to the wall—only in this case it was water—where you have often told me the weakest are sure to go. But let him rest.

"Strolling across the town, I got clear of it about an hour after you left me, and fortunately struck upon the road that led straight to the hut. The track seemed familiar to me—in fact, my mind became clearer as I went along, and I soon hove in sight of the place which my father and I once made our home.

"I am rather what you call sentimental, Will, as you know, and when I saw this rough shanty the tears rose into my eyes, while the form of my father seemed to hover before me."

"As I came up to the hut I saw that it was inhabited, and drawing near I heard voices inside. Now, Will, I am going to tell you plainly and truthfully what passed next, and I am sure you will believe me, for you know I am not given to bragging."

"A long way from it, Jack," said Will.

"I heard the voices of several men inside, and going up straight to the door I knocked.

"'Who's there?' asked a gruff voice.

"'Jack Savage,' I replied.

"Immediately there was a commotion within, and I heard one man say, in a terrified whisper, 'We are all dead men.'

"I could scarcely help laughing, but I had no time for merriment. Minutes are precious sometimes, so I knocked again.

"This time there was no answer, and feeling that promptitude was the best thing under the circumstances, I put my foot to the door and kicked it open.

"I was saluted by a couple of pistol-shots, but neither of the bullets touched me.

"Rather nettled by this treatment of a solitary man, I rushed in and struck out right and left. I suppose there were at least a dozen men in the place, and one went down at each blow. The rest scampered through the open door and tore away for their very lives."

"What fun!" said Will. "And the two left behind—what of them?"

"One," replied Jack, lowering his voice, "will never speak again. I struck him in the temple, and I am sorry for it. The other has lost the beauty of his nose and a tooth or two. He was stunned, but he quickly recovered, and, having in the most abject manner asked leave to go away, he carried himself off.

"I laid the dead man upon the couch in the corner, and then, by the light of a candle, took a survey of the hut. As I looked around my memory grew each moment stronger, and I became certain the place was but little changed.

"The furniture was not the same, but it was quite as rough and rude as that my father owned, and therefore did not distract my mind from the things of the past.

"Oh! the memory of the past, Will—how sad it is at times. But it was never more sad to me than in that hut last night, for I loved my father more than most men are loved by their children.

"I must not trouble you with my sorrows, though. As I told you, the looking round the hut increased the strength of my memory each moment, and forgotten things dawned upon me fast. The day we came to the hut, with the windy blast howling around us, the rain falling in sheets, then the fire my father made to warm me, and the rude meal we both partook of—each detail came back in bold relief.

"I stood musing over the many things I remembered of my life there, until my mind brought me up to the time we left, and then I recollected the last act performed by my father before leaving, an act which I now know concerned me much."

Jack paused, and Will, feeling very curious, waited in silence for him to proceed. It was some time before he went on, and then he spoke in a lower voice than he had hitherto adopted.

"Before leaving," he said, "my father buried a small leathern bag in a corner of the hut, and when he had finished he said, 'If ever you grow up to be a man, and come this way, you may dig it up; if not, let it lie there and rot for ever.'

"I was too young to attach much meaning to the words at the time, but last night they came upon me in full force. I found a spade in the hut, then I dug a hole and unearthed the leathern bag."

"This is getting interesting," said Will.

"It was so interesting to me," returned Jack, "that what I found there kept me busy for hours. The bag contained nothing but papers —things that a year ago must have been dumb to me. But you have taught me to read, Will, and they spoke to me last night."

"And what did they say?" asked Will.

"That I must not tell," returned Jack. "I know you will forgive me when I assure you that I would trust you with anything, but there are reasons why you should not know what I read last night."

"But where are these papers?"

"I have bound them round my waist," returned Jack. "And now I come to what I have to say to you. Should I fall in any accident or fight will you remove these papers and read them? What you learn there will tell you what to do."

"You leave me as trustee to you," said Will, smiling.

"A trustee who will find a thankless office," returned Jack: "but I know you and revere you, and I am certain that you will do as I wish for the love of me."

"I'll drink molten lead and eat fire for you," said Will.

"I do not care to tax you so far," replied Jack, "but I shall want you one day, when I go to claim my own."

"Ho! ho!" cried Will. "I scent a secret. I guess you can wear another name beside Jack Savage."

"Is your name Will Larkin?" asked Jack, smiling.

Will blushed a little, and looked down.

"Any name," he said, "is good enough for this country, I guess."

"Certainly," replied Jack. "I have for a long time thought as much. You are better bred than the generality of the men about me. But you will keep your secret and I will keep mine for the present."

"You know your name, then?"

"Yes."

"And the country where you were born?"

"Yes—I may tell you that much, and a little more—I am a native of Great Britain."

"I was certain of it," said Will.

"If this expedition ends well," said Jack, thoughtfully, "I shall break up my band and cross the seas, but I should like to go quietly."

"It must be done quietly if you intend to settle there."

"I should like you and Tom to go with me, Will—the rest I do not care for. They are good men in their way, but not quite the thing for civilised life."

"I, too, have a longing to go back," said Will, "and before I do so I will tell you the story of my life. It is too long to relate now, for I see Long Tom and the others returning."

"By the way," rejoined Jack, "there is one more I should wish to go with us. Not for our sake but for his. Snip is scarcely the man to be left in such a country as this."

"It will be a great country some day."

"Perhaps so, when Snip's bones are dust, and then the country won't matter much to Snip. The fellow is a great fool, but I cannot help being amused by him. He shall go with us if he will, but he must not know of our going until the last moment."

"Certainly not—one might as well preach

from the house-tops as confide in him. Well, Tom?"

"Back once more!" replied Tom, coming up; "all right except one man."

"Wounded?"

"No—missing."

"Who is it?"

"Snip."

"Snip again!" cried Jack. "I never saw such a fellow. If there is a wrong turning to be taken he takes it, or if there is a hole about he is sure to fall into it."

"Have you looked for him?"

"I shouted and hollered for him everywhere, but not making him hear we thought he had come back to the camp."

"He is not here."

"So Barton tells me. But where is he?"

"Ah! that's the point," said Will; then, turning to Jack, he added, in a low tone, "I am afraid your good intentions respecting our friend are nipped in the bud. He has fallen in with some of the vagabonds yonder, and they have sent him home before us."

"I do not think so," replied Jack; "he will surely turn up again, so we will wait a couple of hours for him."

"Leave him alone and he'll come home," sang Will. "By the way, is anything more to be done to the town?"

"Yes—it is only a nest of gamblers—there is not an honest man in the place," returned Jack.

"But they are all out of it."

"Those who haunt it will return as soon as we turn our backs," said Jack. "They are only skulking in the woods."

"Shall we follow them?"

"No—but I intend to prevent them herding together here for a time. The town shall be fired in every quarter, and I will not move until I am assured that it will be reduced to ashes. The houses are of wood and they will burn like tinder. There are no people in it, and so no lives will be lost."

"I should like to be sure of that," said Will.

"We will march through the streets and cry as we go, 'The town is about to be fired! All those who wish to leave may go in peace!' If none come forth we shall begin our work. Those who choose to skulk must take the consequences. Their lives be upon their heads."

Poor Snip!

CHAPTER XL.

FIRE.

SNIP's disappearance was a mysterious problem, but Tom had afforded a solution which really seemed to be the right one, and the others were inclined to accept it.

"I'm told," said Tom, "that he went ahead of the rest, and it's my 'pinion that he went straight through the town to the hut in search of the captain—that's what he did; and he's been and lost his way in the wood—that's what he's done; and he'll come back afore we start as lively as a cricket—that's what he'll do."

"Tom's about right," said Jack, and then Snip was dismissed from their minds.

The camp was soon busy, all the tents being struck and carefully packed away upon the backs of the mules.

Leaving a hundred men on guard our hero took the rest with him and went again to the town of Marena.

It was apparently entirely deserted.

"Fire!" cried Jack, in stentorian tones. "If any man, woman, or child is hiding here let them come forth, for I am about to fire the town. Fire! fire! fire!"

"Fire! fire!" roared the men.

And the terrible cry echoed far away among the hills, as if some gnome had taken it up, "Fire! fire!"

"Try them again," said Will. "One more shout before we begin. Fire! fire!"

"Fire! fire!" cried the men, and the air was full of the warning.

Then the men marched up and down the first street—or rather rough thoroughfare dignified by that name—repeating the cry; but nobody came forth—the place was deserted.

"Begin with the gambling saloons," cried Jack, pointing to the place where the two Spanish Dons had sat the previous night.

No crowd there now—saloon and balcony alike are deserted. The stillness of the grave was upon the place.

Two men ran forward with torches in their hands and entered the first floor. Others followed, and piled the gambling-tables and chairs in the centre of the room.

Under them they placed a quantity of dry rush matting, and then the torches were applied. The work of destruction had begun.

Slowly the first wreath of fire curled round the furniture, and the first burst of flame sailed towards the windows. As it mixed with the outer air it announced to Jack that the dread step was taken.

After this they went to a place opposite and performed a similar office, then a house a few paces down was honoured with a visit, and soon the street was a mass of flame.

"Nothing can save that," said Will. "We may go on, I think."

"The smoke is rising thickly," returned Jack, "and what a mass is behind yon house."

"That is not smoke," said Long Tom.

"What is it, then?"

"A cloud."

"Impossible!"

"It is, and there's a furious storm brewing. We may not get it here, but if we do we may want the shelter of some of these houses."

"I am resolved upon my work," replied Jack, firmly; "these houses are but the haunts of vice. On to our work. Fire—fire!"

"Sharp's the word, then," said Tom, looking back. "That was a vivid flash of lightning. Did you see it, Will?"

"I did, and it must have been terrible to those immediately near it."

"Perhaps we are not doing good work," said Tom, thoughtfully, "and the storm's against us."

"I have no superstition that way," said Will. "We have but to obey our leader, so come on."

In a few minutes more another of the roughly-constructed streets was fired.

The work was congenial to most of Jack's men, for they were of a rough order of humanity, and, but for the power he held over them, very little better than the men whom they antagonised. Jack knew how to make one evil work against another, and made good use of the material he had at hand.

The cry of "Fire!" went on, and the work never slackened. Up in a room of the largest and only substantial house in the place the cry was heard by two men.

Snip and Don Ricardo.

Through the perforations of that fatal box it came, and fell upon their ears with a significance which was terrible.

Both had suffered fearfully. Half stifled by the heat, and exhausted by their efforts to get out of their strange prison, they were resting in despair when the sound of the voices in the street came to them.

"Fire! fire!"

"What may this mean?" growled the Don.

"Who can tell?" groaned Snip. "When people shout fire there is sure to be a little smoke somewhere."

"Sacre! there is the cry again," hissed the Spaniard, glueing his ear to the side of the box to catch the slightest sound.

"I remember once at home," continued Snip, talking in a quiet, mechanical way, as if he had been set in motion like an automaton, "when the chimbley of the back parlour caught fire.

"My mother was boiling a bit of neck of mutton for dinner, and when she took the lid off to look at it down came a bit of fiery soot, as big as a man's hat, bang into the pot.

"Then we hears a scream outside, and my father rushes out and finds five feet of flames coming out of the top of the pot.

"Off he rushes for the engine without his hat and knocks over a butcher and his tray at the corner of the street."

"I hear the rush of flames!" muttered the terrified Don, quite oblivious of Snip's story.

"When dad got to the turncock's house," pursued Snip, speaking in the same mechanical way, and ignoring the Don's terror, "he finds the turncock out.

"'I think he's gone to the Goat and Compasses,' says his wife, and off rushes my father there.

"'He's been here,' says the landlord, 'but he's gone to the Green Man to play skittles with Mr. Snogges the baker.'

"Away goes my father to the Green Man, and tears into the middle of the ground just as the turncock was throwing the ball.

"It was a fourteen-pound ball and it was well throwed, for it caught my father just under the waistcoat and knocked him down insensible among the skittles.

"They was nearly half an hour bringing him round, and when he does come-to my father tells 'em what brought him there. Then he and the turncock and all the people rushes my father's house, when they finds the chimbley had burnt itself out.

"Then the turncock axes my father what he meant by calling him away from the game for nothin', when high words ensoos, and that night my parient went to bed with a black eye."

"Hush!" said the Don. "Do you hear anything?"

"Eh?" returned Snip, waking up like a man in deep sleep. "What did you say?"

"Do you hear anything?"

"No."

"Listen, then."

CHAPTER XLI.

THE SEARCH FOR GOLD.

SNIP was silent and strained his ears. After a few minutes he said—

"I hear a crackling noise."

"Yes—anything else?"

"A sound like the trickling of water."

"Aye, that's right—both sounds are from the same source."

"Are they?"

"Do you know what they mean?"

"No."

"They mean this," cried the Don, clutching his hair in a frenzy, "that the house is on fire, and we shall be roasted alive. It is too awful."

"It can't be true," gasped Snip. "Who has set the house on fire?"

"Those wretches, Jack Savage and his men. Listen! Do you not hear them? They knew we were here."

"Jack would never do such a thing," said Snip. "I know him better."

"It is done!" yelled the Don, frantically, "and they stand outside mocking us."

The men were still in the street, crying "Fire! fire!" and Snip heard them plainly. His dismay passed all bounds, and he groaned aloud—

"Perhaps they are only joking!"

"The box is growing hot!" yelled the Don. "The flames are around us! Do you call that a joke? Help! help!"

"Fire! fire!" cried the voices outside, sounding as if the men were moving away.

"Help! help!" shrieked the Don and Snip in concert.

"Fire! fire!" cried the men, their voices fading away.

"Help! help!" yelled the imprisoned men.

"Fire! fire!" once more cried the men outside, and then their voices died away.

"Nothing can save us now!" yelled the Don.

"We are dead men!" gasped Snip, and then the imprisoned pair beat the sides of their prison-house like frantic beings, and shrieked madly, but they shrieked in vain, for Jack's men marched out of Marena and left them to their fate.

* * * * * *

Two months have elapsed since the events narrated in our last chapter, and we must now carry our readers to a fresh scene, still keeping before them the old faces.

Under a broiling sun Jack Savage and his men toiled across a sandy plain. The whole band bore signs of hardship and travel, and a few of the faces were missing.

On their way they had oft encountered hostile tribes of Indians, some of whom had merely menaced them and retired, while others had shown more courage and made a fight for the territory of their people.

Stout hearts and firearms had carried the day, but some of his people had fallen, and Jack lacked full twenty men of the number which had marched with him out of the town of Marena.

But these were only some of the rank and file. Jack and Tom and Will had escaped unhurt, and the meeting with the various bands of Indians had only been so many breaks in the monotony of their wandering lives.

Tom was their guide. He knew the direction where gold was supposed to lie, and he kept a western course.

Through forests and over vast plains they had come, sometimes without any impediment, but oft the road was rough and almost impassable, which could only be crawled over at the pace popularly attributed to a snail.

But hardships were nothing to these men—they had surmounted them all, and were now upon a plain which, according to Long Tom, bordered upon the land of gold.

"It's a rich land," he said; "but no man ever had a chance of searching it. We shall be first in the field, lads, and when our pockets are full the rest of the world shall know of it."

"Hurrah for long Tom !" shouted the men, all eager for the promised wealth.

Jack smiled. It was the first time a cheer had been given by his men for any but him.

"Gold is the god of many men," he said, "and great is the pity ; but it is so, and it will be so to the end of time, I fear."

"Men love gold for what it produces," returned Will.

"But there are some who love it for itself," said Jack, "as I know, and my father knew before me. It was the curse of my race, but there, Will, I must not talk further, or I shall be letting out secrets. I only obey my father when I keep them from you—so forgive me, Will."

"Freely, Jack ; but what think you of this expedition—shall we find gold ?"

"Yes, for already I see signs of it here-abouts—signs which my father oft spoke about. He had not travelled in such places as this, but was a great scholar, and knew most things. You see that stone—the one small and rough ?"

"Yes."

"That is a piece of quartz. Crush and wash it and you will find gold."

"I am not over greedy," said Will, "but upon my word I shall not be sorry to set my eyes upon a little of the yellow metal."

"You will fill your pockets before we leave this place."

"Not my pockets, for they are full of holes," laughed Will ; "we sadly miss our little tailor, poor Snip."

"I have often wondered what could have happened to him," said Jack, in a thoughtful way. "There were many knaves in the town ready and ripe for murder, but men seldom murder except for revenge or gain. As Snip was a stranger revenge could not have been the motive, and as for gain, he had nothing to lose."

"It is a mystery," returned Will. "But he was a wonderful fellow for getting into the wrong shop. You remember his miraculous escape from Don Ricardo and his crew ?"

"Yes."

"Then he dished the Pawnees pretty cleverly. But I am afraid he is done for this time."

"He may turn up again."

"Never."

"Sometimes I think he will," said Jack. "He has a great knack of getting out of scrapes."

"But how can he possibly come here ? If he was alive, why did he not show up at Marena ? If dead, he of course lies under the ashes of the town."

"I cannot tell how it will be done," returned Jack, "but I feel convinced that he will crop up again as he has cropped up before. Snip has a genius for such things."

".Danger ahead, captain !" sang out Long Tom.

"Where away ?" asked Jack.

Long Tom came running up, pointing to the horizon. Apparently there was but little to be seen except the rank grass and the setting sun.

"I see nothing, Tom," said Will.

"Run your eye along the horizon and look at that clump in the distance."

"A small knoll of trees ?"

"No, Will, them are Injuns on horseback. They were moving a minute ago, but they've sighted us, and are halting to reconnoitre."

"They are moving again," said Jack ; "but their numbers appear to be few."

"Only a scouting party, captain," said Tom. "The rest aint far away."

"It's a great nuisance," muttered Will. "I thought we had got rid of those fellows."

"The Indians may only be moving to another hunting ground," suggested our hero. "I think we had better rest for an hour or two, and keep an eye upon them."

"In an hour the sun will be gone," said Tom, "and if they've sighted us it will be an easy matter for them to fall foul of us in the dark."

"And an easy matter for us to give them more than they seek," returned Jack, quietly.

The word to rest was given and the men lay down. The mules also stretched themselves at full length amongst the luxuriant herbage.

Jack kept his eyes upon a dark patch on the horizon, and soon it broke up into pieces as the Indians moved onwards in a northerly direction.

In a few minutes another patch appeared on the horizon, then another, and another, until several bands of Indians were moving before his vision.

Apparently the foremost band was satisfied, and went on without making any visible communication with the rest, but Jack knew them too well to rely upon this, and he saw that his foes, if foes they should prove to be, would very far outnumber him.

"I don't like turning tail, but I think it prudent to give those fellows a wide berth," said Jack.

"The men are fatigued," replied Will, "and tired of unprofitable fighting. "What will you do ?"

"Wait until dark and then move on. If they intend to fight us by so doing we may elude them, at any rate we shall be so many miles further on our way."

When the sun sank to rest and darkness came on Jack and the hardy wanderers started and marched throughout the night, halting only just before dawn for a little needful repose.

Eager eyes were ready to take a view of the plain as soon as it was visible. A dense mist lay upon the grass, but this rolled quickly away before the sun, and to the relief of all the vast flat land was clear.

"They did not see us," was the general comment.

"So you may think," replied Long Tom ; "but Injun eyes have grown much weaker this last few years if they didn't."

"They are gone," urged some.

"Gone ! yes—that's the way with them," said Long Tom ; "gone to come back again just when you don't want 'em."

◁◆ GIANT JACK: ▷◆

A Story of the Red Mountains.

"IF THERE IS ONE WHO LOVES THE PAWNEE TRIBE MORE THAN THE REST LET HIM KILL THE MORNING DAWN!" CRIED THE WOLF.

" 'Tis best not to anticipate evil," said Will. "For the present the sun is shining and the coast is clear, so hurrah for the land of gold !"

They rested a couple of hours, then moved on, and presently a range of hills appeared in sight.

The hearts of many beat fast, for Tom had told them that the gold lay among these hills, and the step of everyone involuntarily quickened.

Late in the afternoon they came up to the hills, and entered the range by a gorge, with Jack Savage at their head. Anything more barren and cheerless never was seen.

Huge rocks piled one upon another, heaps of stones, a few blades of rank grass, lichens growing here and there, and nothing more.

But where was the gold? Nothing so bright and pleasing to the eye was to be seen. The whole place was sterile, comfortless, and hopeless.

"I don't see much chance of picking up the dust here," said one of the men.

This remark was overheard by Tom, who looked a little gloomy. The prospect was certainly not cheering.

"I've never been in the gold country," said Tom ; "but I hope we are on the right road."

"The place is enough to give one the toothache," returned Will ; "but perhaps we shall find something better further on."

"Yes—we had better go further on," said Jack, with one of his quiet smiles.

They marched for an hour or two through the gorge, and then came upon a sort of basin between the hills.

Here matters did not improve. The very spirit of desolation seemed to have taken up its abode in the spot, and nothing was visible but ugly and barren rocks.

"This is a good look-out," said one of the men, with a bitter curse ; "we may thank that old fool, Long Tom, for bringing us here to starve and die."

"I did it for the best," said Tom ; "don t fall foul of a man when he does his best."

"Patience, my men," said Jack, "all may not be so bad as it looks ; we will halt here now and move on to-morrow, when we may come upon a better and brighter land."

"If we don't," returned one of the chief grumblers, "I shall make one for going back."

"You will go on," returned Jack, sternly, "when I give the word, and halt when I bid you halt. The man who disobeys me dies."

They knew him well, and every man was silent. Rations were served out, and then the men sought repose.

The morrow saw them again upon their march —Jack being their guide, vice Long Tom retired, for he was disheartened by the country, and gave up his post in despair.

"I'm afraid I've been misled," he said. "There's nothing but stones, and rocks, and moss about here. So why go any further ?"

"Because it is my bidding," returned Jack, and with that Long Tom was obliged to be content.

CHAPTER XLII.

VIRTUE REWARDED.

It is a bad thing to be popular, for unpopularity is but too often only one step behind. The mind of a mob changes with great rapidity, and he who is overwhelmed with praise one moment runs the risk of being stoned and beaten the next.

Thus it was with Tom.

Hitherto he had been the idol of the men, or, at least, had been so on their last march—he was the guide to wealth, the man who was leading them to a land of untold riches, so what Tom said was law, and what he did was the summit of human perfection.

But how soon all changed !

The sterile country he had brought them to looked so unpromising that all hope died at once, and they felt like hungry men who had been promised an excellent dinner and then placed before a table with nothing upon it but dish-covers and empty dishes.

It was tantalising, and it is dangerous work to tantalise hungry men.

On the first blush of disappointment they would have gone back but for Jack, whose commands at all times had to be obeyed.

"March on !" was the command given, and they marched on, with bent heads and sullen brows.

The mules bore upon their backs a number of skins filled with water, but these were soon emptied by the men, who found the barren road a great incentive to thirst, and then eager eyes commenced looking about for a spring.

They might as well have looked for a roadside inn with excellent bitter beer on draught.

"Where are we going to ?" was the general query. "What does the captain mean—does he want to let us all die from starvation and thirst ?"

Starvation was not near, for they still had many days' rations ; but eating when the throat is parched is very difficult, and the longing for food often dies entirely away.

But no man ventured to remonstrate. Jack was not accustomed to it. He was the leader, and would be obeyed. To disobey, as he had hinted, was to risk life.

Poor Tom ! he was sadly dejected. He had been so certain all along that he was on the right track, and had indulged in such golden visions of fabulous wealth, that his disappointment, without the addition of his unpopularity, was enough to break him down.

"It's a mighty blunder," he said to Jack ; "but I can't help it now. I wish you would turn back."

"Why ?" asked Jack.

"We shall starve here."

"It is two days' journey back," said Jack, "and we must soon get through this range of hills."

"They last a mighty way further yet," returned Tom, despairingly. "I climbed a peak afore we started this morning, and, although it wasn't quite light, I could see nothing but those blessed hills running ever so far away."

"Did you see anything else ?"

"The hill-tops was enough for me, Jack. Oh ! let us turn back, and bear the disappointment as best we can."

"I said we would go on," replied Jack, "and go on we will, if we drop and die off one by one. You know me, Tom."

"All my fault," groaned Tom.

"You acted for the best," returned Jack, and then said no more.

Tom's apprehension was shared by Will, but

he said nothing to Jack. If his leader wished to go on, that was enough. He acted in accordance with his wishes, and made no complaint.

As matters grew apparently worse the sullenness of the men increased. They had been nearly twenty-four hours without water, and when they laid down to rest on the fourth night of their pilgrimage in the barren land their bitterness knew no bounds. Under their breath they cursed the man who had brought them there, and the leader who persisted in keeping them marching onward against their will.

There were dark, sullen minds in the camp—men who had done desperate deeds in their lifetime, and were prepared, if pushed, to do them again.

Some of them, enraged against their leader, resolved to murder him to obtain their liberty. Living, they feared him, for they knew that if a man were missing he would be pursued and captured.

But Jack slept not that night. As if instinctively knowing his danger, he kept walking up and down among the men, and none dared lay a finger upon him. Awake he was too terrible to assault, sleeping they might have slain him.

Parched lips and dry throats cursed him with the morning light, but none ventured to disobey his command to move forward, and the band slunk along in silence, with heads bowed down.

Jack, with a look of quiet determination on his face, led the van. Will was by his side, and Tom walked a few paces in the rear, the very picture of disappointment.

"Oh, for a spring of water !" said Will, licking his dry lips.

"I thirst with you," returned Jack; "but there is no water here."

"Some of the men will break down to-day."

"None of the men will break down, Will."

"Why not, Jack ?"

"In an hour we shall find water. It is but a short distance ahead."

"Would that it may prove you speak truly !"

"I am sure of it. Tom climbed a peak the other morning, and saw nothing but barren hills. I climbed one this morning, and saw signs of fruitful valleys. Look at the rocks—see the number of the lichens now, the thickness and softness of the moss, the height of the grass, these are all signs of our approaching water."

"You know about these things better than I do, Jack."

"I know them so well that I am certain of what I say," was the reply.

Their path lay through a narrow gorge, which wound round in a serpentine way, hiding all save the immediate prospect from view, and this, to the general vision, was as barren as before.

But Will, having obtained a clue from his leader, soon discovered a change in little things—the moss and patches of grass were greener and more plentiful, and then they came across a small flower-bearing plant, which seemed to the eyes of Will the very emblem of hope. He would have expressed as much to the men, but Jack forbade it.

"No," he said; "wait a little while, then we will give them cause to shout."

The little while was soon over, for a sudden turn of the gorge brought Jack and his men within view of a fruitful valley, through which

a stream was calmly flowing.

"Forward !" cried Jack; "you who thirst can drink your fill."

With a shout of joy the men ran forward, and soon the banks of the stream were fringed with their recumbent forms, lapping up the cool, glittering water. The mules, too, trotted down to the river and drank to their hearts' content.

The men gathered the fine, luscious fruit, and ate greedily, until satiated appetite cried "Hold !" Then they gave in, and, throwing themselves upon the soft turf, lay like luxuriating Turks.

Their thirst for water was appeased, but their thirst for gold still remained unsatisfied.

"My men," cried Jack, "here is our camping-ground for awhile, for there is fruit and water in abundance, and here we shall find plenty of game, which some of us can catch, while the others get the gold."

"The gold !" repeated a dozen suppressed voices.

"Yes," replied Jack, "the gold—it lies in that barren region behind. We have but to seek and it will be found. I knew it when we were marching across its rugged and sterile wastes, but I feared to tell you until I had found a safe camping-ground. We have the camping-ground here, and now the search for gold need not bring upon us destruction, as it must have done had you halted in that desolate spot."

Then uprose a mighty shout, and all the men shook hands with Jack and Tom until their aching arms could shake no more.

"Now, this," said Tom, as he sat panting upon the ground after his involuntary exercise, "is what I calls the reward of vartue."

CHAPTER XLIII.
WEALTH FOR ALL.

THE sagacity of our hero was duly appreciated by his men. He saw at once, when they entered the barren region, that they had fallen upon the land of gold, but he said nothing about it until he had found a suitable camping-ground, for those who work must eat and drink, and the rocky land between the hills gave neither food nor water.

But in this fruitful valley everything was different. Sheltered by a complete circle of hills, and hitherto untrodden by the foot of man, it was rich in every requirement to sustain life.

There were rabbits and hares by the thousand, birds without number, and fruit enough for a nation. And, to crown all, there was a plentiful supply of pure water.

It was, indeed, a lovely place, and, as far as beauty went, might have been the original Paradise where our forefather and his mate opened the way to sin and misery, and left them as an inheritance to countless generations.

But what mattered the beauty of the place to the main body of the band !

They were glad of it on account of its food-providing resources, but all their ideas were centred on gain. They had no earnest desire for anything except the yellow metal lying under the surface of the earth in the Valley of Desolation through which they had travelled.

Even Will Larkin and Tom had a serious touch of gold fever. Both had need of wealth, especially Will, who had a use for it, as time and our story will reveal.

But Will was not quite dead to the beauty of the Paradise on which the adventurers had fallen.

There was a deal of poetry in the young fellow, which found response in his leader, and the two chose a snug retreat away from the main body, where they swung their hammocks under the boughs of a huge walnut tree, whose branches mingled with those of a prickly pear, and thus placed the rich fruit in their very grasp as they lay at rest.

"Here we abide by ourselves," said Will, "and rub off the rust of the day's work with a little communion, Jack."

"We shall not bore each other, Will."

"No, that is not likely to come yet; but the talk of the rest will be of gold—gold—nothing but gold—that is, if we find it."

"We shall find more," said Jack, quietly, "than our whole party, man and beast, can carry away."

"Some of it will be welcome to me," rejoined Will, thoughtfully, "for if I can only get home with a cargo of it I shall be a happy man."

"I never thought you were fond of gold, Will."

"No more I am, Jack; but I have work to do with it—the wronged to be righted, the weak to be strengthened. It was not for myself I spoke."

"Your pardon, Will. I ought to have known you better."

"You need not apologise," said Will, smiling. "I forgive you."

Their hammocks being swung, and their private properly arranged around, they went back to the men, where the preparations for the gold-seeking were going briskly on.

All the live stock—the mules and mustangs—were stabled under a rough shelter formed of the boughs of trees, and around this the men had set up their tents.

Some were digging hollows in the earth, wherein to construct rude cooking ovens and smelting furnaces, while others were making "cradles" to wash the dirt and gather the gold in, and a few were engaged in making boxes to carry home the wealth they hoped to find.

Knowing the value of order, Jack at once arranged his company into working and resting parties, the so-called resting parties having to occupy their time in cooking and washing the dirt at home.

Some rough wooden panniers were also made by his orders, in which the mules were to carry the dirt to the stream for washing, and these were made very strong and sound, so that none of the valuable soil could escape during transit.

"Gold is very heavy," he said, "and quickly filters through, especially when jolted about. We must have all our tools sound and strong. When they are ready we may begin."

The men were naturally impatient, but Jack was firm, and they knew their man too well to disobey, so they worked for three days in making needful preparations, and then the real work began.

The first party went out with Jack at their head, and they had retraced their steps about a mile only when he called a halt.

They were now in a very deep part of the gorge, where it seemed as if the hills had been rent in twain by some violent commotion of nature. But time and rough weather had pulverised the surface and broken up the face of the rock in many places, giving growing room to various specimens of moss and lichen, which showed great abundance.

Will accompanied his leader, but Long Tom had been left behind with the resting party, much to his inward disgust. But Tom did his best to put on a smiling face as they left him at his post.

"I guess I'll do a bit of digging to-morrow," he muttered, "and I'll bring back such a bag of gold as will open the peepers of all of you."

But let us return to Jack and his men. As soon as he called a halt the men wanted to begin digging there and then, in a helter-skelter sort of manner, without method or any regard to the appearance of the soil. But Jack quickly checked them.

"Order, there!" he cried. "You won't find the metal growing like potatoes. Fall in!"

The men muttered a little, but fell in two deep, and told themselves off like well-drilled soldiers.

"File one and two!" cried Jack, "fall out and fill two boxes with earth."

The foremost mule—they had brought all the mules with them—was led out, and the four men called upon proceeded to fill the boxes.

Jack walked on a few paces, looking here and there. Suddenly he halted and called for the next two files, whom he likewise set to work.

And in this way he went moving about until all his band were engaged.

Will remained by his side, wondering why he selected the spots in which he ordered the men to dig; but he had great faith in his leader, and let him go on until the men were all busy, then he asked him to tell him by what rule he had been guided.

"A very simple one," said Jack. "You see that feathery kind of moss there, mixed with the lichen, which looks like so many cups?"

"Yes."

"Well, where you see those two together in a gold region there you will find gold."

"How do you account for it?"

"I do not attempt to account for it, Will. I have my father's authority for it, and unless he is mistaken we shall find gold here."

"I don't see any at present," said Will.

"Perhaps not, and we shall not often find it in lumps."

"The earth looks wonderfully black and soft. It is a very different sort of stuff I hoped to find here," said Will, handling it. "It doesn't glitter at all."

"Indeed!" said Jack, quietly.

"Not a bit," replied Will, with a disappointed look. I don't think there is an atom of gold in it."

"I am not certain we are in a gold region," said Jack; "perhaps I have spoken too sanguinely, but I have seen signs here which my father's books say indicate the presence of gold. If mistaken I am sorry."

"Oh! don't talk of being mistaken," said Will, turning pale. "That would not do at any price."

"We are men," returned Jack, "and must bear our disappointment, if we are to have one, like men."

Will looked very dubious, and the expression upon his face was reflected by many of the men, who shovelled the earth into the boxes with moody faces, and grumbled and growled like so many bears with very tender heads.

"If there's gold among this stuff," said one, "I'll eat my grandfather's long-tailed coat, and swallow a hundredweight of nails as a sauce to it."

"WE are under orders," growled another of Jack's party, "or I'm blessed if I'd put spade into this rubbish. The captain's wrong for once, I guess. This aint a proper gold field."

"No, I reckon it aint."

"Why I've heerd of men," continued the previous speaker, "who have come across gold in lumps."

"That's how gold ought to be found."

"Ah! and lumps as big as your head—such as one man couldn't lift. I had a cousin, a sailor, who landed on the Hafrican coast and went up country, where he saw houses made of it."

"That cousin of you'rn," said the other, "ought to have brought home a house to live in."

"He would have done it," said the narrator, "but that the natives were so savage. They cut his nose half off and slit his ears, so that he was glad to get away, gold or no gold, I can tell you. But my cousin warn't a liar, if some people are, and he saw them houses or my name aint Jim Spratt and my father didn't deal in horses."

Having thus announced his faith in his cousin's veracity, Jim Spratt threw the final shovelful of earth into the box with an expression of contempt, and declared himself ready to move as soon as he received orders.

"We may as well lay on our backs and eat prickly pears," he said, "as to go on at this game. The captain's having a lark with us."

Mr. James Spratt was not the only grumbler, and some of them talked louder than he did, so that Jack, walking in their midst, could not fail to hear them; but he paid no heed to anything he heard, maintaining through all a satisfied look upon his handsome face.

As soon as all the mules were laden he gave the word to return, and he headed a party almost as sullen and downcast as that which, three days before, had crawled into the fruitful valley.

The "resting" party, having had an easy day of it, came running forward to know what luck they had experienced, and found an answer in the discontented faces of their friends.

Long Tom took Will's arm.

"Any gold?" he asked.

"There is some earth," returned Will, with a half-mournful, half-comical look at his leader, "and it is as black as our hats. If you can see gold in it, Tom, I can't."

"It's roughish," returned Tom, feeling it, "but there s no gold in it."

"Will you bet on that?" asked Jack; "not that I ever bet, but I will do it this once."

"I'll bet my first month's share that there is nothing in this lot," said Tom.

"Done!"

"Done with you!"

"That's a bet," said Will, "and I am witness, but I hope you've not been rash, Tom."

"Rash!" returned Tom, contemptuously; "do you think I don't know gold when I see it? And if it were mixed up with this stuff shouldn't

I see it? Haven't I got eyes in my head?"

"Logically argued," rejoined Will, with a rin, "but the proof of the pudding is in the eating, and the proof of the gold will be in the washing."

"Fill the cradles," said Jack.

So the cradles were filled and the washing began. The process was rather a long one, and had to be carefully performed; but, in spite of this disbelief, the men were all interested, and worked willingly.

With his own hands Jack worked one of the cradles, and as the earth was gradually washed away, Long Tom kept his eyes fixed upon the residuum with an expression of hope and fear which was rather comical.

"You have made a good bet of it, Tom," said Will. "If there is gold you lose your share."

"And if there isn't I gain the captain's," returned Tom.

"Just so—but where will the captain's share come from? If there is no gold there can't be any share."

"I guess," said Tom, wrathfully, "that I've been took in here."

"You made the bet yourself, Tom," replied Jack. "But if you want it off say the word and it is off."

"I'm not the man to go from my word," said Tom. "If there's gold I lose my month's share."

"Don't be pig-headed, man," said Jack; "the bet was a foolish one. Have it off. I don't want any share but my own."

"But it's mean, Jack."

"Not a bit of it."

"Then, if you don't mind," said Tom, slowly, "I'd rather have that bet off, for I'm darned if I don't think my head must have been like an addled egg when I made it."

"It's just as well it is off, Tom."

"Perhaps it is—perhaps it won't make any difference."

"I know it will," cried Jack, suddenly tilting the cradle towards him, "for look here, old boy—here's something to gladden your eyes and send the blood galloping through your heart."

Tom looked, as he was bidden to, and beheld, lying at the bottom of the cradle, a coating of the finest gold.

CHAPTER XLIV.

TOM'S CUTENESS.

AYE! there it was—a quantity of the metal which men of the world too often make their god. Gold, gold!—fine glittering gold, purified by contact with the cold earth, and faintly reflecting the radiant beams of the sun.

The men came crowding round and looked upon this, the first offspring of their work, with beaming eyes, mantling cheeks, and quick-throbbing hearts, as if they had found all the bliss they sought. Then, when they had feasted sufficiently on the welcome vision, they hurried back to their own cradles and rocked them like frenzied men.

"Steady, there!" cried Jack, "you will waste more than you save. This work, if done at all, must be well done."

They paused upon hearing this, and went to work in a quieter manner. Soon cradle after cradle was washed, and at the bottom of all a goodly quantity of the metal was found.

Then what a cry uprose ! Shout after shout rent the air, they tossed their hats about and shook hands with each other again and again, and some even wept in the excess of joy which overcame them. But soon they became calmer and the gold was gathered up and put away.

"If you shout so loud," said Jack, laughing, "you will bring half the world around you."

Absurd as the suggestion was, the men were half inclined to believe it, and actually spoke to each other in a lower tone, as if they feared to bring more people to share with them.

During the evening meal many a story was told, but they were all in the same strain—accounts of fabulous wealth, and of wonderful discoveries made by our forefathers and the old sea captains, who went prowling about the earth and sea in days long since gone by.

Gold ! gold ! was there, and nearly all else but gold was forgotten.

Many there would have given up their night's rest and gone out to dig again, but they were under a wise captain, who foresaw this madness, and bade none of them leave the camp on peril of their lives, so they sat and fretted and frowned until they fell asleep.

Among the impatient, none were more so than our friend Long Tom, who was to command the working party on the morrow. He had been wrong in his calculations, and he thirsted for an opportunity to retrieve his character.

"I guess," he said, "that I'll do good work to-morrow, and bring home a pile of the real stuff."

"I hope you will," said Jack.

"And I don't think you will," added Will Larkin, who felt disposed to be contradictory.

"You don't think so !" cried Tom, very savage, "what's put that into your pumpkin head ?"

"I don't think you know where to look for it," said Will, winking at Jack.

"If there is anything I hate in this world," said Tom, "it is a born young fool."

"You can't be born an old fool," returned Will, "but a man may grow into one, you know."

"That is, you mean I am an old fool ?"

"On my word I mean nothing of the sort."

"If I am a fool I am one," said Tom, rising ; "but if I don't make you sing small arter my work to-morrow I'll eat the first pick and shovel as comes handy."

Tom went away in a very wrathful mood, leaving his young friend in high glee. Will was very fond of " getting a rise out of Tom," but it never resulted in anything serious. A few soft words always turned away Tom's wrath, and peace was easily made.

"It's a glorious night," said Jack, stretching himself upon his back and looking at the stars.

"It is more than earthly, Jack ; we ought to live and die here contented."

"Yes, Will, here is peace itself."

"With one I know," continued Will, "I could live on here very comfortable for ever."

"That is, with one of the other sex ?" said Jack.

"Just so," returned Will ; "here we should be happy indeed." And Will, stretching himself out, looked up at the stars also, and pictured to himself no end of domestic felicity in that

place, little thinking how soon it would become the scene of strife, hatred, blasphemy, bloodshed, and a thousand other sins which have fallen upon our race.

"I have often thought of telling you a story," said Will, after a long pause ; "it is the story of my life—short, and tolerably interesting. The camp is quiet, and all are asleep, I think. Shall I tell it now ?"

"You could not do a thing which would interest me more," replied our hero. "But do not tell me more than you wish."

"I have nothing to conceal," returned Will. "My real name," he continued, "is Eardley Talbot, and I am the eldest son of Sir Eardley Talbot, who owns a very decent family estate in Berkshire. It does not become any man to speak ill of his parents, but I must say a few truthful words concerning my father, or my story will be anything but clear to you.

"In plain terms, my father is a thoughtless, dissipated man of the world. He married my mother for her money, spent it, and then—pardon me, but the truth must out—killed her not as common men kill their wives, with a knife or a hatchet, but with unkindness—inch by inch he slew her.

"I, as a child, was a witness to this, and clung to the mother I loved. For this reason, if for no other, my father honoured me with the most perfect hatred a father ever entertained towards a son, and the unkindness bestowed upon my mother was, with the same liberality, bestowed upon me.

"Many and many a time we—my mother and I—have sat trembling in the upper part of the house, listening to the rioting below, and knowing that the termination of the feast would be the beginning of fresh scenes of misery for us, for it was my father's custom in the afternoon or evening to fill himself with drink, and then seek us out and swear himself sober.

"Such scenes passed within the walls of our house as would make your blood curdle to hear. Young gentlemen with plenty of ready cash, but minus of common sense, were lured there to their destruction."

CHAPTER XLV.

WILL LARKIN CONTINUES THE STORY OF HIS LIFE.

"IN the world my father passed for a finehearted, free, generous sort of fellow—one who would put his hand in his pocket and do a good turn for any man—but we at home only knew him as a violent brute, who never addressed us without an oath, and too often supplemented it with a blow.

"After several years of this my mother died, and her last words were words of regret that she had to leave me behind her. I was then sixteen, and, you may be sure, had no wish to give up my life just then ; but I really did wish at that moment that I could lay down my life in place of hers, and leave the world for her.

"But it was not to be—she died, and I was left. My father followed her to the grave halfdrunk and weeping copiously, but my eyes were dry when I looked at him—my heart alone shed tears.

"My mother's death did him a little good, but in a month he broke out again and was as bad as ever, and now he endeavoured to vent his double rage on me.   But he had reckoned without his host.

"While my mother was alive I had offered no resistance—all that he inflicted upon me I bore in quietude for her sake ; but now that she was dead I had no such restraint upon me, and I resolved if violence was offered me to resist with all my youthful powers.

"One night he entertained a lot of hunting fellows, who drank, and sang, and shouted like so many mad jackasses, until the night was far spent, and then they either rode home like furies or staggered up to bed like the swine they were.

"My father was the last to leave the table, and I heard him coming straight to my room. The time had come at last, and I was resolved to resist.

"Having barricaded my door with a chest of drawers, and other things, I threw myself on the bed and awaited his coming.

"He blundered up to the landing, banged savagely against the door, seized the handle and turned it.   Then he pushed, and, finding he was resisted, swore a deep oath.

"'Open here !' he cried, smiting the door with a heavy hand.

"I lay perfectly quiet, but my heart beat a little faster—that I could not help, but I promise you that I felt no fear.

"My father paced up and down the landing for a few moments, then he came to the door again.

"'Open here, Eardley,' he cried ; 'open the door, or it will be the worse for you.'

"'What do you want, sir?' I asked, yawning, and pretending that I was just aroused from a sleep.

"'Open the door, and don't ask impertinent questions,' was the answer.

"I stood for a few moments reflecting—then I said, quietly, but loud enough for him to hear—

"'You want to beat me, sir, and I am too old to be beaten—I do not like it.'

"'Who cares for what you like?' he said. 'Open the door this instant, or I swear to you I will break it in.'

"'And I swear to you, sir,' I cried, now thoroughly aroused to the resolution I had formed, 'I swear to you that if you touch the door again I will throw myself from the window.'

"I spoke earnestly, and it checked him. For some time he walked to and fro, and I could hear him muttering something to himself, but at last he went down stairs, and came near me no more that night.

"But I knew the contest was not over.   He was not the man to yield to a first impulse, and I was sure that there was more to be expected from him.

"I was right.

"In the morning he came again, and spoke to me in softer tones.

"'Eardley—Eardley !'

"'What is it, sir ?' I asked again.

"'Come out, and let us talk this over,' he said.

"'Will you give me your word not to strike me ?' I inquired.

"There was a pause, and I could hear a tapping, which I knew was the sound of a hunting-whip against a boot.

"'I give my word,' he said.   Then I took down the barricade and went out.

"My father was there with a lowering brow and a heavy whip in his mind.   But I did not fear him—he had given his word, and that a Wilmot dare not break.

"We went down to the breakfast-room, and there we sat down at the table opposite each other.

"'So, sir,' he said, 'you rebel, do you?'

"'No, sir,' I replied, 'but I resist—I am too old to be beaten.'

"'Indeed !' he sneered.

"'Yes, sir,' I said, 'and I will not endure it. In all lawful things I will obey, but if you beat me I will not answer for the consequences.'

"'Perhaps you would strike again ?' he asked, savagely.

"'No, sir,' I replied, 'but I will take means to let the world know what you really are, and they shall read the truth of what I will declare before my death, for live I will not and cannot under such cruelty.'

"I know it was very wrong of me even to hint at such a desperate measure, but I was mad and knew not what I said.   Perhaps I did not mean it—I now most fervently hope to Heaven I did not.

"My father sat looking into his plate in silence for a time, then he looked up and said, quietly—

"Be it so—I will never lay a hand upon you again.   But I will so mortgage the estate that there shall not be a penny left for you when I die.   I cannot take away your name, but you will have that alone to help you through the world.   I hated your mother, and I hate you. Leave the room, sir."

"'I am sorry you hate me, sir,' I said, getting up ; 'but I cannot help it.   As for the estate, do what you please with it.   Mortgage it as deep as you like.   I will go out into the world, make a fortune, and come back and buy it when you are dead.'

"It was a boy's vaunt, and he might well laugh ; but I was in earnest, and really believed that I should be successful.

"Boys are sanguine little fellows, and think they have only to try a thing to succeed.

"From this hour the severance between my father and myself was complete, but I had gained my point, and he struck me no more.

"He left me to myself, and took no steps to give me a profession, or ever said anything concerning my education.

"Once I hinted that I should like to go to college, at which he laughed heartily, but with a ring of sarcastic contempt in his voice, and I never broached the subject again.

"I was left to wander about the woods at my own sweet will.   I had a home, but it was no home, and I saw it going away piecemeal, for my father was carrying out his threat, and spending money right and left.

"What caused this unnatural frenzy I cannot say, and I assure you that I was more grieved than angry when I saw it.   Ruin was fast coming upon my home, and I resolved to make one last effort to save it.

"Choosing a time when my father was suffering from a late debauch, I went boldly into his room and entered straight upon the subject.

"'Father,' I said, 'are you lost to all ties of affection—are you resolved upon this course ? Is it, indeed, your wish that I shall be a pauper?"

"'I will beggar you,' he answered, with an imperious wave of his hand, and I left him.

"I knew it was in vain to argue with him, so I went away to my own little room, where I put a few necessary things together, and stole out of the house, with very little hope within me of ever returning.

"I got a lift across the seas—worked my way over, in fact—and landed upon the new continent, where I was buffeted about, here and there, until you met me, Jack, and the rest you know."

"I feel very sorry for you, Will," said Jack, in a soft tone. "Have you ever heard of him since?"

"Never."

"Have you written?"

"Whenever I was near a post, but that was not often, and if he had replied I do not think I could have received the letter, for I have always been moving from one place to another."

"No, I suppose not," said Jack. "I do not understand these matters, reading and writing are new things to me. Are you tired?"

"Rather."

"So am I, and a few hours' sleep won't do either of us any harm. Good-night."

"Good-night, Jack."

Then they lay down side by side and quickly found the repose they sought, for the great restorer comes to the young and healthy without much wooing.

In the morning they were aroused by Tom, who was calling the men to their task, and they, all eagerness, quickly responded.

Jack and Will, who had slept on the ground, forgetful of their hammocks, were soon moving about, inspecting the camp while breakfast was being prepared.

When the meal was over Tom called his band together and prepared to march, but before going he addressed a few words to Jack.

"I guess I'll bring home something good," he said, "so get your cradles ready, my boy."

Jack shook hands with him and wished him luck.

Then the working party moved away, and the resting party busied themselves until sunset with washing some of the earth which had been left from the day before, when Tom and his followers were seen coming home.

There was a triumphant look upon the old man's face which was good to see, and he swaggered up to Jack with the air of a conqueror.

"I went a little further afield," he said; "but I came across the right stuff, I bet, full of gold, and yellow as a guinea. Now, lads, out with the dust, and put the cradles to work."

Jack went up to the boxes borne by the mules, and handled the earth brought back by Tom with a curious look upon his face. But he said nothing, and soon the cradles were rocking to and fro.

Long Tom worked at one of the largest, and the earth soon faded away under the frequent ablutions he bestowed upon it, until nothing but a gritty-looking deposit was left.

But there was no gold!

No! the precious metal was evidently absent, and as the cradles were one by one emptied, expressions of disappointment and rage were heard on every side. Not a grain of gold in any of them.

Jack felt inclined to laugh, but the woe depicted upon the faces of the men checked him. As for Long Tom, he looked like a man who had been robbed of a large fortune, without the slightest hope of its recovery.

"It is but a day wasted, lads," said Jack, consolingly. "There are heaps of gold hereabouts, only it wants properly looking for. My friend Tom has made a little mistake, and thought that pulverised sandstone was gold. He will know better next time, especially after he has had a little talk with me."

"I want a little talk with somebody," groaned Tom. "Close on fifty years old and took in in this way! It's disgraceful. I'm a duffer! I'm an idiot! I'm an ass!"

CHAPTER XLVI.

AN IMPORTANT MISSION FOR LONG TOM.

HAVING made one grand mistake, Tom wisely followed the teachings of our hero, Jack. Under his instructions the men worked and found their full reward. The gold, if not quite so plentiful as sand upon the seashore, came very readily to hand, and the little bags, heavy with gold-dust, rapidly increased in number.

While the work was in full swing an agreement was drawn up and signed by all, and this was its purport—

"The wealth acquired was the property of all—share and share alike.

"If any man died his share was to go to the general fund, and become a portion of the common stock.

"No man was to harbour in private so much as an ounce of gold, and any man doing so exposed himself to the penalty of being expelled from the community.

"All orders from Jack to be strictly obeyed. Any refusal to be followed with a trial, and his crime, if proved, to be succeeded by the penalty of death.

"All theft, no matter how trivial, to subject the evil-doer to the same penalty."

This was stern, but it was necessary law. They had no prisons, so there was but one way of punishing a man, and that was to shoot him —a rough-and-ready way of getting rid of a criminal, but they were rough men, and required rough-and-ready treatment.

This agreement gave general satisfaction, but there was one clause in it destined to work destruction among them, which none of them foresaw, and of which more anon.

Gold—gold in dust, gold in nuggets, gold in lumps—rolled into the general store, until it became patent that they must have more beasts of burden or else leave some of their treasure behind.

This none of them would consent to do, so to meet the emergency a number of men under Long Tom went out in search of mustangs, which were supposed to be plentiful upon the plains.

He took sixty men with him, and those who remained behind went on working, for the gold-fever was upon them, and they could not rest with it so near. Tom, it was expected, would be absent for nearly two months.

Not being provided with good horses, he could not hunt the wild mustangs, but must of necessity construct a trap, or path, which is generally made of two fences, shaped like the letter V, and terminating in a pit, where the animals can be lassoed, and afterwards tethered to stakes until they become tolerably tame.

Tom took his leave of Jack and Will, exhorting them to keep a sharp look-out upon the precious metal.

"Men are but men," he said, "and one of these chaps may take it into his head to bolt with some of it."

"He must be a brave fellow to do that," replied Jack; "but, if it will ease your mind, I will have the bags moved down to the spot where I have swung my hammock."

"I shall be easy then," rejoined Long Tom, "for there's not a man who would care to take them from near you."

"I will be careful, Tom—good-bye," replied Jack Savage.

"Good-bye, my dear boy," said Tom. "I shall think of you every moment I am away."

"And we shall not forget you—so, again good-bye."

Tom rode away, taking with him the sixty men and nearly all the mules, which were necessary to bring the mustangs into training.

When he was gone the work was renewed, but, owing to the decreased number of men, carried on on a smaller scale. Yet the profit was enormous, and the store of gold vastly increased.

One day Will took command of the working party, and having learned to discriminate between good and bad soil, it took him very little time to set his men to work. This done, it was his custom to climb one of the hills and ruminate until it was time to return home.

On this occasion he selected one of the highest points, and, sitting down, fell to thinking of his old home and the father he had such little cause to love.

But he loved this father, nevertheless, for Will had a true and tender heart, and he could not help thinking that he at least owed his existence to his parent, and that he was not to be his judge.

While he was musing on his home as it had been, and speculating on what it might have been, his eyes filled with tears, and he turned his gaze upon the valley below—not where the men were at work, but on the other side, which had been the scene of operations the day before.

Immediately all thoughts of home were chased away, and he looked long and earnestly downwards.

What was this he saw?

A man!

The distance was so great that he could only distinguish his outline, but a man it was, and it could not be one of his men, for they were at work upon the other side, a distance of several hours' journey from the valley below.

"I hope I am not dreaming," muttered Will, "or troubled with any of those visions which Jack has often talked about. It must be a man—and a stranger, too, and if a stranger, who is it?"

Will lay flat down, and, shading his eyes, gazed at the figure below.

It was a man, undoubtedly, moving to and fro with a stooping action, and picking up and examining particles of earth.

"He has come upon our workings," thought Will. "Now, if he is alone, he must be stopped

and made to join us; one more or less won't matter, but he must not get clear away. It is too soon to let the world know of this golden harvest."

He would have gone down and joined the stranger at once, but that side of the hill was too precipitous, and Will had too much respect for his neck to risk it idly or needlessly.

CHAPTER XLVII.

RIVALS.

"PERHAPS if I shout the stranger will hear me," thought Will, so, putting his hand to his mouth, he shouted, "Hallo, there—hallo!"

His voice reverberated among the hills, and the figure below halted and looked up.

"Hallo, there!" shouted Will.

The figure began to run, as if alarmed, while Will made signals for him to stop, but the stranger only ran the faster.

"Don't be a fool!" shouted Will; "pull up, stupid. Nobody wants to harm you."

Presently the figure disappeared round a bend of the gorge.

Will, cursing his stupidity in giving the alarm, and hastening down to his men, singled out two of the fleetest of foot to accompany him.

"There is a stranger prowling about the other side," he said, "and strangers are not wanted at present. We must stop him."

Had they been called away from the pleasant work of gold-digging for any other office the men might have grumbled a bit, but a stranger in their midst might probably mean danger, so they set forward in company with Will, showing the greatest alacrity.

It took nearly two hours to reach the other side, and then, of course, the man was gone.

Will had relied upon being able to follow the trail, but the rocky ground gave them no clue.

There was one footmark, however, and that was upon some loose earth which had been turned up from under a rock, and this footmark was made by the foot of a civilised man.

"Worn through at the toe," said Will, "and down at the heel, but a civilised boot, nevertheless. Confound the fool! Why did he run away?"

He went back to the men and sent them home, saying that he would follow them shortly. Then alone he went in search of the trail.

Those under him returned to the camp with the proceeds of their day's work, and told Jack what had transpired.

Our hero was startled to hear of a stranger being there, but he did not think it of very much moment.

He was vexed with Will for going in pursuit alone, but he had sufficient confidence in our friend to believe that he would know how to take care of himself.

When the day's work was done, Jack went to the spot where he had swung his hammock, and, getting into his nest, filled a pipe and began to smoke.

This habit was new to our hero; but he had taken to it of late whenever he was at all troubled and perplexed.

He smoked one pipe out, filled another, and smoked that. Then the sun went down, but Will had not returned.

"He may have fallen among a host of them," thought Jack. "If so it will go hard with him.

Why was he so rash ?"

Jack got no sleep that night, for after lying an hour or so, he got up and strolled along the road where he knew he would meet Will if he was returning.

He traversed the gorge until it divided into two paths, and then he halted, not knowing which way to go.

The moon was up, and he could see far on either side, but no living creature was in view.

"To the right or left ?" thought he. "Which shall it be ?"

He stood for a moment, then chose that which lay to the right, and, throwing down his hat so that Will might see it in case he came that way, Jack went on for several miles, occasionally stopping to shout for his friend.

But he saw nothing and received no reply, so retracing his steps he picked up his hat and went home.

Getting once more into his hammock he lay sleepless until sunrise, when he went to the men and announced his determination to scour the country for his missing friend.

"There will be no more delving for gold until he is found," he said.

Will was a great favourite, and, much as the gold-seekers valued every moment of their time, they made no demur.

In a few moments all were ready, and they were about to start when Will came slowly in, his face wrinkled with the pain and fatigue of a long march.

"Give me something to eat and drink," he said. "I am dying with hunger and thirst."

"I have looked for you all night," returned Jack, as he led him to a seat.

"Don't blame me, old fellow," rejoined Will ; "I did what I thought was for the best."

When he had eaten and drunk he asked Jack to send the men, who were lounging about in curiosity, to their work.

"What I have to say is not for them to hear just yet," he said, "and they need not hear it at all unless you wish it."

The men were therefore set to work, and Will, as soon as they were gone, began his story of the previous night's adventure.

"When I left the men last night," he said, "I went back to the gorge where I had seen the stranger, and although there was no trail I kept on, hoping to find one.

"Footsteps in such a place could not be expected, but I found something which did quite as well. The fellow was carrying some earth in a handkerchief, and little pinches of this escaped as he travelled on. These were my guides, and by them I travelled on until sunset, and then I pulled up, not knowing what to do.

"I was loth to return, and unable to go on ; but while I was hesitating darkness came, and then I saw in the distance another clue to guide me—the reflection of the light of a fire.

"At first it did not seem to be far away, but I soon found that I had at least a couple of miles to traverse, and it took me an hour to reach the spot, when, climbing a rock, I cautiously peeped over and beheld a large body of men.

"They numbered at least three hundred, I should say, and were crowding around one, whom I have no doubt was my friend in the valley, a half-caste fellow, who was exhibiting the earth he had brought home.

"'Good gold,' I heard him say, 'as good gold as ever was coined in a mint.'

"They uttered cries of delight, and some capered in a way which proved them to be Frenchmen—one in particular was like a maniac, and reminded me of poor Caderouse. When they had gesticulated and talked for a while they dispersed, and lay about near the fires, the materials for which they seemed to have brought with them.

"There was a small fire not far from me, and three men, drawing apart from the rest, lay down by it. These appeared to be the leaders of the band—their dress was better, and they walked like men of authority.

"'Bernado is right,' said one, 'we have indeed come upon the earth's bank—it is gold.'

"'But how about this stranger,' said the other ; 'this man who shouted to him from the rock ?'

"'A native, perhaps,' said the first speaker, 'one of the many Indian tribes.'

"'I do not think so,' said the third man. 'Bernado says he was well dressed, and carried a gun, he believes. The height was very great, and he may have been deceived ; but if he is not, there are others in the field before us.'

"'And not one alone.'

"'No, or he would not have shouted—we must be careful. When will Luigi be here ?'

"'In three days,' replied the other.

"'Not before ?'

"'No, but there will be two hundred with him, which makes five hundred in all. Then, if we have any rivals here, we shall be strong enough, I hope.'

"After this," continued Will, "they began talking in a language I did not understand, and as I had learned sufficient to know what sort of people we might have to cope with, I stole softly away. It was a long journey, and I had to walk sharp to get here as soon as I did."

"I am sorry to hear this," said Jack, thoughtfully. "We may have strife and bloodshed perhaps."

"Unless we amalgamate with our rivals," suggested Will.

"Impossible !" returned Jack ; "it cannot be done. They would want a share of our wealth, and there would be perpetual bickerings among the men. Our only safe course is to march straight the other way and leave the field to them, but that would not suit me."

"Nor me."

"The next course is to meet them and propose certain arrangements, whereby they shall camp away from us—in another valley, if they can find one—and work in another district. This won't suit them."

"I think not, Jack."

"They would immediately suspect our wealth and covet it, and, being half-castes you say——"

"Most of them, I should think."

"Such being the case, Will, they would prefer money gained by blood in preference to that honestly worked for. No—their coming means danger to us, and we must be prepared to meet it."

"How ?"

"Entrench the gorge and forbid their approach."

"But they can climb the hills, and give us pepper from above."

"We must risk that—at all events they cannot come down upon us without warning. Nay !

I have a better plan. Entrench the gorge and establish redoubts upon the hill-tops.'

"That's better, Jack. We can hold our own then."

"So be it, then," said Jack, and they went out to choose the points of 'vantage."

That night, when the men returned, they were told of the danger, and before going to rest a deep hole was dug near the river and the main body of their wealth carefully buried.

On the following morning a barrier was erected in the gorge, while two redoubts of stone were constructed upon the hill-tops on either side, and then they began to look for the enemy.

"In ten days," said Will, "they will be here." And in less than ten days the enemy came.

The strangers espied our friends about mid-day. Apparently relying upon their numbers, they came marching along as if the all the land was theirs, until they reached the entrench-ment where Will, who was with the working party, was prepared to receive them.

The strangers, mostly half-castes and Spaniards, halted about two hundred yards away, and sent two men carrying a flag of truce.

Will, nothing loth, went out to meet them, and saw that the men were two of those he had seen lying by the fire a few nights ago.

"Your health, senor," said the foremost.

Will bowed and gave him greeting, English fashion, then they eyed each other for a moment.

"The English senor has been at work here," said the other Spaniard.

"Yes," said Will; "we are protecting our property."

"Cattle, probably?"

"No—not cattle," returned Will.

"This should be a high-road," said the first Spaniard. "I see no sign of any culture here."

"Nor I," said the other.

"Culture or not, it is our property," rejoined Will.

"By what right?"

"The right of discovery."

"We are discoverers, too," said the Spaniard, with a shrug; "it is ours also—the English senor is not logical."

"We are logical thus far," said Will; "if you attempt to advance we shall try to stop you. There is plenty of ground for you to work upon, without coming near us."

CHAPTER XLVIII.

A PRISONER OF WAR.

"But why should you be so selfish?" asked the Spaniard, "why forbid us to come? Have you wine or women concealed here?"

"Neither."

"What then?"

"That is our affair," replied Will; "the place is ours—we are the discoverers, and mean to keep it. It is ours by right."

"When there are two discoverers," said the Spaniard, "the question of right assumes another form. Blows generally result, and the weakest goes to the wall."

He spoke with a smile of calm confidence upon his face, which exceedingly irritated Will, and he answered, sharply—

"Here we have set up our barricade, and we say none shall pass. If you attempt to do so you do it at your peril. We are numerous, and strong in arms."

"And I am weak neither in numbers nor weapons," said the Spaniard, haughtily; "nor am I accustomed to be told to go hither and thither at the bidding of any man."

"It may be new to you," said Will, coolly, "and, perhaps not very pleasant. But if your men come forward another pace I shall give mine the order to fire."

"Then it is war to the knife?"

"Unless you turn back."

"As well talk to the Amazon, and bid it turn from its course. As it must be war, take that as an earnest of what is to come."

As he spoke, the Spaniard drew a knife swiftly from his belt and struck at Will.

Our friend saw the attempt, and stepped aside, striking out with his fist as he did so.

The blow landed upon the Spaniard's face between the eyes, and he fell heavily.

The other turned and fled.

Will wrenched the knife from his hand, and, while the Spaniard was yet stunned and bewildered by the blow, he bound his arms and dragged him towards the entrenchment.

Two of his men leaped out to help him, and the trio bore their prisoner safe behind the shelter. Then the enemy began to fire, but they might just as well have blazed away at a brick wall.

They seemed, however, to enjoy the fun, until one of the redoubts opened upon them, and then they scampered away.

"Your attempt on my life was most dastardly," said Will, addressing his captive, "and you have forfeited yours to me. But I shall not judge you—that will be left to my leader."

The Spaniard scowled and bit his lips, and, after a slight pause, he asked—

"Who is your leader?"

"Jack Savage, the hero of Red Mountain," replied Will.

The Spaniard's face became livid, and his frame shook with suppressed emotion—either rage or fear—probably a little of each.

Leaving a sufficient body of men behind on guard, Will took his prisoner to the cave where Jack and the rest were at work.

"Here is number one," said Will, "the first fruit of our meeting."

"A prisoner?" asked Jack, in surprise.

"Yes, a prisoner," returned Will, "and one who tried to settle me quietly before the fight began. But he made a mistake in his reckoning."

Will then narrated all that had occurred, and, when he had finished, Jack had the prisoner before him for examination.

The Spaniard was a swarthy, eagle-eyed fellow, with long hair falling upon his shoulders.

His dress was of velvet, and had once upon a time been very handsome, but it was now much travel-stained and worn.

Round his waist was a cashmere shawl and a belt, in which he had kept his weapons until he got into tribulation and was deprived of them by Will. There were other signs in his attire and demeanour which showed that he was above the common run of his class, and accustomed more to issue commands than to obey them.

"Your name?" said Jack.

The Spaniard hesitated and twirled his moustache, half-defiantly.

◁ GIANT JACK: ▷

A Story of the Red Mountains.

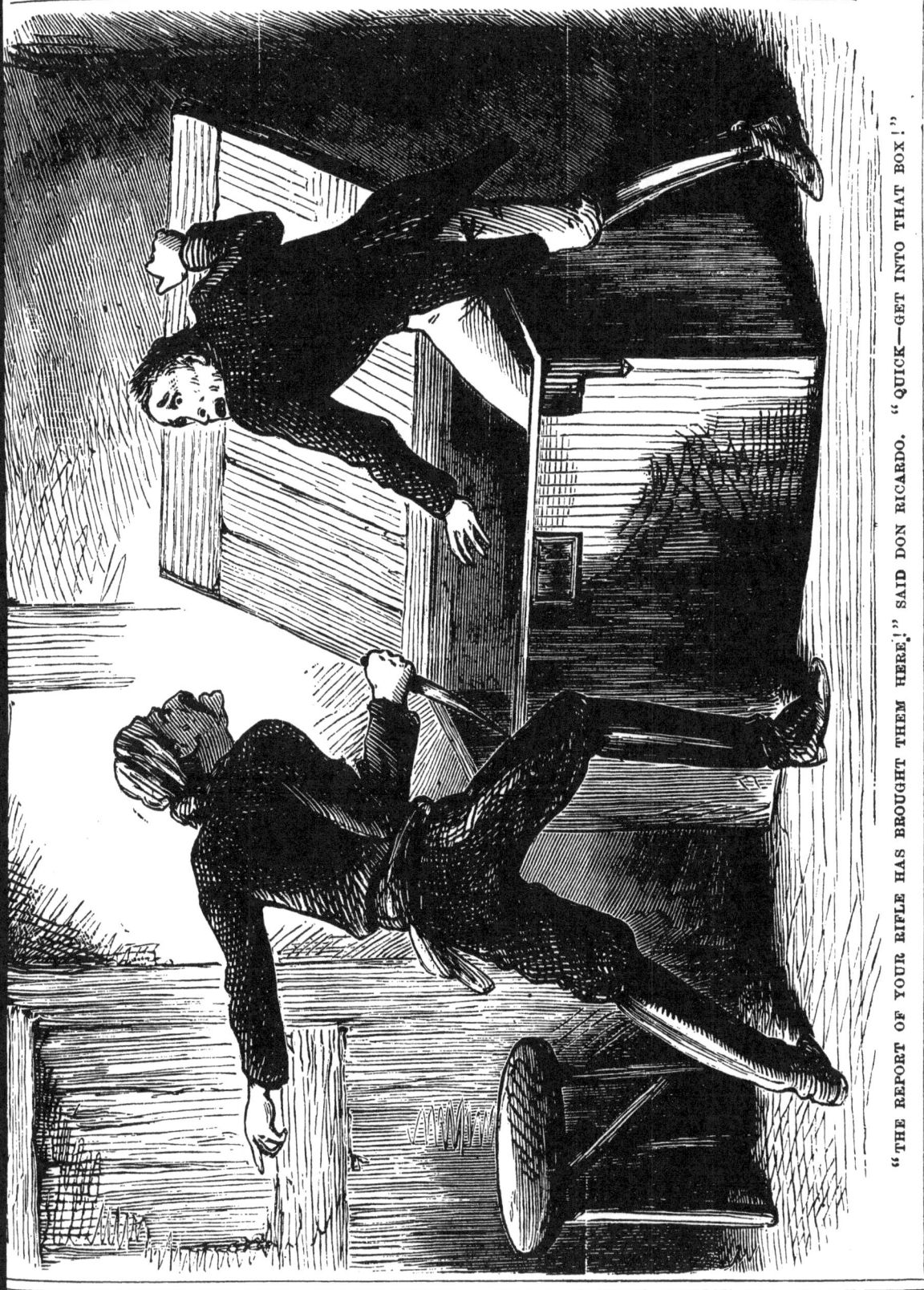

"THE REPORT OF YOUR RIFLE HAS BROUGHT THEM HERE!" SAID DON RICARDO. "QUICK—GET INTO THAT BOX!"

"Quick—your answer!" said Jack.

"Bernado," replied the other.

"You are the leader of this party?" asked Jack, making a flying shot to get at the truth.

The Spaniard hesitated slightly as he answered quietly—

"I am not the leader, but I have a command."

"What is your leader's name?"

Again the Spaniard paused before he answered.

"Don Santa Yuhla."

"And the men under his command—how many has he?"

"Eight hundred."

"That will do," said Jack. "I suppose you are prepared to give your word not to attempt to escape."

"Yes, senor," returned Bernado, eagerly.

"I wish I were equally prepared to accept it," said Jack, coolly; "but there is 'liar' written on your face and beaming in your eye, and I will not trust you. You will occupy yonder tent, and a guard will be kept constantly over you. If you attempt to escape you will be instantly shot."

"A stern and sharp way of dealing with him," said Will, as the Spaniard moved sullenly away.

"The only way," said Jack. "You heard his story?"

"Yes."

"There is not one word of truth in it."

"How can you tell, Jack?"

"How do I know there is honesty in you? By instinct, which never deceives a man, if he will be guided by it. No, Will—our friend is not to be trusted. He is not a subordinate, but the leader of the band—his name is not Bernado, and there are not eight hundred men."

"I saw about a hundred," said Will; "but two hundred would find it difficult to get into our redoubt."

"How many men have you left in charge?"

"Sixty, with Griffith at their head. I think he is a good man."

"He may be trusted, but we must make all secure. Retreat is impossible until Tom comes back."

"Retreat ought to be out of the question, Jack."

"If there is nothing to fight for we will not fight, Will, but until Tom returns we must hold our own. He is sure to come back, and if he did not find us he would either break his heart or fall a victim to the enemy."

"Anyhow," said Will, "I'm for standing our ground and fighting."

Jack resolved to leave a guard in charge of the prisoner, and to march the rest back to the spot chosen for defence. The reason he gave was that probably the new-comers had attacked by this time, and a decisive blow against them ought to be struck at once.

"As they are here, Will, let us face them and give them a drubbing."

"I don't think we shall get a chance just yet, Jack—the beggars are such brutes for bolting."

"Hark!"

"What's that?"

"Firing!"

"Yes—and heavy firing, too."

"We have lost time, Will," said Jack, setting forward at a smart pace. "Fall in there, men! Forward!"

As they advanced the firing became louder and louder, and Will thought he could hear the shouts of men.

Jack was certain of it, but he said nothing.

When they arrived near the scene of action, however, all Jack had surmised, and more, was confirmed.

The Spaniards had attacked and carried the redoubt and trench, and the men left in charge were in full retreat.

They came tearing along, with a look upon their faces which comes upon men when the tide of fear sets in. Some were bleeding, and staggered along holding their gaping wounds, but the main body were unhurt, and had retreated only under the impulse of fear.

"Halt, there!" cried Jack, and his voice fell upon their ears like music, while it sent back the best blood to their hearts.

"Griffith," said Jack, singling out the man who had been appointed to the temporary command, "how is this?"

"I held the trench as long as I could," replied Griffith, hanging his head, "but they came over like a swarm of bees. There are ten of my men dead and as many wounded. What could I do?"

"You doubtless did your best," replied Jack, kindly; "but you must regain our ground. Ready, men—forward!"

Enjoining them to go back as silently as possible, Jack kept on until the trench was in sight, and then with a shout he bore down upon it.

The enemy had taken possession of it, and were resting on their laurels, little expecting a return of their attack. The arrival of the reserve force overcame them with surprise, and, acting upon impulse, they turned and fled.

But Jack and his men were close upon them, and the hindmost had but one moment to regret their temerity and make peace in the world to come—strong arms and swift weapons laid them low.

The air was full of execrations and cries for help, but it was not a time for pity or quarter, and none was given. About sixty fell, but the rest got clear away—the greater portion of their number.

"They are more numerous than I thought," said Jack; "but if the gorge had been wider it would have gone badly with the whole of them."

"As it is," added Will, "we have only scotched and not killed the band."

"They will give us no end of trouble, I fear; but see to the wounded, and carry them back to the camp."

When the muster roll was called, Jack found himself minus forty-two men—twelve of them would fight no more, and some of the rest were dangerously wounded.

It was found that the redoubts upon the hill-tops were of no use during the fight, for in those days long-range rifles were unknown, and the weapons then in use could not reach the field of strife below. But they were useful as posts of observation.

The foe, as Will said, were scotched, not killed, and within an hour they came back into sight and began to throw up a trench as a protection to their position.

Jack would have advanced at once and driven

them back, but night was coming on, and he could not tell what trap they might have in readiness for him.

"To-morrow," he said, "with sixteen hours' daylight, I will make short work of them."

He sent Will to the camp and remained himself on duty all night. He did this knowing that Will was almost broken down by fatigue, and needed rest. As for his own iron frame, he could do with or without it, just as circumstances might avail him.

In the morning a messenger came to Will and told him that there had been no attack during night, but the enemy had been very busy, and had thrown up a stiff breastwork.

"Does the captain attack to-day?" asked Will.

"I cannot say," was the reply. "But he wished to see you about noon."

During the morning Will walked in and looked at the prisoner. He was sitting sullenly in his tent, gnawing his nails like a man half-mad with vexation and terror.

CHAPTER XLIX.

SNIP TURNS UP.

"Is there anything you want?" asked Will of the prisoner Bernado.

"Nothing but my liberty," replied the Spaniard, savagely.

"That you will have if you are lucky," said Will, coolly. Then, sitting down near his captive, he proceeded—

"I say, my friend, Bernado, where have I seen you before?"

"Nowhere—I swear!" said the Spaniard, eagerly.

"Oh! but I have," rejoined Will, positively. "I cannot say where. Perhaps I have only caught a glimpse of that interesting face of yours. But I have seen you before, or may I never see old England again."

"The English senor dreams," said the Spaniard.

"No," replied Will. "I am generally remarkably wide-awake, thank you, especially when I am in the company of men who are too handy with their knives. I have seen you somewhere, and I shall soon remember where. Good-morning."

He went out, and in another hour was on his way to the trench. When he arrived there he found all quiet, but Jack was making preparations to attack.

"I mean to leave nothing to chance," said our hero. "It is no use playing with these men—short and sharp must be our motto."

"How many do you think there are?"

"More than I first thought—there must be at least four hundred of them skulking about; but I do not care for numbers—we are in the right, and that is enough."

The opposite trench gave out no signs of the enemy, so Will went up to one of the redoubts to get a bird's-eye view of the plain. Then he saw them, all ready to defend their stronghold when the attack should come, and a murderous lot of fellows they looked as they lay upon the ground resting on their rifles and swords.

Will soon came down again, and proposed to Jack that he (Will) should take fifty men and work his way round in their rear, but this Jack would not hear of.

"We are strong enough to attack them in front, and attack them we will," he said.

Shortly after noon Jack gave the signal to advance, and the men leaped over the barrier and followed him as he dashed forward. The foe were ready for them.

Fifty rifles rang out, and as many bullets sped upon their course of death and misery. Some were hit fatally, some were wounded, and the rest of the missiles battered themselves flat against the sterile rocks.

"Forward!" was the cry from Jack's lips, heard above all—and there were no laggards in his troop.

Jack and his men were soon amongst the enemy, and hand-to-hand fighting began.

With cries and curses the Spaniards and half-castes fought, until they found they had encountered no common men, but a band of heroes led by a hero chief—one all pluck and sinew.

Then they would have turned and fled.

But a new surprise—a new alarm—was in store for them.

And a surprise for our hero, too.

As the Spaniards turned to flee, a sharp fusilade from the rear dealt death and destruction in their ranks.

Jack heard it, and saw some of the Spaniards falling, while others frantically sought to scramble up the face of the precipitous hills, only to be picked off or to lose their foothold and fall into the gorge below.

What could it mean?

Who were these new assailants, and from whence did they come?

The Spaniards were in a trap—between two enemies—and fear gave them courage.

Quarter they did not expect, probably because they did not intend to give it, and they asked for none, but slashed with swords and fought with clubbed muskets like men demented.

One by one they fell, shrieking and moaning, until their ranks were so thin that Jack could see those from whom he had received this unexpected help.

It was Long Tom and his band, who went out in search of mules.

But why was he returning?

It was no time to debate the question within himself, for some of the Spaniards still fought like the children of darkness, and he was obliged to cut them down.

At last the work of slaughter ceased.

All but a few, who had succeeded in climbing the hills, lay still, or grovelled on the earth in the last agonies of death.

Then Long Tom, still panting with exertion, came forward, dropped his cutlass, and gave one hand to Jack, the other to Will.

Jack was the first to speak.

"How came you back, Tom?"

"I found the horses and mules."

"So soon?"

"So soon, Jack; but there's a yarn to that bit of business. Good fighting here?"

"Good or bad, as a man may think," said Will; "for my part I am almost sick of such work."

"You grow squeamish."

"If it is squeamish to dislike this terrible bloodshed, Tom, I am so; but I am sure you must have had almost enough of it."

"Perhaps I have, but I'm getting old."

" Young enough to look forward to a long life yet."

"Sometimes I think I'm near the finish," replied Tom.

"Now Tom is growing sentimental," laughed Will.

"No I aint," replied Tom, indignantly. "I aint of the sentimental sort. But stop a moment —I've got somebody to show you. Hallo ! come here."

In obedience to his call a little man, dressed in a Spanish costume, but with a face as black as a negro, came forward.

His features, however, were small and of an European cast, and he had a sheepish look which rather amused Jack.

"There," said Tom, "look and tell me if you know him ?"

"Who should know me ?" broke in the voice of the stranger, before Jack could reply. "Would any man know me now who ever knew me before ? Is there any man even in Wapping who could swear to me ?"

It was the voice of Snip, and Jack and Will, after staring at him for a minute, burst into a roar of laughter.

"Ha ! you may laugh," said Snip, dolorously ; "but it is no joke to me."

"Why, then, did you black your face ?" asked Will.

"*Me* black my face ! *Me !*" cried Snip. "No—no—it's none of my work, and, as my favourite poet says, ' thereby hangs a tale.' "

"Which you shall tell when we get back to the camp," said Jack. "At present we have more serious work in hand."

The "more serious work" was the attending to the dead and wounded, and very serious work it proved to be, for the ground was literally covered with those who had fallen in the fight.

By far the greater number of those who had fallen were Spaniards.

Eight to one, at least, was the proportion— but Jack's band had not by any means escaped scot-free.

Many a bold heart was stilled for ever, and many a gallant form writhed under the agony of a deadly wound.

Those who were dead were laid aside for burial on the morrow, and the wounded were carried back to the camp, where every tent but that containing the prisoner was given up for their use, and the men who had escaped unhurt made rough huts for themselves with the boughs of trees.

Every care was bestowed upon the wounded, for among the men were several who were skilled in rough surgery and a knowledge of herbs.

These applied refreshing bandages to the wounds, and then gave in their report to Jack.

Some—most of them, probably—would recover, but many would die, as the wounds they had received were very severe.

"It is the lot of such a life as this," said Jack, with a sigh. "I am sorry for the poor fellows."

"The rest will be richer," muttered one of the men near, and Jack turned upon him sharply—

"Do you think of gold in comparison with life ?" he demanded. "Do you pit the vile dross against a man's existence ?"

"Perhaps I am wrong," replied the man ; "but you know we are all fond of gold."

"Fond of gold ?" muttered Jack. "Aye, that is it. Fond of gold ! Man loves it, and it is too often his curse. Woe to him if he makes it his god, for it will work his ruin."

He walked about, moody and thoughtful, until the voice of Will aroused him.

"I have made a fire near our retreat," Will said, "and there I have left Long Tom and Snip. We have had a rough day of it, and Snip's story will help to brighten our thoughts."

CHAPTER L.

SNIP'S STORY.

THE unfortunate little tailor was sitting by the fire, his black face shining in the lurid light, and Long Tom lay watching him with an air of curiosity, as if his friend was some strange animal from an unknown region.

Jack came, took a seat, and nodded good-humouredly, as was his wont, to Long Tom. Then he looked at Snip.

"You have a story to tell ?" he said.

"Sich a story as never was heard afore," returned Snip. "There, it is a buster, and nothing less."

"Before you begin I wish to impress one thing upon you."

"And what is that, respected captain ?"

"This," said Jack, emphatically. "I wish you to tell the truth."

"Upon my word I will," said Snip, hanging his head. "I know that I have often told lies, but I don't mean to do it again."

"Lying is mean and contemptible," rejoined Jack, "especially when you are associating with people who believe you. It is about as dirty a thing as you can be guilty of."

"As I hope to live," said Snip, warmly, "I will tell the truth. I have gone through terrible things, and the end of them is this black face of mine, which, if any of you think is a lie, oblige me by trying to wash it, and I will be very thankful to you if you can get it off."

"I rely upon you to tell the truth," said Jack, "and I promise to believe you. Now begin."

Then Snip launched into his story, and, strange as it may appear to our readers, he told the truth, the whole truth, and nothing but the truth.

He was nearly an hour getting to that part where he left him—in the box with Don Ricardo, with the flames gathering around him. We continue the story in his own words.

"Never shall I forget that time," he said, "if I live for a thousand years and become blind, and deaf as a doorpost. We lay in that box, sweltering and listening to the crackling sound of the flames, which was all we could hear after you were gone, and the horror which came upon me I shall never be able to tell.

"Burn we must, I thought. There seemed no chance for us, and I lay there dying an awful death of fear every minute."

Snip paused and wiped his face, for the memory still made him hot. Then he went on—

"Don Ricardo was in a terrible way. Sometimes he cursed, sometimes he prayed, and I thought that he must have gone mad. But he didn't, and the box grew hotter and hotter, until I swooned.

"There was a great blank after this, and I

have no recollection of anything until I came to, when I found myself surrounded by a pile of men—fifty at least—who had been throwing water over me until I was drenched to the skin.

"I sat up, thinking I had, as usual, been dreaming. But no—although I was no longer in the house, I was in the streets of Marena, and the box I knew so well was near me, with the don sitting upon it like some imp, curling his black moustache, and grinning at me like a Cheshire cat.

"'Ah, my friend!' he said; 'better now?'

"'I am better,' I said. 'But how did we escape?'

"'These good fellows came round to see what they could find, and they found us.'"

"They looked as murderous a lot of vagabonds as ever I come across," Snip continued. "A great many of them were old friends of Don Ricardo's—wretches who had served under him when he was a pirate on the high seas. You have seen the don?"

"Not to my knowledge," replied Jack. "He escaped me when I attacked his stronghold, and I have not seen him since."

"When you do see him," said Snip, with a savage shake of his fist, "you will see a double-dyed villain and a scoundrel. Now, after what we had suffered together in that box, would you not have thought that he would have treated me with decent kindness?"

"I should have thought so."

"But he did not," rejoined Snip, "not he. The vagabond owed me more than one grudge, and he said he would have it out with me."

"Poor old Snip!" said Will.

"You haven't heard half yet," rejoined Snip. "Well, as soon as I got round a bit the men marched off, with Don Ricardo at their head, and me as good as a prisoner, for when I tried to run away they told me if I as much as thought of doing that again they would knock my head off, so that made my staying a sort of compulsion.

"We tramped off into the open country and marched for two days, when we came upon another body of men living in a wood, but all as comfortable as you please, with no end of luxuries in their tents. There the don was hailed like a king, and he announced that he intended to rest a month or so—and rest he did, bother him.

"When bad men are idle," continued Snip, with a look of most profound wisdom on his face, "they are always up to some game, and the don soon got up to a game with me.

"He made me a sort of body-servant about him, and never gave me a minute to myself. I have poured out wine for him by the half-hour, until he got into a stupid state, and then he generally wound up by throwing what was left over me.

"Often and often I thought of cutting his throat, but I don't like murder, and I am naturally a bit of a coward, so I put up with his games until he played his worst game of all, and that was to give me this precious face.

"One morning he bawled out for a fellow who was always pretty near him—

"'Bernado! Bernado!'

"Bernado comes in—and asks what he wants.

"'Bernado,' he says, 'I am tired of a white servant and I must have a change. Get me a black one.'

"Bernado bows but says he don't know where to get a black servant.

"'If I have not one to-morrow,' replied the don, 'you will lose your head.'

"Bernado seemed in a terrible funk, but all of a sudden he brightens up and looks at me.

"'Will your excellency have a black servant of my making?' he asked.

"The don wanted to know what he meant.

"'I mean,' say Bernado, 'may I make a black servant of him?'

"The him was me, and as I thought a black face would not hurt me I said nothing.

"'But his face will wash,' says the don.

"'His face may wash,' says Bernado; 'but the black I will put on will never wash off!'

"At this the don roars and kicks up his heels more like a mad boy than a man.

"'Good!' he bellows, 'make a nigger of him. Excellent Bernado!'

"'Excellent Bernado' then takes me by the arm and leads me out. I thought he was joking, but deuce a bit—there was no joke in him—and calling a lot of fellows together, they straps me down, and then he sets to work.

"Bernado pricked the skin all over, and when I hollered they gagged me and the beggar pricked me all the harder. He was two hours at work, and he finished off by rubbing some black stuff from a bottle into the skin—then the game was over.

"I lay down a white man and rose up a nigger, and a nigger I have been ever since.

"The don was delighted. He gave Bernado a silver-hilted dagger, and he had me stuck before him to make him laugh if ever he felt melancholy—which is a nice use to make of a man like me. But I could not help myself, so I stood it as well as I could, although there were times when the British Lion had got his dander up and I fairly boiled over.

"I suppose I had spent about a fortnight of this life when a man came and told the chief that he believed gold would be found across the prairies to the west. The don, having got tired of idleness, said he would march that way, and in two days we started.

"I don't want to trouble you with what we did on the way, or how I was riled day after day by that aggravating don, but I must say that I suffered a martingdom, and going to the stake was a fool to it—but it wasn't to last for ever.

"One night, when he was asleep, more than half drunk, I stole out upon the prairie to get a mouthful of fresh air, and wandered further and further away until I must have been a mile from the camp.

"I was very mournful, for my 'art was full, and I was thinking of home. It was a moonlight night, and everything was as clear as day, but I was so full of my thoughts that I did not see anybody near me until Long Tom came up and fetches me a whack behind, and when I goes down he sits upon me, and tells me he will settle me if I move an inch.

"He also called me a 'cussed nigger,'" continued Snip, "but I forgive him."

"You looked like a nigger," said Long Tom, "and any man might have mistaken you for one."

"I forgive you," said Snip; "but you gets me down, and when I says 'I'm Snip' you stares at me wonderful, but at last you believes me, and then we compares notes, and you tell me that you are after mules, and I tell you it will be very easy to bag theirs when my people are asleep, and then we come back together and hide in the gorge until the fighting, when you sallies out and gives the vagabonds pepper. But I am afraid the don is got away, for I can't see him nowhere."

CHAPTER LI.

THE FATE OF DON RICARDO.

" A WONDERFUL story, and wonderfully told," said Will Larkin. " So you did not see the don anywhere ?"

" No—neither living nor dead."

" I am sorry he has again escaped me," said Jack. " The atrocities of this villain merit a heavy punishment."

" He is like an eel."

" So he is, Will, and it is a thousand pities he has escaped."

" Not many got away," said Snip, " and I had my eyes upon those who climbed up the hills, but I did not see the don amongst them."

" I have an idea," cried Will, and then he whispered something in Jack's ear.

Jack nodded in acquiescence, and Will bade Snip follow him.

They went straight to the tent where the Spaniard was a prisoner, and Will opened the canvas folds and peeped in—he was sleeping.

" Who is that, Snip ?" he asked.

Snip gave a little cry of exultation.

" That's the knave—that's Don Ricardo !" he exclaimed.

" I thought as much," said Will, with a smile of satisfaction. " He is safely housed at last."

Snip's cry had aroused the don, who opened his eyes and stared lazily at him. It was evident that he did not exactly realise his position.

" Ah ! my black friend," he said ; " some wine there."

" Fetch it yourself," returned Snip, shortly.

" Am I defied ?" cried the don, leaping to his feet. Then he remembered himself, and a shade of mortification crossed his face as he muttered, " I forgot I am a prisoner."

" Yes—we've got you safe enough," said Snip, complacently, " and now we know who you are you will be tried to-morrow."

" Enough," said the Spaniard, with a savage frown upon his face and a wave of his hand to intimate that he wished to be alone.

So Will considerately withdrew, and Snip followed him.

" They carried the news to their leader, who received it with satisfaction, and he sent for Tom to come to his cabin, which was now sumptuously furnished.

When Snip had withdrawn the three consulted as to the manner the don should be put to death.

" To-morrow," Jack said, " we will give him a trial, and such justice as he deserves he shall receive."

" It would be a pity to kill him before we know where the hidden wealth of the fellow is hidden," said Will.

" He won't reveal it."

" I think he will," replied Will.

" Are you going to try him ?"

" Yes—to-morrow. Stay, there's no time like the present. I will be back with you in a few moments."

Before Will got outside, the sound of a rifle was heard, followed by a piercing cry.

It came from the direction where the don was held a prisoner.

Jack leaped to his feet, and the whole party, fearing the Spaniard had made his escape, ran towards the tent where he was confined. Their fears, however, were groundless, for although the whole camp was in commotion the Spaniard was not gone.

He lay outside the tent, grovelling on the ground. Over him stood the sentinel in charge, with the barrel of his rifle yet smoking in his hand.

" What is this ?" cried Jack.

" Tried to escape," replied the man. " He crept out and seized my gun."

" Is he shot ?"

" The bullet missed its mark, but the smoke has blinded him."

" He will never see again," said Will, raising the wounded man in his arms.

" Blind ! blind !" shrieked the don.

" Blind as a bat !" muttered Long Tom. " The eyeballs are gone."

It was true—the don was blind for evermore. When full inquiry was made it was discovered that the prisoner had crept softly from the tent and fallen upon the sentinel as narrated. But the man saw the Spaniard at the moment he closed, and endeavoured to fire his rifle at him.

The barrel was near his temple, and the bullet sped away within an inch of his head, but the deadly blast of the powder destroyed his eyes for ever.

" Blind ! blind !" was the bitter cry which came from his lips every few moments. " Blind ! blind !"

" I need not try him now," said Jack, turning mournfully away ; " his punishment has come from a greater and wiser hand than mine."

CHAPTER LII.

THE END OF A BAD LIFE.

" I FORGIVE the poor devil," said Snip. " Better a black face than a sightless one."

" Well said, little 'un," cried Long Tom, slapping him upon the shoulder. " I likes your disposition. Hand over your fin and let me give it a grip."

Tom gave him a grip which took his breath away, and then he gave him another slap on the shoulder.

Indeed, he repeated the dose several times within the next half-hour, until Snip's back was sore.

" I like your grit," he said, again and again.

" And I should like yours," replied Snip, at last, " if you did not hit quite so hard. Thank you, Tom, that's better—I can stand that."

One of the men placed a bandage over the face of Don Ricardo, and he was led back to his tent ; but those who were awake in the night heard his dismal groans as he bewailed his lot.

" Blind ! blind !" was his moan, as he tossed and turned upon his couch, and the light of the morning still found him lamenting his fate, but as the day advanced he grew calmer, and at noon he lay sullen and despondent.

Jack came in and inquired if he had need of anything. The Spaniard cursed him, and bade him begone, so Jack left him.

The food they gave him he ate, but he never spoke but once, and that was to ask for a knife. When they wanted to know what he wished to do with it, he answered—

"End this life of mine."

But they did not give him the knife, and he spoke no more that day, but lay with the sin of a desperate life gnawing at his heart and driving him to despair.

*   *   *   *   *   *

Fully convinced that he and his band must soon be moving, Jack laid before his men the entire position of affairs, pointing out that they had gold enough for their own wants, and, if they wanted to keep it, they must soon leave the spot where they had found it.

"Many of the pirate band have made their escape," he said, in conclusion, "and these will soon bring thousands down upon our field of gold, who will not be content to earn it as we have done, but will rob and murder us, perchance. Therefore, I say we had better go with what we have, and rest content."

A few still urged their leader to stay, but the majority saw that they must get well upon the road home before the world learned the secret of the gold-field, and these coincided with their leader and carried the day.

In twenty-four hours all was packed and ready for a start, and then the question arose as to what was to be done with the pirate chief.

Jack went into the tent, and, finding him in a calmer mood, asked him what course he would wish to be pursued.

"If I take you back to civilised life," said Jack, "you are sure to be recognised, and the hatred of mankind is so strong against you that no word of mine could prevent your being hung."

"Would you save me if you could?" asked the pirate, sarcastically.

"I would, indeed," replied Jack, earnestly, "although there was a time when I would have killed you with my own hand. But all that is passed—retribution has fallen upon you, and I have no more to say or do except to pity you."

"I believe you," said Don Ricardo, after a pause. "I have more reasons than one to recognise you as a noble fellow, and I shall not forget you."

There seemed to be some hidden meaning in his tone, but Jack did not remark upon it, contenting himself with having asked Don Ricardo what he would do.

"Place me upon a mule," he said, "and turn my face to the south. That is all I ask."

"It shall be done," replied Jack.

When all was ready for a start on the morrow a mule was brought out, and Don Ricardo, with ten days' provisions, was placed upon it.

"I have no wish that you should starve," said Jack. "You never harmed me personally except in one case." Jack's voice was a little husky, for he spoke of Ximena. "But I have forgiven you. Farewell!"

The don smiled faintly, and held out his hand with an imploring look in his sightless eyes.

"Will you touch it?" he said. "My hand has not lain in a honest one for many a year, and may never do so again. Do not refuse me."

Jack clasped his palm, and then the don asked for Will Larkin. Will came, and the pirate besought the same favour of him. It was granted.

Snip came forward also and volunteered his palm, and Don Ricardo, with the dawn of a humorous look upon his sightless face, took that, too.

"I wish I had spared you," he said. "But better go through the world with a black face than a black heart, Adieu!"

"Fare thee well!" replied Snip. "Adoo!"

Then the don turned his mule to the west and rode slowly from the camp. A hundred yards away he was seen to reel in the saddle and fall to the ground.

Jack and Will both ran forward and raised him up. But on this earth he would never walk more—he was dead! Despair and remorse had overcome him, and his heart-strings were broken.

"Bury him by the side of the river," said Jack, "and let no man judge him, for who, if he carried his sins upon his shoulder, could walk in the light of the sun?"

*   *   *   *   *   *

Two months later a vessel spread its sails to the wind and carried some of the adventurers over the ocean towards the shores of Old England. Some, we say—but, alas! how few.

Of all those who left the gold-fields only four remained together—Jack, Will Larkin, Long Tom, and the hitherto unlucky Snip.

The rest had all perished or had deserted and been left behind.

First a base conspiracy in their midst had led to much slaughter. A few villains, thinking over the clause of the agreement wherein it was arranged that the property of any of the band who died should be divided amongst the survivors, were tempted to murder their comrades as they slept.

The thirst for gold was in their midst, and wrought its usual amount of ruin and desolation.

Men fought and died and were cast away like encumbrances of which they were well rid, and all Jack's influence failed to save a single life. Powerful as he was, there was a devil abroad that overmastered him. Then came fever.

One night the Black Angel came down upon them, and the whole camp, Jack alone excepted, was smitten down. Then a giant task lay before him, and like a giant he executed it.

But he could do little. Pain he could assuage, but life he could not save, and the band which had fought under him melted away like dew before the sun, until only Will, Tom, Snip, and a few others were left to him.

These he just succeeded in saving by the most strenuous care, and, strange to say, Snip was the first to recover and give him a helping hand with the nursing.

The little tailor came out wonderfully well, and did his duty like a man, for although Will in his suffering was petulant, and Tom very rough, Snip made no complaint, but nursed on and brought them through it like a Roman.

"I am not afraid of fever," he said, again and again. "Fever never kills niggers, and since I have been turned into a nigger I am safe."

This idea remained fixed with him through life, and did much to reconcile him to the altered state of his appearance; for the work executed for the amusement of Don Ricardo was permanent, and Snip might safely have been warranted by any manufacturer "not to wash." He was blackened for life.

CHAPTER LIII.

JACK SAVAGE'S STORY.

So Jack Savage and his companions came down with their gold to the coast, and quickly chartered a vessel to carry "lead" for them, long before the great secret was known. Snip, who had been elected one of the band, although he had no hand in the digging, was soon safe on board the George the Third, an undoubted millionaire.

"I shall wake them up at Wapping," he said. "But lor! I don't think I shall care to live there now. A house at Hampstead is more my cut. I have been there several times when I had a holiday, but I never thought I should live there. Fancy, Jeremiah Snip, of Hampstead Heath, Esquire! It sounds like print."

While he indulged in his dreams of ambition, and others forgot not theirs, and many plans were laid out for the future by Will; but until the night when they first sighted the white cliffs of old Albion Jack kept the secret of his birth. Then he revealed his history, which he had found in letters written to him by his father.

It was a peaceful, moonlight night, and Jack and Will remained upon the deck in preference to going to their hammocks below. Jack, after laying for awhile in a thoughtful mood, turned to his companion, and said—

"I have much to tell you, Will—much that concerns myself—and I do not think I could choose a better time."

"Choose your own time, Jack."

"I have had to obey the voice of the dead, Will; but I think we are now sufficiently near home to be released from my bond. Draw nearer, as I do not care for the men of the watch to hear."

Will drew nearer, and Jack, in a low tone, began his story.

"My father's name," said Jack, "was not Savage, for he came of the old English family of Beauchamp, and was the eldest son of Sir John Beauchamp, of Martingtower.

"The place is, of course, strange to me, but that is the name which my father gives me in the papers I found in the hut near the town of Marena.

"I learn from other papers that my father was never the favourite of his sire, Sir John, who preferred his second son, Lewin—a slight, fair-haired boy, much like his mother—whose nature belied his soft and tender looks, for he was crafty, cruel, and remorseless to a degree, and eventually worked my father's ruin.

"My father was always a great student, very fond of ancient books, and he read a deal of Egyptian lore, wherein he learned much of what is known as magic, a thing of which the world understands very little.

"It was this study that brought about, with the assistance of his brother Lewin, the downfall of my father, for it was a dark age in England then, and people were full of superstition.

"Old women—helpless creatures without the brains of a bat—were stoned to death for holding close converse with the Evil One, and dealing death and destruction around them, while all learning not of the plainest possible description was looked upon with distrust and suspicion.

"My father was also fond of the study of chemistry, and he generally worked at night. This was soon observed and commented on in no friendly terms. The country louts took it up, and shunned him as if he had been a wild beast or a pestilence.

"They even abstained from entering the church if he was known to be there, or if he was expected to arrive.

"My father, like myself, was very tall, as you know, and he looked down upon these people, both morally and physically, and laughed at them.

"But it is a dangerous thing to have the mob against you. Martingtower soon became unbearable.

"The servants followed the country folks, and refused to wait upon my father, and so he left his home and took up his abode at our town house in London.

"I have never been in a very great city, Will, but I can picture what it must be like from his description—miles of streets and houses, and no trees. Well, there my father was tolerably quiet for a time, for the city people were not so ignorant as those in the country, and after a year or so he married.

"This was done in secret, but he acknowledged my mother instantly, and took her home to his house, to the great annoyance of Sir John and his brother Lewin.

"In a year I was born, and, my mother dying as she gave me birth, my father was again without a companion. I say without a companion, for my father tells me that reports were so spread about concerning him that no man cared to take him by the hand. I daresay he had a wild look, for he was always poring over his books, and seldom left the house except at night.

"I learn from his written account that during his experiments he discovered a method of making brilliant lights of different colours, and these, streaming out of the windows of his room, soon drew the attention of the people in the street and made him notorious.

"Thus came his brother Lewin's opportunity.

"He went about among the crowd and hinted that my father had dealings with evil spirits, and that he wanted to bring harm upon the town.

"Some believed it and some did not, but, the cholera breaking out, a cry was raised against him, and a mob surrounded the house both night and day.

"This was the mob which fixed itself upon my memory, and which I shall never forget to my dying day—nor the white, upraised faces, the angry cries, and the fierce imprecations they heaped upon his head.

"Once my father endeavoured to expostulate with them, but they stoned him from the window, and then tried to force the door, but they did not succeed or I should not be here to tell the tale.

"Disgusted by such treatment my father sought the aid of his friends, but they repudiated him and called him a sorcerer. Then, heartbroken, he turned his back upon England and left it for ever. He stole out in the night, carrying me as a thief carries a bundle, and took passage on board a ship bound for America.

" 'Books have been my ruin,' he said, 'and my boy shall never know their meaning. If I had lived the life of a dull country fool I should be a happy man, but now, because my learning is above the common standard, they seek my life.'

"So he sailed away, and landed on the shores of America, and the rest, I think, must be pretty well known to you."

"It is a strange tale," said Will. "Can you prove all this?"

"I have some documents with me which will prove what I have told you," replied our hero, "and I am desired to go to our family solicitor in Lincoln's-inn, who will see to the rest."

"If this Lewin Beauchamp is in possession," returned Will, "you will have some trouble to oust him."

"I do not think my identity will be very difficult to prove," returned Jack, with a smile, "for I am very much like my father. My father writes that in all his ancestors there was a great family resemblance. The battles in which they fought—the wars of the Red and White Roses, the Civil War with Cromwell, and so on, which I daresay you understand, Will, although I must confess my ignorance."

"You are speaking of some of the most glorious times of old England," said Will—"that is, what people accept as glorious. Great deeds were done, and men rose from the lowest position to high rank, while all the nation was turned upside down."

"It seems that my family has been mixed up in all these things," said Jack, "and I rather long to get to my ancestral home, for I have had enough of travel and adventure to last my life."

"And I, too," sighed Will; "but it is not a bad thing when you are young. I don't think we shall be the worse for it. It has improved even Snip."

"I doubt much if he thinks his face an improvement," said Jack, laughing, "or his friends will do so either. Come here, Snip."

Snip, who had been leaning over the ship's side watching the water glistening in the moonlight, came over and asked what was wanted of him.

"When you land in England," said Jack, "what will you do?"

"Go to Wapping," answered Snip.

"Yes, I know that; but what will you do Whom will you go to see?"

"I shall go to my father."

"Is he alive?"

"I hope so," said Snip; "he was when came away, and he told me I was making a fool of myself. Then there is my old master—he will be very glad to see me."

"But will you be able to prove your identity?"

"That's uncertain," said Snip, in some dismay, "for there is no telling how they may take my black face. Bother that fellow! No, he is dead and gone, and I won't say a word against him."

"That's right, Snip, for, after all, your being with him has brought you nothing but good fortune."

"I shall never forget that box," said Snip, with a shudder. "Ugh!"

"I suppose not," said Will. "It must have

been a real treat."

"And the worst of it is that nobody will believe me," said Snip.

"You have this consolation," said Jack, as he rose and walked aft, "you know you have told the truth about the box, and although the world is foolish and generally prefers the liar, he who tells the truth gets the best of it in the long run."

A few days later the good ship George the Third reached her port, and our friends, having warehoused their treasure safely, were on the road to London.

In those days steam was yet unknown, and they travelled by coach. Jack, who had been all his life in a rough country, thought it the most delightful and rapid travelling in the world; but he lived to see steam-engines tearing through the land, and then he learned how comparative all things are in this fleeting life.

CHAPTER LIV.

FINALE.

THERE was a smooth path before our hero. When London was reached he and his friends drove to Lincoln's-inn, where Mr. Chichester, the family solicitor, lived.

Men in those days resided on the spot where their business was conducted, instead of affecting a country house in the form of a stucco villa, with fourteen feet of lawn and garden at the back, dignified by the name of "grounds."

Mr. Chichester was in his private room when Jack, unaccustomed to the forms of civilisation, walked unceremoniously in, but the lawyer made no remonstrance, for the appearance of our hero seemed to strike him dumb.

Mr. Chichester was engaged, as our heroes entered, in giving his two daughters a music lesson. He had on a French cap, wore spectacles, and looked every inch a professor of music.

The ladies soon withdrew, bowing as they passed to another room.

"Mr. Chichester, I believe?" said Jack.

"Upon my word," cried the lawyer, "if I believed that the dead could rise I should think that—that——"

"What?" asked Jack, seeing he paused.

"I should think," said the lawyer, "that you were Mr. John Beauchamp."

"So I am," said Jack. "But don't stare, man—I am not the father, but the son."

"The son? The child he took away with him?"

"The same, and I have come back to claim my own."

"You will have no disputant," returned the lawyer, "for ill-fortune has followed your family since your father was unjustly driven away. First Sir John, then Mr. Lewin, and gradually the family all died, some naturally and others by accident. The last broke his neck by falling from his horse on Thursday last."

"Then the estate is mine?" said Jack.

"As soon as you have proved your identity," replied the lawyer. "No very difficult matter with that face and figure."

"I have brought papers with me, too—my father's will and other matters, in his own handwriting."

"Then I may already congratulate you, and hail you as Sir John Beauchamp," said Mr. Chichester. "Permit me to shake your hand, sir?"

This was done, and the lawyer shook hands all round, winding up with Snip, whom he called Mr. Sambo, much to that gentleman's indignation.

"By the way," said Will, addressing the lawyer, "do you know anything of a gentleman named Sir Eardley Wilmot?"

"Poor Sir Eardley," replied the lawyer, "I should think I do. Everybody knows of him. He has, by a course of the wildest dissipation, completely beggared himself, and his estate is now in the market. The creditors have put it up for sale."

"Could you purchase it privately?" asked Will, eagerly.

"If anyone is prepared to pay down the amount of cash," said Mr. Chichester.

"How much is required?"

"About forty thousand pounds."

"I have the money at my disposal," said Will; "lose no time, but obtain it at once."

Mr. Chichester looked surprised, but he was a man of business, and when Jack assured him that his friend was perfectly sane, and able to pay the amount required, he was satisfied, and said it should be attended to at once.

"You may leave both transactions to me," he said, rubbing his hands with an air of satisfaction. "This is a most fortunate meeting for all, gentlemen, I assure you."

Then followed another shaking of hands, and after this our friends received a recommendation to put up at a certain hotel, when they retired.

There they dined, and, as soon as it was dark, Snip announced his intention of going at once to Wapping in search of his father.

"Why not wait until to-morrow?" urged Will.

"Ah!" exclaimed Snip, "you don't know London boys, or you wouldn't advise me to go down to Wapping with my face during daylight. It's an ordeal no man could go through with successfully. I've done a lot, and been through a lot, but I would sooner go through the whole of it again than wentur among them boys with a face like mine, when the sun is shining."

Saying this in his most emphatic tone, Snip took up his hat, made a polite bow, and departed.

The road to Wapping was not then what it is now, but Snip, who knew the way well, reached the spot of his birth without molestation. The once familiar scenes came back upon him and touched him deeply, for if he was a bit of a fool he was not entirely devoid of good feeling.

He remembered the court where his father and mother lived, and, going up to the house, knocked at the door.

"Who's there?" cried somebody within.

Snip's heart leaped within him. It was his father's voice.

He tried to open the door, but it was fastened, so he knocked again.

"Who's that disturbing a respectable man when he is going to bed?" asked the same voice, with a low growl.

"It's me?" replied Snip.

This reply, of course, gave no clue to those within, but the bolts were withdrawn and the door thrown open.

An old man in déshabille, holding a candle in his hand, peered curiously out.

"Now, then," he asked, "who is it?"

"Father!" gasped Snip, entirely forgetting his changed countenance, "don't you know me?"

Then uprose a mighty screaming, and Mrs. Snip was heard to declaim against the wickedness of man.

"Oh! Jeremiah," she cried, addressing her husband, "who would have thought you bad enough to have a nigger for a son?"

Then our friend remembered his little misfortune and rushed towards his mother, who retreated screaming.

"Mother!" he cried, "I am your own darling boy—your only son!"

"Don't tell me that you are my Jerry!" she said.

"I am indeed, mother," he said. "I have been in furrin parts, and got mixed up with people who made me what I am. Aint I your own Jerry? Didn't you 'prentice me to old Rummel the tailor? Come, aint it my voice?"

"It's our Jerry," said the old man; "but look here, my lad, what do you mean by coming back with a face like that?"

"I couldn't help it," returned Snip, humbly; "the people abroad did it."

"And when they had done it," said his father, "why didn't you stop with 'em? Look at him, Mary; would you care to walk about Wapping with him?"

"He is my Jerry," said the old woman, stoutly; "and, white face or black face, I stands by him. Them as don't like to walk with him needn't walk with me."

"That's a woman all over," said the old man; "she allers goes by the rule of contrary."

"Father," rejoined Snip, "I have got something to say to you. I have come back a rich man—a very rich man—and you and mother needn't work no more."

"Jerry," cried the old man, with much emotion, "come to a father's arms. I was allers fond of you. If anybody have got anything to say against your black face let 'em say it to me—don't let 'em sneak about and talk behind your back, but let 'em come to me—that's all I ask. Give me a hug, my boy."

Without staying to question the depth of this new-found emotion, Snip embraced his father, and then, a second candle being lighted to do honour to the arrival, they sat down to talk.

Snip learned a deal about his old friends before he retired that night, and on the morrow his father was up and out early, when he naturally bruited abroad the return of his long-lost offspring. The result was what might have been anticipated—a mob collected round the court, who first cheered their throats dry and then demanded largesse, wherewith to moisten them again.

Snip kept close, but he was obliged to show at last, when they took possession of him, and carried him up and down the streets until he was so limp and exhausted that he might have passed for a Fifth of November guy after a hard day's wear and tear.

At last they let him go, when he quietly left Wapping with his parents, and Wapping for a long time saw him no more.

Readers, the skein of our story is unravelled, and every thread is clear; what little we have now to say can be placed before you in a few words.

Jack came into his estates, not without some trouble, but his proofs were strong, and fortunately the law was not called on to decide in a possible second Tichborne case.

Had he not been the true John Beauchamp they would have settled him in ten minutes, but, being the right man, he was allowed to have his own in two months.

Will Larkin, now Eardley Wilmot, obtained his family estate, and rescued his father from poverty and distress.

This act of his touched the heart of the old tyrant, and he bowed beneath it. He lived only a few months after, but to the day of his death he always looked up to his boy with fear and reverence.

Long Tom took up his residence with Jack, and lived with him all his life. And Jack, like a good old English gentleman, married and raised a family to do credit to his name.

Will also performed that sacred duty, and the name of Wilmot is not likely to become extinct.

Snip's Wapping friends heard nothing of him for a long time, until a butcher drove over to Hampstead one day for a holiday, and came back with the intelligence that Snip and his parents were comfortably located there in a very charming villa, and that he, the said butcher, had seen the trio in a pony-chaise enjoying a drive.

The butcher's remarks upon Snip's driving were not very complimentary, but he was loud in the praises of the trap, the pony, and the villa. Shortly after the butcher saw him he took unto himself a wife who could overlook a black face if it belonged to a decent, good-tempered husband.

What more is to be said? Nothing. Good and ill are alike disposed of, and the author lays down his pen and leaves the friends who have walked and talked with him for so many weeks.

THE END.

THE
BANGWELL BOYS

BEING THE SEQUEL TO

Hardiboy James ; or, Chums and Chappies.

There were four of them, and they were making a horrible mess of it.

www.ingramcontent.com/pod-product-compliance
Lightning Source LLC
Chambersburg PA
CBHW081156170626
46813CB00009B/3215